Architects of
Eternity

Book XIII of The Quietus of Fate

By Brian C. Kershner

ISBN-13: 978-1-942082-25-5

Acknowledgements

The process of writing the *Quietus of Fate* series brings with it both wonder and tragedy. In some ways, each character is a living breathing thing, and sometimes I think they have lives of their own outside of my mind, and I've just been given glimpses into the parts that they want me and the wider world to see. We get to celebrate their triumphs, cry along with their losses, shake our fists at their moral failings, and ultimately give pieces of ourselves to the parts of them that remind of us who we are deep down inside.

Some of these characters have been with me for over thirty years (by the time this is being written), and they are like an odd traveling circus of an extended family. Two of these characters are Logan Ranthall and Pike Rhuiden. Logan and Pike came into being when I was a freshman in high school, and in some ways they were the inseparable friends that saw the world with completely different eyes but always walked together. The events at the end of *Cacophony of Hope* changed that dynamic forever, and dear readers you are about to see the ramifications of that change in the pages that follow.

Tales of loss and sacrifice strike very deep and powerful chords within us, because that is where we all can find the core of our humanity. Ultimately, *Quietus of Fate*, besides posing questions of perspective and perception, asks questions about the nature of humanity, and what any of us would be willing to do to protect the most precious parts of it.

B.K.

Table of Contents

And in the Darkness there is but one light,
There is but one truth and one way,
The Creator tries to block it from sight,
Forcing our curiosity and will to decay.

The Creator is jealous, malicious, and cruel,
Greedy for attention and supplication,
His only desire to oppress and to rule,
Threatening with torment, fire, and damnation.

But despite the Creator's ever-watchful eye,
And his violent and murderous Servants,
From us our freewill He cannot pry,
As we flaunt our defiance for His observance.

Our Light is the fires of our collective will,
That even He cannot douse or extinguish,
A growing rebellion it is poised to instill ,
Under the wings of the mighty Phoenix.

-    *Writings of Kamen*
From the Teachings of the
Order of the Flickering Flame

Prologue

Yet Each Man Kills
the One He Loves

Year One of the Divine Empress and Child of the Creator Marlae Tamerlane, Creator's Calendar Year 1871

The Flying Kingdom of Hedorah was known far and wide with two distinct and largely opposing reputations. The first, and the far more positive was as the most prolific and well-respected trade hub in the whole of the Cadarian Empire. More cargo and trade passed through the ports of Hedorah than the rest of the Cadarian Empire combined. The workers at the docks were renowned for their precision and speed, and without those attributes the whole of the empire could have found itself with shortages of all manner of food and supplies. However whatever stability and professionalism existed in that portion of Hedorahn life did not extend to the royalty or military of the kingdom prior to the arrival of the Divine Empress. Corruption was rampant, vice was the rule, and selfishness was the only code of conduct. The Divine Empress had changed that, and perhaps it was this new standard of care and decency that had enabled the whole of the kingdom to pull itself together as it fled from the advancing fires and destruction that began to radiate from the southern docks. People scrambled together, pulling survivors from the rubble and carrying those who could not run in the direction of the northern docks. The angels who had been protecting the kingdom had all fallen or fled, and only those members of the Flying Guard who remained after the purge and had proven their loyalty to the ideals of the Divine Empress in the eyes of the Lady Anabel Binosear, remained to shepherd the panicked flock. Some fled past the Church of the Creator in the Royal District, and would forever be scarred by what they saw and felt there. The survivors would tell of a green cloud filled with screaming phantoms, and a wail that threatened to melt their brain. Some reported that their eyes and ears bled. Others cried that they choked on blood that poured from their noses and mouths. What they didn't understand was that the nausea, the blood, the sense of impending doom, and the heart-stopping chill that shrouded almost the entire district was generated by the cold hate that smoldered between two men who had been joined by love, blood, and fate since the moment of their births. The green fog pulsed with violence, with rage, and with contempt as the last of the hate and pride filled words tarnished the air between the two men. But the words had faded into the silence, and any love and respect that had once existed had become another spirit silently screaming into the advancing night.

Both men exuded power, but power that could not have been more opposite. Pike Rhuiden, at least the man who had once thought of himself as Pike Rhuiden, had been a hero that was defined by his loyalty, passion, and unflinching desire to make those enemies pay who threatened the people he loved. The days of being an apprentice blacksmith were so far behind him that they were not even a shadow in the corner of his consciousness. Those days of working hard at the forge and then going to the bar and singing until dawn, drinking with the girls, and forgetting the world several hours at a time had been scabbed over by so much pain that it was hard to know where the tissue of his formative life ended and the scars of his years as a so-called hero began. From the very moment that his pride and his trust had caused the fledgling champion to burst forth from the protective cocoon of everything that he had ever known, danger, loss, pain, death, and suffering had stalked his every step. How many times had he cheated death? How many times had he seen those he loved not be able to escape those cold clutches? And then that Pike, that pupa stage of his development ended. In the throne room of their enemy, the vile and evil nightmare of men Shau-ling, Pike paid the ultimate price. He sacrificed his life so that his friends, his allies, and his world could continue. It would continue without him, but it was a small price to pay. But Pike, as he had been from the moment his folly of a quest began, was lied too. He had been lied to by his friend and blood, he had been lied to by his gods, had been lied to by his Creator, and ultimately had been lied to by fate. His fate had not been to die at the hands of Shau-ling, because Shau-ling was not truly the enemy. And so when the Blaze revived Pike from his slumber, he found new purpose. He would meet the world around him with eyes open. It brought him to the sides of his enemies, it put him in conflict with his allies, and ultimately put him on a collision course with himself. The dark shadow of Pike Rhuiden, the one who called himself Lord Rhuiden was a brutal and self-absorbed man born out of devotion to a self-important and misguided destiny placed in his mind by his best friend. It was fitting that that shadow had been destroyed by the reborn version of Pike Rhuiden. But another rebirth and revelation was waiting. Pike found himself once again walking in the shoes of another, one whose path wound through only pain and death. It would take another supposed great enemy to open Pike's eyes once more and make him into what he was always destined to be. Finally he was cast in the role that should have been his from the beginning. As Conquest, he would finally be the hero and bring retribution for all the evil that had been visited upon those he loved.

Like Pike, Logan Ranthall had reinvented himself more times than he cared to admit. A hero, a lover, a husband, a father, a patriot, a rebel, a villain, a heretic, an agitator for peace and understanding, and finally, a facilitator of destiny. No role had ever fit perfectly, and because of that there were many losses and failures along the way. But Logan learned from every mistake, every failure, and while there had always been a part of him that didn't want to follow the path that stretched on before him, he knew that he could not stop until he had reached the end. Even when the path that pushed him forward led him to a conflict with the man that could have been his brother, Logan would never relent. How many more costs would he pay? He lost his brother, the love of his life, a relationship with his son, a relationship with his daughter, his best friend, his father, everyone he had ever loved…and now, perhaps finally, he would lose his life. But Logan had known the cost would be his life from the first day that Aryx Terian stepped into that small cottage on the edge of Aradon. He had made his peace with the fact during his years in exile. However, at the precipice of what might be his ultimate fate at the hands of his best friend, all he could feel was intense sadness. This wasn't how it was supposed to end, but perhaps in the grand scheme of things, it was the only way that it could have.

Time seemed to stand still in the eye of the hurricane of destruction that whirled around the two men, and for the barest instant Logan lost focus on the moment. He was quick to find it once more when the ghostly aura pulsed and the piercing wail went from silent to deafening. Logan was shaken down to his core by the wail, as though the spirits were trying to sap his strength before the fight was joined. Logan reached deep within himself and held tightly to the primal strings of power within him; both the roaring fires of the Blaze and the nearly insubstantial mantle of power granted to him by Aerith Seth. Instantly Logan felt every fiber of his being alive with energy, and his mind whirled with thoughts from too many sources to process. He could feel the danger that surrounded Aerith, Arin, and Hannah. He could feel the tension and the uncertainty that gripped Rhain and the members of the phasia. But there was something else there hanging like a phantom in the back of his mind. In that moment Logan almost reached for it, but just before his mind's eye locked on that hazy image, he pulled away. The conflict with the creature Death had opened a rift within him. Through that rift was the ability to draw upon the powers of his brother and his son. The last time Logan seized hold of those powers, the exertion had nearly ripped him apart. Apparently though the connection had not been severed when Logan relinquished hold on the powers. He inwardly hoped that he would not need those abilities again because if the battle came to that, he wasn't likely to cheat fate once again.

Logan's eyes saw Pike move before his mind was able to process what he was seeing. The impossibly muscular man charged forward, his hands wreathed in deadly power. Logan's reflexes were enhanced enough to throw himself out of the way at the last moment. Pike charged headlong through where Logan had stood only a moment before and continued through the support wall that held the steps to the church. The solid stone wall was obliterated, sending shards blasting in all directions, and dust billowing up into the air. Several of the sharp shards cut at both men, but neither paid the minute wounds any mind. Flesh wounds would not matter in the minutes that this fight would last, and Logan became painfully aware that he was terribly overmatched. The toe of his boot pressed up against the wall of the Church of the Creator, Pike turned his head to find his prey.

Out of the corner of his eye he caught sight of Logan who was taking several steps back toward an alley that cut between two large storehouses across the street from the church. The larger man turned and faced Logan, his face devoid of all expression, but his eyes filled with such hate that they smoldered. Again Pike launched himself forward at impossible speed, but Logan was ready. Instead of dodging out of the way, he channeled a small fraction of power and leapt high in the air over the advancing monster. As soon as Pike perceived the change in Logan's tactics, he too tried to adapt, but the speed at which he moved made it impossible to alter his course, and though he reached up with one of his strong hands, he was unable to land more than the tip of a finger on Logan's boot as the man sailed over his former friend. Logan landed across the street, nearly in the same place as he had been standing when the confrontation began. Pike continued charging forward, his right shoulder clipping the corner of one of the storehouses. The subtle impact sent shockwaves through the structure, shattering the support beam and bringing the whole of the storehouse crashing down. The dust cloud obscured everything in a two block radius and Logan crouched slightly scanning everywhere for his opponent.

The twinge of danger hit the back of Logan's mind the next moment, and the green and gold blur that filled his vision closed the distance with startling speed. Again Logan had no choice but to leap out of the way, but his movement was too slow and too clumsy. The shoulder charge struck Logan square in the left shoulder before he could dodge out of the way, sending the smaller man careening into the wide street beside the church. Logan was able to pop back to a knee, but knew instantly that his shoulder had been dislocated and all three major bones in his left arm had been broken in several places. The flows of power that it took to mend the arm were unconsciously set into motion before Logan even knew they were working. His reflexes had been honed to such a fine point that there had even been flows of wind and stone woven through his bones to deaden some of the force of the impact. But obviously he had miscalculated. He would not make the same mistake again. Once the repairs had been done to his arm, the flows of stone and wind intensified throughout his body. It would make him heartier and more capable of absorbing the crippling blows, but would not make him heavy enough to deaden his agility or speed.

Just as Logan straightened and made it back to his feet, Pike was emerging from the rubble of the church. Logan hadn't seen the massive man collide with the ancient stone building, but the sound of shattering beams and exploding stone could not be missed. Pike stood where the front doors of the church had once been, the aura of the dead now accentuated with pieces of stone and wood that floated around him like planets orbiting a star.

"You're getting slow in your old age, Logan," Conquest taunted. "Or perhaps all of that power you expended with Death has left you at less than your best."

With but a simple motion of his hand, one of the large beams from the church ruins hurtled like a spear across the distance toward Logan. While he had not been exactly prepared for the tactic, his defenses were heightened, and he was able to channel a bit of power to nudge the beam enough off course that it would not come close to striking. Whether this duel would be over quickly or not, the key would be the application of power and who would be able to last the longest. Pike had demonstrated incredible power, but perhaps how long he could keep up such expenditures would prove to be a weakness that could be exploited. To that end, Logan could not be drawn into using his abilities for grand yet ultimately futile displays. There was no need to conjure a boulder when a pebble would do, and in the end he would need to think small and precise. It was clear that Pike had no such intent to restrict or restrain himself. All he sought was power, and so he could not be judicious in its use. Perhaps that too would afford Logan and opportunity to survive.

"We could have settled this anywhere, Pike," Logan said, letting his right fist fill with power so it achieved nearly diamond hardness. "There was no need to endanger all of these people. You didn't have to kill to get to me."

A hint of some emotion that might have been disappointment flickered across Pike's features.

"Not that it matters," Conquest answered, "but I would have killed every person on this world to get to you, Logan. Dorovar will cleanse this world, save them from their bondage at the hands of the Creator and his perverse children, so their fates are already decided, whether they die here or not."

Pike took a step forward and two large beams as well as half a dozen larger pieces of stone lifted from the ground behind him.

"And I thought you would have gotten the message after the Peaks of Patience."

Logan's blood burned. All along Logan had thought that it had been Dorovar who had been responsible for killing all of those people in Menoris. Now it was clear. The destruction of the Order of the Flickering Flame and all of the innocents of Menoris was a message to Logan as well as an initiation of sorts for the fledgling Conquest. Until that moment, until that very moment Logan thought that perhaps there was something good left in Pike. Perhaps there had been some part of him that had not been completely corrupted by Dorovar. Pike had been brought back from his rage, brought back from his depression, brought back from his servitude, and even brought back from death. Now, not only was Pike promoting the wholesale slaughter of innocents, but he had actually done the deed himself. There was nothing left of the man that Logan had once known. There was only the monster. Only Conquest.

Conquest wasted no time in attempting to press the advantage of his revelation. He had hoped that Logan would be shaken by the information long enough to finish the troublesome man quickly. To that end, a fraction of a second after the last word was spoken, it was punctuated by the beams and boulders hurtling toward their intended targets. Taking hold of the string of Air, Logan created a wedge of swirling wind in front of him which easily deflected the incoming projectiles away from him. The first of the two beams was deflected to Logan's right, and it collided with a shop behind him, shearing through the front wall and ripping through the second story and out the back causing more havoc in the adjacent block. Four of the boulders also collided with the shop, obliterating its front wall and threatening to cave in the entire structure. The second beam angled upward, sheering the roof off a storehouse to Logan's left. The remaining three boulders also rolled in that direction, the smaller two colliding with a large wagon that had been left in the road, turning it over before the third larger boulder smashed it into thousands of pieces. However, Logan was not left with an opportunity to celebrate his small victory.

Conquest did not hesitate to follow up his ranged assault with a more intimate one. Wreathed in his glowing ghostly aura, Conquest charged in, his balled right fist speeding toward the smaller man. Logan reacted as quickly as he could, not to dodge the blow, but rather to intercept it. Logan's left hand, filled with as much power as he could manage caught the incoming punch, and instantly Logan wondered if the tactic had been a mistake. Pain rocketed through his entire body and for a brief moment Logan thought that a mountain had fallen on him. The power at Conquest's disposal defied description and the force he exerted was threatening to snap Logan like a branch in a hurricane. But despite the pain and the uncertainty, Logan held his ground. When Pike's other fist came speeding in, Logan's reactions committed him to a course of action before his mind had a chance to weigh the consequences. Logan's right hand caught the more awkwardly angled and clumsy blow, but the force that resonated through Logan's already tortured form was only slightly less. For a moment Logan wondered if his feet and legs would break under the strain or the cobblestone street beneath him would crack open and swallow him. The marks of the extreme exertion were painted all over Logan's face as beads of sweat began to form on his brow, but as he looked into his opponent's eyes, there was no trace of fatigue or concern.

"Impressive," Conquest intoned dryly, "but foolish."

The next moment the crown of Conquest's head came down hard impacting Logan on his forehead just above his eyes. The impact shocked all of the smaller man's system, and for a moment everything went black and an impossibly loud ringing filled both of his ears. Numbness shot through all of Logan's extremities, and for the barest of moments the grip in both of Logan's hands relented and his knees buckled. It was all the opening that Conquest needed. He ripped his right hand free from Logan's grasp and seized his opponent by the front of his shirt. Conquest pulled Logan in and then slammed his head down on the man once more, scrambling all of his senses and causing all of the strength to flee from his tortured appendages. By the time the blackness cleared from Logan's vision, he had only a moment to take in the wicked sneer that curled his former friend's lips. The next moment, Conquest lifted Logan into the air and then slammed him back first onto the cobblestone street. The force of the impact was so great that the stones beneath Logan's body shattered and the hard-packed ground beneath was forced to give way forming a crater. Blood poured from Logan's mouth, nose, ears, and the myriad cuts on his arms and back. He had no concept of just how many of his bones had been broken in the collision, but his powers were already doing their best to knit the most severe injuries. But if Conquest acted too soon, there would be no chance for survival.

As he looked up from the crater, Logan saw the haunting green haze stretched above him casting the sky in the pall of death. Beyond the haze, the sky was beginning to darken in the advancing dusk, and the final traces of the Days of Star Fire were already fading into nothingness. Conquest entered the frame a moment later, towering above like a giant, his face expressionless, and his menace clear in his posture. A moment later a huge piece of stone floated into view. It was easily ten feet in length and had a cruel looking point that was aimed directly at Logan's chest. Conquest meant to end the battle now, and Logan had only a precious few moments to act. The move he had planned was a risky one at best, and one that he had never attempted, but certain death was proving to be a good motivator. The slab of rock sped downward and Logan didn't even have time to hold his breath before the plan of action executed. As the tip of the slab collided with Logan's chest, he formed a shield of wind at the impact point that would cushion the blow but not deflect it. At the same time, he formed a portal a few inches below him, in the soil itself. If his calculations were off, the force of the slab's impact would shatter his chest before the dirt had been pushed through the portal and before Logan himself was saved. Fortunately his gamble paid off, and as the shield of wind broke, the stone slab slammed deep into the crater, and Logan was gone.

Conquest did not have time to wonder what had happened. Of course he felt the portal, and entertained for a brief moment that Logan had thought better of his foolish notions and had fled. That delusion was short lived as he felt power above him. A column of pure Blaze fire laced with as much of Aerith Seth's mantle as he could manage poured from Logan's extended hands where he levitated high above the ground. The column stretched nearly ten feet wide and moved faster than the eye could see and the mind could process. However, Conquest was not a normal man, and he was able to wrap himself in a shield of souls as the attack struck. The sound was terrifying and it drowned out even the cacophony of wails that held the air captive. Intense heat rolled from the conflagration, igniting everything flammable for hundreds of yards in all directions. Though he wanted to continue the assault, Logan began to feel his strength waning, so he released as much of the energy as he dared and floated down to the ground at the far end of the street away from the devastation. He could still feel the menace in the air, and while he had not expected the strike to finish off the monster, he hoped that Conquest was diminished enough that he would now be a manageable threat. As he expected, when the smoke and fire cleared, Conquest stood in the center of a roughly circular burn mark, bearing no hint of damage. This time when Conquest's voice hit the air, the confident tone was clear and unmistakable.

"That must have taken almost everything that you could muster, Logan," Conquest said as he extended his arms away from his sides with his palms facing out. "But as you can see it had little effect. I could kill you a hundred times over and not expend a fraction of the power that Dorovar has given me. If you surrender now, I will make your death quick. Do not let your foolish and misguided pride fuel your last act on this world. For once acknowledge that you are not the spoke upon which this story turns."

Logan considered for a long moment. Conquest was right about one thing, that last strike had taken just about everything that Logan had left, short of opening himself up to the powers that he had used to defeat the creature Death. However, in his current weakened condition, even seizing those powers would probably kill him. It was time to think more creatively. Digging into his pocket, Logan pulled out a small blue stone with black speckles. He had hoped he wouldn't have to try this trick, but it was about all he had left before invoking the potentially suicidal strategy. Logan held the stone in his right hand and extended it so that Conquest could see it. There was a flicker of disbelief across the larger man's features.

"A stone? Is this a peace offering or a joke?"

Logan sighed.

"You've made it clear that there isn't any path for us now but for one of us to die. I wanted to believe that there was a part of you, even the smallest bit that was still my friend. But I know now that all that stands before me is a demon that wears my friend's face. I didn't want it to come to this, but you gave me no choice. Here and now, I promise the spirit of my friend that I will destroy the thing inhabiting his body and give him the burial he deserves."

Conquest began to laugh. If the monster realized what was going to happen before it actually did, he had no time to act upon it. Logan tossed the stone upward from his extended palm, and just before it reached his eye level, it began to open. Long ago Logan had keyed a portal stone to each of his remaining old friends, but he had never imagined using it in this capacity. At a distance, the stones were good enough to get to the target's vicinity because the portal was largely being formed blindly. However at this range, Logan was able to control exactly where the portal formed. The destination portal came into being in the very center of Conquest's throat and expanded outward in a flat disk that bisected the monster's neck. The portal was mostly insubstantial, but utilized in this capacity it acted like an impossibly thin blade passing through skin and bone. When the portal closed, it took the surrounding viscera with it, and blood burst in all directions as Conquest's head fell from its shoulders. Logan looked on, his stomach twisting in revulsion. Blood continued to pour from the sickening wound, streaming down Conquest's body and collecting in a pool at his feet. However, the body did not fall. The muscles appeared to stay rigid as though it was fighting to retain some form of life. The head sat on the ground, propped against the Herald's left leg, its eyes tilted upward toward the sky. Seconds passed, and there was perceptible movement from Conquest's head. Its eyes blinked. At first Logan thought that it was just a spasm of dying muscle, but seconds later they blinked again. The golden crown that had sat upon Conquest's head and lay like a tarnished lump of cheap jewelry several feet away suddenly sparked back to life, its golden luster renewed. It levitated from the ground and returned to its position, floating inches from Conquest's brow. The white cloak that had somehow resisted all of the blood that poured from the severed neck now also began to glow intensely. There was a blinding flash, and when Logan's vision cleared, Conquest stood, whole once more, no sign that any blow had ever been struck. Retaliation came quickly, and the green phantasmal force around Conquest flared and extended outward. Two of the nearly insubstantial spirits wrapped themselves around Logan's arms and pulled them behind his back, holding him as tightly as the thickest chains and manacles. Try as he might, Logan could not move, and no expenditure of power would free him from bondage. Conquest approached, each step careful and measured until he stood face to face with his foe.

"It's a pity that you would not accept Dorovar's offer, Logan, but your delusions would never allow the truth to be revealed to your eyes. But for whatever reason, Dorovar respects the manner in which you fight, and he would spare you his fate. Once he watched his world burn as I did. Perhaps that is why he picked me to be his final Herald, because we were kindred spirits. But in the new Cosmos, there is no room for one such as you, and you will be spared watching everything you fought for ground into nothingness. After all, Logan, you will only ever be that which you are, a mortal playing at being a god. When Dorovar ascends to the Heavens and unseats the Creator, I will stand at his side, and I will be a god."

Conquest's hand extended and his fingertips found the area of Logan's heart. All Logan could hear at that moment was the tortured and ragged beat of his heart. The steady beat of the phasia heart was gone, and once again emotion stirred his pulse. Searing pain hit the next moment as Conquest's fingertips pierced the soft flesh and burrowed deep. In a few seconds it would all be over.

"Close your eyes, Logan. This is truly the death that you have earned."

Chapter C

The Flame and the Phoenix

Year One of the Divine Empress and Child of the Creator Marlae Tamerlane, Creator's Calendar Year 1871

As Kamen had indicated, the brilliant red portal was just beginning to form when Rhain and Jeroch arrived in the audience chamber of the Grand Master of the Shadow Guild. Kamen, Saurn, Taya, Rael, and Trece were several steps behind when the first of the four forms emerged from the portal. Jeroch tensed immediately upon recognition of the woman, and inwardly wondered first how he was going to explain his presence, and second whether or not his life was about to be in danger. Jeroch's history with Leonora Wastri was tenuous at best, but perhaps her recent alliance with Rael and Trece would soften the blow of Jeroch's true identity. Next through the portal was a red-haired woman that Jeroch also had passing acquaintance with. The first time Jeroch had met Jillian Corven, it was clear that she had no idea what she had become mixed up in. But it was clear that her time with Logan Ranthall had an impact on her, and there was a clarity in her eyes that only came from the accumulation of great and shocking knowledge. Only one of the last two women through the portal was known to Jeroch, and the memories that he had of the woman that had been known as Marlae Lorien for the majority of her life were not favorable to say the least. She had been a spoiled brat through most of her childhood, and as she grew into adulthood her appetites for vice and power grew in equal measure. The girl was vain, prideful, and vindictive. She manipulated everyone that came into her orbit, and what she could not possess she sought to destroy. But the woman that stood in the audience chamber had a regal air, one that would have more completely benefited her new station as the Divine Empress of the Cadarian Empire. The woman who stood beside Marlae was dressed as a simple servant, but the power hanging off her could not be ignored. All four women were bathed in blood and looked as though they had been through an incredible fight.

As the portal closed, Jillian ran across the room and threw her arms around Kamen. Though her arms would not go completely around the giant, Jeroch was shocked at the calm and loving nature that Kamen showed by gently stroking the woman's hair. Rael and Trece moved to check on Leonora, while Rhain and Marlae simply stood looking at one another. In another life they had been lovers. In another life, Marlae had been a princess and Rhain had been her servant and personal assassin. Now, Marlae was a vessel of the Creator's power upon Espre, and Rhain was the vessel of one of the Children of the Creator. To say that the relationship was complicated was an understatement. Instantly Jeroch became concerned by the fact that Logan Ranthall was not among the new arrivals. Kamen too seemed to share Jeroch's concern, and as soon as he broke the embrace with the much smaller woman, he looked down at her and spoke.

"The Phoenix?"

Jillian was about to speak, but Marlae's voice cut through the moment of hesitation.

"Logan bought us time to escape. The Herald of Dorovar known as Conquest arrived at Hedorah with the express purpose of killing me and every vestige of the Creator's power that dwelled on that island. From all reports it was making sport of the angels that arrayed against it, and it would only be a matter of time before Conquest laid siege to the palace and killed everyone inside. Logan and Anabel Binosear sought to draw Conquest off and create enough time for the innocents of Hedorah to be evacuated."

Leonora took up the story there.

"We were delayed by someone calling himself Krysis. He was in the palace, supposedly as an advisor to the Empress, but his true purpose was to monitor the Empress on behalf of Talisia."

Jeroch's stomach tightened.

"Anabel Binosear?"

The servant girl spoke next.

"Lady Anabel has been acting as advisor to the Divine Empress since nearly the beginning of her rule."

Jeroch could not suppress his frown. His blood ran cold every time the Binosear name was mentioned.

"And you are?" Jeroch asked.

The girl pulled herself to full height and smiled.

"Isabella Ranthall," she said proudly. "I'm Logan's daughter, Jeroch."

The statement was a simple one but was filled with so many meanings that the whole room reacted. Jeroch could feel tension coming from the woman Jillian, but an air of relief coming from both Kamen and Rhain. Rael, Trece, and Leonora seemed to have no reaction at all, while both Saurn and Jeroch had to be feeling the same thing. Another Ranthall, more trouble. Before there was any further reaction to the girl's identity, Jillian's voice rang out.

"You have to help him, Kamen," she pleaded to the gentle giant, "he's still so weak after fighting that Death creature, and I don't think he'll be able to survive another fight so soon."

Kamen looked down at Jillian.

"Worry not, child, the Phoenix is resourceful. If his intent is merely to give the innocents time to evacuate, then there is little danger."

Saurn's voice rang out next.

"But that isn't his intent, is it?"

Rael was the one who answered.

"No, it's not. We have learned that it is Pike Rhuiden who has become the Herald Conquest from the dragon Aspertis. The dragons are surprisingly well informed, and fortunately at least some of them have formed an alliance with Aerith Seth and his confederate Hannah Ironheart."

Jeroch grimaced. Now he understood.

"If Pike Rhuiden has really gone over to Dorovar, then Ranthall will feel honor-bound to deal with the problem. Pike was his best friend, and in many ways, Logan would not have become what he became without that loathsome braggart. In this Ranthall is consistent. He cannot stand idly by while one of his own falls to darkness."

Kamen looked first at Jeroch and then down at Jillian. He put his massive hand on her shoulder for a long moment reassuring her, and then stepped away. He took a long glance around the room before locking eyes with Rhain. There was a moment of tension that flooded the room that Jeroch could feel but not understand. Then, without a word, Kamen turned and left the audience chamber. Jillian started to go after him, but Rhain's voice held her back.

"Don't. This is family business."

Rhain watched Kamen go, and then turned her attention back to Marlae.

"What are you going to do?" the Divine Empress asked.

Rhain sighed, her thoughts obviously troubled.

"The phasia do not abandon their own," she said shortly, "not again."

* * * * * * * * * * * *

Rhain entered the small sitting room and closed the door behind her. It took a few moments for her eyes to adjust to the lower level of light, but once they did, she had to fight hard against the waves of sadness that swept through her. Kamen sat on the far side of the room, his back against the wall, his legs crossed, and his hands on his knees, palms down. In front of him on the ground was a simple bronze candle holder with a simple white candle. A small flame danced on the end of the wick and gave off a very small amount of light, but that candlelight illuminated the heartbreaking story painted on the face of the gentle giant. Shadows clung to Kamen's face, making him look old and tired. His eyes looked sunken and sullen, and all life seemed to have drained away from his features. Though Rhain knew that Kamen's expression was usually measured and controlled, the barely perceptible frown was magnified in the flickering light. For several long moments they remained like that, Kamen concentrating on everything but the physical world, and Rhain trying her best to balance what she knew was coming and the profound sadness that the memories of the previous hosts of her power conjured within her. Halicon and Sabrina had known Kamen differently, and those opposite impressions collided in Rhain's mind.

From Sabrina, Rhain knew the frightening power of the creature that had been known as the Living Flame. The Flame was a foe that even the phasia feared and had been tasked with guarding the door to Shau-ling's throne room until Draven set him free. Outside of the palace, the Flame was a force of nature whose power knew no bounds for death and destruction. The construct of pure Blaze energy had no conscience, no fear, and a penchant for enforcing its will in the most direct and brutal fashions possible. Halicon's memories were far more layered and complex. Kamen, when he was first formed by Shau-ling was supposed to be the only member of a race that would eventually come to be known as the phasia. Kamen had been given all of the powers and will necessary to stand toe to toe with Emries and bring him to heel. Kamen couldn't have killed the Child of the Creator, but Kamen had enough power to render Emries incapable of fighting so that he could be captured and face the Creator for his crimes. But as the war progressed and Emries created his Erieal and sent armies of innocents to their deaths at the hands of the armies of the Shadow, Shau-ling knew that Kamen for all his power could not fight a war on that level. Kamen had a single purpose, and while he was not simpleminded, he did not have the emotional breadth of complexity that his later siblings would. The key to Kamen was his utter loyalty to his cause, and his devotion to the completion of his soul's purpose. And that, in the later days of the first act of the war was why Halicon began to see Kamen as a threat. Kamen would never betray his cause, but as the war evolved, Kamen could see the rest of the phasia and even Shau-ling as an impediment to that cause. Which is exactly what happened. First the phasia, and then Shau-ling lost their way prompting Kamen to do the unthinkable, challenge Shau-ling to a duel.

There were many memories about that time that filled Rhain with a sense of shame, but there were many memories from the dawn of the war that tempered that shame. There were nights between the long senseless destructions, when Kamen, Aryx, and Halicon would sit and talk together. They would marvel at the tenacity of their opponents and wish for better fates for the human race. Perhaps those talks had been what prompted Aryx to leave the fold and strike out on his own. Perhaps that is why Kamen became the embodiment of peace on this world as a member of the Order of the Flickering Flame. Perhaps that was why Rael and Trece were so eager to live their lives away from the phasia once they were reborn on Espre. After all, Rael and Trece had been made from Kamen's essence, and so in some ways they were one body and one soul. All of that swirling in her head, Rhain finally took a step further into the room, her eyes never leaving the sullen face of the oldest of the phasia. Once she had crossed the room, Kamen finally looked up and met eyes with the Mistress of the Blaze. Neither said anything, and after a moment Kamen looked back down at the candle and then lifted his right hand and indicated to the space across from him. Rhain hesitated for a moment and then knelt across from Kamen joining him in his silent contemplation. Since Kamen's arrival, Rhain had been unable to shake the feeling that Kamen had been holding something back. There was a foreboding in every breath and a sadness that hung around him like a cloak.

"You knew this would come to pass."

Rhain's words sounded louder and more urgent to her ears than she had intended. If Kamen noticed, nothing showed on his face or in his eyes.

"From the moment I was reborn upon this world and the Phoenix found me, my life has been leading to this. The Dark Seer came to me in her final days. She told me that Hedorah would burn in the fires of Conquest, and it would burn the Phoenix to ashes. She said that only through the Flames of its birth could the Phoenix be reborn. Even before those words were spoken, I knew my fate. Even before we learned of Pike Rhuiden's fall, I knew what would come to pass. My only regret is that my time reunited with my sisters and brothers shall be so short-lived. But we were drawn to this moment. Our fates cannot be ignored."

Rhain nodded. While neither she nor Halicon had seen this eventuality, the Dark Seer's words clearly framed what would happen next, and what each of their roles would be. If Marlae was to be believed, time was short, and Kamen was already deep in preparation. Kamen looked up once more, and his tone was grave.

"My path ends here," he said solemnly, "but yours continues, Rhain Seth. For so long you have denied your existence. You have put on other faces and chosen to be something other than your father's daughter. That is a luxury you can no longer afford. It is the very essence of your blood and your family that will turn this war. You must see it through. You must be true to your purpose. Learn from the mistakes that Halicon made. Do not allow yourself to be corrupted by the trappings of war. All that matters is saving what can be saved and using your every fiber of who you are to end the suffering that had been inflicted upon the innocent."

Rhain began to speak, but Kamen raised a hand and stopped her.

"There is no time left for kind words or sentiments of regret. I see no future past the next few moments, and those shall be hard enough to bear. My soul must meet its fate unburdened, and there will be enough loss for all who remain to share. You have much to do. I would say goodbye to you now, Rhain, and wish you luck in what comes next. Be wary of your past, because you are not the only one who has changed, nor are you the only one who must answer to something beyond yourself."

Kamen lowered his eyes back to the candle.

"You know what must be done. Please do not make this harder than it must be, Mistress. But if there is time, I should like to speak to the Shadow once more."

Rhain stood without another word and turned away from the gentle giant, her heart on the verge of breaking. She stopped at the door to the chamber and looked back over her shoulder for a brief moment before opening it and stepping through. She emerged into the dim light of the hallway and had to blink her eyes several times before they would adjust. Blaming the light for the tears in her eyes, she pawed at them briefly before truly taking in her surroundings. She should have realized that she would not be alone in the hallway outside of Kamen's spartan quarters. Jeroch, Rael, Trece, and Taya stood together. Taya's expression was one of confusion and concern. Jeroch's one of determination. Rael and Trece on the other hand had expressions very similar to the one Rhain had seen on Kamen's face a moment before. They were both gripped with a profound sadness, and at the same time a profound peace and understanding. Jeroch took a step forward and stood proud and tall.

"Saurn is ensuring that our new guests have appropriate quarters, but the arrival of our four guests has made everyone a little nervous. I understand that Kamen's behavior concerned you, but you must deal with this Empress soon."

Rhain couldn't keep the frown from pulling at the corners of her mouth.

"Marlae will have to wait, at least for now. I want you to attend to Leonora Wastri and Jillian Corven personally, since you have history with both. I require some time to meditate and ensure that what happens next is successful."

Rhain looked to Rael and Trece.

"You know what is happening next?"

The twins nodded solemnly.

"Good. Time is of the essence. However, before you begin, Kamen would like to speak with Jeroch. Taya, come with me. You must make sure that I am not disturbed."

Rhain did not wait for an answer before pushing past the three members of the phasia and leading a very confused and frustrated Taya toward the other end of the palace where she had co-opted the Grand Master's quarters for her own. Jeroch watched Rhain go and then turned his focus to Rael. He opened his mouth to start to speak, but Rael had turned to Trece and the two were engaged in yet another of their silent conversations. So, he moved to the door and hesitated. The last time he and Kamen spoke privately, Jeroch had sensed a dread and foreboding in his older brother, perhaps he had reached the moment he had been dreading. Jeroch opened the door, not realizing he was holding his breath until he was in the room with the door closed behind him. Kamen looked up and regarded his brother for a moment and then motioned for Jeroch to join him at the candle. As Jeroch was easing himself down to the floor, Kamen began speaking.

"Do you remember the day you were born, Shadow?"

Jeroch stopped his decent into a sitting position briefly, unprepared for the question. The hesitation was momentary but felt like it lasted for several minutes. When he finally sat down, he smiled slightly.

"Vaguely," Jeroch answered. "The one thing I do remember is that you were the first thing that I saw when I emerged from the Blaze."

Kamen looked back at the candle before he spoke.

"I was there when each of my siblings was born. I wanted to help each of you into the world. I wanted you all to see that you were not alone in the tasks that lay ahead. I wanted you to never feel alone."

Jeroch frowned.

"Because you were alone."

Kamen stayed silent. There was so much he wanted to say, but time did not allow for it all.

"My time is short, Shadow, and in a matter of minutes, you will be the eldest member of the phasia, and you will need to shepherd them all through these end times. But I needed to see you, needed to speak to you, and I needed to ask something of you."

There was uncharacteristic emotion in Kamen's voice. He was always so reserved and spoke only when necessary.

"First, I would ask your forgiveness. I acted rashly during the Dragon's time on Onea. I was impatient and did not understand all of the factors in play. I raised hands against my maker and in the process, I injured my brother. For that, Shadow, I would ask that you forgive me so that my soul may pass unburdened into the next world."

Jeroch was bewildered by Kamen's words but understood the sentiment well enough. They had all done things on Onea and again on Espre that they had no reason to be proud of.

"We all lost our way on Onea, Kamen, each and every one of us. Had we not made war against ourselves and kept to the task that Halicon laid out for us in our earlier days, perhaps we would not be here having this conversation, and perhaps Onea would still exist. But after Aryx's defection, your imprisonment, and the dilution of the ideal that the phasia were born to exemplify, there was nothing left of the mission. There was only greed. There was only want. Of course, I forgive you brother."

Kamen's expression seemed to brighten for a moment, but the lightness in his features was short-lived.

"Thank you, Shadow. And I have a kindness to extend to you as well. In the early days of the war, you committed atrocities on the innocent in the name of war. With your Black Tower, you converted thousands into all manner of horrors, and I know you have carried that in your heart for all these centuries. I cannot give you the forgiveness that will soothe your heart, Shadow, but I can help you shoulder some of that blame. Aryx and I helped to feed that furnace of death, and so we shared the burden. It is not yours alone. Perhaps that will help you to find peace before your end."

Jeroch's mind swam, and his puzzlement was not going to find relief in that room at that moment. Any further words that he was going to say, any further sentiment that he was going to express or receive was extinguished the next moment when Kamen sighed hard and then fixed his gaze firmly upon Jeroch.

"Understand, Shadow, that what happens next must happen."

Kamen's words seemed to trigger the door to the small room to open. Rael and Trece entered the next moment. Kamen shifted slightly and then slowly rose to his feet. Without being acted upon by any obvious force, the candle at Kamen's feet went out. Light streamed in from the doorway, and Kamen moved gingerly past Jeroch, pausing for a moment to put his hand on his brother's shoulder before following Rael and Trece into the hallway. As they continued down the hall, Jeroch started to push up to his feet to follow his siblings, but he couldn't. When Kamen touched his shoulder, he must have done something that prevented Jeroch from moving. Jeroch tired again and again to get to his feet, but each time he was held in place by the unseen force. No matter how much power he channeled into his legs, he could not break the hold, until finally, what could not have been more than a minute or two later, the force simply relented and Jeroch was able to stand. The sudden realization of what was about to happen struck Jeroch. That was why Kamen wanted to delay Jeroch, he couldn't take the chance that Jeroch would interfere. As soon as Jeroch was back on his feet, he rushed down the hallway after the trio. He was able to catch a glimpse of them entering Rhain's room, but he was unable to get there before the door closed. Taya immediately stepped in front of the door. Jeroch skidded to a stop less than two feet from the young blond-haired woman, his face a mixture of anger and concern.

"Step aside, girl."

Taya's lips twisted into a snarl.

"Rhain doesn't want to be disturbed."

Jeroch's cold eyes burned.

"Move aside, or I will move you."

There was murder in Jeroch's eyes, and Taya suddenly realized that there was nothing that she could do to impede his will. Grudgingly she took two steps away from the door and Jeroch barely waited until she was out of his path before advancing on the door. He tried the handle, but it would not respond. It was not that the door was locked, but simply that the handle would not respond. He pushed at the door, threw his shoulder into it, but still the door would not budge. The door was as sold as a mountain face. With his fists he hammered at the door, more out of frustration than expectation of change.

"You don't have to do this!" he shouted at the door. "There has to be another way! We can all go together to save Ranthall. We can take the fight to Dorovar."

There was no answer, and for anther few moments, Jeroch's adrenaline would not relent, and his fists pounded at the door until they were bloody. Finally whatever strength was compelling him fled. He thought he heard Kamen's voice in the back of his mind telling him that it needed to be this way, and that there was no need to struggle against fate. Finally, Jeroch's knees went weak, and his legs collapsed under the weight of his body, his guilt, and his shame. He slid down to the ground, his back to the door, and it wasn't until the first teardrop dropped from his chin that he realized that he was crying, perhaps for the first time in the entirety of his existence.

No Action Without Balance
or Sacrifice

Year One of the Divine Empress and Child of the Creator Marlae Tamerlane, Creator's Calendar Year 1871

Pain. Pain flooded through Logan Ranthall's body as Conquest's fingers pierced the skin of his chest and pushed between his ribs on their inevitable collision course with his raggedly beating heart. But pain had been the one constant in Logan's life, the one true companion that he had with him since the moment of his birth. He had been born into pain, the very act of his birth setting off a chain reaction that would haunt his steps for the rest of his days. Logan's birth had cost him his mother, and also cost him any positive relationship with his brother. In the years that followed, new pains echoed as the relationship between his brother Korrd and their father deteriorated to the point that Korrd would leave home. New pain emerged upon the supposed death of Logan's brother at the hands of common bandits. Then there were the disappointments of youth, the failure in young love, the loss of a father, the self-imposed exile from everything he knew, and a war that was not his to be waged. At every turn he would lose friends, loved ones, and pieces of himself. Whether it was Dreamscape, or Illimar, or Sarmeel, or Falke. Through Taren, and Marcwell, Frontier, and the Island of Mist. Every step, the one constant was pain. But even after what should have been the end, the pain did not stop. In one reality, he had had time with the woman he loved, watched as she gave birth to their child, and thought to have the quiet life that he had always dreamed of. That dream was shattered with Emries' hands around his throat. But that was not the world that Logan remembered, at least not completely. The love of his life died, and a chance at that family and quiet were stolen away. The intervening twenty years were bereft with pain, depression, and self-loathing. And of course there was the war. He could not stay away from it forever, and eventually he exposed himself to more pain and the death of more innocents. Following rejoining the war, Logan found new ways to suffer, and new ways to lose. He had even lost his humanity in the transition to something between human and phasia. The pain should have ended with his death on Onea, but it didn't. That was only the second act in the on-going play staged by the Creator. So when the Creator pulled Logan's strings once more and brought him to Espre, Logan tried his best to stay out of the conflict. At least, for a while. While Cedric and Gwydeon were hunting down the Erieal and the phasia, Logan remained on the periphery, just providing information to Sabrina when he could. But just like his time in self-imposed exile on Espre after the second generation of the prophecies, it was only a matter of time before Logan would be dragged back into the conflict, and the pain would begin anew.

The sound of one of his ribs snapping under the pressure of the invading fingertips brought Logan back to the present moment. He knew he only had seconds left to live, and only one gambit left to play out. It however was as risky as simply doing nothing. Pike's hand would find his heart and kill him in a matter of seconds. If Logan opened himself up to the powers of his brother and his son, the exertion would probably kill him just as quickly. The only chance would be to draw on the powers and then detonate them before they could eat him from the inside out. If he was fortunate, he would be able to eliminate Pike in the ensuing conflagration. There was no other option. Logan closed his eyes for the briefest of moments and then filled himself as full as he could manage with the powers of both the Blaze and that of the Chosen One. He didn't make any effort to hide the gathering of power. Pike would have seen it as some last ditch effort to stave off death. Pike had already shattered all of Logan's defenses and in his mental state, he would not see this gathering of power as a threat. By the time he would feel the new powers blooming in Logan, it would be too late. At the edge of Logan's consciousness was the brilliant golden chaotic rain of Emries' powers and the bright joyous powers of Pyrrus. In a moment it would all be over, all the pain and all the torment. Inwardly he regretted the pain he would cause in those left behind, but there was no other option. Not for the innocents he was trying to protect. Not for his children. Not for his friends, or his family. And not for the woman that he was just beginning to love. He took one final deep breath and opened himself up to the powers just at the edge of his consciousness.

* * * * * * * * * * * *

Rhain Seth stood in the middle of the Grandmaster's quarters in the Shadow Guild's stronghold, bathed in the full and unbridled powers of the Blaze. The column of brilliant green swirled around her like a flaming cyclone, unrelenting and eternal. At equidistant points around her, three of her semi-adopted family sat. She still had not had time to sort out the strange relationships that the inheritance of her new position as the Mistress of the Blaze had created. With most of the members of the phasia, it was less complicated, but still strange. While they were her aunts and uncles by blood, they were her children and her charges by her new connection to Halicon's mantle. It was even more awkward of course when it came to her mother. As her thoughts shifted to these anomalies of relation, she felt her concentration began to wane, and the powers within her flutter. The slip was momentary, and she snapped herself back to the gravity of the situation that needed her complete attention. Lives hung in the balance, and perhaps the fate of the war the raged on around them. While it was easy for anyone to say that the future stood precariously on a knife's edge, few could feel it as clearly as Rhain. The Children of the Creator, and those who held their powers, felt time and fate in a very substantial way. Now it felt like a noose around Rhain's neck that was tightening slowly. She brought herself back to the task at hand, trying to push away the feeling of inevitability. If Kamen's plan was going to work, it was going to take every bit of Rhain's power, concentration, and all the luck they could muster. The plan was as simple and elegant as it was dangerous. Even now, Rhain could feel Logan's desperation rising as his life force failed. What no one knew, except for Kamen and Rhain, was that Logan had always been perched between two worlds. He was no longer mortal, because of his arrogant presumptions and Halicon's interference, but he was also not completely a member of the phasia. Four members of the phasia had assisted Logan in his transformation, but only three had become intrinsically linked to their new sibling. It was a fluke of fate really that those three phasia had been there at that moment in time, but as Rhain felt the phantom chafing around her throat again, she knew there was no such thing as fate.

Humans who believed in and worshiped the Creator had a concept of a grand design, some plan that charted the course of every event that touched and shaped every single life on the face of Espre. But the human mind could take that belief only so far. Once terrible events started entering a person's life, they could no longer reconcile the hand of the Creator in those events. And so, the construct of fate came into being. Fate was the confluence of events, neither intentional nor foreseen, that inexplicably altered the grand design. It was a fluke, a quirk, an unexpected consequence of the order of Creation. The Creator didn't want any of his faithful flock to suffer, and so it must have been a quirk of life. People created fate, not the Creator. That fate expressed itself in myriad ways; evil, the Great Dark One, demons, restless spirits, and the like. Only in contradiction and incongruence could the human mind find peace.

Kamen, Rael, and Trece were three parts of the same whole. Kamen was one of the original members of the phasia; in a time when the war with Emries was new and the roles to be filled by the children of Halicon were not as well defined. Kamen had been made with power enough to shake the whole of the world if he wished, perhaps even enough to stand toe to toe with Emries. In those days, Halicon did not foresee the possibility of the phasia becoming a fractured body with designs on creating their own dark empire. All Halicon wanted was to end the madness that his brother had wrought. To that end, the first six phasia were special, and their ability to draw not only upon the primal strings but also the Blaze was without limits. They were only limited by their imaginations, much like the humans they were modeled after. But time changed the war, time changed the phasia, and Halicon made his mistakes in creating soldiers whose failings were the same as those they fought. Aryx was lost to the forces of the Light. Grawn, Bryn, and Ellis were in exile. Jeroch was desperately trying to hold the fractured members of the phasia together. And the one member of the phasia that Halicon had always known he could depend on had been reduced to a guardian because Shau-ling was paranoid and faltering in the face of a conflict that was spinning out of control. So

Kamen became fuel for the war effort, sacrificing himself so that a new more pliable member of the phasia could be created. But the amount of power that Kamen possessed coupled with Emries' interference in the war gave birth to the twin phasia Rael and Trece. In every way that mattered, Rael, Trece and Kamen were one being, one incredible power that was capable of almost anything. That capability was on display at the death and rebirth of Logan Ranthall into his new role as the Lord Phoenix of the Brotherhood of Phasia. It was their combined powers that facilitated the transition, but Caris had interfered before the process was complete. She forced Rael and Trece to stop pouring their powers into Logan, and thus he was only a fraction of what he should have been. It was Kamen's plan now to finish what they had started all those millennia ago.

Rhain marveled that Rael and Trece had fallen into line so quickly. The two had always been so staunchly independent. When the option was given to the phasia to walk away from the fight as Aryx had once done, it was only Rael and Trece that had taken the opportunity to see how life was away from the constant fight. They had established something in their hundreds of years together that had filled Halicon with the most pride. But as independent and special as they were, at their core, they were the most loyal of the phasia. They were cut from the same cloth as Jeroch and Kamen, ready to do anything for their brothers and sisters. So perhaps it wasn't so surprising that there had been no conversation needed, and no convincing. However, as Rhain's glance shifted between the three faces, she knew that there was communication on-going. Rael and Trece were always literally in each other's head, a background conversation that never stopped. They always knew what each other were thinking, feeling, and needing. But what Rhain had not guessed, not until this very moment, was that there was a third track running through each of the twin's heads. Kamen had been planning for this moment for a long time, and he was not going to leave anything to chance.

"It is time," the giant's calm and low voice rang out. "The Phoenix is very weak now, he only has moments."

Any nostalgia that clung to Rhain's thoughts was instantly banished to the back of her mind. The procedure that she was about to attempt was dangerous and precise, and she did not like the fact that she now was going to be forced to rush. Her eyes shifted first to Rael, and the dark-haired man held her gaze and then shut his eyes tightly. Rhain could feel Rael open himself fully to the powers of the Blaze. Rael drew so deeply that the Blaze suffused every fiber of his being. It was not a sustainable connection, and in a matter of moments, the Blaze would burn Rael like a torch. A moment later, a dark stream of energy wrapped in Blaze fire burst from Rael's chest and lanced into the cyclone of Blaze that surrounded Rhain. Next, Trece was wrapped in the powers of the Blaze, and a white stream of power wrapped in Blaze fire burst from her chest and joined with Rael's in the spinning conflagration. Rhain turned her attention back to Kamen, and he too opened himself to the powers of the Blaze. Unlike Rael and Trece however, Kamen did not fill himself to bursting. At first Rhain thought that the gentle giant was hesitating, but from the pain she saw on his face, she guessed the truth. Kamen was not as practiced with his abilities as the younger members of the phasia. In Kamen's time they relied more on strategic applications of power rather than overwhelming their opponents. Even as the Flame, Kamen did not draw upon the Blaze for incredible feats. Kamen was mission oriented. He used enough power to complete the task at hand. Nothing more, nothing less. That had been Jeroch's failing for a long time as well, but Jeroch had the advantage and disadvantage of being pushed to his limits by his more power-hungry bothers Saurn and Zarsi.

"When I was born," Kamen said softly, the level of power in his body rising, "I was but a flickering flame, unsure of my direction but yearning to be more. From my infancy, I grew, I learned, and the flickering flame changed; it spread its wings and became the mighty Phoenix."

Peaks of brilliant green flame grew around Kamen as he continued to speak. It filled the room with a brilliant light unlike Rhain had ever seen. The strength and ferocity of the flames grew until they rivaled that which surrounded Rhain.

"But from the day those wings spread to catch the air, I knew that there was a great fate waiting beyond; beyond what I knew, beyond my perception. I would make the most of my time as the Phoenix; learn all that I could learn, live a life that would make me worthy of what would come after. The Phoenix is not eternal. It returned to flames when its life is ended, only to be reborn once more to continue its work."

A brilliant green string bathed in Blaze fire slowly extended from Kamen's chest and merged with the column of Blaze that circled Rhain. When Kamen continued speaking, Rael and Trece's voice joined his, a harmony that resonated within the pulsing Blaze.

"We do not live but one life. Like the Phoenix we live many; some ending in fire, others in ashes, but all ending and beginning anew. My life before was the Phoenix. Now I am but the flickering flame waiting to be reborn. Only through my deeds shall I become the majestic Phoenix once more."

Peaks of green fire appeared around Rael's body the next moment, causing his hair to stand on end and brilliant light to emerge from his eyes, ears, nose, and mouth. Every inch of his skin tingled with power, and every fiber of his being sang with the peace of his new purpose. There was a brilliant flash, and Rael was gone, everything that he was traveling down the dark string of power into the storm of power that surrounded Rhain. Kamen and Trece's voices broke through the tumult once more, but their harmony was not diminished by the loss of Rael's voice.

"I shall walk this world, the flickering flame. I shall raise up those who cannot rise by themselves. I shall use this flickering flame to bring comfort to those who have none, to shelter those who know only the ravages of the world. I am the flickering flame, and yet I am so much more."

Rhain saw Trece's long curly red hair lift away from her body until it was standing straight up from her head. Tendrils of green flame wove through the scarlet rivulets, making the woman's head look as though it were a brilliant bonfire. Light seemed to stream from all of her pores, and at the last moment, Trece opened her eyes and her pupils had been replaced by flame. A flash of green light engulfed Trece, and her essence flowed through the white string to join that of her twin. Now when Kamen's voice rang out once more, he spoke not in just his voice, but in all three voices.

"Let this flickering flame be a beacon to all those lost in the darkness and let it lead them back into the light. Through these deeds and through grace, this flickering flame shall spread its wings once more to become the mighty Phoenix whose might shall protect all those who take shelter in its magnificence."

Kamen's body flared again, the aura of Blaze around him now matching the intensity of that around Rhain. He raised his head and slowly made his way to his feet until the two were standing looking into one another's eyes. His face devoid of all expression, Kamen spoke again, and this time the voice was his alone.

"Until again I shall return to the flames of my birth."

The light flared and Kamen was absorbed by the roaring fires of the Blaze. Tears streamed down Rhain's face, but she paid them no mind. It was taking every bit of her concentration to keep the incredible powers flowing around her in check. For Halicon, this would have been a much simpler task, but Rhain, despite her special parentage, was still mortal. The memory of Sabrina's failing frail form tried hard to emerge from the back of Rhain's mind, but she resisted its influence. There was not much time left for any of them, and the invisible noose tightened the more Rhain manipulated the incredible power. She looked up to the ceiling, and her eyes forced shut as she let one image form in her mind. The Blaze flashed and flared, threatening to grow out of control. It filled the room with its power, scorching everything in its path. Just before it broke through the thick walls of the room, the flames flared once more and were gone.

* * * * * * * * * * * *

Conquest could feel the triumph rising inside of him. In a matter of moments the last obstacle to his ascension to his rightful place in the Cosmos would be removed. Logan Ranthall had been the cause of so much suffering for so long. He had twisted fate around himself for a burden that was not his to carry. But now that would all come to an end, and Pike could make right everything that had gone so wrong. Dorovar had decreed that Talisia was not to be touched, but there were so many other targets left to remove. The other Ranthall brother would need to be destroyed as well, another puppet whose strings would need to be cut. Piece by piece Conquest would remove all of the armor that protected Emries from direct attack. Then, finally, Pike would be able to take the truest measure of revenge for all the crimes that robbed him of sleep every night. He would reach into Emries' chest, rip out his heart, and then stuff it down his throat and laugh as the creature finally died. Last of all, the last piece of the puzzle would be Aerith Seth, the genesis of this stage of the conflict. Conquest only hoped that as he had done with Raenera, Dorovar would give him the privilege of the killing blow.

The phantasmal green force that surrounded the two old friends had grown and surged as the fight continued. Now that Conquest had a peaceful few moments, he could sense the spirits of the dead from his march through the streets of Hedorah. There were hundreds more spirits that ripped and clawed their way out of their broken mortal forms to be free of the shackles that the Creator had imposed on them. Each of the newly dead added their voices to the song that was wrenched from their spectral throats. The wail was beautiful and chilling in the same breath and as it froze Pike's blood, it made Conquest's heart race with pride and passion. Blood poured from Logan's chest, and Conquest could hear his soul beginning to cry out. At that moment, Conquest found himself caught between the desire to follow his master's mandate and add Logan's soul to the growing Chorus, and the desire to destroy everything that Logan was. Certainly one soul would not be missed. Certainly Dorovar would forgive Conquest for ripping his former friend's soul to shreds. He had already added hundreds of souls to the Chorus, and its power was so great now that the world would shake. It was almost over now, and Conquest could feel the beating of Logan's heart at the tips of his fingers. There was an unexpected electricity that jumped between his outstretched fingers, like lightning that jumped between clouds as a storm gathered. Would there be thunder when his hand finally closed around Logan's heart, or would there only be a whimper as the last breath died in his throat. Either way, the sound would live forever in Conquest's memory.

* * * * * * * * * * * *

A spasm rocketed through Logan's body and for a moment, just for a moment, his hold on his powers wavered. He had been trying to use Aerith Seth's powers to delay the invading hand that was approaching his heart while at the same time using the Blaze to weaken the spectral force's hold on his arms and legs. When he seized the additional powers, Logan had to make sure that he was able to surge forward and take hold of Conquest. He had to maximize the potential of the explosion that was about to happen. However, he seemed to be losing the battle on both fronts. Conquest didn't need to use much power to push through Logan's weakened form, and even at full strength, Logan's power paled in comparison to what Dorovar's Herald could bring to bear. The spectral force also was incredibly strong. Though Logan knew in the back of his mind that there was no way that this Chorus of Souls had the same amount of strength that the Blaze did. However, in many ways, the Blaze mirrored the strength of the person who wielded it, and as Logan's strength waned, his control over the Blaze would as well. Time was short. He would have to either act now, or not act at all.

The process would take less than a second, but inside of Logan it felt like an eternity. All he had to do was reach through the smoky gates and take hold of the disparate powers. But just as he was about to reach out, a spasm of pain shook every part of his form, breaking his concentration. Logan forced his eyes open and saw the knowing and vindictive glare in Conquest's eyes. In his weakened state, Logan was unsure if he could concentrate long enough if Conquest knew what he was trying to accomplish. It was then that Logan heard the quiet voices in the back of his mind. Conquest's eyes narrowed slightly, and the prideful and confident smile turned into a vicious frown. It was then that Logan realized he was smiling. From somewhere deep inside of Logan, he felt a familiar tingling. It spread from some invisible and insubstantial part of himself and blossomed in his chest. As the tingling strengthened to a burning in the center of his chest, it spread down his arms and his legs and up into his face. By the time his toes began to tingle, the burning in his chest had grown so intense that he didn't know if the enervating spectral fire would consume him. Suddenly Logan's mind exploded with the brilliant emerald flames of the Blaze, and they burned away every thought, every doubt, and every fear. There was only the Blaze. He needed nothing else. The Blaze bloomed brighter and brighter inside of him, suffusing every pore, duct, and cell. After a moment, Logan's skin began to glow, and small peaks of flame began to blossom from his pores; the hairs on his skin standing up, bristling with power. Fire slipped and slid across Logan's skin like oil on water. After a moment, the flames burned brighter, and the phantasmal force that held Logan's arms struggled to keep the man still. The Blaze fires flared and the ghostly servants of Conquest were burned away, and the Herald of Dorovar had to shield his eyes from the impossibly bright explosion of power. Conquest didn't see Logan's hand come up, but he felt the heat and the blistering of his own exposed skin as Logan grasped Conquest's wrist and pulled it away from his chest. Conquest's vision cleared in time to see the wounds in Logan's chest instantly heal as soon as the invading fingers had been expelled. Conquest's shocked and angry gaze found Logan's suddenly confident eyes.

"I am the flickering flame," Logan said in a voice that was his own, but was laced with voices that Conquest could not place, "and yet I am so much more."

And in the Twilight be
All My Sins Remembered

*Year One of the Divine Empress and Child of the Creator
Marlae Tamerlane, Creator's Calendar Year 1871*

A casual observer at a safe enough distance might have perceived a shift in the conflict between the two ancient men who stood staring one another in the eye. Conquest's gaze was full of hate and disdain, while the tinges of suppressed shock could be seen at the edges of every expression. His opponent should not have been causing him this much trouble, and a matter of heartbeats earlier, the battle had been over. But now, Logan's eyes were not filled with the desperation and the growing acceptance of his fate, but rather a quiet almost unnerving confidence and peace. Whatever had happened that last moment before Conquest's hand was to crush Logan's heart had filled the troublesome man with new power. The burning had stopped in Conquest's arm, less about the application of his own powers and more about the retreat of the flames of Blaze fire from Logan's body. The aura was still visible, but it was not the raging bloom of power it had been. Logan released Conquest's wrist and took a careful half-step back, never breaking the eye contact. Conquest did not let his mind spin, but could not contain the question that wanted to explode deep in the recesses of his unconscious mind. Dorovar had given him the ability to negate Halicon's power through his absorption of Caris into the fold. As long as Jerah was a loyal member of Dorovar's flock, the Blaze was not a hazard to be feared. And yet, something was different about this version of the Blaze. It was not as confined as it had been in Caris. The phasia, for all of their power, feared what they were capable of and were limited in how much of the seemingly infinite power that the Blaze represented. Logan too had this restriction, more so because he was not born into the bastard family that was the Brotherhood of Phasia. This new power was a threat that Dorovar had not foreseen, and if it could not be harnessed, it would have to be eliminated.

"Impressive, Logan," Conquest's voice boomed. "But utterly futile. You may have been able to out-think Death, but you cannot out-think your oldest friend. I know every tactic you could employ. In fact, I taught you most of them. You were never comfortable with your powers. They scared you, and what they could make you capable of. You were never a killer. Remember what I did to Taron? Remember what I did to all of the other enemies that stood in our way? I've killed entire cities. I could kill entire worlds. Nothing can stand against me."

Logan's expression was blank.

"Whatever death you have caused is nothing to what I have been the architect of."

Logan's voice was different now, a full bass with power to spare.

"So you destroyed a city by dropping a mountain upon it. So you tortured one mentally defective phase to death. So you ripped apart a Servant of the Creator. I have been the death of hundreds of thousands. I have been the death of whole generations of humans. Cities were consumed by my wrath, and a world shook with my footsteps."

The voice shifted again, but instead of one voice, there were two, one higher pitched than the other, but operating in perfect harmony.

"I have killed dragons, men, women, children, the old, the young, the infirm, and the seemingly immortal."

Again Logan's voice shifted, and it sounded more like Aerith Seth when Logan spoke again, but again it was not a singular voice, it was tinged with two higher pitched voices, and one lower, this not a perfect harmony, but rather a discordant mass that somehow fit perfectly together.

"I have slain angels and demons by the hundreds, and I have ripped the wings from more than one Servant of the Creator."

Logan closed his eyes, and when he opened them again, his eyes had been replaced by the dancing flames of the Blaze.

"Dorovar may have made you to be an efficient killer, Conquest, but I am death incarnate!"

Logan charged forward the next moment, his left hand coming up to slam palm first into Conquest's chest. The strike was accompanied with as much Blaze as Logan could channel into that small point of impact. The strike became an explosion whose shock-wave leveled every building in a three block radius, and sent clouds of dust so high into the sky that they could be seen from everywhere on the mainland of Cadaria. Conquest flew back several hundred yards before finally striking the ground where he left a long furrow in the ground like a meteor that had fallen from the sky. Unhurt by the explosion of power, Conquest rose from the crater, lightning flaring in his eyes and the phantasmal aura flaring again around him. Logan had not moved from where he stood by the ruined church, and Conquest levitated back to solid ground. The part of Conquest that was still Pike wanted to let a jibe fly across the distance, but there was not time for that now. There was only the climax of the battle that remained, and the bloody and broken corpse of Logan Ranthall would be the last best insult. Conquest leapt into the air and was carried by the Chorus of Souls high into the air above the debris. He extended his hands to his side, and the sickening green aura around him began to intensify. As the seconds passed the mass solidified like a gigantic green storm cloud. However, this cloud was made of the ghostly bodies of the dead, churning in a mass of intertwining limbs, bodies and faces with horrific expressions. Each face that pushed to the surface of the mass was locked in a silent scream and twisted visage of pain and torment. The cloud grew and grew until it blocked out the twin suns overhead. Energy crackled between Conquest's extended and spread fingers, and Logan braced himself for an attack. The shield of Blaze fire flared back into existence, and the living flames danced across his hands practically begging to be used.

From out of the cloud a dozen of the spectral forms emerged, streaking like falling stars toward Logan. The screams that emanated from these spirits were not silent, and they threatened to force Logan to his knees. Both the force and the mind-numbing effects challenged his fortitude and balance. The first two spirits streaked by, just inches from Logan. The next two were closer, and they extended their claws and one of them ripped through Logan's shoulder while the other raked jagged claws across his face. Before Logan could think about what had happened, a fifth slammed right into him, passing through his torso, breaking half a dozen ribs in the process. They seemed completely unfazed by the shield of Blaze fire, and if Logan didn't come up with a tactic soon, the spirits would rip him to shreds. It was then that Logan saw the glint from his forearms. The bracers that he had been given by the dragon Aspertis were so light that Logan had forgotten he was even wearing them. In fact, had he had more time to think, he would have wondered if he even remembered to take them off when he slept. But rogue thoughts could not be entertained. All of his mind was consumed by remembering what the dragon had told him about the light pieces of armor known collectively as Flame.

Again, the rogue thoughts would have wanted to dwell on the nature of coincidence or fate, but they too were pushed away. Thoughts poured into the bracers and they flared from the nearly transparent crystalline structure to ghostly flames that extended up his arms, mixing with those of the Blaze. The two sets of flames seemed to battle one another for a time before they fell into a rhythmic harmonic dance like two strangers finding their feet together on a crowded dancefloor. When the next spirit came toward Logan, its claws extended and the baleful scream was replaced by one of pain. The claws streaked across the surface of the flames, and they reached out to claim the spirit, consuming it like dry brush in a wildfire. Not even ash was left. It was too late for five other spirits to pull up from their now suicidal dives, and Logan lashed out with a gout of flame that consumed them all in a single burst. A group of the spirits hung in the air between where Conquest perched high in the air and where Logan stood firmly on the ground. The mass of spirits flared again, and more joined the phalanx that was preparing to once again test the defenses of their dangerous opponent. The mass melded together, forms become indistinct, faces disappearing and emerging. The wail peaked and Logan steeled himself against the inevitable charge.

When the mass dove at him again, they came from all sides like swarming insects. Some ripped at the shield of flames while others sent forceful screams from his flanks and from behind. Logan struggled to keep his balance, his knees buckling and the ground under his feet becoming unstable. Blood streamed from his ears and nose, the sonic force threatening to turn his insides into soup. He knew that almost all of his bones had miniature fractures, and he could taste the mixture of bile and blood forming in the back of his throat. The time for restraint had ended. The explosion power that came from Logan was accompanied by a scream, one a mixture of pain and rage, which was inaudible above the wail of the circling spirits. The aura of flame extended in all directions, creating a perfect sphere of brilliant and terrifying power that obliterated everything in its path. As fast as the spirits were, the advancing barrier of flame was faster, and no matter which direction they flew, they were eventually enveloped and destroyed. The sphere expanded until it had almost reached the massive bank of phantasmal power that now wreathed Conquest, and then it contracted back upon itself. Logan now floated above a pit that rapidly filled with water from the sea that surrounded the island nation of Hedorah. The sphere of flames had broken completely through the crust of the island, and the lake of sea-water that now existed covered most of the area of the city where the Church of the Creator had been located. No buildings stood for dozens of blocks in all directions, and nearly a tenth of the total landmass of the island was completely gone. But Logan didn't have time to think of the level of destruction, and he hoped that the evacuation had gotten as many of the people out of that part of the city as possible. He bought as much time as he could during his parley with the monster Conquest, whatever happened now was beyond controlling. If Logan failed now in destroying the Herald of Dorovar, the amount of death he would wreak upon Espre was incalculable.

If Conquest was concerned by Logan's display of power, nothing showed on the Herald's face. However, there was a reaction from the mass of spectral energy around him. The cloud of spirits seemed to shrink away from Conquest, becoming more and more insubstantial until only the aura that clung to the Herald like smoke remained. Regardless, the power emanating from Conquest was still beyond definition, and Logan braced himself for the counter attack. He did not have to wait long for reprisal. Black clouds appeared out of nothingness around Conquest, and as the background filled with formless darkness, the golden crown shined like the sun and the flowing white cloak crackled with energy. The sparks of power jumped from Conquest's fingers into the clouds, bouncing from invisible border to invisible border. As the energy jumped, it forked and grew in intensity. Some of the bolts jumped to the cloak and then back to the clouds, gaining a blueish hue, while the bolts that touched the crown ended up with a reddish tint. Without warning, a bolt of the blueish lightning lanced out from the clouds and nearly struck Logan. He was able to cast himself to one side and avoid the worst of the strike, but the heat and the intensity of the bolt of energy was enough to singe the skin on his left arm black. The wound was gone nearly as quickly as it was inflicted. The bolt of energy struck the newly created lake, and danced across its surface, as though the lake was suddenly comprised not of water, but of electricity. Massive bolts of electricity and power rained down from the sky, some as thick as tree trunks. With the amount of power that they contained, Logan could not chance trying to deflect or block one of the bolts so he concentrated all of his power into his body to increase his speed and reflexes. The bolts came faster and faster, with Logan bobbing and weaving, unable to touch down to the electrified lake below, and unable to flee the area of attack. Because of the density of the attacks, he also couldn't ascend toward Conquest to take the fight to the monster. The air sizzled with power, and Logan's hair stood on end as he dodged more and more of the bolts. However, each one seemed to be getting closer. He felt a pang of panic strike his mind, and at the last moment he was able to dodge a smaller bolt of power. This one however had not come from above, but rather from the lake below. So much of the lightning had struck the water that it had begun to leap back into the sky toward its source. Conquest's cackling laughter could be heard high above, but the bolts of light were so bright that Logan could no longer see his opponent. Logan pirouetted through the air, dodging another dozen bolts from above and below, the last grazing his arm as it passed far too close for comfort. He could no longer afford to be on the defensive.

Letting the full powers of the Blaze fill him, Logan dove for the lake of lightning beneath him, pouring all of the speed that he could into his dive. At the last possible moment, Logan pulled up from the dive, and almost miscalculated. The searing heat from the lightning and the sheer force of gravity that held him to his suicidal descent were nearly enough to rip him from the sky and envelop him in the destructive light. But with an eyelash's width to spare, Logan pulled out of the dive. His insides did not react well to the change of direction, as his sternum and newly repaired ribs cracked and broke under the strain. Even his skull felt like it was going to spilt apart, but he would have time to worry about the damage later, if he survived the attempt. As he had hoped, a wake of lightning collected around him and began to follow him as his flight turned skyward. Reaching inside himself, Logan reached for the strings of Air and Fire, mixing them with the powers of the Blaze and creating a shield of lightning around himself as he had once seen Aryx Terian do so long ago. He felt rather than saw his target hovering high above him, and as he sped toward the sky, he increased his speed as much as his rapidly failing body would allow. The gambit was dangerous, and if he timed it wrong, there would likely be nothing left. As he ascended, Logan began to spin, ionizing the air around himself and hoping that it would have the effect that he wanted. Finally, Conquest was in sight; the flashes of lightning far enough from his form that he could be made out clearly. A dozen yards from Conquest, Logan curled himself into a ball and channeled all of the power he could manage with the string of Stone and hardening his bones and skin until they were almost diamond. The maneuver also increased his density and slowed his momentum. The trail of lightning that had followed him from the lake below sped past scorching his skin even with the increased density. The damage was incredible, and as each ragged breath dragged in and out of his lungs, Logan wondered if it would be the last. Ultimately, Logan's powers failed and he plummeted to the ground, but not before he saw the result of his plan.

Conquest could feel the moment of victory approaching. Logan's new powers were impressive, but the struggle would ultimately be futile. No matter how fast he moved, the lightning was faster, and it was only a matter of time before the foolish man made a mistake and was struck down. He saw Logan dive toward the surface and then pull up in what must have been a last suicidal attack. It would take no effort at all to avoid Logan's ballistic strike, and that would put an end to the foolishness for good. Conquest channeled all of his power into the banks of clouds behind him, charging them with more and more of the lethal lightning. Logan would speed past Conquest and fly right into barrier of power. If the impact didn't vaporize him, Conquest would be surprised, but regardless Conquest would have the pleasure of scattering the foolish man's ashes on the wind. However, at the last moment, Logan stopped advancing and before Conquest knew what was happening, a massive trunk of blue and red lightning sped past Logan's form and slammed into Conquest's chest. The force of the blow threw the Herald backward until he collided with the banks of clouds. Lightning sparked all around him, burning through his armor, his skin, his bones, and his organs. Huge burned patches of skin were scorched to ash in a matter of seconds, and the skin that wasn't directly subjected to the power bubbled with blisters that popped under the intense heat.

The cry of pain that ripped from Conquest's chest was followed by a wave of force that disintegrated the clouds and dispelled the lightning. The sky remained dark, the light of the suns completely blocked as two forms fell from the sky. The two lifeless and limp forms toppled uncontrolled from their heights, pushed and pulled by the winds that had been tortured by the incredible application of power. The amount of turbulence and instability in the sky had created a hurricane-like vortex that threw the two men in opposite directions. Conquest hit the ground just at the edge of the lake crater burying him nearly six feet deep in a crater of his own. Logan hit the water near the center of the lake, his instincts releasing the flows of Stone as he fell. The shield of wind cushioned some of the impact, but not enough to prevent practically every bone in his body from being broken. As he sank, the bubble of Air and Water formed around him preventing him from drowning, as his powers went to work repairing the extensive damage. Logan didn't know if Conquest was alive or dead, but he knew that he didn't have much time either way. Either his powers would give out and he would drown, or Conquest would recover enough to electrify the lake and finish him off. He wouldn't have time to heal completely, so as soon as enough of the damage was repaired that he could swim, Logan pulled himself toward the surface and the nearest edge of the lake.

Logan broke the surface and scrambled up the unstable shore until he pulled himself panting fully onto the broken land. There was little but rubble strewn around him, patches of ground burned to ash while other areas looked like they had been hastily assaulted with hundreds of shovels. Massive pieces of stone had erupted from the ground, like the island of Hedorah had suddenly sprouted dozens of broken teeth in an effort to devour the two creatures that were tormenting it. Logan's first attempt to get back to his feet was a failure. His legs would simply not support his weight. Logan tried to draw on more power in an attempt to repair his shaking legs, but at first there was nothing there to draw upon. Panic set in along with the pain, but finally a trickle of the Blaze reemerged and the healing began again. The second attempt to stand got farther, but still was unsuccessful, and Logan ended up seated on the ground once more. Breathing was hard, so was thinking, but he needed only one thought. He had to find out what had happened to Conquest and determine the level of threat that still existed. But in order to do that, he had to get back to his feet. The third push managed to get him upright, and while Logan felt as though he could topple over at any moment, he began scanning the shore for any sign of his opponent. Finally, as the healing to his broken body continued, Logan saw the unmoving mass on the opposite shore, the crown laying several feet away and the white cloak ripped into a dirty tattered version of itself. Smoke rolled from the form, and Logan couldn't see any movement. However, he wasn't going to let his guard down or investigate further until he was in better fighting shape. All he needed was a few more seconds. He wouldn't get the time.

Logan was quick to recognize that Conquest had begun moving, smoke rolling from his skin as he pushed himself to his feet. The hulking form looked like a shell of its former self, but the power rolling from it could not be ignored. As soon as Conquest caught sight of his opponent, he launched himself forward faster than Logan's eyes could follow. The Herald's foot barely skimmed the surface of the water as he flew over the entire width of the lake and collided with Logan on the opposite shore. Conquest's hand seized Logan around the throat and Logan's hands instinctively wrapped around the wrist and forearm of his attacker as the two continued to sail through the air. They had flown to the opposite side of the island kingdom of Hedorah into the abandoned and nearly completely destroyed port district before Conquest brought them both to a sudden stop. It was clear to Logan that any fine control of Conquest's powers had been lost, but that the Herald had more than enough raw power to spare. Conquest held Logan in front of him above the ground, his feet dangling, and Logan could see only red rage on Conquest's deformed features.

"WHY?"

The shout was deafening, a roar that felt to Logan as though he had been punched in both ears simultaneously. Suddenly Logan was lifted higher and then slammed hard into the ground. As Conquest pulled Logan up again the roar came again.

"WHY!"

Logan was violently slammed down again, the sounds of breaking bones evident. He was pulled up again.

"WON'T!"

Slammed again to the ground, blood flowed from eyes, ears, nose, and mouth, all of the air driven from his lungs by contact with the hard unforgiving ground. Logan knew he was pulled up again, but the ability for rational thought was nearly gone.

"YOU!"

When he was slammed to the ground again, the impact caused his vision to go black and his hearing was filled with the roar of the blood that flowed through his ear canal. It sounded as though Logan was on the shore of the ocean and the waves were pummeling his head. All of his limbs were limp. He became vaguely aware of being lifted again, only because of the stress on his neck and his head lolling backwards.

"DIE!"

This time Conquest released Logan's throat when he was slammed to the ground. Broken and bleeding, his vision gone, Logan reached for his powers, and there was nothing there. Not even the sustaining powers of Aerith Seth were available to him. He couldn't even perceive the shadowy gates that could give him access the powers of his family. His mind was quiet again, for the first time in thousands of years. It was at that moment that the fear truly set in. Even though he could not see, Logan could feel Conquest standing over him, the red seething rage like waves of heat pouring from its body. The ground began to quake, and Logan could feel Conquest using his abilities. Near his head, the ground shifted and pushed up as though something was being forced through the ground to the surface. There was a stab of pain in the back of Logan's head, and he could feel his eyes beginning to force themselves open. He knew his eyelids were so swollen that they were nearly shut, but as a slit formed, he could see light above him and the shadowy form that must have been Conquest. In that back of his mind, the ghostly mantle of Aerith Seth weakly reappeared. There was not enough left to heal himself, or even launch an attack. In fact, Logan wasn't sure there was enough there to do much of anything. The next moment Conquest's hands were on him again, and Logan was being dragged across the ground, jagged rocks and stones ripping at the skin of his back and legs. Finally, Conquest stopped again and the Herald's other hand took hold of one of Logan's legs and he was hoisted high into the air. As he dangled, Logan got a glimpse of what was below him. Conquest had forced a spike of diamond out of the ground, its cruel sharp point glimmering in the little bit of light that broke through the dark clouds above. Conquest was going to impale Logan on the spike and end the battle. There were no words, no taunts, nothing, and Logan found himself speeding downward.

The flash of power was reflex, nothing more. It shouldn't have worked, but perhaps Conquest was so far beyond the borders of logic that he no longer could feel Logan's minute uses of power. Logan pulled on the little remaining strength from the mantle of Aerith Seth and formed a small portal. There wasn't enough for him to create one to escape his fate, but he could use Conquest's plan against him. The portal dropped over the top of the spike of diamond and opened a fraction of an inch from the center of Conquest's chest. The Herald had already committed all of the force that he could muster into his forward motion, and as Logan tumbled helplessly to the ground, the spike of diamond pierced Conquest through the chest and erupted from his back. Conquest's arms spasmed and Logan fell from his grasp, crashing to the ground in a heap, his head hitting the base of the diamond spike. His skin split wide open, blood gushing from the wound, the skull beneath cracked. Despite the damage, Logan pushed himself up to a sitting position, his eyes barely open, cast up at Conquest. The Herald was standing perfectly still, blood pouring from around the diamond spike. Expressionless, Conquest looked down first at the spike and then down at Logan. Both hands went to the spike and he tugged at the wide edge, impotently at first, and then with a second and third effort was able to shift it and rip it away from where it was lodged. As more of the spike pulled away, it was coated with blood and viscera; each inch extricated met with a gout of blood spurting in all directions. In the end, the gruesome instrument of death had been ripped away from the gaping wound, and Conquest took a step toward Logan. The fallen man was completely defenseless, no more power left. Conquest tried to take another step but faltered, falling to his knees, the flow of blood continuing unabated from the hole that had been ripped completely through his body. Logan could see that the wound was not healing, and that the aura of phantasmal green energy was gone. On his knees, Conquest still struggled forward, dragging the diamond spike every painful inch. Finally, Conquest stopped, looming over his immobile opponent. With great effort the Herald's bloody hands were able to lift the slick blood-stained diamond spike above his head, its cruel point poised to thrust downward and pierce Logan's vulnerable heart. The hate-filled eyes locked onto the nearly closed and resigned gaze of his rival.

Time stopped. There was no sound, no pain, no future or past. There was only the moment. Two men's fates had been intertwined since the moments of their births, one indistinguishable from the other save for the choices they had made. Their places in the cosmic order could have just as easily been reversed. They each fought for a better world, for a better future, for love, for family, for respect, and against forces that they struggled to understand both from the outside and from within their own hearts and minds. They had both lost their way. They had both struggled to find their way back, but always their paths would cross. Always their paths had been leading to this moment. And as Conquest held the diamond spike, Logan knew that after this moment there would be no more path to follow, and an emptiness worse than death flooded through him. He closed his eyes and waited for the pain. But it never came. Instead, there was the sound of something hard hitting the ground and then a weight fell onto Logan's weakened body. When Logan opened his eyes once more, the diamond spike could be seen rolling slowly away in the bloody mud, and Conquest's dead form was draped across Logan's body, his head wrenched to one side so that his vacant dead eyes stared up at Logan. With great effort, Logan was able to lift his hand and reach out. His hand trembling, his fingers fluttered over the open eyes, finding the eyelids and gently forcing them shut. Finally, Logan's hand rested on Pike's head.

"Goodbye, old friend."

Logan's voice was raspy and muted by blood and bile, barely above a croaked whisper. He too shut his eyes, and the world dropped away into nothingness.

CHAPTER 100

Chapter CI

On Wrongs,
Swift Vengeance Waits

*Year Four of the Just Emperor Kaitain "Dragonsbane" Lorien,
Creator's Calendar Year 1871*

The suns were just beginning to set in the west over the Pritan Islands and long shadows stretched across the landscape of broken stones and shattered mountain ranges. As the suns faded from view, the last streaks of the Days of Star Fire became more brilliant. They would only last another few days and would be gone for another hundred years. As Dorovar looked up into the sky he knew that this world would not see another hundred years. It would most likely not see another year. His hands clasped behind his back, Dorovar pondered the sky. At first his eyes shifted between the streaks of light, the stars, then to the vast blackness. But his eyes did not stop with the blackness that stretched above. His gaze passed through the ephemeral veil that separated the material world from the realm of the Creator, perceiving not with his eyes but with his immortal soul the celestial palace and the Golden Throne that lay within. For several minutes Dorovar stood there, his impassive and unbreakable stare boring through the impregnable defenses of the Creator's stronghold, trying to see what lay beyond the Throne. What would await Dorovar when he pierced through the lies and betrayals and paper towers to the creature behind the death and pain? Was there even a form for Dorovar to seize with his hands? Was there a neck to squeeze? Was there blood to spill? Was there a heart to crush in his bare hands? Were there eyes to watch the life slowly fade from? Pain filled Dorovar the next moment, a familiar pain, but one that he had become far too accustomed to. How could he concern himself with the obstacles that awaited him in the next world when he still had trifles that demanded his attention in this one?

Dorovar's eyes lowered from the heavens, and it took several moments for them to refocus on what was before him. The scenery on the island that was serving as a makeshift base of operations would have been considered beautiful, if chaotic. There was no symmetry or pattern in the outcroppings of stone, or the swirl of the grass in the wind, or the waves that beat against the beach. To the calm and ordered mind of the members of the Adhradair the lack of pattern was an assault on the senses. On their home-world of Loinn, everything had its place, its purpose, and its pattern. The goddess Raenera had decreed that everything would follow her plan, and so even the wind blew as it was ordered to do so. The grass swirled in perfect harmony, always in the same direction, and stone burst from the ground at proper angles, and always at proper distances and with proper parallel or perpendicular angles to their fellows. For every thing there was a purpose, for every place there was an arrangement that had been in place since the moment of the world's creation. It was a pattern that would have continued for eternity if it weren't for the interference of the traitorous Emries and Talisia, and the blind faith of Dorovar and the other Adhradair in their goddess. It had cost them so much, and now, once again, Dorovar felt the pain of loss.

Faelara had been the first of the Adhradair to come to him after she had been released from the prison imposed upon her by Talisia's continued treachery. She had been there when he broke from his own prison and took his first steps onto this new chaotic world. She had been there when the oldest of the dragons took its last breath and the first measure of vengeance was paid to the overgrown lizards. It had been Faelara who had suggested expanding Dorovar's influence in the world of the mortals, and it had been Faelara who had offered her former companion Jaccob Aldora as the vessel by which Dorovar's mercy would be shown to the brutish little girl Marlae. To Dorovar, it had been a waste of his time and power to spare the woman, but if Faelara wished such a boon as the price for her continued service to Dorovar's will, then so be it. Faelara, more than any of the other members of the Adhradair had felt the fickle pull of the primrose path of providence. On Loinn, she had tried to warn them all of a great test that was coming, a test that would prove who was truly faithful and who was unworthy. Each of the Adhradair, including Dorovar, had failed that test, and it had cost them all their world. But the rest of the Adhradair had taken Faelara's prediction to heart, and had seen Dorovar as the most faithful of them all. Again, it was the demands of Order that pulled at them. They could be no more or no less than what they were made to be. The Adhradair were shepherds of Order, but they were also shepherded by the very Order that they enforced. It was a delicate and perfect symmetry as envisioned by Raenera. And it was a symmetry that they would be forced to adhere to until the whole of the Cosmos was brought to heel and was reborn under Dorovar's watchful gaze. But Faelara had also seen the future when it had come to the girl Marlae. She had seen that the Creator would touch the petulant girl and make her into something more. And so, Faelara had set about to plant a seed within the girl, a seed that at the right time would blossom into something that would spread a disease through the body of the Creator's faithful. It would be a slow and painful death that would slowly rob the Creator of His strength and feed more imprisoned souls into the growing Chorus. In time there would be enough voices and enough power to raise Dorovar beyond the mortal world and the Creator would finally be toppled from his Golden Throne.

Dorovar's eyes dropped from the Heavens and his thoughts returned to the world around him. There were so many sounds, so much chaos, even on the quiet remote island. He took several long strides forward, his hands still clasped behind his back, until he was standing at the edge of a cliff overlooking the sea. To the north lay the mainland of Cadaria, and beyond that, burning like a beacon on the edge of his vision was the island kingdom of Hedorah. Just as Dorovar had known the moment of Faelara's demise, he also had felt the moment of Conquest's defeat. Perhaps it had been hubris to send the newly minted Herald to destroy the mortal vessel of the Creator's divine mandate. But it had not been the Flying Guard of Hedorah, or even the angelic host that had brought about the end of Conquest's march of destruction. No, that honor had gone to the imminently frustrating and increasingly fascinating Logan Ranthall. Already the tarnished hero had cost Dorovar two very effective tools in the Heralds Conquest and Death, and had been the one who had banished Faelara's soul to the void. But as much of a nuisance as Logan Ranthall had proven himself to be, he was no longer worth the resources it would take to destroy him. He was merely a cog. Once the wheel was broken, the fallacy of his existence would be resolved. Distractions could no longer be afforded, and there was no time for petty vendettas. All focus needed to be on freeing the remaining members of the Adhradair, restoring all of Dorovar's power, and locating the soul of the High Priestess.

It was then that Dorovar felt that he was not alone in the advancing darkness. Unlike the mortals that called themselves Dark Gods, or the ones who claimed to be touched by the rebellious Children of the Creator, the freed members of the Adhradair needed nothing as pedestrian as portals to travel across the face of Espre. They were not truly mortal, nor as Dorovar reflected upon it, were they by any definition alive. Much like his heralds, the remnants of the Adhradair floated between life and death. Using the ether that lay between the dimensions, they could move like ghosts, simply willing themselves where they wished to be. More of his brothers and sisters had been freed from their prisons, and though Faelara's death had been a great loss, it would not prevent the rest from accomplishing their tasks. Victory would be at hand soon enough, and so would the final and complete redemption of the Adhradair.

When Dorovar turned, five faces greeted him, two of which were the recently freed. Standing with Coriden, Redissa, and Haricos were two of the more enigmatic members of the Adhradair. The first, and oldest member of the group was Luigsech. The dark-eyed man with sickly yellow sclera around black irises always had a dour expression and a furrowed brow. In life, Luigsech had been the member of the Adhradair who was tasked with overseeing the wild and natural areas of Loinn. As the years passed Luigsech's visage began to more closely resemble the natural world that he had been tasked by the goddess Raenera to maintain. His skin was ashen and coarse like the bark of a tree, and the long hair that cascaded from his head had grown long, thick, and stringy like vines. Luigsech was also an extremely sturdy man with thick muscular legs and powerful willowy arms. When the incursion upon Loinn became war, Luigsech had become the most deadly of all of the Adhradair, bending the forests to his will.

Branches and vines pulled dragons from the sky, snapped their necks with incredible force, and strangled them with brutal efficiency. The malice and hatred had formed dark circles under both of the man's eyes that served as a reminder to all of the other members of the Adhradair just what their compatriot was capable of. Once Dorovar would have counted Luigsech among his closest allies and staunchest friends. But the war had changed all that, and it had created a rift between Luigsech and the others that would never be mended.

The other newly restored member of the Adhradair was perhaps the most physically gifted of all of the group. Maedoc was the chosen protector of the High Priestess. Even though the role was primarily ceremonial, Maedoc took the position very seriously. Every waking hour Maedoc devoted himself to the training of his mind and his body, honing them into a tool that knew only one purpose. If there were ever to be a threat against the High Priestess, Maedoc would be able to meet and defeat it. In the days before the invasion of the dragons, Maedoc could be seen wearing brilliant white armor with a flowing white cloak trailing his steps. He was a symbol of all that was best in the Adhradair. Once the war with the infernal lizards began, Maedoc's armor never shown brightly again. Each and every engagement, the armor was stained with more and more blood of the enemies of Order, and Maedoc wore the blood of his enemies like a badge of honor. It took only a matter of weeks for his once brilliant armor to turn black. Now, in his reincarnated form, Maedoc's thick armor was still black, and the cape had long since been abandoned. Long dark hair framed his face and flowed to the level of his shoulders and were matched by a thick mustache and beard.

Redissa bowed her head for a moment and then spoke.

"We followed the trail of the seers and discovered two of the Maldovrin sisters in hiding. Before we were able to approach them quietly, one of Emries' minions appeared and tried to take information from the seers by force. The Will appeared and prevented the seers from divulging the information to anyone."

Dorovar frowned.

"What information?"

"The location of the fourteenth weapon," Haricos answered. "And with it the location of the soul of the High Priestess."

The frown deepened on Dorovar's face.

"This is most troubling. Either Talisia has decided that she is no longer capable of carrying out the tenants of her scheme and requires the assistance of her treacherous brother once more, or Emries has not allowed the wool to be pulled over his eyes and intends to use Talisia's scheme without her intervention. Regardless, they know that without access to the soul of the High Priestess I will be unable to attain my full power and leverage the Chorus of Souls to ascend to the Heavens. It is an unacceptable turn of events."

The displeasure was clear on Maedoc's face.

"I cannot allow the High Priestess's soul to fall into the hands of either of those traitors. The Order must be preserved at all costs. Please Dorovar, let me take up the search for this fourteenth weapon. She is still my charge, even after all these years in prison."

Dorovar did his best to suppress a sigh. Of course he knew that this would be Maedoc's position, and though he wanted to refuse there was no point in it. Even if Dorovar chose to send Maedoc on another mission, he would feel duty bound to pursue information about the High Priestess no matter the cost. So, Dorovar had no choice but to use that zeal for the betterment of all.

"Very well, Maedoc," Dorovar relented, "but go with Luigsech. I have a feeling that you will need his strength and tenacity when the time comes. The loss of the seers leaves only two options for finding the information. We know that the third member of the triplets had been given shelter by Raenera before the fall of her refuge. She has since disappeared, and none of my attempts to divine her location have borne fruit. That leaves only one option. The Dark Seer."

Coriden crossed his arms.

"Is she not dead?"

Dorovar tilted his head slightly, looking past his compatriots to the south.

"These mortals continue to surprise me with their need to cling to life in the face of overwhelming odds. Jehna Feris was touched by the Creator more strongly than any seer in history, with the exception of the First Empress who was herself a servant of the Creator. And yet this woman has survived with her sanity still intact. She has touched the minds of gods, demons, dragons, and has stood against the mortal elite with no fear. Were she not an impediment to our cause I might find it within myself to grant her mercy. But she has opposed us by suppressing the information about the soul of the High Priestess, and for that I cannot extend any protection. Find her, Maedoc, and make her tell you what she knows, no matter what it takes."

Luigsech's rough and gravelly voice filled the silence next.

"And do you know how we are to find this resilient and formidable woman?"

Dorovar's glance returned to Maedoc.

"The last creature to track down the Dark Seer when she did not want to be found is the monster Shadowweaver. If Shadowweaver had a method to track the Dark Seer, he would have left the actual work to his trusted minions. That means Stormbane the Traitor and Derelor the Manipulator are the most likely to have the information. I know how long you have ached to bring death to those creatures, Maedoc. Now is your chance."

Maedoc's expression was one of determination rather than pleasure, but Dorovar quickly saw the murderous look in Luigsech's eye. Derelor and Stormbane had burned dozens of forests during their time on Loinn, and Luigsech wanted nothing more than to make them burn for their crimes. The assignment given, the two hunters disappeared. Dorovar's attention then shifted to Redissa and her brother.

"We must accelerate our efforts to free our remaining imprisoned brothers and sisters. The difficulty however is that it seems as though Aerith Seth and his followers have gained possession of three of our compatriots. We cannot act against Aerith Seth directly, not yet. Stalk his protégé, Hannah Ironheart, isolate her, and then remove her from this war. Free our sister and strip Aerith of one of his followers."

Redissa and Haricos both bowed slightly and disappeared. Dorovar was left alone with Coriden, the one member of the Adhradair whose hate might have pushed him to act against Dorovar and put the whole plan at risk. The two men regarded each other silently for several moments before Coriden finally spoke.

"Things are not going as you foresaw them, are they, Dorovar? Has your vision once again been compromised by your desires?"

Part of Dorovar wanted to be offended by the words, but there was no purpose behind it for two reasons. The first, and least important, was that all of the transgressions that lay between Dorovar and Coriden happened millennia ago. While Coriden's soul would not have been aware of the time that had passed, Dorovar was painfully aware of every single moment. The second reason, and the one far more relevant, was that Coriden was right. Dorovar had been blinded by his faith and his belief in Raenera. He never once asked why he was being directed to give shelter to the dragons or what the ramifications of that act would be. Regardless of what came before, Dorovar knew that he was the sole member of the Adhradair responsible for what came after. Even though his fellows were tied to him in death, it was not truly penance for their actions in the war that followed. The penance was Dorovar's. For the rest of his days he would be tied to his brothers and sisters in the Adhradair, the ones whom his duty it was to protect; a duty he failed miserably.

"This time, Coriden, my eyes are open wide, and I have no illusions about the future."

Coriden's dark features did not change, and there was significant anger in his eyes. His long wild white hair fluttered in the evening breeze and his posture spoke of violence barely restrained.

"The others are ashamed, Dorovar, ashamed of what we became at the end. They are ashamed of the death and of the loss and destruction. They all took the loss of our world very hard, and they have all been changed by our captivity. We were not awake like you, but we do have memories from our time. We know every hand that our prisons passed through, and all of the events that revolved around us. We remember being in the Heavens before the fall and the peace that the dead must feel. But we were not free to find solace in our deaths. Even in that peace, we were imprisoned. Even in eternal rest we knew no respite. But you and I, Dorovar, we are different than the others. You became a killer to get revenge for our fallen world, but I have always been a killer. I was born to this calling, born to this life, and born to take the lives of the enemies of the Adhradair. Raenera made me this way, not to be loyal to her and to punish her enemies, but to be loyal to my brothers and sisters and to punish our enemies."

Dorovar nodded and began to speak, but Coriden raised a hand.

"I may be a weapon, Dorovar, but I am not a witless one like your Heralds. And while I feel this compulsion to follow your plans without question, I will not allow the darkness to be pulled over my eyes and be led around like a child. You will have my cooperation, Dorovar, I have no choice in that matter. You could dismiss me now and send me on the next murderous spree, and I could do nothing to oppose your will. But if you are as you say, wishing for a better world, a better reality where the Creator does not view all within his domain as expendable pawns serving at His pleasure, then you must here and now explain to me what this grand plan is and how you intend to accomplish it."

In another life, Dorovar might have found Coriden's words insulting or perceived them as a challenge. However, after millennia of pride shattering loneliness in the void between worlds, Dorovar felt the words as nothing more than a need for validation. There were many times that Dorovar felt as though he were alone in his quest, very much as he had been at the end on Loinn as he watched his world burn. The rest of the Adhradair had already fallen, and Emries and Talisia had left Dorovar to impotently watch the final death throes of everything Dorovar believed in.

"The Creator is not just a being that can be assaulted and toppled by force of arms, Coriden. He is as much an idea as he is a creature. In all these centuries of study and thought, I have yet to even be able to determine if the Creator has a physical form. I may not know how to kill a formless entity, but I know how to kill an idea. We learned that on Loinn.

Emries and Talisia showed us the way. We must strip away every implement of His will, we must break the faith of His followers. The Children must fall first, as they are direct conduits of the Creator's power and intention. They have made all of this possible, and so they must be removed. Three have already been silenced, and we have saved Talisia and Emries for last."

Coriden frowned.

"But these vessels of the Children, and their chosen…"

Dorovar shook his head.

"We were the only true Chosen, Coriden, and look how easily we were misled and used for ill purpose. These mortals are no different. Whether it is Halicon's phasia, Emries' puppets, or Talisia's so-called children, they will be cleansed of their delusions. Soon enough we will openly hunt these unfortunate souls and give them the rest they deserve. With the Children and their throng eliminated, that will leave the last of the Servants, the one they call the Will. His destruction will serve two purposes. The first will be to rob the Creator of the last of his defenses short of the pathetic angelic warriors, and the second will be to strike a blow against Aerith Seth."

Coriden glowered.

"We should have already eliminated that thorn in our heel."

"Aerith has proven to be a great advancer of our agenda, even if he does not fully realize it," Dorovar said waiving a dismissive hand. "While I shall not go so far as to say that the enemy of my enemy is my friend, what I will say is that as long as Aerith is fighting against the Creator, the dragons, Emries, and Talisia, he is serving a purpose. The moment he stops serving a constructive purpose, we shall eliminate him, his family, and his followers."

Coriden smirked.

"Your Heralds did not prove capable of that task thus far."

For a split second, rage surged in Dorovar, but he was able to keep it out of his eyes, and out of his tone.

"Logan and Arin Ranthall have proven to be interesting opponents, but ultimately their victories mean nothing. Pestilence redeemed his failures by sacrificing himself to free Drust from her prison, and while the loss of Death and Conquest are unfortunate, both have shown me how much the enemy knows about the nature of this war and the ultimate victory that lies within my grasp. The knowledge that they had accumulated died with Logan Ranthall. By the time they reconstruct what he knew, it will be too late, and I will be seated upon the Golden Throne."

Dorovar did not like lying to Coriden, but there was little choice now. Whether Logan Ranthall was alive or dead was still to be determined, as the whole of Hedorah was wreathed in so much power that it was impossible to determine the fate of the man. Dorovar would have sent one of the Adhradair to determine for certain, but even if Logan survived his confrontation with Conquest, he would be no threat for some time. As to how much of the information about the manner in which to unseat the Creator had fallen into the hands of Aerith Seth or other members of the opposing forces was still unclear. Talisia and Dorovar both had the knowledge to make the plan work, and if Talisia knew, there was no doubt that Emries also knew. However, if Aerith Seth had learned of the information through Logan Ranthall, the race for power became far more tenuous. Perhaps Aerith and his family would need to be eliminated before they outlived their usefulness to the cause. None of that mattered however if Dorovar was unable to regain all of the power he had stolen over his years floating in the nothingness of the void. He had learned the power of the Cosmos, and had siphoned as much as he could of the forgotten energy of Creation before he was imprisoned. Of course, his jailing had been by design. However, Dorovar had not foreseen his power being stripped away from him by the traitorous Talisia and distributed among the souls of his fellow Adhradair. It complicated matters, but only earned the Creator a short reprieve.

"We must focus now on our brothers and sisters that still languish in their prisons," Dorovar said finally. "Your lady love, Judoc, and her prison Patience has fallen into the hands of the woman Chelsea Zarova, the former wife of my Herald War. Seraph thought he was being clever by hiding the weapon with his wife, but once he became my Herald, all of his secrets became mine."

Dorovar laid his hand on Coriden's shoulder for a moment, closing his eyes and concentrating on his connection with the Herald War. When he removed his hand, Dorovar took a step back and continued speaking.

"Chelsea should not be a challenge for you, Coriden, but should she pose a problem, use War's knowledge to take the woman off-balance. There should be enough incendiary material there to force her to strike at you and free Judoc."

Coriden considered for a moment, nodded his ascent, and then was simply gone. Dorovar was left in silence once more, and he turned back toward the cliff and looked once more in the direction of the Cadarian Empire. As he closed his eyes, he reached out his mind looking for one who was about to be useful to him once more. Jerah in her defiance had discovered an opportunity, one that Dorovar was not going to hesitate to use to his advantage.

No Change Without Upheaval

Year Four of the Just Emperor Kaitain "Dragonsbane" Lorien, Creator's Calendar Year 1871

Work. Work. Work. Arturious Demascious had known only that singular word drumming in his head for almost two thousand years. Even in the sub-freezing temperatures, sweat rolled down the sides of the ancient man's face as the hammer once again came down upon the forge. Thousands of swords, spears, axes, and thousands more pieces of armor lay in odd piles throughout the room. Thousands more were in a storeroom that lay feet away from the forge. While Arturious didn't know the exact count, for it didn't really matter, what he did know was that his time was coming to an end. Arms and armor for Raenera's army of the dead were almost complete, and Arturious knew that once the last hammer fell on the last item, his pain would end, and the fear would end. But there was the crawling in the back of Arturious mind. The blinding fear that seeped through every thought continued to claw at his mind, and the green glow of Dorovar's might tangled with it. The work kept away the doubt, but it could do nothing with the fear. Had Dorovar in any way guided Arturious' hand? Were there flaws in the weapons or armor that he had been so fanatically creating for so long? But how could any of those fears be real? Would Raenera have let his work continue for so long if any part of it were corrupted? Would she have let it be compromised by such an obvious lecherous influence? Now that Raenera was gone, would that be the siren song for all of the dark forces aligning for control of not only the world of Espre, but also for the Heavens that stretched above?

While Arturious worked, the world continued to turn, continued to change, but the darkness would never relent, it simply grew and fed on all it could touch. It was always touching the back of Arturious' mind, driving him forward. Each time one of the Heralds of Dorovar set foot upon the face of the world a cold like the wind of the grave wrapped around Arturious' slow beating heart. Arturious lived by the grace of Raenera, as did Dorovar, as did each of the Adhradair, but now that grace had changed; diminished. Of course, Raenera's power still existed, and would exist so long as the universe existed, but now it was imprisoned in the body of a mortal. At least the man wearing the name Gideon Viruci was partially mortal. Over the centuries, Arturious had gained the ability to truly see the world around him. Some of that was from the touch of Dorovar, some was from the influence of the powers of Raenera, the rest, was simply time. Mortals to Arturious' eyes looked like hollow shells, within which bloomed the smallest piece of the living Cosmos' consciousness. There were other things of course, the web of power that came from the being's creator, and a slight haze of divine influence. Humans, by and large were confused things, a shell filled with the clinging and crawling conflicted morass that came from their brutal architect Emries. There was so much of the confusing mass in fact that it made it difficult for Arturious to see the glimmer of the Cosmos at all. Fortunately for this Gideon Viruci, the piece of him that was Emries was tempered by a brighter streak of the Cosmos that burned within him, something that Arturious had seen only one other time. But that was so long ago, and only in passing. Perhaps he had not really seen it at all, or perhaps Raenera had removed so much of it from his memory. It mattered little. His time was at an end and there would be no one to which his knowledge and pain would be passed. The millennia of torture would end in blood, and Arturious wondered if there was really peace waiting beyond the veil for him.

* * * * * * * * * * * *

Gideon stalked around the frozen cave like a caged beast. A war raged inside of him unlike any he had known in his life, and he had had more than his fair share of moral quandaries to deal with and reconcile. Being a thief had its advantages when it came to moral equivalence, so too did being a spy. Gideon had been both, and he had excelled at both. But that was in a time where he always believed he was serving the greater cause, and he always drew a moral line. Murder was beyond the line. Even when murder would have made situations better, he could not bring himself to do it. Then he became a father, and the thought of taking a life in cold blood was unpalatable. Of course, as he raised his daughter, the world fell apart around him. Monsters and demons lurked around every corner, and Gideon tried hard to teach, protect, and retain his humanity as the shadow continued to tighten its grip. He regretted that his daughter grew up a warrior; a killer. But perhaps that was inevitable. She was descended from a long line of killers. And his father had shown him a long time ago that there was a very thin line between killing for a cause and simply killing. One man's hero is another man's villain, and a champion and a murderer are only separated by point of view. Aerith would have laughed off the rationale as the idle thoughts of someone who had never had to fight and kill for something they loved. Just because history was written by those who survived didn't mean that they were in any morally superior position, it just meant that they were still alive. Circumstance was a terrible dictator, and it was one whose reign was continually unchallenged. And it was circumstance that Gideon now found himself squarely set against. Could he set aside everything he believed to do what needed to be done?

How could it have come to this? But perhaps he shouldn't have been surprised. How many times during this war had it come down to one life? One life to save, one life to sacrifice, one life to take. Out of context, which is so often how information came, it seemed so simple, just as it seemed simple now. All Gideon had to do was track down one girl and kill her. With all of his new abilities coupled with his experience there was little that should have been able to stand in his way. However, what chance should Cedric or Korrd or Nathaniel have stood against Shau-ling and the phasia? What chance should Terrik Lorien stood against Grawn and his warlords during the Founding Wars? How many obstacles would be standing in the way between Gideon and Jillian, and how many of those could Gideon have at one time considered friends? Was that a cost he was willing to pay?

Gideon turned to face the frost-covered wall and placed his forehead against it. Ever since he had become the vessel of Raenera's power, he had felt increasingly warm, as though a great fire now burned where his soul had been. His rational thoughts knew that he was being slowly consumed by Raenera's powers, and if his thoughts were quiet enough he could hear Raenera's calm and ordered tone speaking the thoughts he was sure were his. But how could he know for sure any more? Where did he end and Raenera begin? Did it even matter? Was it her disdain for mortal beings that made it so easy for him to rationalize killing? Was it the training he had received from Basille and Bryn? Was it the piece of him that shared Aerith Seth's blood, the monster of all monsters whose death toll could never be fully reconciled with his aims? Was it the necessity of killing in the Dark Mirror world? Or was he just a coward who was unwilling to find another way?

His mind immediately went to the day before he collided with the people who would change his life forever. Gideon had been sent at the behest of his mentor and his adoptive father Basille Mystic to keep tabs on a rag-tag group of would-be heroes that seemed to stumble from one crisis to another without any clue of how they were going to get out alive. Basille was very familiar with the creatures known as the Tarnae, and he had become aware of Jeroch and Shau-ling's plan to trap Logan Ranthall and the rest of his companions in the woods outside of the city of Aradon. The Tarnae agreed to 'capture' Gideon and put up enough of a fight that the do-gooder in Logan would not question how this potential ally found his way into such a fortuitous position. However, from the moment Gideon met Logan Ranthall, he knew that his life would be different.

As the son of a member of the Brotherhood of Phasia, and raised and trained in that world, Gideon had a different view of humanity. Gideon's father had been a great hero, a great martyr. His mother was villain who had slaughtered humans by the thousands because that was what she had been bred to do. Basille had been something in between. He loved and cared for his people as though they were his own family, and then at the same time turned his powers to killing mortals at the orders of his master Shau-ling. It was a duality that Gideon had always found hard to process until he spent time with Logan and his companions. Gideon, like many of his generation, grew up with the legend of Cedric Binosear. Cedric, the tragic figure, overwhelmed by grief and saddled with a need for vengeance, gathered behind him a legendary group of adventurers and toppled the demon Shau-ling. If he was never heard from again, that alone would have made him a figure of immortal status. However, it was what Cedric did after the war was over that elevated him to heights that no hero on the world of Onea had ever seen. Much of the countryside had been devastated by the attacks of Shadowwalkers and Jeresei, and a great deal of usable farmland had been decimated. Many towns and villages were shattered, more homes burned to the ground than there were those still standing. Cedric toured the countryside with his advisors and with a core of carpenters, farmers, and masons. For years, Cedric devoted all the money and resources that he could gather to rebuilding the ravaged countryside. Cedric became beloved beyond measure. There was great hope that the next hero of the prophecies would not only meet the expectations that Cedric's reign had created, but exceed them. It was through these expectations that Gideon first tried to look at Logan Ranthall, but soon realized how both unfair and inadequate those expectations were.

Logan Ranthall by most measures was not a hero, nor would anyone confuse him with one. He was confused, conflicted, and consistently did everything for the wrong reasons. He was loyal to his friends even when their faults would have prevented him from doing the right thing. He was in love, and that love prevented him from seeing clearly or making the sacrifices that needed to be made. But in the end, even though he was not the hero of the story, he stood at the end and was willing to make the ultimate sacrifice. At every turn he should have failed, and yet he persisted. Logan was a man to be admired, and one that every person should have aspired to be like, even though he would have been the last person to advocate for that. Reluctant to lead, reluctant to be more than he was, and yet by his very presence he elevated everyone around him and pushed beyond the bounds of the possible. Perhaps that was the influence of Gideon's father in Logan, or perhaps that was just the nature of the man. Gideon didn't want to credit any of Logan's success to Aerith, but at times it was impossible to separate the two.

Gideon banged his head against the ice once more, trying to jar his mind into working. He kept going around and around again, and it kept coming back to the same problem. Could he kill a defenseless girl for the sake of everything? His father was willing to sacrifice his own life. His mother had been willing to sacrifice her own life. His mentor had sacrificed his life. Everything in his life had been the product of sacrifice. Even Raenera had sacrificed herself so that he could continue her work. And now that work called for one more sacrifice. However, this one probably would not be a willing one. But why did it have to be murder? Couldn't Gideon simply explain the situation to Jillian and then hope she made the right decision? And then what if she didn't? What if she ran or if someone got to her before Gideon could act? The advantage of taking swift action was that it would likely be the most painless approach. Whatever Gideon decided, he needed to act quickly. Arturious was almost finished with his work. Another murder, but this one certainly one of mercy. Arturious had suffered long, and Gideon would be happy to put the man out of his misery. It was then that Gideon became aware that he was no longer alone in the cavern.

His head still resting against the ice, Gideon reached out with his awareness. Arturious was still in his workshop hard at work, but his pace was slowing with every hour that passed. Jerrica was asleep further into the cavern, exhausted by the exertion that had given Gideon the identity of his victim. The newcomer radiated a power that was familiar to Gideon, one that filled him with a sense of dread. Snow and ice crunched under heavy riding boots as the interloper approached, and Gideon made no move that would spark the conflict before he was ready. He too was feeling the pull of exhaustion, not just from the moral quandary that held his heart, but also from the incredible weight that Raenera's powers. He felt stretched and squeezed at the same time, his body on fire and freezing.

"I wasn't sure what to expect," the young man's voice rang out. "But the longer I am on this pathetic ball of dust, the more I realize that the People of the Dragon's most pathetic trait was their inability to simply die. Don't you realize that there are no heroes anymore, Gideon? We have all become villains simply because those who are willing to do anything to survive, will survive. Those who remain shackled to outmoded morality will be crushed."

Gideon kept his head against the wall of ice, and he felt the droplets of water as they melted away from the pristine ice and ran down the sides of his face. He did not turn to face the interloper, instead he let his voice remain calm and even.

"Nathan Sandar. I had hoped that I would never have the misfortune of crossing paths with you again. But then I suppose that none of us are getting what we want this time around. But you are right about one thing. I have survived. I have survived when many others didn't. We have killed in the name of saving the innocent. We have murdered and called it noble and necessary. And the losses we have incurred along the way have only made us fight harder. And in the end, here we are, once again."

Finally, Gideon straightened and turned fully to face Nathan. The young man looked exactly as he had the last time the two had crossed paths, the same cocky and self-assured posture, and the same knowing smirk. He had the eyes of a killer.

"Do you know, Nathan, why Emries sent you to me? Do you know why he risked your life?"

Nathan rolled his eyes.

"Because you are yet another ancient nuisance that needs to be removed from the path, old man. Just like Logan, and my so-called parents, and the rest of the filth of that thankfully extinct world. Emries is the logical heir to the throne of the Creator, and no one and nothing will stand in the way of that. We, his chosen champions, will ensure that when Dorovar unseats the Creator it will be Emries who stands ready to reshape the Cosmos in his image."

Gideon sighed and shook his head.

"That is the thing I never understood about you, Nathan. You grew up in a world shrouded in darkness, a place that you would have been a king if you would have followed the path that your parents blazed. But you could not simply be another cog in the wheel of the forces of the light, could you? You felt yourself being overshadowed in the war by Logan, Gwydeon, Midarin, and Pike. You were supposed to be the hero, and you were just another fighter. At least until you sold your soul to Emries, and turned your back on everything your parents fought for."

Nathan's face was an impassive mask.

"My so-called parents didn't understand the significance of what they were attempting to do, nor did they understand the folly of it. All they had to do was stand aside, let Emries win. The phasia would have wiped themselves out and we could have picked off the stragglers. But no, they had to rescue Sabrina from Draven, they had to follow that pretender Pike into places where they never should have walked. And worst of all, that damnable Logan Ranthall just would not die when he should have. He embraced Shau-ling and threw you all on the wrong side of the war. If Emries had won, Onea would never have been destroyed. If Emries had won, the rebellion in the Heavens would have resulted in more than just the death of Pyrrus. Together Emries and Talisia could have made a move on the Throne with the heroes of Onea behind them. We could have been there at Emries' left hand when he unseated the Creator and took Talisia's head to ensure that he would never be challenged. Then we could have hunted down Raenera, Halicon, and Dorovar and ended them. The Cosmos would have been ours to rule as the new Children of the Creator. But this outmoded sense of nobility and mercy stood in the way. They had to do what they thought was right in the moment, never seeing the long game. They were fools."

Gideon could not keep the frown from turning the corners of his mouth.

"We did many unwise things in the name of nobility and mercy, Nathan, but we were never fools. Perhaps we were uneducated and unaware of the greater war that was being fought, but that was because we were lied to at every turn by your patron."

Gideon opened his mouth again to speak, but thought better of it, shook his head, and then closed his mouth again. He saw the direction this conversation was headed, and he knew more than Nathan could possibly know about the task he had been sent upon. It was a fool's errand, and Emries expected Nathan to fail and to be destroyed. However, Gideon had other plans for the hot-headed young man. Plans that perhaps could help the boy redeem himself before he would face the judgment of his betters.

"Emries cannot change what he is," Gideon said somberly. "All things considered, I don't believe that any of the Children can change. Perhaps that is why we are here. Halicon came the closest to seeing the end before it came, but he too was trapped by the pattern that the Creator had made. That is why we fight this war, Nathan, not because they are unable to do so, but because they don't know how. Emries and Talisia make these grand gestures about ruling the Cosmos, and still they play down here in the dirt with the mortals, trapped just as we are on this ball of death, waiting to be snuffed out at the Creator's whim. We are all disposable pieces in a sad play, Nathan, and perhaps the most disappointing part of it all is how there are still those that would follow blindly the ravings of a would-be messiah."

Nathan made a move to retort, but Gideon's raised hand cut him off. Nathan could feel a new power radiating from the man, and he choked on his own words with every half-breath. His chest would simply not expand, his body rebelled, and he gripped at his throat trying to channel his abilities to counteract the assault. Gideon knew that his shock tactic would not work against more seasoned members of Emries' cadre, but Nathan was too reliant on his abilities and did not think laterally. If he only would have realized the exertion required to rob him of breath, he could have launched a counter-offensive against Gideon and taken back the advantage. There were benefits in knowing the failings of one's opponent, a lesson that Gideon had only learned after far too much bloodshed.

"Are you starting to understand the fallacy of this action, Nathan? I knew you were coming here long before Emries gave you this suicidal task. You don't even know why he wants my heart. All I have to do is close my hand and your neck will snap and you'll be removed from the game."

Nathan's throat was raw, and he struggled for every bit of breath that he could drag in and out of his tortured lungs. His body rebelled at the lack of nourishing air, and his knees began to buckle. Conserving his strength to fight against Gideon's spectral grip, Nathan fell to his knees and focused all of his powers on the grip that was crushing his neck and chest. But the more he pushed at the suffocating force, the more it tightened. Gideon approached his fallen opponent slowly, fearing the retaliation that thus far had not materialized. Perhaps Nathan was as dim as Emries thought he was after all. He had eschewed all the tactics that his father had tried to drill into his head, instead falling into the seductive trap of unbridled power. Gideon bent low so that he was at eye level with the young man, his voice calm and remorseful.

"In a few moments, Nathan, you're going to be thankful for this mercy and nobility that you have railed against. In these past few days, I have lost friends that I have known for thousands of years, and more recently I have lost two men that I loved like brothers. As much as it would give me temporary pleasure to kill you, it serves no purpose, and in fact it may even advance Emries' schemes. And so, I will allow you to live today, and I will give you a choice. I am going to send you far from here and I'm going to suppress your ability to portal. You can live out the rest of your days away from this war, saved from the fate that your patron chose for you, or, you can try to restore your powers and return to him. If you do have the courage to face your maker on his terms, then I give you this piece of information. He should look in on his secret weapon. He may find that she is not growing in to the terrifying instrument of destruction that he intends. Let us see how devoted you are to your master when you know that this failure means your death."

Before Nathan could protest, Gideon snapped his fingers and the irritating young man was simply gone. Gideon stood looking down at the place where the son of one of his closest friends had been only a moment before and was about to turn back toward the deeper portions of the icy cave when a spasm of pain wracked his body. His stomach and chest seized at the same time, a half stifled cough bringing a plume of blood bursting from his mouth. Gideon fell to his knees, his insides on fire as blood began to trickle from his nose, his mouth, and the corners of his eyes. His vision became blurrier as the seconds passed, and his head felt as though it weighed more than his entire body. The next thing Gideon knew he was collapsed onto the cold ground, unable to move, and unable to call for help. When the blackness took him, he was not sure that he would see the next dawn.

* * * * * * * * * * * *

Jerrica wasn't sure how long she slept, but she did feel more rested than she had since she had left her sisters to go on this fool's errand. Why did she ever think that she could change the darkness that was coming? How did she not see Tolon's death, or the deaths of all of those people at the refuge in the middle of a desert of ice? But she knew that she was nothing more than a pawn in a greater game, her visions a gift and a curse given by the Creator. And now, a Child of the Creator had taken information that was the most guarded secret of each generation of Seers. Now that her purpose was fulfilled, perhaps she would no longer be cursed with the visions, or perhaps she would simply be washed away and forgotten like so many of the bit players in the Cosmic game.

Wrapping the blanket firmly around herself, Jerrica went to look for Gideon. Now that he had gotten the information he needed, perhaps he would let her go, or maybe he would have further use for her. Either way, she did not want to be left in the dark any longer. She was so shocked when she found him crumpled to the ground that she dropped the blanket and forgot how cold it was in the icy cave. She was at his side the next moment, ripping a sleeve from his shirt and dabbing the copious amount of blood away from his face. A great deal of it had pooled on the ground, but she could find no wound that accounted for that much blood. Just as she pulled his head into her lap, his eyes began to flutter open. For a moment she could feel his confusion, and there was a brief moment when he didn't know who she was. Finally, the fog cleared from his eyes, and the knowledge flooded back into him. Gideon smiled a weak smile and tried to sit up, but was unable to summon the strength. Finally, Jerrica helped Gideon to a seated position. By the time he waved off her assistance, more color had returned to his pale cheeks.

"What happened, Gideon? Are you alright?"

Gideon tried again to smile broadly, but it came through as nothing more than a smirk.

"Simply overexerted myself," he said in a simple truth that almost certainly sounded like a lie to her ears. "I need to be more careful if I'm going to accomplish my task."

He tried in vain to get to his feet, and again Jerrica found herself helping the ancient man. Once Gideon was standing, he put his hand on her shoulder and gave it a reassuring if weak squeeze.

"I'll recuperate while Arturious finishes his work. Soon, I'll unleash Raenera's army, and the whole of Espre will be cleansed of all of the Children's influence. Even if that means there will be no one left standing when their grim work is done."

Jerrica smiled weakly, and helped him to a chair that was nearby.

"But you, Jerrica, I need you to take a message to my daughter for me."

Dignity, Honor, Family

Year Four of the Just Emperor Kaitain "Dragonsbane" Lorien, Creator's Calendar Year 1871

It was just after sunrise when Midarin returned to the command tent. Gwydeon could immediately see that she had been crying, but the trails of the tears were beginning to be erased from her cheeks by the heat of her rage. The way her eyes flashed was usually Gwydeon's clue to steer clear of his wife's fury, but in the moment, Gwydeon knew that she needed him. She didn't say a word as she crossed to where he still stood by the map table, and when she threw her arms around him and hugged him tight, for a moment he thought she was going to break him in half. Gwydeon had lived so long without the abilities granted to him as a member of the Dark Gods, that the simple applications of strength in times of emotional stress had nearly been forgotten. Midarin on the other hand had lived so long with her abilities, so much longer than a human being was supposed to live, that she used them without thinking. They had become natural, and she was so strong now that she could have snapped him in half. A reflex caused Gwydeon to pull on the powers of the Blaze to reinforce his bones and muscles against the unintended consequences of his wife's embrace. She clung to him as though he was keeping her from drowning in the sea of emotions that held her. Finally, Midarin pulled away and looked up at Gwydeon with tear-filled eyes.

"She's gone," her voice wavering but clearly filled with anger, "Camille's gone."

Gwydeon tried to keep the grimace from coming to his face.

"So the twins were right, and it was only a matter of time before the Creator started to use the Heaven-born against us. Maybe we should have considered finding something else for the twins to do."

Midarin's eyes narrowed.

"We don't throw away family. And there has to be a way to prevent the Creator from using them. We'll come up with something we always do."

Gwydeon's lips curled into a sly grin.

"I thought I was supposed to be the optimist."

Midarin could not repress her own smile.

"I had to spend a millennium as a counter-balance to Pike, Aryx, and Lissa. You learn very quickly to try to find the better options. I don't know how you did it all those years keeping everyone's head on straight. Between Logan, and Pike, and Eldar, and even me. You dragged us through when things were their darkest. I guess you rubbed off on me."

Gwydeon kissed her lightly on the forehead and then held her until he felt Midarin begin to pull away. After she had taken a step back, Midarin produced a piece of paper from her pocket and handed it to Gwydeon.

"I found this in Camille's tent."

Gwydeon took the simple white piece of paper and looked at it for a brief second. After a first glance and a moment to process the single word written there, Gwydeon turned back to the map table and dropped the paper on the map. Pieces were finally starting to fall into place.

"I should have known," Gwydeon said finally shaking his head.

He took a long silent look at the table and then brought his fist down on the table hard, surprised almost instantly that it didn't shatter under the force of the blow. Then he stopped, pushed himself back from the table and put his hands on his hips.

"And if I hadn't been so blind I would have seen it before now. I've been so stupid."

Midarin was struck by the defeat in Gwydeon's voice. Gwydeon was a practical man possessed of a dry wit and unwavering loyalty and belief in his friends. Moreover, he was pragmatic and calculated. And while he could be self-deprecating and humble, he was not one to be defeatist.

"You may be a lot of things, Gwydeon," Midarin said after a moment, "but you are not stupid."

Gwydeon shook his head.

"No, Midarin, this time I'm stupid. Sabrina tried to tell me. Even Aerith tried to tell me. But I just wouldn't listen. I've been out of the war for too long, and all that time I should have been learning about what was going on rather than sulking and trying to make a difference as one of the humans."

Midarin's blood ran cold. To hear Gwydeon use that word, human, as though he were apart from them shook her. Gwydeon had marked himself as special on Onea because he fought against gods and demons with only his sword and his wits, not with powers like his childhood friends. He was a champion because of his heart. Midarin could sense there was a conflict growing inside of Gwydeon, one that pitted that human side with the side that had once been called the Brother of Angels. The conflict had been there at the last days of the war on Onea, and it had intensified during the rebellions in the Heavens. Now, Midarin could sense that the conflict was nearing its end, and whatever Gwydeon did next would determine the course their lives would take for the rest of the war.

"What did they try to tell you, Gwydeon?" Midarin said, the exasperation clear in her voice, "What does this have to do with Camille?"

The frown on Gwydeon's face caused his brow to furrow. He suddenly looked so much older, as though the realization of whatever he had figured out in that moment had aged him. He looked tired, ever so much more tired than Midarin had ever seen him.

"After the fight with the dragons, when you and Camille were recovering, Aerith came to see me. He tried to warn me about Camille, tried to tell me the Creator could use her. I should have listened, but I was so angry at him. Just the sight of him incited such hatred in me, and I couldn't understand why. It wasn't until I saw how Mirana and Liara reacted, and now this revelation about Camille and the note. The Creator has gone to great lengths to set up this conflict, and though we thought we knew all that he was doing, it wasn't until right this moment that the complexity of it truly dawned on me."

Gwydeon returned to the map table and brushed all of the markers aside.

"We've been looking at this war all wrong. We see the lines and the barriers and the movements, but none of it matters. This isn't where the war is being fought. I've been acting like we're fighting the phasia all over again. Kingdoms and strongholds and armies throwing themselves at each other trying to gain advantage on one piece of land or another. The Creator doesn't think that way, neither does Dorovar, and now the Children have stopped worrying about winning battles and have turned their attention to the war. And the war isn't here. It's in the Heavens. It's all for the Throne now, and no one is trying to veil their intentions."

Gwydeon picked up a marker and placed it in Galateria.

"Talisia. We know she's been using Galateria as her base for some time now. What we don't know is what her intentions are. She never acts openly and always works through intermediaries. I would be surprised however if she wasn't behind some of the dragon attacks on the kingdoms that aren't loyal to Kaitain. What better agent of chaos than our power-mad emperor?"

He picked up another marker and put it in the area of Bellnoc.

"Halicon's gone, Sabrina's gone. Rhain, Aerith's daughter is in charge of the phasia now. I don't know what she's planning, but I'm sure she has her hands full with Jeroch and Saurn and the rest. Their numbers are few, but you know how crafty they are. At least this time they're on our side."

Two markers Gwydeon picked up and put to the edge of the map.

"Pyrrus and Raenera. We know from the girls that Wolf has Pyrrus' powers now, but he disappeared after the fall of the Citadel of the Dark Gods. His motivations have always been his own, and I'm sure at some point he'll resurface. We also know that he'll be on our side. As far as Raenera, that's anyone's best guess. No idea her motivations, no idea her goals, and no idea whether she has her own designs on the Golden Throne, or if she'll simply oppose Talisia and Emries."

The fifth marker Gwydeon turned over in his hand several time before he brought it down on the piece of paper that Midarin had found in Camille's tent.

"Emries," Gwydeon said hatred tinging his voice. "He's been all over the map, and I fear what he's been doing behind the scenes. What is clear is that he's marshalling his forces and getting ready for a major move. This isn't the same Emries we fought on Onea. He's ruthless and he's efficient, and he intends to win."

He picked up two more markers and put them in the center of the map.

"Aerith and Dorovar. They are the wild cards. Dorovar because of his power and his followers, Aerith for the same reasons. Two sides of the same coin."

Finally, Gwydeon stepped back and looked at his wife.

"And none of them can be allowed to win."

There was a moment, just a brief moment, when Midarin was shocked. But it faded as soon as she understood the point of Gwydeon's words, and knew them to be true. Midarin moved to the table and looked at the map and the markers.

"You know what this means don't you?"

Gwydeon nodded.

"It means we're going to have to kill some of our friends."

Midarin's eyes went wide. That was not what she meant at all. The fact that Gwydeon's mind had immediately gone there made her heart sick. Finally, a tear falling from her eye, Midarin shook her head and spoke softly.

"Do you know what you just said? Do you know why you said it?"

Gwydeon stayed silent, his jaw set. Midarin recognized that his mind was working, but there was something in his eyes, something that told Midarin that he didn't really understand what he had said.

"Think Gwydeon," Midarin continued, keeping the distance between them, "go back to what Aerith told you in that little cabin. What did Aerith say? What did he try to tell you?"

Gwydeon's jaw tightened and he ground his teeth together. His eyes filled with hate. Midarin could not believe what she was seeing. It was just the same way that Mirana and Liara had reacted. It was then that the truth of it dawned in Midarin's head.

"He tried to tell me about Camille," Gwydeon said finally, his voice sounding small and unsure. The tone of his voice rattled Midarin even more. She was not accustomed to hearing him so vulnerable and unsure. "But I wouldn't listen. He tried to convince me she was compromised and that the Creator had plans for her, and all I could see was him trying to manipulate the situation so he could win. But that wasn't what he was saying at all. And now I know why."

Gwydeon turned to the map table and put both of his hands on it and hung his head.

"Sabrina wanted me to go to Evan not long after we were sent here. It was before I knew that we were the reason the dragons were going to be stuck here. It was before I knew anything about the political nightmare we were about to cause. But Evan wouldn't listen to a word I said. It was as though the man we knew had simply disappeared. Aerith told me that the Creator had changed him, lied to him, changed his memories. The Creator made Evan think that we rebelled and tried to take the throne and that he showed up just in time to stop us. In Evan's mind he defeated us all and threw our limp and broken bodies down from the Heavens with his bare hands. He couldn't see us as friends anymore, or as allies. All he could see were enemies and threats to the Creator."

Midarin was aghast.

"To what end?"

Gwydeon pointed to the markers on the table.

"Because of this. Aerith was right. Evan would never have knowingly betrayed Aerith, or Logan, or any of us unless the Creator made it impossible for him to do anything else. He had to insure Evan's loyalty."

Midarin's blood boiled.

"But why Evan? I mean, I know he was important in the last days of the war, but why not you or me? Why not Pike?"

Again, Gwydeon pointed at the markers.

"It's Aerith at the center of it all. Sabrina was tapped as the Spirit because of her tie to Aerith. Evan became the voice because of his ties to Aerith. Ayden is the new Will because he's Aerith's son. Rhain ended up with Halicon's powers, I suspect, because she's Aerith's daughter. And the Creator didn't want me to listen. Didn't want me to put the pieces together, so he made me feel only rage at Aerith's words. He manipulated me like he manipulated Mirana and Liara and Camille. The Creator, like the Children, has been trying to keep us divided. The Dark Gods, the Forgotten, Aerith and his family, Logan, the phasia. Keeping us apart, keeping us from thinking. Making it the opposite of how it was on Onea. Our strength was when we worked together, and the Creator has tried very hard to prevent us from doing that again."

Midarin nodded.

"So the note…"

Gwydeon picked up the note and held it with the scrawled word facing toward Midarin.

"It means Cedric is back on the board."

Midarin shook her head.

"How is that possible? Everyone knows that Jeroch killed him. Sabrina was sure to let everyone know so that we wouldn't waste our energy hunting him or trying to protect him."

Gwydeon shook his head.

"I may not understand it all, but what's clear is that anyone who has any connection to Aerith is a major player in the closing of this war. And I guess that means even if they're dead."

There was a rustle that came from the direction of the tent flap on the far side of the command tent, and by the time both Midarin and Gwydeon turned to the entrance, two people entered. While neither were surprised to see Rhionna enter the tent, however both were stunned speechless by the appearance of the man who trailed Rhionna. Duncan Rhuiden let his gaze move first from Gwydeon and then to Midarin and let an uneasy smile come to his lips.

"Well I guess that would explain why I'm here."

Gwydeon looked first at Midarin and then back at Duncan. While Gwydeon had not known Duncan in life, Midarin had told many stories about the boy who had raged against his father and attempted to murder him. Duncan was the spitting image of his father, though not nearly as muscular. But the eyes were the same. The four stayed silent for a long time, until finally Duncan cleared his throat and spoke again.

"Isn't anyone going to say anything?"

Midarin was the first to answer.

"I'm sorry Duncan, but you have to understand, you're the last person we expected to see."

Duncan nodded.

"And one of the last you wanted to see."

Midarin shook her head.

"No, Duncan," she said as genuinely as she could manage. "Whatever you did on Onea was then, and we don't have the luxury of judging anyone. If anything, Pike has proven yet again everything you said about him to be true."

Duncan frowned.

"I take no pleasure in it," he said finally. "I didn't understand then what was at stake. There was so much hatred and resentment for my father and my mother, as well as my sister. And that resentment cost me. I've had a long time to think about what I've done, and fortunately I had a chance to get to know the woman who in some ways was my sister. Sabrina sought me out and forgave me for my transgressions, and she brought me to the attention of a man who taught me how to be better than who I had once been."

Gwydeon leaned back against the table, turning one of the map markers over in his hand.

"How long have you been on Espre, Duncan? What can you tell us that we don't know about what's been going on?"

Duncan looked pensive when he began to speak, and his gaze moved from Gwydeon to Midarin but centered mostly on the ground between them.

"I wasn't really sure what was happening when I first arrived here on Espre. I didn't recognize anything, and I didn't understand how it was that I was cut down by my father and then suddenly standing in a field in the middle of nowhere. The next thing I know, this woman is standing in front of me radiating light. I thought she looked familiar, but it wasn't until she started speaking that I knew who it was. Sabrina was very kind, and she stayed with me for several days, trying to explain to me what had happened. On the third day, another man arrived, one whom I knew by reputation and the disdain that my father held him in. Sabrina said that he would be the one to help me find my place in the world, and who could teach me how to make peace with the man I had been on Onea."

Duncan paused, as though he was unsure of his next words, and then finally continued.

"So I was taken to the Kingdom of Menoris, and made the journey down below the Peaks of Patience into the settlement that had been created there. It was there that I met the gentle giant named Kamen, and I spent many years learning from him and Logan Ranthall about the nature of forgiveness and the nature of selflessness. Kamen took his time in educating me about the war that I was too stubborn and too blind to learn about in my first life. He taught me about the phasia and the battle between Halicon and Emries. He taught me about the role that my parents had played in the war, as well as the role that I shunned in my arrogance. Then Logan took up my education, showing me the better way to fight this war. And so, after a hundred years or so as a member of the Order of the Flickering Flame, working in the Kingdom of Menoris, I went out into the world to try to redeem myself by helping those who could not help themselves, and making little contributions that my arrogance and my paranoia would not allow me to make as a selfish prince."

At this point Duncan looked up and seemed much more assured of his next words.

"I wandered for a long time. Of course I caught rumors and stories of the wars with the Dark Gods, the movements of the Children and the Servants, the coming of Dorovar and his Heralds. In the end, Logan came to find me and put me on the path that led me here. I wasn't sure that I was cut out to be a soldier, but Logan assured me that Lordhill was the best place I could be. And now I'm here."

Gwydeon started to respond, but Duncan held up a hand.

"No, wait," Duncan said, his voice adding a hint of discomfort and barely repressed pain, "hear it all first. There are those that think that Aerith is only still fighting because he wants to remake Creation in his own image. But that couldn't be farther from the truth. According to Logan, Aerith doesn't want to unseat the Creator for himself, and he understands that if he were to ever sit on the Golden Throne, he would become every bit the tyrant that the Creator is, even though his desire would be to do things better. He believes that he has become a monster that cannot be redeemed. However, there is something that Aerith does not know, and something that I don't think anyone knows. It was information that Sabrina entrusted to me just before she died, information she swore to me to keep to myself until the time was right. And I believe that time is now."

Duncan fell silent. After a moment, he nodded to himself and then began to speak again.

"Sabrina told me it was no coincidence that I was brought back. Every member of Aerith's family has been brought to this world. The Creator lied to you Gwydeon. It was never about the humans on this world. It was never about winning their loyalty. It was never about which of the Children could bend this world to their view of the Cosmos. It was about Aerith and his family, about their connection to the living Cosmos and the pieces of Aerith's abilities that the Creator does not understand. He seeks to use them for his own purposes, to make himself stronger, to learn from the mistakes he made with the Children, and to start over. He wants to use Aerith and his family as some sort of template to remake Creation."

Gwydeon and Midarin had different reactions at the same time, but it was Rhionna's reaction that came out first in the form of a blurted disbelieving curse. Once the vehemence and violence of Rhionna's reaction faded, Midarin let her thoughts fill the empty space.

"So no matter what happens, we lose. The Creator is going to destroy everything and start over no matter what we do."

Gwydeon shook his head.

"No, it's much more insidious than that. Aerith has something that the Creator wants, and He's trying to pull every member of Aerith's family closer to Him in order to extract whatever reaction he wants out of Aerith. And if He can't get it through coercion or corruption, He'll get it through blood, lies, and murder."

Duncan nodded.

"And unfortunately there are a lot of us to attempt to exploit."

Gwydeon immediately understood the implication and shook his head. Midarin's eyes went wide.

"Who has been brought back that we didn't know about?"

Duncan smiled.

"Of course you know about Cedric, Sabrina, and myself, but also my mother Cairyn, and my grandmother Anabel. And also Gideon."

Midarin murmured the name.

"Gideon. I should have known,"

Gwydeon turned, took a handful of markers from the corner of the map table, and let them fall onto the map. His frustration was clear. Finally, Gwydeon shook his head and turned back to his three companions.

"My head hurts, I've had no sleep, and the troops I'm sure are anxious to continue towards Aldere. We should pack quickly and start our journey. When we camp again at nightfall, I look forward to continuing this conversation. Until then, not a word of this to anyone, especially Mirana and Liara. Until we find some way to remove the Creator's influence from them, I'm not sure that we can trust them with sensitive information."

Midarin frowned.

"That's not like you Gwydeon."

He nodded.

"I know, and that's why it has a chance to work. Duncan, I need you to keep a low profile, and keep using whatever identity you've been using to this point. You've been able to escape all of our notices up until now, I'd like you to keep that discretion for a little while longer."

Duncan nodded his ascent.

"Rhionna, I have to give you the worst job of all. I know that your first priority is to keep Quyhn safe, but I also need you to find some way to keep Mirana and Liara busy. Add them to Quyhn's protection detail if you have to, but make them feel useful and not isolated. If they suspect for a second that they aren't trusted, I shudder to think the damage they could do."

Rhionna wanted to argue, thought better of, and then finally nodded.

"Alright," Gwydeon said finally, "let's get moving. I have a feeling that we've only just begun to discover the kind of danger that we're about to walk into."

Chapter CII

Courage is Knowing
What not to Fear

Year Four of the Just Emperor Kaitain "Dragonsbane" Lorien,
Creator's Calendar Year 1871

Arin Ranthall's head ached. His ears still rang from the incredible scream that had deafened everyone within a mile radius. He wasn't sure as he pushed up from the blood-stained ground if he had lost consciousness, but even if he had, he was still alive. Every solider knew that even a moment of lost attention could mean death, so the loss of consciousness was assuredly fatal. He pushed himself up again and that was when the pain hit. When he first put his hand down on the ground to push up, the lightning rush of pain sped up his arm and seized his muscles. Arin's elbow buckled and he collapsed back to the ground again, his face going straight into the mud. This time instead of pushing up, Arin rolled onto his side, taking as deep a breath as possible. His chest ached, and he felt as though he had been kicked in the ribs several hundred times. When Arin brought his hand up to try to determine the source of the pain that had caused the most recent collapse, he was greeting with a dozen pieces of steel shrapnel in his palm. Arin turned his hand over, and one of the pieces of shrapnel had completely penetrated his hand and a sharp point was sticking out between the third and fourth knuckles. He felt the rasp in his chest the next moment, and the cough that rattled his body produced a spray of blood. Arin's bottom lip burned, and he realized that it had been split during the fight. He felt an ache between his eyes and when he reached up and his fingertips brushed the bridge of his nose, the spark of pain was like a dagger to his brain. That next moment there was heat from the blood that ran down the side of his neck. It didn't take long to realize that the blood was trickling from his ear canal, and that moment Arin feared that his skull had been fractured. That would have explained the loss of consciousness. As Arin reached inside himself to draw upon the powers granted to him by his connection to Aerith Seth, panic filled him. There was nothing there. It was as though his connection to his powers had been severed. Nausea twisted his stomach and his chest heaved as though he was about to vomit, but nothing came up but more blood. Arin began to feel light headed, his vision blurring. He thought he would close his eyes for a second, just to refocus, but when he tried to open them again, his eyelids were rebellious to his will. Unconsciousness tugged at his mind, and no matter how hard he tried to fight it, it kept drawing him deeper into the blackness. After only a few seconds Arin's will shattered, and he could no longer resist the emptiness that beckoned him. As he faded into slumber, perhaps for the last time, he tried to think of how it all went so wrong.

* * * * * * * * * * * *

As Orren and Felicia got back to their feet, Zaraven released his hold on Arin Ranthall and moved in front of Drust. Drust, though a member of the Adhradair who fought against dragons on Loinn, was not a warrior. Her role on Loinn had been as a mediator, and she was an expert at settling disputes quickly without upsetting the perfect Order. Even on a world dedicated to an effortless and smooth Order, there were times when the people of Loinn came into conflict with one another. Carpenters and farmers had to know who had rights to certain patches of land. Foresters and hunters had to know which areas of forest were to be cut down for lumber and which were protected for hunting. It was Drust's responsibility to ensure that the perfect Order was respected and each person was told exactly what they were allowed to do and what they were not. Drust was extremely accomplished in her role, but when the dragons came to Loinn, there was no mediation that she could offer in disputes between the people and the great winged beasts. In Drust's mind she was relegated to uselessness, denied her role in the perfect Order by the traitorous monsters. That was why she was one of the first to embrace the powers that Emries offered. At first all she wanted was to reclaim her role, and force a peace between the people and the dragons. However, when that failed, her wrath was as fierce as any of the Adhradair, and she ripped more than one of the arrogant beasts apart with her bare hands. But Zaraven knew that this was not Loinn, and Drust was not defending her home. There would be a time for her kind of warfare once again, but not on this field, and not at this time.

Zaraven was no stranger to killing. Along with Luigsech, Zaraven was one of the guardians of the wilds, responsible for enforcing the perfect Order in the natural world, away from the eyes of the people who roamed the civilized lands. While Luigsech's responsibility was to ensure that all of the species of plants grew and evolved in harmony, Zaraven was entrusted with ensuring that all of the species of animal existed in their appointed roles and that no one breed grew out of control. The primary responsibility that took the greatest amount of Zaraven's time was ensuring that the alpha predators did not over hunt their designated areas, and that they did not become too numerous that the prey animals would not be able to keep their numbers at high enough levels. And so Zaraven was the greatest hunter on Loinn, tracking and killing the most dangerous predators on his world to preserve the perfect Order. It was the ultimate protective role, ensuring that the defenseless had a chance to flourish while at the same time ensuring that the strong remained strong. But then the greatest predators in Creation came to Loinn. In the first years of their residency on Loinn, Zaraven was constantly frustrated by the limitations placed on him. He could not intervene against the dragons as they destroyed the delicate balance, killing prey animals and predators alike without any regard for the perfect Order. Zaraven simply had to sit and watch as everything he had worked his whole life to protect was torn apart. When Zaraven was given the opportunity to act against the dragons, his first thoughts had not been ones of revenge, but rather to reset the perfect Order, including the dragons. However, that quickly proved to be an impossibility. The dragons were too numerous and too powerful. If even one of them were living upon the face of Loinn, that would be enough to upset the Order. And so, they all had to be exterminated, one way or another. Zaraven proved to be the most efficient hunter and killer of dragons.

As he stood against Orren Eldrath and Felicia Lorien clad in her Nightwing armor, his thoughts went to his brethren who were tracking the dragons responsible for the fall of Loinn. His blood burned to track down and slaughter every last one responsible, which was why he could not have been assigned to that mission. And so, he would have to take his frustration out on these people. In his mind he saw them as predators who had grown beyond their usefulness, and therefore they needed to be removed in order to promote the new Order that Dorovar was trying to build.

"Why can you not see the truth of your situation," Zaraven growled. "You are like rabid wolves storming across the plains killing all that come in your path. You do not kill for food, you do not kill to protect your young; you kill only because you are uncontrolled and there are no consequences for your actions. In your minds you think that the actions you take are justified, but the unrepentant killers and alpha predators always believe that their mere existence is justification enough. If you were truly interested in saving this world, you would surrender Orren Eldrath and his Sacred Weapon."

By this time Arin Ranthall had made his way back to his feet and tried his best to take stock of the situation. Orren Eldrath and Felicia Lorien had power to spare, that much was clear, and they felt as though they had access to powers similar to those of the Dark Gods. It took only a moment to access information from Aerith Seth's mantle and fill in the missing pieces. Aryx and Diana Terian had passed their power on to this new pair, and in addition Diana had passed the creature Nightwing to Felicia. The pair were formidable for sure, but right now they were unpracticed with their abilities, and fought instinctively. The pair of Adhradair on the other hand were much more imposing. Arin couldn't feel their powers the same way he felt Orren and Felicia's but he knew that they were extremely powerful and practiced with that power. Like the Heralds, they were extensions of Dorovar, but something told Arin that they were far more dangerous than the Heralds. Going one on one with a member of the Heralds at full strength had nearly cost Logan his life, and Arin knew that he was not anywhere close to Logan's equal in the use of power. What Arin had that Logan didn't have was the capability to utilize the military tactics that he was taught as a member of the Lion's Mane. To that end, Arin was probably the only member of Aerith's extended family, with the possible exception of Hannah Ironheart, who could fully utilize Aerith's extensive study of military tactics. The problem was that he needed time to impart his strategy to his new allies. Of course, the greater problem was how to impart his strategy once he figured one out. He could criticize Orren and Felicia all he wanted for not being practiced with their powers, but Arin was truly no better in the grand scheme of things.

"And you believe your path is better?" Arin countered; his voice raspy. "How is Dorovar any different than the animal you describe? His Heralds kill indiscriminately, by the hundreds. Are these just more sacrifices to the greater glory of Dorovar or are they this unchecked aggression that you claim to stand against? Truth is the first casualty of warfare, so is what you are saying truth or just more of Dorovar's self-serving hypocrisy."

A gentle laugh came from Drust.

"Finally someone with a spark of intelligence on this rock. Whom do you serve, soldier? It's clear that you are not in league with these children."

Arin brushed himself off and tried not to let too much of Aerith's irreverence into his posture or his voice.

"Firstly," Arin said as calmly as he could manage, "I would not so quickly discount the abilities of my companions here, and secondly I would gladly claim them as my allies. As to who I serve, I don't think that would take you much to figure out, if you are half as intelligent as you claim to be. After all, I just sent your Gray Man Pestilence back to Dorovar with his tail between his legs."

Zaraven sneered.

"Another one of Aerith Seth's fools."

Both Orren and Felicia turned their heads in Arin's direction for half a moment before returning their gaze to the opposition. Arin could feel both relax slightly at the discovery of the man's identity, even though part of them already knew. Even unpracticed, the information eventually would have come to their minds if they were calm. But even in the height of battle, the information would have found a way through.

"I won't dispute that we can be a bit foolish, or that Aerith himself has been taken for a fool once or twice in his life," Arin retorted. "But you can't dispute the impact that he has had on this little conflict, or the damage that his allies have caused to Dorovar and his Heralds. I seem to recall that Death didn't fare very well when he faced my son."

Drust put her hand on Zaraven's shoulder, a move that Arin interpreted as an effort to restrain him from taking any rash action.

"You accuse Dorovar of self-serving hypocrisy without knowing anything of his motivations beyond what you have gleaned from the Heralds. But in your rush to judge their actions as cruel or harsh, did you stop to truly examine them? Has your Aerith Seth? Have any of you?"

Nightwing's metallic voice ground out accusations like an assault.

"How could their actions be judged any other way? The murder of innocents is the murder of innocents. Or does your Dorovar somehow see these people as something else?"

Drust smiled.

"The fact that you are even able to ask that question demonstrates more intelligence than I thought you capable of little princess. And as to the answer to your question, it is quite simple. Dorovar, though imprisoned, has had a long time to study the conflict between the Children of the Creator and their father. He has also had time to study the Dark Gods, the factions in the dragons, and the faction that calls itself the Forgotten. You have all been so sloppy in your actions, thinking that you have somehow escaped notice. But if Dorovar has marked nearly every action that every person of power has taken on this insignificant rock, do you not think that the Creator is aware as well? He sees everything from his Golden Throne, and while the stakes of the game being played on this world are quite obvious to the educated observer, the potential outcomes are not. Will the Creator truly allow one of the Children to win their childish conflict over the true fate of the Cosmos? Will the outcome of their ideological war have any bearing on anything beyond their own destruction? What happens when one of the Children stands victorious? The answer is simple, and the Children are finally no longer blind to it."

Arin swallowed hard.

"The Creator will wipe the board clean and start over."

His voice was calm and did not betray the horror in his heart. The words of course had not been his, they had come from Aerith and Sabrina and the pieces of the conflict they had been able to put together. Drust nodded, her expression impassive.

"And so these innocents as you call them are already dead, they just don't know it yet. So how would you like their lives to end? Would you like them to die meaningless deaths, erased from existence by the uncaring Creator who has no further use for them? Dorovar does not want that to be their fate, and so he has gifted them with a purpose in their deaths. They have the privilege to take vengeance upon those that see them as insignificant. Freed of their mundane husks, they join the Chorus of Souls and will forge the path by which Dorovar will ascend from this world into the Heavens. There he will stand before the Golden Throne and cast down the Creator, freeing every world and every being from His tyranny."

Orren quickly interjected.

"Replacing one tyrant with another."

Drust's response was calm and measured.

"Do you know what tyranny really is, Sapphire Knight? Do you know what it truly looks like? You have equated it to what Dorovar shall be without first recognizing it in what the Creator represents. Did you see it in your Kaitain Lorien before his madness was revealed? The Creator is the tyrant to be sure, his absolute abuse of power that he applies arbitrarily without conscience or restraint. But that is not what Dorovar seeks. We Adhradair come from a world where the abuse of power is impossible as the perfect Order itself is the power, not one individual. And while the High Priestess was the core of our Order, even she did not dictate. We were all equal, we were all the same. We were born to our purpose, we lived that purpose, and we died when that purpose was fulfilled. A child born had his whole life mapped out for him. He would know from the moment of his birth whether he was meant to be a blacksmith, or a carpenter, or a farmer, and once known he would live that purpose without question and without longing for anything else. There was no dissatisfaction or disappointment because all knew their place. There was no anxiety or sadness, because everyone in the community served their purpose and lived for the betterment of the community. There was only the harmony that can be forged through order and predictability."

Orren could not believe what he heard, and could only question.

"What good is life without the ability to make your own choices? How is life worth living without free will and self-determination? Even under the tyrant that you call the Creator and Kaitain Lorien, we have the choice of what we accomplish in our lives. We love, we create, we fight for the things we believe in. It seems like your perfect Order robs life of all of the things that make it worth living."

Drust smiled.

"And how has this free will benefited this world? Or the world that your Dark Gods came from? Yes, you can make choices, but your choices are not for the good of the community, are they? You are selfish. You are cruel. You will stab your neighbor for a morsel of bread when the famine hits rather than sharing what little you have evenly among you. Greed consumes you. In the perfect Order there is no avarice. There is no need for the accumulation of wealth. You prey upon the weak like animals with no thought of what you are destroying. What if the beggar in the street who had been robbed of everything he owns was in truth possessed of talent to create art that would bring tears to your eyes were he only given the means? And yet because you crave status, and because you are cruel you spit on the unfortunate. You curse them. You act as though they do not exist."

Drust's words rattled Orren, and though his mind could not process her words, he hit back regardless.

"Our foundation is the teachings of the Church of the Creator. That informs our morality and teaches us to love our neighbor, to honor them, to honor all life."

Drust's eyes flickered with a knowing fire.

"Does it? Are those the core tenants that the Church of the Creator teaches, or are they something else entirely? Is not the first tenant to believe in the Creator and to offer him your complete fealty? Does not this informed morality begin from a command to be a submissive supplicant to the will of the Creator? Is not the second tenant to believe that to follow the commands of the Creator will bring rewards in the Heavens while failure to surrender your will to the Creator will bring only punishment? Is not the third tenant that the rule of the Creator and the teaching of His Church are absolute? That the Church of the Creator speaks with the voice and authority of the Creator making questioning their will akin to questioning the will of the Creator? And so, you surrender your will to people whose own free will and staggering self-interest could create nothing short of endless opportunities for abuse and graft. Do you even know if these tenants were dictated by the Creator? Did they come from one of the Children? Or were they written by vain and selfish men who were carving out unimpeachable power for themselves."

Orren was about to answer, but Drust raised her voice and his protest died in his throat.

"How can the teachings of your Church, the teaching that you base the whole of your so-called morality upon, be true when they have lied to you about your own origins? It was not the Creator that made the race of human that walks upon this world. The Children are responsible for the creation of humans. And while the mewling sheep will say that the Creator made the Children and thus by extension the Creator made humans, that ignorance is nothing more than hollow chatter to those who understand the conflict between the Children and the Creator. And so you would rather base your society off of a lie that empowers the few to abuse your belief rather than basing your society on a true equality of all of its members?"

Silence held the field for several long moments before Zaraven let his voice be heard once again.

"You waste your words, Drust. These creatures are too dim and arrogant to admit that our way is better. We should just take what we want."

Nightwing's growl came in answer.

"We will not submit to you, we will not submit to Dorovar, and we will not submit to the Children. If there is going to be a way forward, we will find it ourselves."

Nightwing shot from the ground and climbed high into the air before raining down a beam of white fire upon where Zaraven and Drust stood. Zaraven pushed Drust back and extended one hand toward the sky, intercepting the beam of fire with a stream of ghostly green energy that burst from his outstretched palm. The ghostly haze spread, absorbing the fire, a keening wail growing in intensity as the moments passed. Finally, the sound was so cacophonous that Arin's ears began to ring from it. His body shook, and his bones felt that they would break under the force of it. Nightwing too felt the effects of the sonic wave, so much so that it changed the way that the air caught under her bladed wings and forced her to fall from her elevated perch. At first, Felicia was able to control her fall, but then tendrils from the spectral force reached out and took hold of her legs. She was slammed to the ground with such force that she lost consciousness almost immediately. Not content with simply incapacitating his opponent, Zaraven used the power of the Chorus of Souls to drag Nightwing toward him. He lifted her limp form into the air and the spectral force wrapped itself around her.

"There were predatory birds on Loinn that were very much like your Shadowwalkers. Unchecked they could devour whole villages. They were not as destructive as dragons because they were simple instinctual beasts. They did not possess the intelligence to do real damage, but that did not prevent them from being fierce opponents. I underestimated one once, and it nearly was able to end my life. But they taught me tactics that I would later use to drag the petulant dragons to their death. They thought nothing could touch them in the air, but I taught them the price of their arrogance. Your little friend here is no different."

The spectral green tendrils began to flare, tips digging into Nightwing's armor probing for weaknesses. One tendril found a tiny crack in the armor between the neck and the shoulder and pushed its way inside. A shriek came from deep inside of Nightwing, followed by a long, tortured moan of metal being ripped by impossibly powerful forces. Orren did not wait for more of the tendrils to find their way into Nightwing's hide. He let loose with twin blasts of fire and lightning, both aimed at Zaraven's head. Drust stepped in front, weaving a shield to protect Zaraven from the assault. Another scream came from Nightwing, but this time it was in Felicia's voice. Arin didn't hesitate, letting twin blades of fire appear in his hands before charging in. Steps away from Zaraven, the spectral Chorus expanded outward and slammed into Arin, taking him off his feet and tossing him through the air. At the last second Arin righted himself, landing on his right foot, which he pushed off immediately toward Zaraven. Just before reaching his target, he juked to the left, leapt over Orren's assault and dove downward toward Drust. She was able to slide away from the assault for a moment but only enough to save herself from the fatal blow. Arin pressed his advantage, forcing her further back. She had only time to weave a shield of the spectral energy as Arin battered it with strike after strike from the twin swords of fire. Arin's goal was to keep Drust off-balance so that Orren could have a clear shot at Zaraven.

Orren poured on the power, but no matter how much he channeled in Zaraven's direction, the cloud of phantom energy seemed to either block, deflect, or absorb every bit of it. Yet, even defending against Orren's attacks, the tendrils of the Chorus continued to rip at Nightwing, bringing more blood-curdling screams from Felicia. Orren was quickly running out of options. That was when the glint of steel caught his eye. Courage was lying at his feet. In those moments he did the math. There was no calculation that was worth Felicia's life. Taking the chance, he let power flare from his hands, a blinding flash that stretched out in all directions brighter than a dozen stars. In the half-second that he created for himself, Orren ducked down, collected Courage, and then as he stood in a single deft motion let the blade fly like a javelin toward Zaraven. When the flash of light finally faded, Orren saw what his strike had accomplished. At first, he wasn't sure Courage had been able to penetrate the shield of spectral energy, but when he saw the glint from the center of Zaraven's chest, he knew he had been successful. The blade had stuck true, passing through Zaraven's body, piercing his heart.

"Fool," Zaraven called. "You have accomplished nothing but your own failure."

The hilt broke free from Courage and fell to the ground, a piece of the blade still connected to it. Even as Zaraven began to fade from view, he turned his gaze to Felicia and closed his fist. The tendrils of the Chorus redoubled their efforts, ripping at the exposed cracks in Nightwing until the groan of the metal became a cry of such terror that it exploded in a deafening wail in all directions. The wave of pain and torment was followed a second later by an explosion that sent shards of metal flying in all directions. One struck Orren in the shoulder with such force that he fell backwards and as his head struck the ground, he only hoped that Felicia was still alive.

Love is Friendship
Caught on Fire

Year Four of the Just Emperor Kaitain "Dragonsbane" Lorien,
Creator's Calendar Year 1871

It was just before dawn when the tent flap of Dominique Lorien's tent opened and both she and Chelsea Zarova emerged with their small satchels packed with what meager supplies and traveling clothes they would need for the several days' journey to Iltorp and the Keep of the Serpentine Knight. It would be hard for two women of such renown as Chelsea and Dominique to travel without notice, but they would do their best by traveling light and only stopping at remote villages that had the best chance of being less informed about the state of political unrest in Cadaria. However, any stop would be risky. After all, Dominique was the Empress of Cadaria as well as a wanted criminal, and Chelsea was a member of the Knights of the Flashing Blade who had been stripped of her title and branded a traitor to the Throne. But then the list of criminals and traitors grew by the day, and the more Emperor Kaitain Lorien tried to tighten his grip around the throat of the Cadarian Empire, the more stood to resist him openly. The problem seemed to be that there was too much resistance to Kaitain's rule, and the disparate factions were not united in the method to remove the monster who wore the crown. Some would have championed keeping Dominique on the throne, while others would have preferred Quyhn Lorien, the poor ward of the Empire. Still others would align behind Feyd Lorien, the overlooked brother of the emperor or perhaps his daughter, the warrior princess Felicia Lorien. The transformation of the selfish and abusive Marlae Lorien into the paragon of virtue and patience Marlae Tamerlane had been nothing short of spectacular and unexpected, and had won the young woman a great many of supporters amongst the faithful to the Creator. However, no matter how startling her transition to responsible adult, there was no competing with the virtue of Hannah Ironheart, and should the woman want the Throne of Cadaria, a great many would line up behind her. Perhaps the Empire would fall to the Dark Gods to rule in the absence of a responsible human to steer it forward. Either Gwydeon Sandar, Midarin Sandar, or Logan Ranthall would have been fine choices given the impact they had been upon the face of Cadaria, working from the shadows. But the more the factions struggled, the more Kaitain was able to consolidate his support. He might not have controlled the largest military force in Cadaria any longer, but those that did follow him would do so until their deaths, and as he conquered more of the unaffiliated or wavering kingdoms, more fanatics would find their way under his sway. Gwydeon's plan to install Quyhn in Aldere was a risky one, one that would need all the support that could be mustered, and was the first shot in the dark against Kaitain's iron fisted approach to rule. If Dominique and Chelsea could swing Iltorp, Thorigald, and Saldarine behind Quyhn, it could be the start of uniting the factions.

Dominique was struck by the chill in the air almost immediately. Another year was coming to an end, and the last Day of Starfire had passed in the long and eventful night. It was the final day of a year that would seemingly never end, and was already full of more hope than had been present during the darkness marked by the rule of Kaitain Lorien over the past four years. As Dominique stretched her neck and looked to the east to see the first light of the twin signs rising, she almost could not believe that it had only been four years that Kaitain had ruled over Cadaria. How could it have not been a lifetime? How much had been lost and destroyed at his hands? How many innocents would never see another sunrise because of his actions? And how many of those deaths had Dominique been complicit in during her time as Empress? The stain upon her soul would never be wiped clean no matter how much she did to resist her husband, and perhaps that more than anything was the reason that she decided to step away and let Quyhn take the mantle for the Cadarian Empire.

Dominique looked over to her companion and marveled once again at how unflappable the woman was. Dressed in only simple travelling clothes, a light shirt and simple pants, she did not seem to be effected by the cold at all. Dominique was wearing twice as much and she still felt herself shiver with every slight motion of the breeze. One of the saddlebags that Chelsea had draped over her shoulder hung low, and must have contained her light and flexible armor. The armor itself was too recognizable to be worn, and though Chelsea had complained about packing it, she knew it was the best course of action. The one concession that she made to her station was wearing Seraph's Sacred Weapon Patience on her hip. Most would never be able to recognize the blade or differentiate the hilt of the weapon from any other ornate blade. Only other members of the Knights of the Flashing Blade, or members of the royal families would be able to tell with any certainty. Of course Dominique knew the blade on sight, after seeing it every day for so long. Chelsea wore it differently than her estranged husband did, slung low on her hip, the middle hilt tie just above her knee rather than at the middle of her thigh. Chelsea had explained that she was still getting used to the weight of the blade, but Dominique felt there was something more. For so many years, Dominique had tried to get Seraph to explain what was so special about the Sacred Weapon, and he constantly was evasive and secretive. Though once he did let it slip that the Sacred Weapons had personalities of their own and it wasn't so much that Seraph wielded the weapon so much as he negotiated with it. Perhaps Chelsea was feeling out her own way to work with Patience.

The camp was still mostly quiet with only the barest hints of movement beginning in the orderly rows of tents. The rebel army would begin the march to Aldere at first light, and Chelsea had wanted to avoid any unpleasant entanglements during their exit. She was sure that at least a small detachment of soldiers would want to accompany them, orders or not, and the last thing that Chelsea wanted to do was foment any misconduct or disloyalty in the ranks. The margin of error became almost impossibly small the moment that the rebels of Lordhill aligned themselves with the Dark Gods, and it would be all Quyhn could do to hold them together under the watchful eyes of Gwydeon and Midarin. However,

Chelsea had no doubt that the forces of nature that the married couple were could withstand any dissent; it was just an additional distraction that Chelsea would like to spare them if she could. She had already moved their horses to the far edge of the encampment in order to keep the disturbance their leaving would cause to a minimum. When Chelsea's eyes met Dominique's a slight smile came to the corners of her mouth, but it was fleeting. With a curt nod, Chelsea turned toward the edge of camp, wordless taking Dominique's pack from her along with her own. Dominique frowned for a moment and then let a small laugh escape her lips with a slight shake of her head.

As the pair approached the edge of camp, Chelsea felt the presence before she actually saw the man standing by the horses. She resisted the urge to drop one of the bags and reach for the sword at her hip because she sensed no ill intent from the man, however, it did not stop the annoyance from building within her. When she recognized the face of the intruder, the irritation did not abate, but she began to dent it with rational thought. Chelsea was a practical and strong woman and did not relish the idea of needing a protector. However, in subsequent engagements, Chelsea had been exposed to what one might describe as true power. On the battlefield surrounded by other mortals, Chelsea was a force to be reckoned with and could inspire fear in all of her opponents. However, faced with the Dark Gods, the Heralds of Dorovar, and the other mystical and divine forces that had arrayed against them, Chelsea knew she was hopelessly overmatched. She couldn't very well fulfill her responsibilities in protecting Dominique if she were killed at the onset of the first battle. Which was undoubtedly the reason that Alderin Terian was waiting for them. Chelsea was sure that the Dark God had heard them coming as they left their tent, but he neither raised his head nor made any obvious notice of their approach. When the two women were a matter of steps from the horses, Alderin lifted his head, nodded to Chelsea, and then swung himself up into his saddle and started his horse slowly walking in the direction of Iltorp. In Chelsea's mind, the implication was clear. He didn't want to be there any more than Chelsea wanted him there. Another arrangement of convenience in Chelsea's life. The Dark Gods would look very bad indeed if early in their alliance two of the architects of the peace were slaughtered. Despite herself, Chelsea felt the smile break through the annoyance, and quickly fastened the saddlebags into place before helping Dominique onto her horse.

Dominique had just put her foot into the first stirrup when Chelsea's hands found the slender woman's waist. Dominique shut her eyes and smiled widely before looking back over her shoulder at Chelsea. The younger woman had been riding horses since she was a small child, and had never needed much help to get into the saddle, but there was something within Chelsea that saw Dominique as nothing more than a frail and pampered noble who barely saw the outside of a palace. When Chelsea's eyes found Dominique's both women laughed. However, Chelsea's grip did not relent, and any casual observer would have seen the gesture as a dutiful protector helping their charge. However, that moment, between the two women, it was an expression of something deeper; something perhaps that there could never be words for, at least not ones spoken openly. How could anyone understand when they themselves didn't even understand. But then, Chelsea thought as she moved to her own horse, perhaps there was nothing to understand. They were what they were, and maybe that was what made it special. There didn't need to be labels or titles. No one could ever understand the circumstances, and in the end no one's thoughts mattered other than Chelsea and Dominique's.

It took only a moment for Dominique and Chelsea to catch up with Alderin, as he was not truly trying to make time away from his charges. The three horses fell into a steady rhythm, one that would not tax the horses, but one that would not set any records in making the journey to Iltorp. For the first few hours, Alderin said nothing. He kept apart from the two women, staying several lengths ahead, obviously scouting the way with his enhanced senses. Chelsea and Dominique made small talk sparingly. Finally, near midday, Alderin pointed to a small inlet in the tree-lined road. The three slowed their pace and found the inlet led back into a small clearing that would shield them from any prying eyes that might happen by on the road. The conflicts across Cadaria had seriously impacted travel by merchants and others that made frequent trips between kingdoms, and the loss of the Imperial Palace of Aldere had thrown much of the empire's economy into disarray. The impact on traffic on the road from Aldere to Iltorp would prove advantageous for those who wanted to escape notice, but would not protect them from bandits or partisan loyalists who wished nothing more than to make trouble for those who could be branded as disloyal.

Safely into the secluded clearing, Alderin quickly dismounted and began to stretch his back. A thought suddenly came to Chelsea's mind.

"You don't ride a horse much, do you?"

Alderin turned his head slightly to regard Chelsea and then let a small, almost imperceptible laugh escape his lips.

"When you can instantly travel from one place to another, there isn't much call for riding on horseback for long distances."

Alderin finished stretching and then recovered some bread and dried meat from his saddlebag. He also unslung two waterskins from his saddle and walked toward Chelsea and Dominique who had yet to dismount.

"A light meal," he said handing the food first to Dominique and then to Chelsea. "According to the map, we should make a small lake by nightfall. I think we can risk a small fire and some freshly caught fish."

Chelsea regarded Alderin for a moment as he moved back toward his horse and swung effortlessly into the saddle.

"No need for riding a horse, but knows how to fish," Chelsea remarked skeptically to Dominique.

This time Alderin smiled.

"My father insisted on my knowing a lot that was unnecessary for my day to day life in the Citadel. But then again, my father was quite unique even among the Dark Gods."

Alderin turned his horse toward the road and Chelsea and Dominique quickly fell into step behind him. This time however, Alderin didn't separate himself from the two women, instead he rode between them. There was silence again between the three while Dominique finished the meager meal that she had been provided. Honestly she was not very hungry. The intervening days had left her quite nauseous and with very little appetite. But, her position required her to keep putting on the brave face, and as strong as Chelsea was trying to be for her, Dominique knew that Chelsea needed Dominique to be strong too. The two women would have to depend upon one another more than either of them could imagine in the days and weeks to come, and while Dominique knew Chelsea would be up to the task, Dominique felt in her heart that she might be the one to falter. She was in danger of getting lost in her thoughts and the rising disquiet in her stomach when Chelsea's voice snapped her out of her introspection.

"You were saying about your father?"

Alderin looked at Chelsea for a moment and then returned his gaze to the road ahead.

"I suppose that is what passes for subtlety for the Wolf of Saldarine."

Dominique could not stifle her laughter, and Chelsea gave them both a withering stare before breaking into a smile. Alderin remained silent a moment longer, and then as the three horses fell into a steady rhythm on the hard-packed road, the quiet Dark God began to speak.

"I'm sure you know by now that the Dark Gods have a lot more in common with you Cadarians than you ever thought possible."

Chelsea nodded.

"The twins told us that most of the Dark Gods were humans. Of course they said that they were exceptions, like Camille, and you."

Alderin nodded.

"The twins always did like to talk. We're similar, but different. They were born in the Heavens, like Camille. I was born here. One of the few non-divine Dark Gods. All the power, none of the ties to the Heavens. There aren't many of us; Serrina, Tess, myself…Darrien. Though Tess and Darrien are half Cadarian. My father was similarly different. He was never really human. He was the creation of a Child of the Creator, and some of his powers mixed with the powers he inherited as a member of the Dark Gods creating something unique. He led so many lives, fought for so many sides, and nearly lost everything. But there were times that he was the most human of all the Dark Gods, because he never wanted to forget what had come before. He had been corrupted by power, and didn't want the others to be corrupted by powers they had only been able to imagine before their ascension. So he tried to be humble and grounded. Insisted that all of the children learn to do things without their powers and not become lazy and dependent. Turned out to be very fortunate lessons in my case."

Dominique frowned.

"I'm not sure I understand."

Alderin looked down at the ground for a moment, his brow furrowed.

"The closest analogy that I can draw is how your Cadarian government is supposed to work. The Emperor is supposed to be the center of power, and there is no authority higher than him. I guess that is analogy enough to the Creator. Then you have the Emperor's inner circle, his Court Sorceress, his Voice, his Captain of the Guard, the Master of the Shadow Guild, et cetera. Those are like the Servants. They have only as much power as the Creator gives them, and they have specific roles that they fill. The next layer I guess would be like the Emperor's children and successors. They have power, but their position is a little tenuous. Similar to the Children of the Creator. Unfortunately, this is where the analogy starts to break down. I suppose you could draw a parallel from the Knights of the Flashing Blade to the Dark Gods. Once ordinary people elevated to positions of power that could be taken from them at any time. Regardless, the point I'm trying to make is that where you fall within the organization, whatever it is, dictates how much power you have. The same can be said in theory when it comes to real power."

Chelsea frowned.

"So, following your analogy, the way the system is set up, a Knight of the Flashing Blade, or one of the Court would never be able to challenge the Emperor. They just wouldn't have enough power."

Alderin nodded.

"That's the theory. A Dark God shouldn't be able to stand against a Child of the Creator, and so on."

Here a small smile cracked Alderin's impassible features.

"Theory rarely holds up to practice," Dominique offered.

Alderin nodded.

"No system is perfect. The Children of the Dark Gods, and the Dark Gods themselves have learned ways to bend the rules to their favor, and like in the Cadarian Empire, there are enough wild cards that continue to make things interesting. One of those wild cards unfortunately has the ability to change the nature of a person's power. And so, the powers that I once had as a unique Child of the Dark Gods was taken from me. However, in our world, it is just as easy to be born with power as it is to have it given to you."

Chelsea concentrated for a moment and then shook her head.

"This is starting to make my head hurt," she said after a moment, "and ultimately it means nothing to us. As proficient as I am on the battlefield, any of you would be able to tear me apart in a matter of moments, no matter how you got your powers."

Dominique was disappointed. She found the information fascinating and would have listened for much longer with many more questions. However, Chelsea was the pragmatist. If the information would not benefit her or further her goals, she rarely found the use in engaging in idle conjecture. However, what Alderin said next surprised both Dominique and Chelsea.

"And it's thinking like that that has consistently held you Cadarians back and has kept you from being what you could be. You could be what my parents were. You could be like Gwydeon and Midarin, but you are all too quick to accept your limitations and not push against them. Perhaps that was how Emries wanted it this time around. He didn't want to chance any of you rising against him."

Color immediately came to Chelsea's cheeks, but before she could retort, Alderin continued, his eyes never leaving the road.

"For thousands of years you humans have squandered all of your opportunities. You've warred against each other when you could have built a towering civilization that could have overshadowed any ever built. But instead you did exactly what the Children wanted you to do. You became the pawns that you were designed to be. You all wander through the wilderness thinking that you are special, that you are somehow better than the other beasts that call this world home. You think that you are morally superior to the Dark Gods, you think that you're somehow entitled to this world more so than the dragons or the other creatures. And all of you, all of you point back to the Creator. You're special because the Creator made you so. But even that is a lie. The Creator didn't make you. You aren't molded in his image to the be the inheritors of his gifts. You were created by one of the Children, Emries, to be his slaves. You're nothing more than an experiment in servitude, put forth by a selfish and vengeful god in an effort to topple his siblings."

Dominique's stomach turned.

"But what makes it more insulting is that you aren't even the first world to be enslaved. Dorovar was no different than any of you. He was a slave just like your Kaitain. My parents' world was no different. They were all slaves caught in a battle between two of the Children. The difference is that they didn't stay blind. They rose up, they fought away from their chains and they sacrificed everything they held dear for freedom. And in the end they weren't afraid to sacrifice. Do you think for one moment that my father or my mother stopped to think about how terribly they were overmatched? Do you think my sister thought about how she stood no chance when she fought toe to toe with beings whose powers dwarfed her own? Do you think for one second that Gwydeon or Midarin were willing to let innocents be murdered just because they had no powers? My father always taught me that as long as there is a will, there is a chance."

Here Alderin pulled his horse to a stop, and Chelsea and Dominique did the same, both completely stunned by Alderin's brusque words. This time when Alderin spoke, he didn't direct his words to the empty landscape before them, he instead turned and spoke directly to Chelsea.

"Maybe when this world was created, Emries engineered everything out that made humans special. Maybe he took out the fire and the power that allowed ordinary people to stand up to him. Is that the reason it took the intervention of people like my father and Logan Ranthall to turn the tide all these years later? Or is there more fight in the human race on this world than you have shown so far?"

Chelsea's face was red with anger and her fists were clenched on the reins of her horse. Before she could retort however, another voice cut through the uneasy silence.

"You waste your words on the mortals, Dark God," the gruff and violent voice said with clear disgust. "They are a pale imitation of what humans once were."

The three travelers looked back to the road that stretched before them, and a man stood in the center of the road looking back at them. He was dressed head to toe in white, with white pants that looked as though they had never seen a moment of travel, a long white coat that stretched to the ground and covered a white vest and sparkling silver armor. His skin was dark, topped with a full head of white hair that moved around freely in the breeze. Everything about the man had an air of violence, and his eyes held a malice unlike Chelsea had ever seen. The man was not visibly armed, but the danger that hung around him told Chelsea instantly that this was not someone that should be taken lightly. The stranger held his hands out to his side as though in a gesture of harmlessness, but Alderin regarded the gesture as one more of challenge and insult rather than one of friendship.

"These creatures aren't worth your time or the investment in protecting them," the white-clad man growled. "They should be regarded as nothing more than the mindless cattle that they are, obliviously leading themselves to their inevitable slaughter at the hands of their betters. This chaotic and mindless shadow of civilization they have created is an abomination and an affront to everything that a true society should be. We of the Adhradair were the truest bastions of what a society could be. There was no famine, no murder, no hatred. We all knew our duty and we all served the greater good. At least until the criminals Emries and Talisia descended upon our society like a plague. And so they took our world apart, they made a mockery of everything we held dear, and then they reduced us to servants to the will of those who are our inferiors."

A haze of power appeared around both of the man's outstretched hands.

"These humans are a shadow of what we were. They are a shadow because that is what Emries made them. He took their hearts, he took their will, and made them into nothing more than sacrifices to his greater glory. Where do you think Dorovar learned how to harvest the souls of the faithful as fuel for his ascension? Talisia and Emries invented the technique. They have been gathering power to overthrow the Creator. They were thwarted on my world, and they were thwarted on Onea. But they have had almost two thousand years to ensure that their gambit will be successful. How many souls have I damned to their service during my time imprisoned in that damnable weapon? I felt every skull that cracked under the weight of blows from the weapon your people so ridiculously called Faith. And those deaths, those murders were not in the service of some shining example of civilization but were in the service of a perverted delusion. Now, my young Dark God, if you were truly interested in ensuring that this war is not won by the villains, then you would take that so-called Sacred Weapon from your companion and hand it over to me. I have no quarrel with any of you."

Chelsea's lips twisted into a malicious snarl.

"Over my dead body."

Coriden smiled.

"As you wish."

Faith and Foundation

Year One of the Divine Empress and Child of the Creator Marlae Tamerlane, Creator's Calendar Year 1871

When the Brotherhood of Phasia came into being, they were possessed with great ability to destroy. They could create massive tidal waves hundreds of feet tall, send streams of lightning and fire pulsing from their outstretched fingers, bring lethal needle thin rains of ice falling from the sky, and swallow whole cities with quakes and sinkholes. In the end, they could also use the limitless powers of the Blaze to transform human flesh into abominable creatures whose only aim was to serve and to destroy. But along the way the phasia also developed uses of power that were not destructive, more out of novelty then out of necessity. It was Jeroch who first created the portals. The initial goal was to have a way to move the giant Kamen quickly in an out of battle. The tactic was simple; when facing an army of considerable size, Jeroch would open a portal to the center of their ranks which Kamen would emerge from. Kamen would then use his powers to open fissures in the ground all around him, which would swallow the army before they had a chance to run. Kamen would then step back through the portal to safety. The tactic proved effective for not only Kamen, but for the rest of the phasia, who were able to engage in battle on multiple fronts at the same time, confusing the enemy and making it possible to conquer half the world in a matter of hours. Once Emries and his Erieal adjusted their tactics, the portals became less of a tactical advantage, and the phasia became complacent once they developed armies of their own. By the time the second generation of the phasia were born, the portals had become part of the tapestry of the Blaze, and became second nature, the memory of their tactical capability ignored and the convenience and complacency embraced. However, the Blaze remembered everything that the phasia forgot, including the fear of that first portal.

Modern phasia would describe portal use as three moments. The first moment was the formation of the portal; keeping the image of the destination in mind until the portal completely formed. The image didn't have to be perfect, as intention tended to fill in gaps in the details. The second moment was actually stepping through the portal, as the intention had to hold in the mind of the person who created the portal. For those who used portals consistently, this part became second nature. The third moment was exiting the portal, as there was always a few moments of disorientation transitioning back into reality. As Anabel Binosear exited the portal into the brisk air of Albitonin, she reflected that there was a fourth moment, one that existed within the portal. Of course, the phasia would never acknowledge this moment existed, likely because of their somewhat stilted emotional condition; but for a human being, there was a moment of fear and trepidation as to whether there would be an exit from the portal at all. Deep inside of course, Anne knew that she had nothing to fear from one of Logan's portals. He had had centuries to perfect his technique, even if he did tend to use Aerith's stones more often than not. Yet the fear still clawed at the back of her mind. Perhaps the fear had something to do with the uncertainty that faced her once she appeared in Albitonin. Perhaps it was just a manifestation of the uneasiness that Anne felt with any use of the Blaze's power. Or perhaps it was just the human instinct to fear the unknown. Whatever it was, as she stepped into the light, her stomach churned with it.

Immediately Anne was struck by the fact that Logan must have known the layout of the Heart of Stone very well. Then she chided herself. Logan knew because Aerith knew, and Aerith knew because Hannah knew. The extended web of Aerith Seth's connection to those who carried his mantle was worrisome and advantageous in the same breath. At first, Anne didn't understand how the connection worked, but fortunately Sabrina was patient in teaching her. Now that Sabrina was gone and Anne found herself embroiled in the war that she never wanted to be part of, it was clear that Sabrina knew that all of this was going to come to pass. Sabrina knew that her time in the war was growing short and that Anne needed to be educated on the state of the war and the use of her powers if she was going to survive the storm that was coming.

Anne took a moment to take in her surroundings. The space they were in reminded her very much of the private garden that she had once upon a time back in Trelon. It was a place that she could go and escape the rigors of running a kingdom. A place where she could be alone with her thoughts. She could envision Hannah Ironheart here; the strong woman tasked with carrying the spiritual burden of a whole world upon her shoulders. Anne could see her sitting on one of the low benches, her eyes closed, her mind filled with the troubles of one who lives wrapped in the trappings of authority and responsibility. This was not a place of tranquility. It was a place where the troubles of the world could be dealt with out of the public eye, when emotions did not have to be controlled. But Anne did not have the luxury of time to revel. There was trouble in Albitonin, and Baeata would be walking into it blind.

It was in that moment that Anne knew there was something wrong. There was a presence, a force that she could not understand but could feel pressing down upon her. For the moment, Anne put the thoughts away and turned her attention to the High Priestess, who it seemed was even more shocked by their destination than Anne had been.

"There are very few people who know that this garden exists," Baeata was saying to Aelind, "and fewer still who would dare to set foot within. How is it that this man, Logan, would know to send us here?"

Anne smiled.

"You'll find that Logan is very resourceful, but he cannot take all of the credit. He gets his information from Hannah Ironheart."

Baeata's eyes went wide.

"Lady Ironheart is still alive?"

Inwardly Anne cursed. Of course, everyone still thought Hannah was dead, that's why Baeata was elevated to High Priestess. Anne would have to be more careful in the future, at least as long as she could. There was going to be so much that Baeata would have to handle that she was not prepared for, and sidestepping the unnecessary was going to be Anne's role for a while.

"Baeata," Anne said, dispensing with the formality, "I apologize, but you have to understand that there are forces at work that you are never going to be able to understand, you must simply accept."

Aelind's voice came like a growl.

"How dare you insult the High Priestess…"

Baeata's calm voice cut off Aelind's rebuke.

"The Creator teaches that to seek to understand the mind of the Creator is folly, and to believe that there is nothing beyond understanding is a sin against the teachings of the Church. I accept that I do not know, and so I stay within the Creator's love."

Baeata paused and let Aelind drink in her words. That would be enough for the faithful of course, but in that place, in that garden it was not enough for Baeata. As she began to speak again, Anne felt that tug again in the back of her mind. The presence that she felt was getting stronger and closer.

"Here I stand, in this private garden that few know exist, brought here by means outside any that I could ever understand, wielded by a man who now stands against a creature that effortlessly destroyed the forces of the Creator and sought to murder the embodiment of the Creator's love and leadership upon this world. I did not recognize the man at first, and now upon reflection, I know him. He wore another name of course, but he is the one who espouses to not believe in the Creator and instead places his faith in the mortals of this world. Our clergy would seek to have him silenced, and in many circles he is viewed as the most dangerous threat to the faithful."

Baeata stopped and looked first to Anne and then locked her eyes firmly on Aelind.

"It was not the warrior angels of the Creator who delivered us from danger and risked all to save the innocents from the path of the monster bent on destruction. It was a non-believer. One who curses the name of the Creator and yet does not abandon those who still believe. In a way I think he pities us for our naivety."

Anne wanted to suppress the small chuckle that escaped her lips, but was unable to. When Baeata turned back in her direction, she also could not keep the color from coming to her cheeks.

"You disagree, Lady Anabel?"

The formality of Anne's title struck her in the chest like a blow, but the pause lasted only a moment. Anne immediately recognized not only the tone, but the purpose of it. Baeata, a woman who had massive authority thrust upon her suddenly felt that strength slipping away from her. She was desperately trying to hold on to what she could of her faith and her station, both in her eyes, and the in eyes of her subordinate. In that moment, Anne had slighted her with the small chuckle. It was a bridge too far of disrespect, one that if the positions were reversed, Anne would not tolerate either. However, perhaps in a nod to Logan and to her father, Anne straightened her shoulders and took a step forward. There was no time for saving face, and there was no time to soften the blow to Baeata's ego. The congenial Anne had been instantly replaced by the Lady Anabel.

"Logan has no time for pity, High Priestess, and even if he did, he would not waste it on those who have the capacity to do better than they do."

The words were harsh, the tone was stern, and Anne could feel her patience thinning. Was she really upset with Baeata's ignorance or her own?

"Don't you see what is going on around you? Don't you see the suffering being caused by that kind of blind faith? Kaitain has declared war on the Church of the Creator. An abomination called Dorovar seeks to burn Creation using the souls of the faithful as his tinder. The only ones fighting for that which the Creator has made are the ones that you have spent millennia vilifying. It's the Dark Gods, their children, and their allies that are taking the fight to all those who are bent only on destruction. Logan does not pity you, High Priestess, he is ashamed that you are not willing to see the truth and fight for those who cannot fight for themselves. You wall yourself off from the world, holding up your faith as a shield that you think will protect you when the wolf is at the door. But faith alone is not the answer. The Creator's love will not protect you when Dorovar's forces attack the Heart of Stone."

Anne refocused herself and let her tone soften slightly.

"No one wants you to abandon your faith, Baeata, but please do not let it blind you. You have allies all around you, if you are only willing to let them help you."

Anne's voice trailed off, and the realization of what she had been feeling broke upon her like a wave. She turned slightly, her eyes drifting skyward. There was a glint, just for a second. A bright red eye shaped glint in arch above them. Letting some of the powers granted to her as a child of Aerith Seth fill her diminutive form, Anne let her vision pass from the concrete world around her into the ethereal. Freed from the bonds of mortal perspective, Anne could see more. Above them, wound through the architecture was a serpentine form, massive but elegant. Glaring down at her were the gigantic red eyes of a dragon. For just a moment Anne thought her heart stopped. But then she remembered Logan's words. Aerith had lived up to his reputation and had caused an immense amount of trouble in the Heart of Stone. Cursing herself for being so ignorant, Anne reached out with her perceptions and felt the tumult all around her. There was fear in the Heart of Stone. But it was fear tempered by hope. Massive creatures circled the whole of the Kingdom of Albitonin, but they were not the cause of the fear, not really. In fact, perhaps they represented the new hope that had been stoked in the people. There was something in the center of that hope; a presence that Anne partially recognized. She had felt that power before. Someone who had been touched by Aerith Seth was at the center of the change, and Anne needed to find that person quickly. But the more immediate issue was that of Baeata and the dragon. Steeling herself against the next moment, Anne spoke again.

"Aelind," Anne said as calmly as she could manage, "there is a woman in the Heart of Stone who has come a long way and has brought a message for the High Priestess. Would you go an find her please and bring her here?"

Aelind could not hide the indignation from her face, but with a wave of Baeata's hand, the impertinent servant bowed slightly and quickly left the small garden. It was clear that Aelind did not like the idea of leaving Baeata alone with Anne, but she knew the limitations of her position enough to know when not to defy a request from the High Priestess. However, Baeata's next words once Aelind was out of earshot surprised Anne.

"Aelind believes you intend to murder me."

Anne tried not to let the surprise come to her features.

"She brought her concerns to me our first night in Hedorah. It was her contention that you had too much influence upon the young Empress and it was only a matter of time before you turned her away from the path of righteousness. If then you could murder me and make it look like either an accident or the act of some zealot who served Kaitain Lorien, then you could convince the Empress to appoint you as the new High Priestess and dismantle the Church from the inside."

A small smile came to Anne's lips.

"Aelind has a devious mind. I can see why she is valuable to you. And while you have no reason to believe me, such a plan is both outside of my character and my interests. I was advising Marlae because I was asked to do so, and I slowly agreed against my better judgment. I have no lust for the power that Aelind prescribes to me. In fact, nothing would make me happier than if I could simply retire to a quite villa in the middle of nowhere to live out the rest of my days in peace."

Baeata considered for a moment.

"Then why don't you?"

Anne moved to the edge of one of the towering arches that served as the dragon's perch and leaned lightly against it. It was intended as a disarming gesture, and was completely out of character for the regal Lady Anabel Binosear.

"For you, Baeata, this war is an abstraction. Your beliefs against those who threaten them. You shepherd your flock, you bring them ease and peace against the storm that rages outside of these walls. Even those faithful who have been stripped of everything they know have you and this place to lean upon in the darkness. It is their beacon. For me, this war is personal. My entire family is involved in this war and has been for longer than I care to think about. The people fighting and dying are people I have known most of my life. Your faith is a foundation upon which is built hope for a better tomorrow, a better life for those who come after and a fate befitting the good works of a person's life. But this war, the very essence of it, is to ensure that there is a tomorrow to be better. We are fighting and dying for those who would call us villains and abominations. We shed blood without hesitation for those would wish we would all simply die. We ask no thanks. We ask no consideration. We merely fight for what is right, not what we are told is right. Our sacrifice allows you your ignorant world. Safe from the demons that live just at the edge of what you are willing to see. And if we step aside, if we relent for even a moment to entertain thoughts of our own comfort, then we betray everything that our friends have fought and died for. I didn't understand that for a long time. I was petty, and self-absorbed, and I did a great disservice to those whom I love. But that time is over. Now I know that I must fight, and I know that in the end I will die to ensure freedom and prosperity for the people of this world, whether they believe in the word of the Creator or not."

Anne could feel the tears beginning to well in the corners of her eyes, but she did not let the emotion take her. She pulled herself back to a more regal pose and pulled her shoulders back hard. When she spoke again, her voice was filled with conviction.

"And now that I am part of this fight, I must embrace my role in it. While my family has chosen to act directly against our enemies, that has never been my strength. As I did on my world, so too shall I do here. This place shall hold, with the Divine Empress at the center, and I shall ensure that all forces who are dedicated to ensuring the best outcome to this conflict will have a safe haven."

Baeata hesitated for a moment.

"I have yet to find comfort in the fact that the Divine Empress counted a member of the Dark Gods among her highest councilors, but you have demonstrated nothing but honor when it comes to the Divine Empress. Therefore, if you will forgive our trepidation and suspicion, you may count the High Priestess of the Church of the Creator and all of the forces of the Heart of Stone as your allies."

Anabel smiled. However, she did not have time to revel in the small victory. She instead turned her attention to the invisible creature that coiled itself around the arches high above.

"I'm happy to hear you say that, Baeata, but I'm afraid you're going to have to adjust to many new things very quickly, not the least of which is our new friend."

Anabel turned away from Baeata, silencing any question before it could be voiced. She turned to the dragon and addressed it as formally as she could.

"I know that you have been listening since our arrival, and I'm sure it was the portal that drew your attention. Would you please reveal yourself so that the High Priestess can also have the benefit of the conversation?"

That next moment, the great coiled form of the dragon appeared, its large head and brilliant ruby eyes peering down from high above. It was impossible to judge the true size of the dragon because of the way that it was arrayed before them, but the term gigantic did not do justice. Anne felt Baeata freeze behind her, but Anne gave her a reassuring glance and then returned her attention to the dragon.

"manners….." the dragon hissed, "unusual…….child of Aerith….."

Anne wasn't sure if it was a jab at her or at Aerith, but knowing the reputation that Aerith had, she was sure that he was not nearly as polite in dealing with the ancient creatures.

"Aerith Seth has many bad habits, not the least of which is his inability to behave in a civilized manner when it would most benefit him or those who are working to advance his agenda. I trust that you are the surprise that Logan Ranthall warned me about."

"heretic......surprising......great loss......."

Anne's blood ran cold.

"He's not lost yet," she replied without thinking. "He's going to keep fighting and he's going to be there with us at the end, and as long as there is hope, I am going to believe that he is alive."

The dragon blinked very slowly, its dual lids sliding over the great ruby eyes in an expression that Anne interpreted as pity.

"hope......flickers......time.......short.......darkness moves......."

The dragon shifted its attention in the direction of the door to the chamber and then promptly disappeared from view once again. Anne could still see the dragon, but she knew that for Baeata the great creature was simply gone. It was the next moment when Aelind returned with another young woman in tow, one dressed in the garb of a priestess. As soon as the new arrival saw Baeata, she bowed low, probably lower than necessary, and waited to be addressed before straightening. Aelind announced the new arrival a moment later.

"High Priestess Baeata Catrinel, allow me to present Priestess Rhya Edel late of Aldere."

Rhya kept her head low until she was acknowledged by Baeata.

"I understand you have a message for me from Hannah Ironheart?"

Rhya straightened. There was still so much that she did not understand about all of the information in her head. What she was clear on however was that her role had been important, and that all that mattered was what she said next.

"The message is from Lady Ironheart, High Priestess, but not directly. It was relayed through an intermediary."

Baeata considered for a moment.

"Have you seen Lady Ironheart, Priestess?"

Rhya frowned.

"No, High Priestess."

"Then how can you know for certain that this message is genuine?"

Rhya paused, and then her voice came out, as though she was reciting some obscure passage from the Book of the Creator that she had rehearsed to the point that she could recite it in her sleep. There was no emotion in the words.

"High Priestess, as proof of my words, the Lady Ironheart requests that you check the right arm of the chair in the Lady Ironheart's quarters. There you will find a secret compartment that holds hand-written copies of passages from the Book of the Creator in the Lady Ironheart's own hand. The papers will also bear the signature of the previous High Priestess, as the Lady Ironheart wrote them when she was only an acolyte."

Aelind turned her attention back to Baeata.

"Should I verify that these items exist, High Priestess?"

Baeata considered for a moment and then waived a dismissing hand.

"No. I have no doubt that the items exist, as anyone who would dare tell such a tale would know how easily it could be verified or disproved. Instead, Aelind, I think the best use of your time will be to arrange for a mass for all the faithful. Any who are here within the Heart of Stone, and any who still dwell within the Kingdom of Albitonin will be welcome to hear the words of the Divine Empress and the High Priestess. There will be much demanded of the faithful in the days and weeks to come, and they have the right to know what is being asked of them by their leaders."

Aelind bowed and turned to leave.

"And see that we are not disturbed," Baeata continued. "I fear that Lady Anabel, Priestess Rhya, and I will be in serious discussion for some time and those discussions should not be interrupted."

Aelind bowed again.

"As you command High Priestess."

This time Aelind left the garden and Anne could hear the woman giving instructions to guards who must have been stationed outside. Anne wasn't sure if the guards had been there the whole time, or if they arrived when Aelind brought Rhya. Baeata moved to sit on a low bench and once seated motioned for the other two women to do the same. Anne could hear the dragon above them move to a position where the three women would be able to see it, and then the creature reappeared. If Rhya was disturbed by the appearance of the ancient creature, it did not show upon her face.

"Now," Baeata said finally, "let us find a way forward."

Talk of the Devil and His Horns Appear

Year Four of the Just Emperor Kaitain "Dragonsbane" Lorien, Creator's Calendar Year 1871

Kaitain Lorien stepped from the portal and immediately felt the salt-water filled breeze against his skin. In his younger days, when he was solidifying support for his eventual rule with the nobles of the Kingdoms of Cadaria, Kaitain traveled to each and every major city across the face of the empire. His father had once tried to teach him that the best way to rule a people was to understand what it was that they loved and desired to protect. By relating to these base needs, a true and fit ruler could inspire loyalty that would bring civilization to incredible heights. But that was his father's way. During his travels, Kaitain found a way that better suited his aims and dispositions. Of course he could have appealed to love and value, but such base platitudes were lost on Kaitain. He saw such connections as weakness. What was loved could be taken away, destroyed, corrupted. What was valued could tarnish, fade, or be ripped asunder. Love was fleeting; value always degrading and never more than that first special moment. What was eternal was the application of power. People were greedy, selfish, and while they could feign interest in the well-being of others for a limited period of time, eventually they would revert back to their selfish natures. The destitute sought to improve their position in the world, and those with privilege always hungered for more status, more wealth, and more power. The more power one had, the more people wanted, and it was that access that Kaitain sought to leverage during his travels. Those who would swear their loyalty would stay loyal so long as their desires were placated. The secret of course was to not give too much too quickly. To not be over-eager for the advantage that loyalty would bring. Kaitain had to stay above the fray, to be just unapproachable enough to make the eventual capitulation seem that much more valuable. Manipulation of human greed was Kaitain's true gift, even more than his penchant for cruelty.

Kaitain turned back to his companion just as the portal closed behind her. While Alise had been impressive in her service thus far, Kaitain could easily find fault. She had been unable to eliminate Vallic Ultiv, the farmer called Wynne had continued to elude her attempts to track him, Feyd and Felicia were still alive. Her recent string of failures belied her rich history of service, and until she had been sent to murder Feyd, she had never missed a target before. Perhaps removing minor functionaries was the extent of her usefulness. On the other hand, she did have a considerable amount of other skills that made her useful, like the portal she had just conjured. The Shadow Guild had trained her well, even though there were some abilities that she had been denied because of her utter loyalty to the Emperor. On many occasions Kaitain had considered eliminating the leadership of the Shadow Guild, but they had proved loyal thus far. However, it had become clear that even they had turned against Kaitain with their complicity in smuggling Dominique out of Aldere. The number of traitors around Kaitain were continuing to increase, and he could not sacrifice those who were still remaining loyal. The Academy of Arcane Arts had gone rogue, the Shadow Guild were more interested in pursuing their own interests, the Knights of the Flashing Blade had fallen into darkness, and even his own Dark Academy had seemed to turn against him. All that was left was Alise and the imperial Guard. But now the ranks of the Imperial Guard had been thinned by a man wearing Ivan Quicksilver's face. Ivan was gone, Korin was gone, and Calindria was gone. But as long as Kaitain had his Lorien blood and his guile, there was nothing that could stand in his way.

Alise turned to face Kaitain and immediately fell to one knee. Supplication was not a natural action for her, but in the face of the Emperor, considering what had just happened, it seemed the right thing to do to keep his anger in check. Kaitain may have viewed her as a disposable tool, but Alise saw herself as considerably more.

"What orders, my Emperor?"

Kaitain considered for a moment. The remnants of the Imperial Guard would be on their way to the capitol of Zevarit, which from the surroundings should have been over the nearest rise to the south. Even now he could begin to smell the smoke from the chimneys in town. What was left of the army would be in position to march on the town in perhaps two days. There was a garrison several hour's walk from their current position, and Kaitain would find rest and shelter there. There would also be small convents and outposts of the Church of the Creator that could be raided while the rest of the main force arrived. It would take time to rebuild the strength in the army's ranks, and without the support of the Black Academy, Kaitain would have to be more tactically careful. Still, there were other considerations. Who was the mysterious mistress that Yaron had been obeying? Why was the Grey Man Pestilence on the battlefield? How was Marlae able to infect the minds of his soldiers and turn so many to her cause? What happened to the Masters of the Academy after it fell? Too many questions, not enough answers, and too many enemies arrayed against him. At least one member of the Dark Gods had been eliminated, and Kaitain could use that to his advantage. Perhaps Alise was not such a failure after all. She had given him a victory that no previous Emperor of Cadaria had had since Terrik "Godslayer" Lorien had slain the leader of the Dark Gods in personal combat. If he only had a trophy of that victory to claim as his own, that would make it perfect.

"We must move north to the garrison. With our forces diminished by repeated treachery we will need to ensure that if there is a battle for Zevarit, that it is over swiftly to conserve our forces."

Alise remained on a knee. She looked down to the ground for a moment and then back up to Kaitain.

"Permission my Emperor to continue my hunt for Wynne. I must destroy him and reclaim my honor."

Kaitain had half-expected the request. Alise felt the sense of her failure more keenly even than Kaitain did, and as much as he wanted her to cleanse the stain from her reputation, there were far more pressing matters. This Wynne, while an annoyance, was not a threat. Kaitain was about to speak when he saw Alise tense. The long claws appeared on the backs of her hands, and she eased into a crouch like a predator about to pounce on its prey. However, Alise did not move, in fact, to Kaitain's eyes the woman was not even breathing. She stood, placid and unmoving like a statue, eyes fixed, breath arrested. Kaitain turned, slowly, not wanting to appear distressed by his servant's incapacity. When he finally turned, in the distance Kaitain could see a figure in flowing white robes approaching. The figure was not simply walking across the distance. It would take several steps and then simply be several yards closer. Again, several normal steps, and then simply appear to be much closer. It took only a half-dozen of these jumps before Kaitain could see the face of the man, his dark eyes, and the haze of spectral green that floated around him. Setting his feet, Kaitain's hand fell to the hilt of the Imperial Sword, but the blade felt cold and lifeless in his grasp. It did not want to be pulled from its sheathe, it did not want to strike at the man that approached. Kaitain felt for a moment that the blade was perhaps afraid. When finally the man was a matter of a dozen strides from Kaitain, he stopped and regarded both Kaitain and Alise for a moment before raising his left hand. Kaitain heard Alise gasp behind him, and he turned his head slightly so that he could see the woman out of the corner of his eye. Alise had fallen back to her knees, all of the energy drained from her, and the vicious blades were gone from the backs of her hands. Whoever this new arrival was, it was clear he had abilities that were not to be trifled with or underestimated. Kaitain was about to demand the identity of the new arrival when he did something that Kaitain did not expect. The man slowly bowed, stayed for a moment and then straightened. The bow was perhaps just low enough to be respectful, but no more. Whoever the new arrival was, he knew protocol but was only going to adhere to it to a point. This man was clearly once a servant, but would never be so again.

CHAPTER 102

"Emperor Kaitain Lorien of the Cadarian Empire," the man said in an accent that Kaitain could not place. "I would ask for your time and indulgence to discuss a matter of some importance to both of us."

The words were clipped and proper, probably designed to make Kaitain feel at ease, but there was nothing about the words that seemed to fit the man. It was a persona, a disguise designed to ingratiate. However, for someone with an eye for human weakness like Kaitain, such deceptions were glaring and off-putting. Kaitain did not abide pretenders, nor did he abide those who would seek his indulgence by farce and cajoling. However, there was one thing about the man that was genuine, the tone and timbre of his voice. Moreover, Kaitain latched onto that voice. It was a voice that he had heard before, a voice that haunted his dreams. Nevertheless, if the man wished to play games, Kaitain decided that he would indulge the man, for a time.

"I'll indulge you only so far, stranger. It is clear you have abilities that make you formidable, and I am sure that if you had intended harm you could have dispatched both my assassin and myself with little difficulty. That alone should grant you some measure of leave, however, speaking of something that benefits us both intrigues me. What could someone like you, with all of your abilities at your disposal, require my aid in that you could not simply take yourself."

The stranger in white folded his hands behind his back and regarded first Kaitain and then Alise before speaking again. This time the words were not clipped, but more lyrical, and its hypnotic drone bored its way into the very base and primal parts of Kaitain's mind.

"Abilities, Emperor Lorien, do not often translate to power. Power requires ambition, drive, and a vision to do what others will not. Abilities can be the road to power, but they are not power unless they are applied properly. Do you not agree?"

Kaitain nodded.

"Power is not something to be regarded lightly. It must be cultivated to match the abilities of the one who is to wield it. Power can be created for ones-self, or it can be created for another. Power can be wielded through love, through fear, or through hate. Power is not only expressed through one's ability to destroy, but one's ability to command loyalty, to command respect, and to command life and death on a scale that is impossible to predict."

The man in white smiled slightly.

"Spoken as one who was raised at the foot of power. I have watched you for a long time Emperor Kaitain Lorien, and I have seen the boy become the man. I have seen you try to find a different way from your father. Where he wanted to be loved and respected, you wanted to be feared and needed. You cajoled all who thought they had power and tempted them with more. You took what you wanted without repercussions, especially those things that were not yours to have. Like your brother's beloved."

Kaitain grimaced slightly behind his cold mask.

"You have let nothing stand in your way. Not Alistair Ravenheart, not the whole of the Academy of Arcane Arts, not the Shadow Guild, the Knights of the Flashing Blade, your own brother. You have proclaimed yourself the singular arbiter of your future and the future of this Empire, and the future of this world. It did not matter that the dragons are superior to your forces in strength and intelligence. It did not matter that the Dark Gods had more power than you could even imagine. Your desire to dominate all has been the driving force behind every action. And now, Emperor Kaitain Lorien, as I stand before you I am left with but one question."

The way the man spoke intrigued Kaitain, and he could not help the next words that come from his lips.

"And what is that question?"

The man in white's mouth curled into a slight smirk.

"Just how far are you willing to go to have the power which you seek?"

Kaitain turned slightly and pointed to the southwest.

"In that direction lies the remains of a small church and its surrounding community. My soldiers killed all who stood against them, stripped the faithful of all of their belongings, their dignity, and their freedom, and then we defiled the grounds and burnt the place of worship to the ground. I have made worship of the Creator a crime in my Empire, and I will see all who continue to worship reduced to nothing more than cattle and playthings for those who are loyal to the laws of the Empire. There can be but one authority in this world. I cannot abide anyone serving two masters. There will be no Masters of the Arcane Arts. There will be no Grand Master of the Shadow Guild. There will be no High Priestess of the Church of the Creator. Those days are over. All subjects will have loyalty to the Emperor first and only. If they cannot abide by this absolute rule, then they shall be relieved of their status as citizens, or they shall be relieved of their lives. This is the measure of my resolve. This is the measure of my dedication to furthering the Empire."

The man in white nodded softly. When he began to speak again, there was almost a note of pity in his voice.

"Long ago, I lived on a world that was designed to be perfect. Everyone upon the face of my world was born to a purpose. That purpose was written within the blood of each person, and that purpose could not be abandoned or changed. Each person knew that role, and accepted that role. There was no need for strife or jealousy, because all people were provided for equally. No one wanted for food. No one wanted for shelter. There was no need for currency or bartering because everyone had what they required. But there was a flaw in the society, one that was not seen until it was far too late and the death of our perfect society was assured."

The man in white turned away from Kaitain and fixed his eyes on the stars that were just starting to take hold in the sky as the light from the twin suns faded.

"If that had been the root of it all, our purpose, then perhaps my world would not have ended. But the central tenant of our world was not our work and the order and harmony created by it, but rather the order decreed to us by the religion of our goddess. The religion, like a sickness, consumed us. Everything revolved around it. Our schedules, our families, our ambitions. We venerated this thing that stood apart from us, rather than venerating each other. We elevated a small group of us, stood them apart because that was what was decreed by the goddess. In the end, it was this faith in the goddess, the belief in her design, that allowed us to be betrayed. It allowed the dark goddess Talisia to corrupt our beliefs. It allowed the dragons to corrupt our lands, and it allowed the demon Emries to corrupt our souls. We begged for power to fight the dragons, begged for power to take back what was ours. And Emries gave us exactly what we wanted. Power. The power to destroy. But we did not know how to use such power, and so the very beings who were tasked with protecting, directing, and promoting order in our civilization were the ones who ultimately tore it apart and sentenced our world to death. By the time the dragons were defeated, there was nothing left of my world."

The man in white turned back to Kaitain.

"And thus a life dedicated to promoting order while at the same time supplicating to a higher power was forged anew. Now my life is dedicated to ensuring that no other world meets the fate that mine met. That no other people will be tasked with false faith to the Goddess Raenera. That no other world must trade their safety and prosperity for fear in hosting the dragons upon their world. That no other community suffers the vile machinations of Talisia, and no other peoples fall to the temptations of Emries. Finally, there must be no place for the one called the Creator upon any of the worlds in His dominion The Golden Throne must crack, the pillars of the Divine Palace must fall, and the Heavens must be silenced. The Creator must die."

Kaitain did not react to the man's words, but was immediately clear of the man's intent and his identity.

"And what would Dorovar wish of the Emperor of Cadaria?"

Kaitain could feel Alise tense beside him, but if the man whom Kaitain believed to be Dorovar had any reaction to the words, it did not show on his face.

"I should have expected that you were clever," Dorovar responded. "Though you have determined my identity, you have not made threats, you have not shrunk in fear. You simply continue our parlay. I am intrigued."

Kaitain smiled behind his mask.

"I recognized your voice from when I slumbered, stricken by a would-be assassin's poison. Since my awakening, I have had time to reflect upon the lucid dreams of that perturbed sleep, and the bolt that put me there. I remember a woman's voice, a woman who wanted to use me for her purposes, a woman who spoke of treachery and deceit, who spoke of all those arrayed against me. She thought I was weak. She thought that I would blindly accept her transparent deceptions. But then another voice joined. Your voice. You called me to come to your side, to become your herald, and to help you rip this world apart. I refused both advances, and forced my way back into the waking world. But now, seeing true machinations around me, and knowing the traitors not only of my blood, but those who should have been loyal to the words of the Emperor, I have seen through the lies to the truth."

Dorovar nodded.

"And what is this truth that you have discovered?"

Kaitain's voice was calm, but Dorovar could feel the man's impatience and malice growing.

"It was the woman who invaded my dreams who was behind the assassination attempt, not Seraph Kore. She had orchestrated the whole play in order to recruit me to her cause. You were simply taking advantage of the opportunity that she opened. I assume that is because she is your enemy, and that you would go to any lengths to deny her another soldier to her cause."

Dorovar nodded slightly.

"As I said, Emperor Lorien, you are quite clever, and also quite insightful. However, you have had the luxury of time. I have learned that time is the greatest teacher. In the moment you were ruled by your rage. Now, you can find your opportunity to take vengeance upon the one who struck you and sought to control you like a pet. And have you, in your deliberations, concluded who it was who attempted to fool you?"

Kaitain shook his head.

"I have suspicions, but unfortunately, I do not have enough information to know for certain. However, since she is your enemy, I believe you can give me her identity."

Dorovar nodded.

"I can certainly give you her name. She is Talisia, Child of the Creator and the vile witch who is complicit in the death of my world. While some might say that she was responsible, I however hold the goddess Raenera responsible. She failed us when we needed her the most, so the death of my world was upon her head. I have since absolved her of her crimes and sent her to wherever her kind goes when they die. Talisia has thus far served her purpose as a foil for the Dark Gods and your Knights of the Flashing Blade as well as her brother Emries. However, I believe that usefulness is at an end, and thus I have come to find you to help you fulfill your part in this grand charade."

Dorovar could see Kaitain's eyes narrow.

"My part?"

When Dorovar spoke again, his voice was more wistful and mysterious.

"Have you not seen it in your dreams, Kaitain? All the blood and all the death? There is always this young girl, and she seems to be at the center of it all. Every night you get closer to seeing her face, every night you get closer to hearing what she is saying. However, the dreams keep changing. Sometimes it's you with your arm around her throat and laughter drowning out her words. Sometimes it's the Dark Gods. Sometimes it's a member of the Knights of the Flashing Blade, standing on a mountain of the dead as the world tears itself apart."

An involuntary shiver ran through Kaitain and his blood ran cold. Dorovar continued, painting a picture so vividly with his words that it seemed to float in the ether between them.

"The sky above the battlefield blood red, clouds of smoke blotting out the sun. The smell of death thick in the air, and all across the ground lay the broken bodies of soldiers. Many different banners and colors littering the battlefield, all of the major kingdoms represented with dead. The Imperial Palace of Aldere in ruins, a smoking crater where the throne room had once been. You, clutching a young girl in your arms. She struggles against your grip and screams. All around on the bloody ground are the broken bodies of imperial citizens, the armies of the empire. Approaching you see Hannah Ironheart, and behind her a contingent of creatures from Mythryn and a group of the Dark Gods. And you call out: 'You cannot stop me now! I have it, it is mine! You will never prevent my ascension to god-hood! I will unseat the Creator and this world will become mine! I will save us all from the Dark Gods!' At your words, fire emerges from thin air, and breathable air becomes poison. The next moment the world turns mad, ripped upside down and inside out. And then everything goes black."

Kaitain's mind spun, but before he could form his thoughts into a question, Dorovar continued.

"I have seen these visions too, Kaitain, and I know what it is they mean. You are destined to find the Dragon's Tear. You shall use it to destroy the enemies of your empire. You will vanquish the Dark Gods. You will kill Talisia and her brother Emries, and then you will use the power of the Dragon's Tear to unmake all that the Creator has made, and destroy the Golden Throne. This is the prophecy that has been in your soul every night, screaming to be heard. And I have the one piece of information you need to make that vision a reality. I can tell you where to find the Dragon's Tear."

Kaitain did his best to suppress the elation that was building in him. Obviously Kaitain did not trust Dorovar, and did not trust the seeming magnanimity that the demon was demonstrating.

"And what is the price for this information?"

One corner of Dorovar's mouth lifted slightly, for just a moment before the placid façade returned.

"The price, Emperor Kaitain, is that you must use the Dragon's Tear. You cannot simply hide it away to prevent others from possessing it. There must be a reckoning. There must be a war. And there must be so much blood that the seas turn red with it."

Kaitain's voice betrayed the wanton desire burgeoning in him.

"The war has already begun, Dorovar, but the Dragon's Tear will hasten its end. I shall wipe all worshipers of the Creator from the face of this world, and I shall use their blood to cleanse the Empire of Cadaria of their lies and betrayals. The dragons shall have their wings ripped from their backs, and the Dark Gods will be made to kneel one by one before their heads are severed from their bodies. All that will remain are those who are loyal to the true Emperor. And on a leash, kept in my parlor will be my former daughter, brought low by her own hubris."

Kaitain's voice trailed off. Finally, he refocused his attention on Dorovar.

"I accept your terms, Dorovar. Tell me what I must do to recover this treasure."

Chapter CIII

May Flights of Angels Take Thee To Thy Rest

Onea, The Time of the Coromor, Time Unknown

There was formlessness. There was power. There was burning. Even before there was acknowledgement of consciousness or anything that resembled recognition and thought, there was brilliant green. The green faded and resolved into the features of a place, a place filled with darkness except for the brilliant green. Thoughts and consciousness came like a torrent, but were not overwhelming. The budding intellect drank in everything the Blaze taught, everything the Blaze knew, and still was left wanting more. It was then that the green glow began to recede and let the features of the room become crisper. Words instantly attached themselves to the images that clarified, and the lifetimes of knowledge began to have context. A face came into the foreground, and again the disjointed information coalesced into knowledge.

"I know you."

Another explosion of understanding and meaning hit the growing and maturing consciousness. Words, speech, a voice. The ability to speak had been instinctual, seemingly like so many other abilities. Thinking, understanding, seeing, smelling, remembering. Strange concepts with strange names that fit together into the newly formed being, held together with the brilliant green flames. The voice was strong, proud, feminine. The idea of gender and identity detonated in the new brain; her new brain. The face before her pulled back, revealing a monstrously large form, but his kind eyes belied whatever menace his form projected. The familiar looking man reached out with a large brutish hand and waited, his eyes still kind and understanding. Acknowledgement of her limbs became real, and she reached out with one hand toward the giant; slender, delicate fingers coming into the field of vision. Her hand would have barely circled around three of the giant's fingers, but he let her steady her balance against his strength as the concepts of balance and walking took hold. She took a step out of the warm green glow and into the cold harsh world.

"I am Kamen," the giant said finally. "Welcome to this mortal world, my sister."

From out of her field of vision another voice spoke, one that had a hard edge, but was eerily similar to the soft whispering voice of the green flames that had molded her.

"She is my first daughter, Kamen," the voice said to the giant. "She is the Lady Fox. Bryn Rhaine."

* * * * * * * * * * * *

Year Four of the Just Emperor Kaitain "Dragonsbane" Lorien, Creator's Calendar Year 1871

Bryn got to her feet and before she even knew what was happening, she raised her hands skyward and let a massive torrent of fire burst forth from her fingers. The warrior angels that flooded through the portal high in the sky tried to scatter away from the assault, but many were caught by surprise and almost instantly incinerated. The new power that she had felt in the Heavens had not left her, and it seemed that the more she used her power, the more powerful she became. The burst of fire struck the portal and detonated sending a corona of heat spreading in all directions. The portal closed violently, but not before an innumerable host of angels had followed Bryn and her husband back to the mortal world. Bryn took a quick sideways look to where Aerith had also made it back to his feet, and she was shocked to see a large black ball of fur sitting on his shoulder, and a wide gloating smile upon his face. She knew that smile, and it filled her with dread and terror. He was enjoying himself, and that meant death to their enemies. As Bryn's eyes drifted upward again, she felt herself begin to smile as well.

* * * * * * * * * * * *

Onea, The Time of the Coromor, Time Unknown

The assault had gone better than expected, but as Grawn settled back onto his throne fashioned from the bones of the servants of Emries that he had slain with his bare hands, he could not help but feel as though more could have been accomplished. Kamen, Aryx, and Jeroch were off working on their secret experiment out in the plains near some obscure city, the newly born Ellis spent more time prattling on about the nature of the war between Shau-ling and Emries and the reasons behind it, and so Grawn was saddled with the oldest of the women, the so-called Lady Fox. She was an irritant at the best of times, and at the worst, he wanted to choke the life out of her with his bare hands. But he had to grudgingly admit that she was quite adept at killing. The sisters came strolling in; arms entwined their hushed voices clearly discussing something that Grawn could care less about. When they came to a stop half-way into the room, Ellis' eyes moved from her sister to where Grawn sat on his throne of bones. Grawn didn't need to see her eyes roll, he felt them, and he could care less.

"I know that we must kill these pathetic excuses for life," Ellis began, her low calm voice stirring something within the gruff man, "but must you revel in it?"

Grawn let his fingers run over the arms of the throne, the index finger of his right hand tracing across the surface of a thighbone. His left hand rested on a skull that he slowly pulled free and turned so that he was looking into the dead sockets of the eyes.

"For all of the things you understand, Ellis," Grawn began, the violence thick in his voice, "this war is not one of them. Yes, these creatures are fragile and pathetic, but they fight with every bit of will and ferocity that they can manage. Emries has given them something to fight for, something to hate, and has incited them in a way that is hard to combat. So, it doesn't matter how many of them we kill, maim, destroy, disembowel, and burn alive, they will keep coming like an angry swarm of hornets. The only way to truly defeat them is to take the hope that Emries has instilled within them and replace it with fear. They must believe to stand against the Brotherhood of Phasia and the Living Nightmare Shauling is folly, and that there is no chance of victory. There must be great monuments of death so horrific that the very sight of them turns their blood to ice. They must be moved with such horror that they soil themselves at the very mention of our names. In their minds we must dine on their hearts, drink their blood, and use their corpses as the foundation for great palaces of death. Despite all of their other failings, our brothers understand this, which is why Jeroch is building his monstrosity. Rumors of the death that will occur in that place will bring sleeplessness to the humans for generations."

Grawn crushed the skull to punctuate the last word and then let the pieces fall to the ground, an evil smile tugging at the corners of his mouth. He looked up in time to see Bryn shaking her head.

"A fine speech, Grawn, but I don't think many will see your effigy of death here in this palace. What fear are you striking into the hearts of men with this abomination you call a throne?"

Grawn leaned back, his eyes going cold.

"Oh this isn't for the humans," he said dryly, "this is for the rest of you."

Ellis looked as though she had been struck, while Bryn simply put her hands on her hips and waited for Grawn to continue his explanation. Grawn was not known for being overly verbose, but when he chose to speak, he ensured that his point was made. It was not within Grawn's nature to be cryptic.

"We all have been given a talent by our Master. Mine is to be able to see treachery before it will happen. What the humans call paranoia, I call an ability to understand the motivations of those so powerful they can shake the world. And as we have fought and killed together, my sense of each of you has become clear, and the more I see, the clearer your natures have become. Each of you is a danger to that which we fight for. Kamen will turn against our Master, Aryx will betray us all, and Jeroch will constantly battle a nebulous duality in his nature to the point that it makes him completely and totally useless in the advancement of our goals. You, Ellis, the more you use your intellect, the more you will become a danger to the Phasia. Even though you think you are doing what is in the best interest in our cause, your machinations will cause death and destruction."

Whatever Ellis thought of Grawn's implication, she did not react and her eyes were devoid of all emotional queues. Bryn however could no suppress laughter. She folder her arms across her chest and let the frown curl her lips.

"And what of me, Grawn? Do you think so little of me that you won't detail my supposed treachery?"

Grawn sighed.

"I have not the words to describe the depths of the tragedy that your treachery will create. And yet, while I can see that you have the capacity to be the greatest villain and the utter downfall of the Brotherhood of Phasia, there is also within you the capacity to be the greatest hero for our cause. I do not fully grasp that which I see, but you are a tragedy, a plague, and horror to every creature that walks upon this world."

Once again, Bryn could not resist the urge to laugh.

"Perhaps our Master made the mistake in starting this war, Grawn, if what you say is true. If we are as doomed as you believe us to be, why do we even fight at all?"

Grawn stood and slowly but deliberately crossed the distance between them until he stood face to face with the Lady Fox, only the barest space between their noses. Bryn did her best not to flinch, but she felt the intimidation begin to rise within her. Grawn was not a blunt instrument, he was a harbinger of death; violence and bloodlust barely restrained.

"Because I was made for one purpose, Bryn, and that is to kill. And I shall keep on killing until there is nothing left on this world for me to kill."

Finally, Ellis found her voice again.

"And it seems that Emries has seen fit to accommodate your desires, Grawn. Rumors have persisted for quite some time that Emries has been seeking a way to combat us on our own terms."

Grawn held Bryn's gaze for another few seconds, before returning to his throne and letting his dismissive reply hit the air.

"Good. Thus far the only challenge these humans have posed is how to dispose of all of their bodies. Their weapons are no match for our armor, their paltry magic is no match for the Blaze, and their fanaticism cannot compare to our righteous cause. Let them come."

Bryn scoffed.

"Did you know that bravery and stupidity were close cousins, Grawn? Do you not think that Emries would have the ability to imbue some of the humans with powers in the same way that Shau-ling created us? They might perhaps even be our equals."

Grawn's laughter echoed through the chamber.

"Preposterous. At best, they are pale imitations. Their humanity makes them weak. No matter what power Emries imbues a human with, they could never hope to match, let alone surpass us. We are perfection."

Ellis' chiding tone rang out.

"You contradict yourself Grawn because you do not have the mental capacity to understand the complexities of this war. Lord Shark you may be, and a terror on the battlefield you are truly, but a student of the sociology of this war you are not. After that morose speech about the traitorous future of each of the phasia, you then espouse that we are perfection? We are born and bred to be reflections of the darkness in humanity, and still you think that they cannot be made to be our equals?

Perhaps they could have the capacity to be every bit as ruthless as you believe yourself to be, Grawn."

Grawn dismissed Ellis' words with a flip of the hand. Bryn however turned to her sister and implored her to continue.

"Obviously you know more than you've shared to this point, Ellis. Ignore the grumpy old man and tell me what you've learned."

Ellis clasped her hands behind her back and leaned forward slightly as if to give her words far more weight.

"Emries calls them his *Erieal*. There are four of them, his most trusted generals, that he has invested at least some measure of his power within. Some of the information I have been able to gather includes stories of these *Erieal* moving mountains and drowning massive fires with towering waves from the sea. Even factoring in the obvious exaggerations that all humans are prone to, the descriptions of these abilities sound similar enough to feats that we ourselves have accomplished in the last year. The fact that Emries has not unleashed these *Erieal* against us yet to me indicates that he is still testing their power. Much in the same way that Shau-ling held us back until he was ready, I believe Emries is biding his time, sacrificing the mewling fodder, and waiting for the perfect chance to launch his secret weapon upon us. It is only because not all of the humans are mindless sycophants that any of this information has come to me."

Grawn slammed his fist down and let loose a primal growl.

"I shall not wait until our enemy is ready. I shall take the fight to them. I will kill so many of Emries' followers that he will have no choice but to unleash these creatures upon me. And then I shall tear each of them apart with my bare hands and bathe in their blood to show Emries the folly of trying to match the might of the Brotherhood of Phasia."

Bryn rounded on Grawn.

"Don't you think this requires a little more in the way of subtlety and tactical thinking rather than your blind and blunt destruction? What if all four of these *Erieal* are unleashed upon you at once? What if you cannot handle them because you had no idea what they were capable of? What if there are more of them than Ellis knows about?"

Grawn frowned.

"Think. That is all you and Ellis do is think. The enemies attack, and instead of fighting you think. Jeroch, Aryx, Kamen, and I burn whole villages, and you sit and think. If you were running this war, we would already have been overrun by these pathetic humans."

Hands on hips, Bryn scowled.

"You've never thought that I was capable of fighting Emries' forces. You've always believed yourself superior."

Grawn rose and took a step toward Bryn.

"Why Shau-ling made something as weak as you I will never understand. After all, you're only a woman."

In less than the span of a second, the ball of flame crossed the distance between Bryn and Grawn and slammed fully into his chest. He flew backwards and crashed into his throne of bone, sending pieces of it scattering in all directions. Bryn was atop Grawn the next moment, a blade of flame in her hand, the tip pressed to his throat.

"I'll happily remove that doubt right here and right now, Grawn. No one will miss you."

Grawn opened his mouth and a stream of scalding hot water burst forth and sped straight for Bryn's face. The Lady Fox's reflexes however were up to the task, and Bryn was able to propel herself backwards several feet, landing in a crouch, blades of flame appearing in each hand. Grawn was to his feet before the second blade was in Bryn's hand, his balled fists glistening as they shifted from flesh to diamond. Before another blow could be landed or a harsh word spoken, Ellis stepped between her two siblings.

"Enough of this. You two at each other's throats only makes Emries' forces stronger."

Grawn tisked.

"Even if I were to slaughter both of you here and now, it would be no great loss to Shau-ling. Neither of you have the skill or the will to do what must be done against our enemies. Besides, you are only women, and useful for only one thing."

Bryn could feel her blood burn at the characterization. She straightened, letting the twin blades of flame disappear from her hands.

"If you believe me to be so inept, Grawn, perhaps Ellis' information grants me the opportunity to show just how wrong you are. I wager that I can kill one of these *Erieal* before you can. And if I succeed, then you must acknowledge before the rest of the Brotherhood of Phasia that I am every bit your equal."

Grawn frowned.

"And if you fail?"

Bryn's face was a mask of anger and determination.

"Then you can kill me."

A harsh chuckle escaped Grawn's thinly drawn lips.

"I could kill you now, those are no true stakes."

"Then what stakes would you consider worthy of your time and attention?"

Grawn didn't hesitate.

"If I must acknowledge you as my equal, then you must acknowledge your proper place if you fail. You will become my subservient little wife, and you will take my name as your own."

Bryn tried hard to suppress the grimace, but she knew she could not keep the burning hatred from her eyes.

"We have terms."

* * * * * * * * * * *

Year Four of the Just Emperor Kaitain "Dragonsbane" Lorien, Creator's Calendar Year 1871

Bryn could no longer feel her arms or legs, but she knew that she was still breathing. The fight in the Heavens had taken more out of her than she had realized, and now, the fight continuing on the mortal plane, her body was starting to feel the effects. Out of the corner of her eye, she could still see Aerith, a sword in each hand, taking on half a dozen warrior angels. All around Bryn the bodies of angels and Snags could be seen, broken and bleeding, their lives sacrificed for the greater war that Bryn was only just starting to understand. Nearby Bryn could see a gigantic dragon ripping angels to pieces while a young woman with an unwieldy looking mace crushed skulls by the dozens. The stench of death and blood was thick in the air as Bryn let loose another torrent of flame into the skies. On Onea, before her rebirth, to use so much power would have burned her from the inside out. But now Bryn's body sang with the power of the Blaze and she felt as invulnerable as Aerith had always carried himself on the battlefield. But through the numbness and the strength a new sensation hit. The tip of a burning blade emerged from her chest, plunged through her back by a warrior angel that had somehow escaped her notice. Before the shock of the moment set in, Bryn had already spun about and separated the angel's head from its shoulders. The last thing she saw before darkness descended over her eyes was a flash of brilliant white light and the flutter of perfect feathered wings.

* * * * * * * * * * *

Onea, The Time of the Coromor, Time Unknown

The hour was late, and Grawn had just finished his dinner. He relaxed back onto his reconstructed throne of bone and stared into the darkness. The phasia did not require sleep, nor did they require food, but Grawn had learned to enjoy the decadent pleasures of humanity when his boredom and need for blood would not relent. Of course, he also had learned to enjoy sharing his bed, even if it did require listening to Ellis drone on for hours about things he could not possibly care less about. How he had prevented himself from letting his hands wrap around her fragile throat and squeeze until that low incessant voice ceased he would never know. It was then that Grawn felt the portal form not far from his throne room. The other members of the phasia did not stand on formality, and cared little for the human convention of privacy. Torches lit in the hallway outside the throne room, and when the woman in a red dress turned the corner into the room, the six massive braziers throughout the room exploded into life. Grawn felt no malice from Bryn as she strode into the room, but he could feel her pride beaming. Bryn stopped several paces short of the throne before recovering the bag that was slung over her shoulder. In one deft motion she reached into the bag, withdrew its contents and tossed them toward Grawn. The severed head landed at Grawn's feet, dead shocked eyes staring up at him offering up the horrors of his last moments of life.

"And what is this?" Grawn asked, already knowing the answer.

Bryn could not contain her smile.

"This is the culmination of our wager, Grawn. The head of one of Emries' precious *Erieal*. He was a powerful opponent, but unpracticed with his powers. He was hesitant and unfocused, and in truth he was not a match for one who has known power from birth."

Grawn rested his foot on the head for a moment, letting the news pass through him. He had not expected Bryn to take their wager so seriously, but then she was a member of the Brotherhood of Phasia. She was a killer, and now she had undoubtedly proven her worth.

"I am a man of my word," Grawn said finally. "At the next gathering of the Brotherhood, I shall announce you as our equal, as my equal, and ensure that all know your deeds."

Bryn put her hands on her hips, and an evil smile curled her lips.

"No, Grawn, I have thought much about our little wager, and as the victor I am altering the terms of our arrangement. I don't need your validation in front of our siblings, they shall quickly know what I have accomplished, and your words do nothing to elevate my status then. No, I think I shall accept the terms you have offered and I shall become your sworn partner in this life, and I shall take your name."

Grawn's shock broke through his careful façade and colored his cheeks.

"Why?" he stammered.

Bryn took a step forward.

"If you only had to accept me through your words, Grawn, it would mean nothing. But this way, from this day forward, every time you look at my face, every time you hear my voice, you will know that I have bested you. Even if you kill me, even if you outlive me, from the moment I take your name it will become a monument to the failure that I have delivered to your feet. The name Aplee will from this day forward consecrate the victory of the Lady Fox. It will become a testament to the reality that women are superior to the bumbling arrogance of their counterparts. That we take their name not to be subservient to their wills, but to elevate their existence. For as long as you draw breath, you must live with the ignominy of your failure, and each time you hear your name it will be revisited upon you anew, like salt ground into the wound. No one shall ever again doubt the tenacity and superiority of the Lady Fox, Bryn Aplee."

* * * * * * * * * * * *

Year Four of the Just Emperor Kaitain "Dragonsbane" Lorien, Creator's Calendar Year 1871

Aerith watched Bryn fall, and quickly dispatched the three warrior angels in front of him. He turned to run in her direction and just before he was close enough to scoop her into his arms, there was an explosion of brilliant white light. When Aerith's vision cleared, horror filled his heart. The winged creature held Bryn's limp body in his arms. The man stood silent for a long moment before wrapping his wings around himself and disappearing in another burst of brilliant white light. Aerith could do nothing but cry out in that last moment.

"Ayden!"

Fallen Leaves and the Bloody Ground

Year Four of the Just Emperor Kaitain "Dragonsbane" Lorien, Creator's Calendar Year 1871

Once upon a time Loinn was a beautiful world. It was a world dedicated to Order, pure and perfect. But it wasn't just the people of Loinn who expressed the tenants and virtues of Order. The landscape too was crafted by the goddess Raenera to display perfect symmetry and the beauty of unwavering and eternal uniformity. Mountains displayed their majesty in precise angles to catch the light and allow water to travel from the high peaks down into the valleys where the water could be used to irrigate the fields arrayed in their proper grids of a size decreed by Raenera's laws. The sun rose and set at the same times every day. Seasons began on the same day every year, and weather patterns could be planed for to the minute. There were never any surprises, there was never any uncertainty. Even death was not a mystery to the people of Loinn. In the book of Raenera kept by the High Priestess, the times of birth and death of every person who was and every person who would be was written. In the days before a person's appointed time, they would be summoned to the Grand Temple with their family. There they would be honored and prepared for their passing into the next life. There was peace and comfort to be found in the certainty. However, the dark machinations put into action by the treacherous Emries and Talisia used that symmetry and perfection against the members of the Adhradair. Dorovar would never question the dreams that he believed came from the goddess Raenera. Why would he? If they came to his mind, they were part of the pattern decreed by Raenera's Order. And if Raenera decreed that the dragons were to be welcomed on the world of Loinn, then how could any member of the Adhradair object?

While the people and wildlife of Loinn were dedicated to Order, the dragons who came to make Loinn home were not. The dragons adhered to their own codes of conduct, the codes varied from breed to breed of the ancient creatures. Some would have been content to acknowledge the strictures of Raenera's laws, while others would simply have broken the laws for the sake of breaking them. That was what eventually led to the war between the Adhradair and the dragons, and what would lead to the destruction of Loinn. Luighsech could not help but think about the final days of his world as he and Maedoc tracked the creature known as Derelor the Manipulator. It was Derelor's progeny who first began their hostile invasion of the lands of the farmers in the southern reaches. They would raid the surrounding farms, stealing cows, oxen, and other necessary creatures in order to satiate their hunger. This of course was not required, because there were more than enough wild beasts to fill the bellies of even the largest of the dragons. It became clear after the third or fourth raid that the dragons took the action because they could, a sentiment that was totally alien to the poor farmers who simply wanted to continue with their ordered existence.

Luighsech was the first of the Adhradair dispatched to discover the issue with the dragons and the farmers. This would be the first time that the simple warden of the forests would be faced with such naked disregard for Raenera's perfect order. Luighsech had tried his best to reason with the young beast, but no matter the words the sage brought to bear, the dragon responded with venom, condescension, and bile. The dragon insisted that it would take what it wanted and there would be nothing that the pathetic, cowed people of Loinn could do to stop it. The dragons would make Loinn their home, even if it meant wiping out every member of Raenera's flock. The people of that world were no different than cattle as far as the dragons were concerned, and to die at the claws of a dragon should have been considered a great honor. Luighsech's failure at diplomacy, if it could be called a failure, began the first act of the war with the dragons on Loinn. For a long time, Luighsech believed that he had truly failed his people, and so he had been one of the first to accept Emries' offer of power in order to atone for his crime. However, his years of imprisonment in both the formless void, and then in the weapon known as Strength taught him the most valuable lesson of his life. The war with the dragons was destined to happen and there was nothing that he could have done to prevent it. No matter what words he would have used. No matter what bargain he would have offered. No matter the threat, the concession, the recrimination or the adulation, there would be war. Death and misery were their reward for dutiful service, and it was bitter medicine that still burned the pit of the stomach of every member of the Adhradair.

Luighsech was on the front line from the beginning, moving from slaughter to slaughter, fighting pitched battles against impossible odds in the early days. He saw so much death, held the broken bodies of so many innocents as they died. And then, when the balance of the war shifted and the Adhradair shook the ground and the air with their power, Luighsech became the thing he had never imagined he could become, a killer. For Luighsech's companion, the war with the dragons unfolded in a much different way. From his birth, Maedoc had been groomed and trained for a singular purpose. He was the last line of defense for the High Priestess. No matter what, he would protect her with all of his strength, all of his love, and every drop of blood that flowed through his body. So, when the war with the dragons began, Maedoc could not join his Adhradair bothers in glorious combat. No, he was confined to the grand temple, at the side of the High Priestess, ensuring that no harm could ever come to her. Confined there by his duty, Maedoc thirsted for battle. He would not have to wait long.

Though the forces of Loinn had lost every major battle against the dragons in the early days of the war, they had been able to inflict some casualties to the ranks of the winged beasts. The dragons felt every loss deeply. For one of their number to die at the hands of a lesser lifeform was a sacrilege of the highest order, and required the visitation of vengeance a thousand times over. After Coriden led the first successful raid on an egg clutch, the dragons launched a devastating attack on the Grand Temple with the aim of killing the High Priestess and ending the war before the dragons' losses became something that they would not be able to quickly recover from. One of the elder dragons, one called Seladrin the Endless Depths, sent a flight of her progeny to destroy the Grand Temple. There were only six of the creatures, and they were not yet fully grown, but they were more than enough to overwhelm the defenses of the city. With barely a hundred of his personally trained guardians, and his own peerless abilities, Maedoc stood on the steps of the Grand Temple, his pristine white armor gleaming in the sunlight, and called for the creatures to withdraw or they would not live to see another sunrise. Three of the purple-skinned beasts, their black eyes shining with malice and killer intent, slowly advanced up the steps, snarling and belching forth noxious fumes from their salivating mouths. By the time it was all over, all of the guardians were dead, but so were four of the dragons. The fifth was able to escape with its life, but was seriously wounded. Maedoc survived the battle with barely a scratch, his armor stained from head to toe with dragon blood so thick that the metal began to tarnish. From that point forward Maedoc was allowed to leave his post and take the fight to the dragons, leaving his responsibility to his Adhradair brother Dorovar.

Maedoc was a revelation on the battlefield, and fought as though he was possessed by the spirit of Raenera herself. When the time came to accept the gifts from Emries, Maedoc was at first hesitant to embrace the offer, but it took only a nudge from Coriden and Redissa before he joined with the rest. Once he had those powers at his disposal however, Maedoc developed a reputation for ripping dragons apart with his bare hands. He struck terror into beasts who had terrorized the innocent for years, and while he would never admit that his motivation was vengeance, the results could not be denied. In the end however, Maedoc waded so deeply into the strongholds of the dragons that he lost touch with the forces who tried to fight at his side. He was unaware of the disaster that was befalling their world, and was unaware that the Grand Temple had been destroyed until it was far too late to take any action. And so, when the end came, Maedoc carried his shame into his imprisonment. His sacred charge, the High Priestess had gone missing in the last days, and no member of the Adhradair knew what had become of her, not even Dorovar. All through his captivity in the Sacred Weapon called Perseverance, one thought kept resounding, redoubled by time and echoing into eternity. What had become of the High Priestess? Perhaps now, all these millennia later, he would find and answer to his question.

Ultimately, there were five beings responsible for the downfall of the world of Loinn. Talisia, who orchestrated the entire plot to undermine Raenera's society and to corrupt her most trusted followers. Emries, who conspired by giving his power to the members of the Adhradair knowing that they would either destroy the dragons or destroy themselves. The Demon Dragon Shadowweaver, Talisia's ally who used the deception to defy not only the Council of Winds, but to spark an open rebellion against those loyal to the Elder Dragon Tarot. Stormbane the Traitor, the dragon who was tasked with bringing the offer to Dorovar, the one who lied to his face and swore that the dragons wanted nothing more than to coexist with the people who called Loinn home. He kept up the deception that they were there at Raenera's behest, and that they would help the further the perfect Order of her faith. Lastly, Derelor the Manipulator was the one who convinced many of those dragons who were uneasy about defying Tarot to cast their lot in with Shadowweaver. She sold them a story about a world of their own with a limitless food supply and a place where they would be safe and unchallenged, away from the machinations and manipulations of the Children of the Creator. These demons with pleasing faces and voices laced with honey and poison were the engine that drove the fall of Loinn, even if it had been the hands of the Adhradair that had been the instruments of its demise. And those five beings would be the only ones who would know the final disposition of the soul of the High Priestess. Was there another one of the Sacred Weapon prisons hidden somewhere in the world? Was there somewhere else that the soul had been spirited away to? Emries and Talisia were untouchable, at least for the moment. Dorovar would deal with them in due time, and if Maedoc and Luighsech failed in their task, he would rip the information from them in due course. There was a chance however, by the time that one of them would use the soul against Dorovar in some scheme to harness his power for their own aims, or possibly even dissipate it completely. It was still unclear how Talisia had intended to use the High Priestess's soul as leverage against Dorovar, but it was clear that was her aim.

As for the three dragons, tracking Shadowweaver directly, while possibly the most prudent course of action would also likely be the most difficult. As an elder member of the dragon race, one of those who was actually present at the beginning of all things, the creature would pose a significant challenge for two members of the Adhradair should the confrontation turn physical. Given the information that they were seeking, the possibility of a physical altercation was very high. The other problem was the fact that Shadowweaver was a cagey opponent. Though he had the intelligence, strength, and guile to see all of his schemes to fruition himself, he preferred to work through intermediaries, like Derelor and Stormbane, in an effort to keep his prodigious claws clean. The only way to approach Shadowweaver was through an ambush, but without enough information as to his schemes and his motivations, that would be impossible. For similar reasons, Stormbane was a troublesome quarry. Stormbane never strayed far from his master's side, and while he was not a sycophant by any means, he understood the application of power and the desire to be by one who accumulated it. He also knew the appetites and proclivities of his master, and because Shadowweaver chose to work almost exclusively through intermediaries, the most successful and committed of those intermediaries would reap the most benefits. Proximity created challenges, but the benefits far outweighed them. And so, tracking Stormbane was akin to tracking Shadowweaver. That left Derelor as the most likely first target for the dragon hunting pair.

Unlike the other two draconic members of the conspiracy against Loinn, Derelor was not one to keep a low profile. She made alliances freely and quickly and then found a way to betray those alliances when it suited her without taking the blame upon herself. Her true passion was starting wars, and found glee in eroding long-standing alliances until they exploded into warfare. It took little effort for Luighsech to feel the tensions coming from the southern island of the Empire of Cadaria, the home of the Kingdoms of Menoris and Oradrim. The two kingdoms had been close allies for generations. However, recent events, many of them orchestrated by the Heralds of Dorovar, had allowed ancient rivalries and bigotries to fester. With the loss of the Peak of Patience and the leadership of the Order of the Flickering Flame as well as the Tiger's Eye Knight, great debate had begun in the halls of power in the capital city. Members of royal families from the ages before the leadership of the Order worked to fill the vacuum of power, while clinging to the banners of the would-be rulers of the Empire. A small minority championed the continued rule of Emperor

Kaitain Lorien, but most others fell into camps calling for the rule of the Marlae Tamerlane, or Quyhn Ravenheart, or Dominique Lorien. There were some who even supported Feyd or Felicia Lorien as the rightful heirs. This internal division and squabbling had pitted the great houses of Menoris against one another. In Oradrim, similar divisions were taking place. Without the Academy of Arcane Arts and the Jade Knight, Leonora Wastri, rule of the Kingdom fell to a twelve-year-old boy and his senile aunt who served as his regent. The inexperience of the ruler coupled with a power-hungry cousin who had taken over command of the Jade Legion created an environment ripe for the kind of manipulations that Derelor was infamous for. Through missives and other means, she stoked the fires of conflict within the royal families of Menoris, while at the same time allowing those missives to be intercepted, implicating agents within Oradrim. On the other side, Derelor enticed and extolled the General of the Jade Legion, feeding his madness for power by showing him the divisions in the neighboring kingdom. Should Oradrim be able to conquer Menoris, a shrewd man might be able to declare himself the rightful heir to the empire, or perhaps forge a new empire of his own. The conflict had grown to a tipping point and it would take only the barest nudge before it would fall into the flames of madness and burn so brightly that it would drive all who were engulfed by them insane.

Because the manipulation was at this stage, Derelor would want to be close to watch the fulfillment of her meddling. At least, that was what Luighsech and Maedoc hoped. Derelor enjoyed nothing more than to see her schemes come to fruition. From a plateau overlooking what once was the capitol of Menoris at the foot of the Peaks of Patience, Luighsech and Maedoc closely studied the surrounding landscape. During the war on Loinn, the Adhradair took great pains to learn all they could about the habits and habitats of their enemy. While some dwelled in caves, others preferred the depths of the sea, while still others chose to make their homes in the treetops of the densest forests. Derelor preferred to perch upon the highest peaks looking down upon those that she wished to manipulate. For hours the two stoic men watched the remains of the Peaks of Patience, the broken stone and craggy cliffs that had once formed the majestic skyline of the Kingdom of Knowledge. Finally, just before the light of the twin suns receded from the highest remaining cliff-face, Maedoc spotted a large shadow moving under a large outcropping. The area was comprised of little more than dozens of broken rocks that resembled pillars that had been sheared off at odd angles. An early evening mist had just begun to roll in as one large clawed foot came into view. The massive appendage curled around the top of one of the broken rocks and took hold, balanced precisely like the goats that stand upon the smallest peaks in the high mountains. The green skin was mottled with black, and each long talon on the foot was black with green streaks that shown with a sickly glow in the dying light. As the dragon drew itself out of its covered hiding place, one of the massive bat-like wings emerged next. Unlike many other dragons, Derelor's wings attached at the top of the creature's fore-shoulders, knotted with thick muscles that thinned into the sinewy fabric of the wing itself. At the top of each wing was an appendage that looked like a crooked finger with a long thin needle-like talon at the end of it. The top structure of the wing to which the thinner canopy membrane was attached was also thick and muscular, and as the dragon moved out into the early morning light, the wing was used more like an arm than a wing. The far tip of the wing had two of the crooked finger appendages at its base, and they too twined around rock holds to help stabilized the monster's weight as it walked. Finally, the great head of the beast came into view. Smaller than some of its brethren, Derelor's head was clearly made for battle. Thick bony protrusions ran in five distinct rows from the top of the short neck all the way down to her snout, the center row the tallest and the sharpest. The protrusions looked more like rows of teeth than anything else, but dulled by time and use. A beak-like shield that came to a point that glistened in the light protected the snout of the creature. Razor-sharp fangs cascaded down from the over-sized top jaw of the beast, hanging over the thinner lower jaw. The fangs that ran down the entire length of the creature's massive mouth looked like deadly icicles; round, grooved, and glistening. Glimmering black eyes peered out from armored lids, taking in all that surrounded the dragon, while massive fin-like ears could hear the heartbeat of prey miles away. The rest of Derelor's long lithe body was similarly armored and intimidating, culminating in a muscular tail that ended in a trio of the crooked finger appendages that held fast to anything they touched. This was a creature made for the most unforgiving and treacherous environments and one built to survive anything that was thrown at it.

As soon as the dragon had fully emerged from its den, the massive snout sniffed the air and took in its surroundings. Nearly immediately, the head turned in the direction of the two Adhradair. Derelor looked directly at the pair, and her stare would not relent. For a moment Luighsech thought that she was going to lift into the air and flee, defeating any chance they had of obtaining the information that they sought. But instead, she simply stared at them for a long few minutes before turning her attention back to the settlement below. It did not appear that the dragon had any intention of fleeing from the two dead men, and perhaps she even welcomed the confrontation. Or perhaps it was something more. Derelor was a master of manipulation, but manipulation required information. Someone such as Derelor would not be able to resist finding out what her deceased visitors wanted, and so she stayed on her precarious perch, practically daring the two members of the Adhradair to approach. Taking their cue from the dragon, the Adhradair concentrated on what appeared to be a stable platform of rock and soil.

One of the advantages of their undead condition was that the members of the Adhradair who had been freed from their prisons had the ability to simply be wherever they wanted by thinking about their destination. It was similar to the way that the Dark Gods and others traveled by using their powers to create portals that tunneled through the fabric of space and dimension in order to nearly instantly be in another place. Dorovar had learned the ability through his study of the artifacts in the Vault of Terror and through an understanding of how the Children of the Creator interacted with the Cosmos. Because the Adhradair were linked to Dorovar and could utilize a fraction of the abilities he had learned, they too could simply will themselves to where they wished to be. For Maedoc and Luighsech, it made their hunt far more expeditious. When the two men appeared several hundred feet away from the dragon, she did not regard them, instead continued to look down at the city and the people who were beginning to light torches and lanterns in advance of the coming night.

"Look at them," the dragon's voice came, like honey running over sandpaper. "For all of the intelligence and wisdom that they believe they have, they have no concept of what is actually happening around them. They are like children playing at the feet of giants, unaware that they could be stepped on at any moment. It would be tragic if it wasn't so laughably pathetic. These creatures are no different than you were not so long ago.

And you saw what happened to your world. You were responsible as it died around you. That world didn't have half of the factions vying for its control. This place is doomed. As we are trapped here, we are doomed along with it, unless the Creator grants us mercy and releases us from our bargain."

Maedoc took the bait before his intellect allowed him to hold his tongue.

"Would you have us pity you, demon? Would you have us weep for the very creatures that destroyed our world? Even if we fail in our task, it will be worth it to watch you all burn right along with us. That was denied us long ago, and shall not be denied us again."

Maedoc moved as though he was going to attack Derelor, but Luighsech restrained him. If the confrontation became physical, they would lose their chance to extract the information they required. A more delicate hand was needed than the enforcer Maedoc had fashioned himself into. Luighsech took a single step forward and tried his best to keep his tone level.

"It was long ago, Derelor, and you're correct we were not wise enough to see what was happening to us before it was too late. But this world is different. Dorovar can prevent the same cataclysm from befalling this world. Dorovar has seen a future without the Creator, without the Children, and without the bonds that control all life within the Cosmos. He would even forgive the dragons and allow them to live in peace on a world of their own, away from any who would do them harm."

Derelor finally turned to face the two men, but only so far that the gigantic left eye could peer down at them. For a moment, Luighsech felt as though the dragon was sneering at them.

"Dorovar has made plain his hate for all dragons. He would no sooner allow any of us to live as he would allow Talisia and Emries to escape justice. This vendetta of his will not be put to rest until the blood of every dragon that draws breath is shed. For you to attempt to manipulate me with this fiction is a waste of both of our times and an insult to my considerable intelligence. Speaking with you is tiresome and keeps me from my machinations that are entering their final phases. Ask what you wish to know from me. Understand though that the information you seek is not the information you should be seeking. But I doubt you have gained enough wisdom over these millennia to realize that."

Derelor turned her head back in the direction she had been looking previously and waited for the question that she already knew was coming. Luighsech steeled himself against Derelor's barbs and asked the question they had been dispatched to ask.

"We have come to find out what became of the High Priestess in the last days of the war, and what Talisia did with her soul."

Derelor kept her focus on the city below, but her shoulders slumped slightly.

"How disappointing. You still haven't figured it out yet. But no matter. Perhaps you will gain enough foresight to see the folly you are chasing before it's too late this time."

Derelor finally turned to fully face the two Adhradair, a snarl lifting the top of the dragon's upper jaw displaying rows of impossibly sharp teeth.

"If you want the information you seek, Adhradair, as useless as it is to you, you are going to have to take it."

The next moment, the dragon lunged at them, snapping for Maedoc's head.

No Regrets Only Lessons

*Year Five of the Just Emperor Kaitain "Dragonsbane" Lorien,
Creator's Calendar Year 1872*

It was still before dawn when Cedric Binosear felt the twinge of danger that woke him from his sleep. However, it took him only a moment to realize that he was not in any mortal danger and no enemy was waiting to slit his throat in his sleep. He needed to only stretch out a sliver of his perception to realize that the threat came from high above him. In his mind's eye, Cedric could see Tess perched precariously in the branches of the tree, a small bucket of water clutched in her hands. Tess has been progressing well in just the handful of days that she had been under Cedric's watchful tutelage. If the situation had been of his own making, he would have been bringing Tess along slower, working with her to control her rage and learning to make it work for her. However, Cedric knew that as soon as Emries thought she was ready for his purposes, he would return to claim her. Cedric knew that Emries wanted the girl to be a weapon. Emries didn't care if she was unstable, or violent, or even pampered and spoiled. All he cared about was that she was able to use her powers in ways that would be useful to Emries. He didn't want her to be responsible or to ask questions. He wanted her servile and docile, willing to do whatever Emries told her. In many ways Emries was gambling that Cedric would not have time to civilize the girl. Of course, Emries knew that Cedric would have to instill some measure of stability in the girl otherwise she would never be able to reach her full potential. However, what Cedric feared was a thought that he buried so deep, that even a powerful being like Emries would not be able to extract it. The fear was that Emries wanted Tess not as a simple weapon, but as a vessel for his will and power that he could use to displace not only the Creator, but to literally reshape both history and the very fabric of reality.

Though Cedric had been pulled through the fabric of reality, he seemed to have access to the memories of everything his doppelganger accomplished as well as the memories of the nightmare reality he had come from. During his crusade in the early years of the Foundation Wars to eliminate the phasia and the rogue members of the *Erieal* from the battlefield, Cedric ran across one of the men who served as temporary hosts for Halicon. As a Child of the Creator, Halicon did not need to take physical form. He could exist as thought or energy if he chose. However, his form at times dictated what powers he had access to. What was clear though was that the abilities of the Children of the Creator always far outweighed the understanding of those who fought against them. Now the endgame of the monstrous Emries came into clear relief. Once the feral emotional morass that was Tess Annis had been sufficiently pacified, it would enable Emries to subsume her personality and absorb all of her powers. Whatever limitations had been placed on Emries or any of the other Children would mean nothing with the reality warping powers of the Dragon's Tear. The Creator would simply be an impotent pretender waiting to be cast aside.

Cedric's thoughts came back to the moment, and he carefully considered how to handle what was about to happen. The girl was still fragile and bound to fits of anger and impatience. Though she was several hundred years old, there were still parts of her that had not progressed beyond being a teenager. Cedric didn't have much experience with children, though he had two children of his own. Unfortunately, Cedric proved to be more like his father than he wanted to be. That level of explosive frustration had been firmly on display only a matter of days earlier. Cedric pushed Tess farther than he had ever pushed her, making demands on her concentration and focus that would have been considered common in the war that was spinning around them, but was in reality an almost unrealistic demand on her fragile psyche. When she failed in the exercise she had been tasked with, her rage exploded in a wave of fire and lightning that threatened to burn down half of the forest in a matter of minutes. Cedric himself had barely been able to protect himself from the onslaught. To her credit however, Tess came to her senses quickly and froze the destructive wave in mid-air. In that moment Cedric could see the burning trees locked in their death throes, ash hanging like errant splatters of paint on some sadistic painter's canvas. With a gentle gesture the wave of power disappeared and the trees that had been damaged were suddenly as they had been only a few seconds earlier, as though the outburst had never occurred. The display was impressive and frightening at the same moment. When Cedric got back to his feet, there were tears in the girl's eyes, and she was about to sputter out an apology. Cedric simply shook his head, patted her on the shoulder and reinforced her ability to quickly correct her mistakes. He was quick to shift his attention back to her exercises and banish his own fear deep down into himself where she could not find it.

Tess had become very adept at feeling Cedric's thoughts, and if he was not careful she could easily interpret his unconscious reactions as disappointment, fear, or pride. Though he continually scolded the girl against reading his thoughts, he did not have any realistic expectation that she wouldn't take every opportunity to try to please her tutor, even if it meant breaking his rules. Cedric knew from experience that reading minds was something that took a great deal of effort, even for those who were practiced in the art. Cedric knew that seers had that ability, and so did the Children of the Creator. However, what he didn't know was how far that ability extended. The fact that both Halicon and Emries could be surprised by the actions of those who were supposed to be their servants meant that the power was not absolute. That was why Tess's power was also extremely disconcerting. The girl did not seem to have any limitations to her power except for those imposed by her own imagination. In the hands of someone whose only goal was the subjugation of the Cosmos, her abilities would know no bounds. It was no doubt this uncanny ability to read Cedric's thoughts enabled Tess to uncover Cedric's predilection for waking Leah with cold water dumped from a bucket high in a tree during her training.

His eyes closed and his awareness as tight as possible, Cedric felt the bucket above him being tipped and the water falling quickly toward him. Because Tess was becoming more observant in the use and application of power, Cedric's timing would have to be close to perfect. He was counting on the possibility that the girl would be slightly distracted congratulating herself for her ingenuity and not feel his activation of his abilities until it was too late. Mere inches before the water would have struck Cedric, a portal opened sending the water back to where it came. The other end of the portal opened high in the tree and splashed down on Cedric's diminutive mischievous attacker. There was a stifled scream as the cold water gushed over the girl, instantly soaking her hair and clothes. Her precarious perch shifted beneath her feet and Tess tumbled through the branches, a stifled shriek escaping her lips. The bucket crashed to the ground and Cedric was able to arrest the girl's fall enough that she landed with only the slightest bit of momentum. Of course he could have caught her and spared her any impact had he wanted to, but he also had to take the opportunity to teach the girl that mistakes and miscalculations were often met with pain.

By the time Tess had made it back to her feet, Cedric too was standing, and he calmly looked down at the shorter girl, trying to keep any emotion out of his eyes or his facial expression. He had to resist laughing when she looked up at him, her hair wet and matted to her face at odd angles, and her simple dress clinging to her body in spots. However, when her golden eyes found his, any desire to laugh was gone. He could see the rage there. It covered the embarrassment and the questions of what had gone wrong, but as with so many of her failures, rage was the first and most powerful reaction. Cedric though knew how to stave off the storm that once had been unavoidable.

"What was your mistake?"

Tess wasn't prepared for the question and her eyes went wide for a moment. The rage had been squelched, and only embarrassment lingered.

"I shouldn't have tried to surprise you," came her reply in a tone barely above a whisper and mumbled quickly to avoid easy understanding.

Cedric shook his head.

"No, that's not it. I commend your attempt, and if you wouldn't have made one simple mistake, you might have stood a better chance of succeeding. Now think carefully and tell me where you made your mistake."

Tess's nose wrinkled in annoyance, and then she let her emotions go as Cedric had taught her to do and focused on the events leading up to her very embarrassing failure. She remembered waking up early and being shocked that she was actually up before Cedric. The day before had been grueling with lessons, and she was quickly learning that it was much harder to do things without powers than they were to do with. But there was value to the work, that much was for certain. She had gotten the idea from something she had seen in Cedric's mind, even if she didn't understand the context. She saw him working with another young woman, one who looked familiar, and the way that he would wake her up in the morning when she overslept. There wasn't anything malicious in the gesture, and it seemed almost like an expression of love. Since the opportunity had presented itself, Tess decided that she would take it. It was half an effort to prove to her teacher that she had been paying attention to his lessons, and half an attempt to show how much she appreciated him. She could not say that she loved him, but she did care a great deal for him. But those feelings confused her. Most of the time, Tess felt as though her emotions came from someplace else; as though she were just a conduit for someone else's feelings. She had talked to Cedric about that once, and he had told her that the Blaze was not just a source of power. It was a place where the emotions of everyone who had ever touched it mingled. He had told her that as long as she did not have strong defenses against her emotions, it would give those outside feelings an opportunity to take hold. It would happen more often when she was distracted.

Naturally that thought made Tess realize that she was distracted. She was supposed to be focusing on where she had gone wrong in her plan, not in how she felt or even why she had done it to begin with. Or maybe that was the mistake. Could that have been the mistake? Tess's brow furrowed at the thought. No, that couldn't have been it. Cedric's lessons were never that subtle. So she began to run through the sequence of events in her mind. She had awoken early, saw that Cedric was still asleep, and quickly hatched the plan. She moved quietly across the ground toward the small lake, where she recovered the bucket they used to fetch drinking water. Tess hadn't used any of her powers to keep her movements silent. Cedric had been teaching her to quiet her mind and her heart so that she could use her lithe frame to her advantage. It was discipline only, nothing supernatural. The hard part had been recovering the water from the lake without making too much noise. Had the situation been different she could have just silenced all sound and there would not have been a concern. However, she knew that she couldn't use any power, otherwise Cedric would have been alerted immediately. With bucket of water in hand, she returned to the tree that sheltered them during the night. She put the rope of the bucket around her neck and then began to climb up the far side of the tree, the farthest point away from where Cedric slept. To this point she felt that her tactics had been perfect. Getting up the tree proved to be more of a challenge than she thought, and the added weight of the bucket made the ascent too slow for her liking. She kept her hands near the bases of all of the branches that she clung to, and kept her toes from digging into the soft bark which would have made too much of a sound. She stayed close to the trunk of the tree to keep the leaves from shaking too much and was quite proud of herself when she finally made it into position above where Cedric slept. Tess was able to easily get the bucket from around her neck, regardless of the instability of her footing. And then she dumped the bucket, which is where things went wrong.

But as Tess replayed the events over and over in her mind, there was a moment that tugged at her. It was that last moment before she dumped the bucket, a moment when her anticipation and pride swelled and she saw the outcome of the action she was about to take in her mind. When she opened her eyes again and found Cedric's gaze, she knew that she was right. She had projected her triumph into the ether, and it was that confidence that had triggered Cedric's finely honed danger senses. In the end, Tess had not been able to contain her emotions, as had been the case in so many of their lessons together, and it had resulted in her and not her teacher being soaked by a bucket of cold water. She couldn't prevent the color from coming to her cheeks, and as she brushed back her soaked hair, she could feel the shame of her failure begin to take hold. Cedric however would not let her fall prey to her own internal struggles. He rested his hand on the girl's shoulder and smiled.

"You did well, and you almost had me. What's important is that you are remembering your lessons and adapting based upon what is in front of you. Think about all of the places that you could have failed, but didn't. Don't focus on the place where you did not control your emotions beyond the fact that you know what to correct next time. We spend so much time talking about the things we can improve, we forget to remember all of the things that we did right, or at the very least prevented from going wrong. This was not a failure, Tess."

While it was not overwhelming praise, it caused the girl's face to light up and the joy radiated from her like the rays of the sun.

"Now," Cedric said turning his attention to the rising suns, "you should get yourself dried off, we'll get some breakfast, and then time for lessons. And don't think I'm going to take it easy on you today. You did try to ambush me."

Tess frowned for the barest of moments and then quickly realized that Cedric was teasing her. It was so hard to tell because his tone of voice rarely changed, and he was always so gruff and grumpy. The frown vanished, the girl stuck her tongue out at her teacher, and then bounced away to begin the process of gathering the items for breakfast. It hadn't taken long for Tess to take over the cooking tasks, because she didn't like Cedric's methods. The deal was that Cedric would hunt and gather, and Tess would cook. It was either that, or Cedric would have to allow her to try to conjure food out of thin air. The only application of power that Cedric would allow her was the creation of some cooking utensils. Any fire that she lit, she would have to do the mundane way. On several of her first attempts, Cedric monitored her. She failed, and became frustrated and tried to cheat. He would let her think that she had fooled him, only to immediately extinguish the flame and tell her to try again. To the girl's credit, she proved to be a quick study, both at her attempts to do things as a mundane would, but also in her attempts to fool her teacher. In another world, in another time, Cedric would have been proud to be her teacher.

Now that the morning routine had begun, Cedric had his own chores to accomplish. He needed to gather enough firewood for the day and whatever berries and small game he could quickly catch and then skin. Tess didn't have the stomach or the patience for hunting, and her attempts tended to frighten off the easy catch. It didn't take long for Cedric to amass a pile of branches and sticks for the fire, which he tied together with a simple leather strap. He left them at the edge of the thicket and then waded deeper into the brush to find the catch of the day. Tess had said the previous night that she was getting tired of fish, so he hoped to catch a rabbit or two for a stew or perhaps a simple grill. As Cedric moved farther into the deepening wood, the ancient man began to concentrate on slowing his heartbeat and his breathing. Each step became more deliberate and almost no sound could be heard coming from the stalking predator. Finally comfortable with his position, Cedric crouched low and waited for some unfortunate creature to happen into his range. Several minutes passed and Cedric began to become unnerved by the silence in the wood. It was as though the landscape was being held by some unknown dread that had not yet descended but was just at the edge of perception and inevitable. At the very farthest edge of his perception, Cedric felt something move. Whatever it was, the creature was quite large. Cedric prepared himself for the lumbering form of a bear or perhaps a large moose or deer. However, as the thing continued to move through the brush, it was clear that there was no elegance in the movements. It was not concerned with the amount of noise it was making, nor was it concerned with alerting other predators to its approach. Whatever the thing was, it clearly was not interesting in hunting. After several uncomfortably long minutes, the lumbering presence was almost in sight. Cedric saw the radiant aura long before he saw the actual form, but when it did finally emerge from the thicket, the ancient man found himself both disheartened and not surprised.

The first thing to emerge from the brush was the tip of a bright white feathered wing. However, the first thing that Cedric noticed was the fact that the wing did not look completely intact. In fact, it looked as though the wing had only recently been repaired from nearly catastrophic damage. The only shock that registered through Cedric was the lithe body that accompanied the wing and the young woman's face that was etched with barely contained rage. When the young winged woman stepped fully into the clearing, she turned in the direction of where Cedric crouched still out of sight.

"You needn't hide, Lion, I know you are there."

Slowly and carefully Cedric stood from his position. The warrior part of him screamed that he should take hold of his powers and defend himself. The statesman part of him wanted to find out as much information as he could before the situation devolved. The minute he armed himself, any chance at gathering intelligence on the woman or her chore there was lost. Additionally, Tess would feel the action and be moved to assist her new mentor. In her current state of mind, Tess could not be trusted in combat. She would be just as liable to kill Cedric as to kill their uninvited guest.

"I would say that you are in the wrong place," Cedric said slowly and evenly, keeping all emotion out of his voice, "but you clearly came here with an agenda. From the wings, I assume you are either on a task from the Creator, one of the Servants, or one of the Children."

The woman simply stared in Cedric's direction. She wasn't staring directly at him per se, more through him. It was then that Cedric noticed that the woman's eyes were completely white. He had seen that once before in a warrior angel that he had run afoul of in the early days of the Foundation Wars.

"You are not of this world," the woman intoned, her voice both distant and malicious. "You should not be here, and your presence is a hindrance to what must be. In order to ensure the proper execution of the Creator's vision for the Cosmos, you must cease to be."

As threats went, Cedric hadn't heard many better, and he had been threatened by some of the most dangerous people to ever draw breath. It was the chilling matter-of-factness in the woman's voice that made the threat absolutely believable.

"I had no intention of being a part of this war," Cedric replied, speaking more truth than he wanted to admit to himself. "I died. I was done with this whole conflict. But I was brought back to do a job. I'm sure that once that job is done, Emries will try to eliminate me himself. This just seems like an unnecessary use of the Creator's resources. I hear there's a war going on."

A frown came to the woman's face.

"Your assertions are meaningless. The corruption has grown, and your involvement cannot be prevented so long as you live. This eventuality cannot be allowed to fester. This avenue for the heretic must be removed. Do not make this more painful on yourself than is necessary. Your service to the Creator and to the greater stability of Creation has rewarded you with a swift death. Submit, and you shall feel no pain. Resist," the woman said with death her in tone, "and your suffering will be considerable."

Cedric took a step away from the brush, clearing his feet for the conflict that was about to start. He may not have been the warrior that he once was, but he still knew enough of the old lessons from Aryx and Arathorn to not make himself easy prey. Cedric could feel the diametrically opposed powers in the back of his mind begin to flare. Both Emries' power and the Blaze wanted to be used. They both thirsted to taste the blood of this divine messenger. But there was something else there. Something that Cedric had never felt before. It felt like a door had been cracked in the back of his mind, a tiny sliver into something that was beyond. There was power there, an unfamiliar power, a power that was wrapped in fear and pain and uncertainty. But that would have to be a mystery for another time, when his life was not in imminent danger. In a battle against a divine being, there could be no doubt, and so Cedric could only rely on the powers that he knew, and the skills that he had accumulated over his very long life.

"Regardless of the reason I was brought back," Cedric said easing into a defensive stance, "I am back. I wasn't one to shy away from conflict in my life, and I'm not going to stop now. Whatever corruption you think I've been exposed to, or whatever eventuality you think I represent, you're going to have to kill me, because I'm certainly not going to let you."

A pair of short, thin crystalline blades seemed to extend from the woman's palms. She did not change her stance, and the look on her face spoke of annoyance and resignation.

"Time and again you mortals are given every opportunity and every advantage, and all that is required of you is that you show your appreciation for the gifts you are given and not question the manner in which they are given to you. Even those few of you that are touched by the hand of the Creator through the works of His Children consistently question and rebel against those who set you above the mundanity of your race. You question, you argue, and you think that you, in your narrow understanding of the concepts of time and reality, know more than the one who crafted everything that is seen and unseen. Because you have seen a sliver of truth behind the veneer of normality presented to the slobbering masses that pass for civilization on your worlds, you think that it somehow entitles you to a voice in the direction of the Cosmos. And now, staring into the face of the madness that you yourself have created, you have the audacity to blame those who were trying to lead you down a path of prosperity. You have traded comfort for misery, peace and contentment for war and strife, sanctity for torment. And even now, faced with the enormity of your crimes against your own kind, you refuse to show even the barest measure of grace."

Anger flared in the woman's white eyes.

"You are every bit the villains you claim to fight against."

Conquered We Conquer

Year Five of the Just Emperor Kaitain "Dragonsbane" Lorien, Creator's Calendar Year 1872

The Herald War finished pulling itself from the muddy chasm that Gwillim and Korrd had created to contain it. Korrd was horrified to see that there was no visible damage to the Herald, and whatever impact they thought they had up to that point had been completely erased. The heavy mottled black and bronze armor drank in all light except for the spectral green glow that seemed to emerge from every joint. War's eyes glowed a dark blood red, its face completely emotionless. The sounds of combat had faded away to nothing, and though the Army of Fire was still willing to fight, their numbers and their morale had been deeply damaged by their confrontation with the Army of the Dead. Korrd looked to Arin Domae and the wordless order passed between them. Arin, a professional soldier all of his adult life quickly turned and focused his attention on rallying the remainder of Korrd's troops. While they were no match for the Herald, they could at the very least slow the advance of the Army of the Dead and prevent them from reaching Thorigald. It was clear that Dorovar's aim was to destroy yet another of Cadaria's kingdoms, adding Thorigald to the likes of Rashaleb, Menoris, Hedorah, and Aldere. As much as the Saldarine's forces had been raised on hatred for their neighbor and eternal enemy, they would not allow Thorigald to be destroyed by Dorovar's forces. That privilege was reserved for the Kingdom of Fire alone. No matter what they had seen that day, there was no fear in the men of the Army of Fire. They had confronted dragons, angels, and now the dead. Nothing would shake their resolve, and nothing would break their confidence in their commander.

"Pawns of Emries," War's voice dripped with malice, "your petty powers pale in comparison to the gifts Dorovar has bestowed upon me. Dorovar has decreed that the Kingdom of Water shall fall, and then the Kingdom of Fire. The Kingdom of Steam is already on its way to becoming a wasteland, its royal family dead, and its civilization about to be ground into dust by Talisia's dragon allies. Soon there will be nowhere left that Talisia can hide the High Priestess's soul. Dorovar will be whole, and the Heavens with shudder with his fury."

War's pronouncement hung in the air like a chilled wind, and Korrd prepared himself for the next stage of the fight. The glow around War intensified, and the next moment the horrific creature seemed to double in size. It now stood well over thirty feet in height and as it took a step forward the ground shook with the sheer force of it.

There was no further preamble as tendrils of the spectral force lanced out toward Korrd, Talon, and Gwillim. The three men scattered, and the tendrils found nothing but air. Talon rolled through his dive and circled around to War's right, while Gwillim pushed up off the ground and circled to War's left. Gwillim, though slightly slowed by his armor, got into position only a step slower than Talon, and the two lashed out with their powers as soon as they had flanked the impossibly large opponent. Gwillim created waves in the ground designed to unbalance the monstrous beast, while at the same time Talon created cyclones at the level of War's head. But as the cyclones approached War's head, the ghostly energy flashed outwards and dissolved them before they could cause damage. In answer to Gwillim's attack, War brought one foot up and then stomped down hard on the ground creating a fissure that swallowed the waves and would have swallowed Gwillim had he not leapt to his right. His new position, outside of War's peripheral vision behind his left shoulder, gave Gwillim a direct sight-line to Korrd, but restricted his view of Talon. Korrd took several steps back and to his right so that the three men created a nearly perfect triangle around War. This time when the three men lashed out, it was not with abstract forms of the primal forces, but more direct ones. Beams of pure energy shot from each of the men's hands, colliding with the shield of green energy that immediately formed around War. The more power they each poured into their assaults, the further the shield pushed against them. From the southeast a fourth beam lanced out, striking the shield. Arin had quickly returned to the fray, adding his powers to those of his fellows. But regardless of how much power the four men brought to bear, the shield of spectral energy simply pushed it back. When the ghostly shell flared again, it expanded so quickly that it nearly engulfed both Korrd and Talon because they were the closest to War. Gwillim and Arin both released their flows of power, and Arin moved quickly to Korrd's side while Gwillim circled behind War. Talon only took a few steps backwards staying perpendicular to War's right shoulder.

"Do you see now? Do you see the futility? Emries' powers have no sway here. The Creator's power has no sway here. There is no power beyond those granted by Dorovar. You are nothing against War. I will consume this world. I will free every soul from its prison. And in the end the Chorus of Souls will sing Dorovar to the Heavens where he will conquer the Creator. Submit now to the will of Dorovar, and spare yourselves the ignominy of dying at my hands in a fruitless endeavor."

There was a barely perceptible nod from Talon in Korrd's direction and then the next assault began. Arin broke from Korrd, circling around to War's left, so that the four servants of Emries surrounded the Herald. Before War could react, both Gwillim and Talon struck out with pure beams of elemental energy, supplemented by more abstract uses of power. Four cyclones sprung up around War, and pillars of stone sprang up. Some of the pillars appeared to be attempting to pin in the Herald while others erupted from beneath the towering behemoth with the aim of throwing him off balance. Both of Arin's strikes were far less precise, but no less powerful. The twin gouts of flame that burst from Arin's hands were aimed only at causing destruction. However, the streams of flame each had separate targets. The first stream was aimed at War's face, intended to hamper his vision and his ability to counterattack. The second stream collided with Talon's cyclones setting them ablaze and sending waves of heat and smoke in all directions. Korrd let twin beams of light and dark energy erupt from his hands, pouring every bit of power he could muster into the strike. War teetered back and forth, his footing uncertain, and he made no move to counterattack. The shield of souls however continued to defect and absorb much of the energies directed into it, and it showed no sign of relenting under the ever-increasing pressure. Korrd knew that they could not keep up the assault indefinitely, and the more time they gave War to adapt to their tactics, the greater chance that they would fail. Sensing the tide beginning to turn in their favor at least for that moment, Korrd pulled on the innate connection he had with the three members of the *Erieal* and drew as deeply as he dared on the raw power granted to him by Emries. The ground beneath War roiled and heaved, and the air around the massive Herald became a poison smoke that would have meant death to any living being in a matter of seconds. Heat poured through the unbreathable fog, until the air nearly ignited. Sweat squeezed from every pore on Korrd's body, and drops of blood began to emerge from his ear canals, his tear ducts, and his nostrils. If he kept up the exertion much longer, it would likely be the death of him. And so, he planned the last strike.

"Scatter!"

Each of the three members of the *Erieal* obeyed immediately, releasing their assaults and moving quickly to get to a safe distance. They had no clear picture of what Korrd had planned, but they knew instinctively that it was going to be devastating. Gwillim knew that he could not move as quickly as the others so he dropped to the ground and summoned a shield of diamond from the ground below. Talon sped away from the combat and wrapped himself in a cocoon of wind as an added measure of defense. Arin dropped to one knee and wove threads of fire around himself like a shield, and looked on in horror as Korrd followed through with his plan. Korrd's heart felt like it was going to burst in his chest and every nerve ending in his body was on fire, but still he channeled more and more power into the growing morass of energy that surrounded War. His only hope was to overwhelm the shield of souls with one strike so massive that it would vaporize the shield and perhaps even decimate the Herald. The air all around War ignited and blazed as hot as the fires of the twin suns. Korrd was forced to release the assault as soon as the light blazed so intensely that Korrd had to shield his vision or be blinded. The incendiary ball of fire continued to burn even after Korrd ceased his assault, and as the light faded enough to be tolerated by Korrd's vision he had hoped that there would have been a cry of pain or at least some kind of reaction from the Herald. The only outward sign that anything had changed was that the low keening wail from the shield of souls had faded to a nearly inaudible volume. But whatever Korrd had hoped to accomplish, his hopes were dashed mere moments after the assault.

The miniature star in the center of the battlefield started to cool and change hue. After a matter of minutes, the color faded from a brilliant hot white to a ghostly green. Once the change in color was complete, the ball of light disappeared completely. Standing in the center of the crater carved by the heat of the flames was the Herald War, unscathed by the desperate assault. However, as Korrd wiped some of the blood from his face, he thought that the green glow coming from inside of War had diminished. It was slight, but it was something. Perhaps they were beginning to make a dent in the power that War had been allotted by Dorovar. No matter how powerful the demon Dorovar claimed to be, his power was not limitless. It was becoming clear that the only way that Korrd and the others were going to defeat the Herald was to simply overwhelm him. The only issue was that Korrd was unsure that the four of them had enough left to bring to bear. Time however was not on their side. If Korrd and the others took time to recover they would give War time to recover as well, and that could mean the end of all of their lives.

By this time, Talon, Gwillim, and Arin had made it back to their feet. Korrd could feel the exhaustion pulsing through them, but there would be time enough to rest if they were victorious. Korrd's arms rebelled as he tried to raise them, and his stomach turned as he reached deep inside of himself again for the flickering white light that was the tie to Emries' power. At first the power would not respond and it fled from his touch. Korrd recognized in the moment that doubt had crept into his heart. Emries' power would not come to him as long as he doubted his chances for success. Emries had become greedy and cynical since his defeat on Onea, and he would not allow any of her servants to show weakness ever again, as it could lead to rebellion. In his mind, Korrd visualized the defeat of the mammoth opponent, and finally the white light intensified inside of him and allowed itself to be touched. The sweet rush of power filled Korrd with a sense of purpose and peace, and while its first inclination was to knit the wounds in his body caused by the overexertion, Korrd suppressed the wasted use of time and power and instead filled himself to the brim with the intoxicating energy. Wordless communication instantly went out to the *Erieal*, and it took only a moment for each to respond. Talon, Gwillim, and Arin struck War again with beams of pure energy. However, Korrd could feel that the power of these attacks had been severely diminished. If Korrd was going to have any chance to bring his plan to fruition it would have to be soon, otherwise the three members of the *Erieal* would either burn themselves out figuratively or literally in a matter of seconds. None of the three were practiced with using their powers in this capacity, and none of them had the kind of endurance that was required to fight a creature like War. Korrd had known immediately that if they didn't overwhelm War quickly, the chances were good that they would all be destroyed.

There was a marked difference in this stage of the conflict. The shield of souls did not extend as far from War's massive frame as it once had. In fact, it even appeared as though some of the assault was passing through the ghostly green haze and impacting directly onto War's thick armor. War turned his attention toward Talon and lashed out with a tendril of the green energy. The strike caused Talon to stop his assault for a moment as he dove out of the way, but as soon as he scrambled back to his feet, he resumed his attack. This was the opening that Korrd was waiting for. Rather than lashing out with a beam of directed energy, Korrd channeled a small fraction of the power that he had gathered within himself into his legs to increase his speed. Korrd knew he would only have one shot at this type of attack, and if he failed, it would most likely mean his demise. As soon as War turned to lash out at Gwillim, Korrd charged in, drawing into himself as much energy as he possibly could both from the brilliant white flame inside of himself and from his allies. The energy he was able to draw from the *Erieal* had been reduced to a trickle now, and Korrd hoped it would be enough. Korrd closed within three long strides of the gargantuan Herald and he thought for that brief moment that his plan had succeeded. But then, at the last moment, just as Korrd broke through the spectral haze, War spun around and caught Korrd by the throat. As Korrd was being lifted from the ground by his throat, his hands instantly and instinctively came to the armored wrist of the creature War. Their leader captured, Gwillim, Talon, and Arin broke off their assaults, and each tried to figure out what they could do to free Korrd. Korrd found himself dangling two dozen feet in the air, gasping for breath, and fighting off unconsciousness.

The next second stretched out and felt like it lasted an hour. Gwillim charged War from behind, an axe of diamond appearing in his hands. The axe crashed hard into the seemingly invulnerable armor of the Herald, but caused no damage. Gwillim brought the axe back to strike again, but from behind him three tendrils of spectral energy grasped Gwillim by the throat and around his upper arms. Gwillim cried out in pain as his hands went numb. Instead of dropping to the ground, the diamond axe simply vanished from Gwillim's grip. The next moment, the tendrils lifted Gwillim off the ground and then slammed him back down repeatedly. By the third time he was slammed to the rocky ground, battered and bloody, bones broken, Gwillim lost consciousness. The expenditure of energy had prevented Gwillim from erecting any kind of defense against War's assault. Gwillim was slammed two more times into the ground even after he lost consciousness, and then was tossed through the air, discarded like a piece of trash. Gwillim landed with a sick dull thud, blood flowing from his mouth and nose in a growing pool. His breathing was ragged and slow, each breath threatening to be his last.

Even as Gwillim was being repeatedly slammed to the ground, Talon too charged in, a phantasmal spear appearing in his hands. Channeling as much power as he could manage into his body, Talon increased his speed and agility allowing him to barely dodge the tendrils that continually attempted to seize the *Erieal* by his arms and legs. Just as he made his way close enough to strike War, two tendrils shot out and grabbed for Talon's ankles. Talon attempted to leap over the attack, but War had already sprung his trap. War pivoted slightly, the back its right hand crashing into Talon. The sound of bones breaking echoed in all directions as Talon was sent flying through the air, his limp form twisting in midair. His right shoulder, arm, ribs, and hip broken, Talon passed out from the pain even before he struck the ground. The impact forced him back to consciousness for several moments, but he could not hold on to the threads of wakefulness. He passed out just as the next scream of pain echoed in his ears.

Korrd felt the life being squeezed out of him by the spectral tendrils that continued to constrict around him like snakes. He tried repeatedly to release the energy that was stored inside of him, but he couldn't manage to concentrate long enough for the attack to take shape. Gwillim and Talon's attacks did not create enough of a distraction to give Korrd even a second of breathing room. But even as Talon sailed through the air, Arin leapt in, twin blades of fire crashing down on the wrist of the hand that held Korrd by the throat. If the attack had any impact at all, it did not show either on the face of the monstrous Herald or in the power of its grip on Korrd. Arin landed and turned quickly, ready to launch another attack; one that would hopefully free Korrd from his tenuous predicament. But War was prepared for the tactic and the moment Arin's feet left the ground, War's right hand dashed in, impossibly fast, and snatched Arin out of the air. The fingers of the hand closed around Arin's head, and his body hung precariously in the creature's powerful grip. Not ready to concede defeat, Arin thrashed around violently using the twin swords of fire to slash and stab at the armored hand in an attempt to win his freedom.

"Such infantile gestures," War's cold voice rang out as its red eyes bored into Korrd.

War lifted Arin up higher and slowly began to squeeze the soldier's head with its massive hand. Even before Korrd heard the sickening sound of bone beginning to snap under the pressure, Arin's anguished cry of pain rang out. War did not turn his head or let his gaze leave Korrd for even a moment as he slowly tortured Arin Domae over the next few seconds. Then there was a loud pop, and Arin's scream went silent. The twin swords of fire disappeared from his hands and his whole body went limp. War didn't even regard the former hero before tossing him to the ground like garbage. Korrd felt the rage build up inside of him and finally he found the opening to release all of the stored energy that he had been gathering over those moments. In one huge burst, the blast exploded from inside of Korrd, flashing in all directions. The next thing Korrd knew, he felt the sensation of falling and though his blast had temporarily blinded him, he knew that he had at least managed to get himself free. Korrd was barely able to orient himself in time to land on his feet in the mud. It took several more seconds for the bright spots to clear from his vision, and when they did, his heart sank.

War had been nearly unmoved by the attack, though the ground beneath the Herald's feet was now a six foot deep crater. Though the hulking armored form was largely unscathed, Korrd had managed to vaporize the creature's left hand and forearm. But the Herald had not cried out, and did not seem to be the least bit concerned by his missing appendage. Korrd on the other hand was feeling the full effects of what he had done. Already the string of Fire was fading in the back of Korrd's mind, his connection to it weakened at Arin's grizzly murder. The strings of Stone and Wind were also weakened, but they were at least still there. That meant Gwillim and Talon were still alive, though he could tell from the ripples of pain radiating through their connection that both men were suffering greatly. Though Korrd was largely physically unharmed, the release of power had sapped every bit of strength left in his body, and he knew it would be a simple thing for War to simply crush the life out of the extension of Emries' will. The flickering white flame deep inside of Korrd had been reduced to less than the flame of a candle and it stood rebellious to his call. For all intents and purposes, Korrd had no more power than a normal human had.

"And this is the limit of the strength of the Children of the Creator. Using their puppets for as long as they can channel power, and then discarding them like broken toys once they have outlived their usefulness. Is this what you aspired to be when you became a slave to the will of one who cared nothing for you?"

Korrd wanted to respond, wanted to thunder back his righteous indignation and proclaim the justness of his cause. But his protests died in his mind before they even reached his voice. He felt empty, conflicted, and cold. Suddenly Korrd felt a great weight settling in upon him, pressing down on him as though time had suddenly thrust every year of his life down upon his tired frame. The sudden existential exhaustion buckled his knees and Korrd stumbled down to one knee, sweat rolling from his brow and blood trickling from his nose and the corners of his mouth. His body was beyond fatigue, beyond pain, and beyond numbness. There was only thought that confirmed that he was even still alive, that and the ragged breaths and beat of his heart.

"This is the gift of Dorovar," War continued. "When I was a man like you, an idealist who desired to bend the world to his will regardless of the cost, Dorovar came and freed me from my delusions. Those in power will always exert that power, no matter what name they wear, no matter what good intentions they attempt to wrap that power in. Power itself is the criminal, and the people who think that they wield it are in fact wielded by it. They are victims of a construct created long before they existed in the imaginations of their forbearers. Priests, Kings, Emperors, heroes, gods, dragons, and villains. They are simply the instruments of power. Power that comes from beyond a place of imagination, to the very source of all misery on every world. The Creator. Dorovar does not wish power for himself, he simply wishes to free us all from the shackles of power. To remove the source of it. To create a place where power is not needed. Where all will know their place. Where all will know peace and prosperity in the perfect Order. There will be no fear. There will be no recrimination. There will be no hate. There will be only Order. All will live as they are made to live, and all will function as part of the greater whole; each working for the betterment of the whole. No oppression. No slavery to the ideals of another. No mysterious distant father who threatens to visit punishment for failing to follow a set of vague and archaic rules. There will be peace."

War knelt down slowly, bringing itself just above Korrd, lifting his chin up so that the two could look each other in the eye.

"And now, Korrd Ranthall, you have been brought low. The façade of your bravery and invulnerability have been shattered like your faith, and the would-be god you worshipped has abandoned you like so many before you. What use to him are you now? Broken. Beaten. Fallen. Failed. The only mystery now is whether or not he will waste his time and energy to snuff the rest of your life from you; you and your band of refugees from another failed world."

War stood and looked down upon his fallen opponent.

"This, Korrd Ranthall is how you meet your end? On your knees? How disappointing. I thought you would at least show as much fight as your younger brother. He now has stood against two of Dorovar's Heralds, and he has defeated both of them. You have been reduced to this pathetic shell of a man with just one encounter. And you were meant to be the great champion. The anointed one. Look at you. Servile. Docile. Your men are willing to die for you, and you surrender. Think on this from now on, *Coromor*, as the last days of your life fade into insignificance."

War turned away from Korrd and resumed his march toward the Kingdom of Water, Thorigald. With every step, more corpses pulled themselves from the ground and fell into ranks behind the monstrous Herald. As Korrd watched the massive shape grow smaller as it strode away, he could see the ghostly green glow intensify again around War. Thorigald had been sentenced to death by Dorovar, and War was going to rip the kingdom apart, and there was nothing anyone could do to stop it. Pain suddenly returned to Korrd's body, and the shock of it nearly stole consciousness from Korrd's mind. He fought to stay awake even as the darkness tugged at the edges of his vision. His thoughts went to his brother Logan, and the trials that he must have undergone. How had Logan defeated two of the Dorovar's Heralds? What advantage did Logan have that Korrd could not see. If he survived the night, Korrd would have to find out how his brother had triumphed where he had failed. And perhaps, perhaps, it was time for the Ranthall brothers to take the fight to Dorovar together.

CHAPTER 103

Chapter CIV

Swirling Shadows

*Year One of the Divine Empress and Child of the Creator
Marlae Tamerlane, Creator's Calendar Year 1871*

Jeroch was still sitting on the floor with his back against the door when he felt it begin to move behind him. Feeling every joint in his body ache with the exertion, he managed to get to his knees facing the slowly opening door. Jeroch had not yet channeled any of his abilities to heal the wounds on his hands, and blood still oozed from the small cuts that ran up and down the ridges of his hands. Once the door had opened fully, there was nothing for several moments until Rhain Seth appeared, sweat streaking her face and hair, drops of dried blood caked in the corners of her eyes and under her nose. She leaned heavily against the frame of the door, the solid wood supporting all of her weight. Rhain looked down, and her eyes found Jeroch's. She saw the pain and anguish carved into his features, the tears staining his face. Rhain's knees wobbled and threatened to give out under her as she shifted her weight, but she managed to sink to her knees in front of Jeroch so that they were at eye level. So much passed between the two in the silence: rage, lack of understanding, disappointment, fear, and sorrow. There were other emotions; ones that Jeroch did not have the words for, yet he felt the hurt of them deep inside. Sharper than the sharpest sword they were, and more brutal than the thud of a hammer striking bone. He was hot and cold all at the same time, his heart gripped with the biting cold of loss while his blood burned with the futility of it.

When Rhain laid her hand on his shoulder, Jeroch didn't feel it. His insides were in so much turmoil that his outsides were numb. As though her touch thawed his heart, the ache in his body melted away, but it did not cure his numbness, nor did it remove the crushing sorrow that enveloped him like cloak. Finally Rhain spoke, her voice cracking, nearly all energy drained from her.

"I know you don't understand now, Jeroch," she said softly, "but there was no other way. Kamen, Rael, and Trece all understood. They all knew what was at stake."

Jeroch opened his mouth to protest. His tongue felt like cotton, his mouth dry. The protest died in his throat, not because of any physical restriction, but rather the one in his heart. He knew she was right. He had known it from the moment that he sat across from Kamen with only the single candle between them. Perhaps he had known before then, but seeing the candle, and understanding what the symbol meant was more powerful than any word or emotion. It was the essence of everything that Kamen had come to believe about life and faith. It was everything that he believed the phasia could be. Simple and yet so powerful. Jeroch closed his eyes and centered himself. When he opened his eyes again, he noticed immediately that the color was beginning to return to Rhain's face, and that the dried blood had disappeared. Jeroch was able to find his voice the next moment.

"No, Rhain, I don't understand. We sacrificed three of our most experienced and powerful weapons in this war. Instead of sacrificing their lives, we all could have descended upon Hedorah and taken the fight to Dorovar's puppet. No matter how much power Rhuiden may have gained, he could not have stood against the combined might of six full-fledged members of the phasia as well as two more who can touch the Blaze. That much power brought to bear in one place at one time could have shaken the world."

Despair was clear in Rhain's eyes and she shook her head.

"As I said, Jeroch, you do not understand. The path that was chosen was as much Logan's as it was Kamen's. For the future to unfold as it must, we cannot rush blindly in for the sake of meeting our enemies. Yes, we could have brought the entire weight of the Brotherhood of Phasia to bear, we could have met the emissary of Dorovar on the field of battle, and perhaps all together we could have defeated him. But what would be the cost? Look beyond the moment Jeroch."

Jeroch's mind was a jumble. He was still angry, but the sorrow of the loss was beginning to set in. He tried to push it away and tried to tap into the logical and reasoned side of himself, the side that had spent lifetimes plotting and planning against his adversaries. He was not perhaps as skilled at complex interwoven intrigues as some of his siblings, but Jeroch knew he had a more-than-adequate mind for such things. Regardless of how adequate his mind may have been, it was not up to the task of the moment as emotion overpowered reason. Sensing Jeroch's hesitation, Rhain continued.

"There was no way to guarantee that our losses would have been any less if we would have engaged Conquest openly. We don't know if Dorovar would have reacted to the opportunity and sent more of his forces to engage us, or if he would have taken the opportunity to launch an assault on some other target that we did not foresee. Perhaps he would have committed Jerah to the fight in a manner that would prevent us from recovering the part of her that is still Caris. I believe as Logan did that there will be a time to bring the Wolf back into the fold, but the time is not now, and the conditions certainly are not on the field of battle."

Jeroch nodded absently. All of the points were well founded.

"What would be gained in revealing the extent of Taya's abilities, or those of Leonora? Yes, Jerah has seen Leonora in action, but we do not know how much of that has been relayed back to Dorovar, and how much he actually knows about her powers. Then there is the complication of Marlae, and the Ranthall girl. Where are their loyalties? And of course there is the information that Saurn has made us aware of regarding Jillian. There are too many unknowns, too many questions, and by far too much doubt for us to be effective in our charge. We must work slowly, and intelligently, and we must work together. The sacrifice Kamen, Rael, and Trece have made by becoming one with Logan Ranthall will not be forgotten, nor will it be squandered. But we must take advantage of this time that Logan has given us."

Rhain pushed her way back to her feet, and seemed in that moment to be as regal and powerful as the moment she revealed herself as the new leader of the Brotherhood of Phasia.

"There is much to do, and little time to do it. I need you to speak to Leonora and Jillian. Explain to them the situation, and explain to Jillian the importance of her role in this war. Leonora will make that easier, I believe. I will be giving many of you assignments over the next few hours, and then I will deal with Marlae and Isabella. Remember Jeroch, time is our enemy as much as Dorovar and the remaining Children of the Creator."

* * * * * * * * * * *

Jillian stalked around the semi-opulent room that had once been the personal quarters of the Sunstone Knight, Natalia Pressen. The man with violet eyes named Saurn had shown Jillian to the room shortly after their arrival to what Jillian had quickly learned was the headquarters of the Shadow Guild. So much had happened in such a short time, and Jillian found herself struggling with accepting it all. Her life had seemingly been on a straight path since the loss of her home and her family at the hands of the dragon that had called itself Shadowweaver. Everything that she learned, everything that she did, was all to further her goal of making the giant lizards pay for what they had taken from her. She could have joined the military, or learned a trade and moved on with her life. But those pursuits would never fill the gap in her life, and would never be a salve to the wound that had been ripped in her heart that day. Many times over the years she had been questioned by those who had temporarily shared her path if there was any wisdom in living a life for revenge. Her answer to the question was always the same. She was not motivated by revenge. She was motivated by justice. She would exact justice upon the dragons for every life they had taken since they made Espre their home.

But then the war against the dragons started at the hands of Kaitain Lorien, she was branded a traitor, she was targeted for assassination by creatures she could not comprehend, and then he came into her life. Logan Ranthall showed her wonders and terrors that she never imagined existed, and he even brought her to a point in her life where there was something more dangerous than the dragons. She had stood feet away from one of the monsters she had dedicated her life to destroying, heard it speak, and did not feel compelled to visit death upon it. Logan had changed her heart and impacted her soul in a way that she never would have thought possible. And now, she was filled with a worry and doubt that her formerly singular purpose never allowed to enter her mind. So now all she could do was wait, and stew.

Her reverie was broken by a knock at the door, and before she had even turned to face the door, it opened to reveal the former member of the Knights of the Flashing Blade, Leonora Wastri, and the man who Jillian knew as Vallic Ultiv but whom Kamen had called Jeroch. Leonora entered the room first, leaning against the wall beside the door with her arms crossed like a teenager who wanted to be anywhere else. Jeroch closed the door and faced Jillian, his hands clasped behind his back. However, before Jeroch could open his mouth to speak, Jillian took two steps forward, her eyes hopeful and sorrowful in the same moment.

"Is there news on Logan?"

Jeroch's expression was blank, but his eyes were filled with a mixture of anger and confusion. When he spoke, his voice was even and calm.

"Whatever happened to Logan, it's over now, and as soon as Rhain knows something, I'm sure she'll tell us. She more than anyone would know if Ranthall survived his confrontation or not."

Jillian's heart fell, and while she did not completely understand the feeling, something inside of her told her that Logan was still alive. Before she could process the feeling or why she was so confident, Jeroch continued speaking.

"I'm not here about Ranthall, Jillian, I'm here about you."

Jeroch motioned in the direction of the bed, and Jillian resisted for a moment but finally sat on the edge of the bed farthest away from where Jeroch stood. Leonora made no move, and while her posture spoke of a petulant child, her eyes were focused and attentive.

"There is much you don't understand about this war, Jillian, and it appears there is much I didn't know as well. Unfortunately the time for ignorance and naivety is over, and the more we take our eyes from the truth of this war, the more we will lose. And so, as much as this will be difficult to hear, you have to accept this and move on. What happens next is up to you."

Jillian sat frozen for a moment, but then finally nodded. Logan Ranthall coming into her life had opened her eyes to a whole new world, a world that had existed longer than she could imagine, and yet had been just out of sight. Like a splinter in the mind's eye, it gnawed at the consciousness but never fully came into focus. Now she needed to see everything, and she needed to find her place in the madness that had replaced the sanity of the world she once knew.

"I'm listening," Jillian said finally.

Jeroch held his breath for a moment and then began his tale, not knowing how anyone in the room would react, including himself.

"There's no easy way to say this, so I'm just going to say it. I know who your father is, and his identity is why you are being hunted. Now before you ask, I don't have all the answers, and I don't know everything, but I will tell you what I know."

Jillian started to answer, and then bit her lip. Color filled her cheeks, and Jeroch could see rage in her eyes. Finally, she closed her eyes as though centering herself and then she started to speak, her eyes still closed.

"Do I need to know who he is?"

Jillian's eyes opened the next moment, and her gaze was filled with steel. Jeroch had not prepared himself for the eventuality that Jillian would not want to know the identity of her father. Before he could process the new information, let alone devise a response, Leonora interjected herself into the conversation for the first time.

"You really are just a silly girl, aren't you?"

The steel left Jillian's gaze, and her eyes widened in shock. Leonora continued, completely disregarding Jillian's reaction.

"People are trying to kill you because of something you don't know. People are trying to kill you simply because you exist. If you hate your father so be it. If you want revenge for his leaving your life, you can't get it unless you know who he is. At the very least, you should know who it is that you should hate."

Jeroch felt an emptiness in the pit of his stomach. Would Leonora have reacted in the same way had she known the identity of Jillian's father? Would she be so quick to advocate for the hatred of and vengeance against her mentor and the man she loved? Jillian hung her head for a moment, and then as if surrendering to the battle she did not understand raging within her, she slowly nodded. Half of Jeroch cursed the fact that he now had to reveal what he knew, and as he opened his mouth to speak, he felt Leonora's gaze upon him. With every word that gaze intensified, the heat nearly unbearable.

"You've heard rumors for a long time I'm sure about an artifact known as the Dragon's Tear which is supposed to grant its bearer the ability to alter the very fabric of the Cosmos and bend all of reality to its will. For a long time we thought that the Dragon's Tear was a thing to be possessed, however, the truth was far more sinister; the Dragon's Tear is and always has been a person."

Jillian's cheeks filled with color, and she opened and closed her mouth several times, but no sound emerged. Jeroch waved off the silent question.

"No, Jillian, it's not you. But that was what Logan suspected when he brought you to me in Iltorp. He thought that was why the forces of Dorovar were hunting you, and why the knowledge of the identity of your father had been blocked from you. Despite all of his failings, Ranthall can be quite astute at times. No, the answer is much more insidious. The Dragon's Tear was designed by one of the Children of the Creator to be a weapon. It could potentially give the Children or one of their creations enough power to destroy the Creator."

Jeroch could see the idea explode in Jillian's mind.

"Dorovar."

Jeroch nodded.

"We may never know for certain if Talisia intended for Dorovar to be granted the powers that he now possesses, but considering her very long and close ties to the dragon Shadowweaver, we have to at least assume that she understood the potential possibilities of the deal the dragons made to take refuge on Dorovar's world. She and Emries baited Dorovar into accepting the deal, and then again baited him into releasing the dragons from it. If this was indeed a long game, it eclipses any that I have ever seen, and I have been party to some that have spanned centuries."

Jillian picked up the story from the pieces in her head, and from the revelations that her time with Logan had brought.

"So Dorovar is the first piece of the puzzle, a creation that was not beholden to the Creator, and one that could wield incredible power because of his deal with the dragons. The second piece is the Dragon's Tear, a weapon that would allow Dorovar to wield enough power to take down the Creator. So if that happens, and Dorovar wins, Talisia can't think that she can control him, right? He's got to hate her more than he hates the Creator."

Jeroch was impressed. He often had a low opinion of the intelligence of mortals, not purely because of any racial prejudice, but more because of the practical realities. Humans lived for maybe sixty or seventy years. Some of the more gifted humans might have lived twice that amount. And even if they spent every day of that lifespan accumulating knowledge, they could never hope to amass that which a member of the phasia had access to. Even without the thousands of years of knowledge that Jeroch had personally acquired, he had access to the nearly limitless knowledge of the Blaze, a cosmic force that he didn't understand, but would not exist without. He nodded absently before continuing his portion of the tale.

"Dorovar's motivations are not as important as those of the person that created him. Talisia of course would know that she could not directly control Dorovar's actions, and she would also know that given the chance, he would seek to destroy her as retribution for the death of his world. Someone who makes plans that stretch over millennia do not leave such things to chance. Her plot utilizing Dorovar we think began after his first deal with the Dragons, and shortly before the second. When Emries and Talisia granted powers to the other members of Raenera's Adhradair,

Talisia tied their life forces to Dorovar's, using Raenera's own elements of control and order against her. Then, the abilities that Emries and Talisia gave to the unwitting and revenge-crazed Adhradair give Talisia the opportunity she needed to place at least temporary control over the powers that Dorovar would eventually accumulate. As each of the Adhradair died, their souls were imprisoned, and with each imprisoned soul was a small portion of Dorovar's soul and his power. The portion was so small, of course, that Dorovar would not realize what was happening until it was too late. Talisia had instigated a plan that would ensure that Dorovar could not realize his full power until the rest of her scheme had played out the way she wanted. While I was able to uncover most of this with the help of the knowledge of the Blaze, even with Saurn and Logan's information gathering and the information I was able to retrieve from Irene Drage's mind, much of Talisia's endgame is still unknown to us."

Even laid out plainly, Jillian was having trouble making all the pieces fit. For the little she did know, there was still so much that Jeroch had just summarized that she only had the vaguest of knowledge of. In the end what would matter most was how she fit into the greater scheme. And so she tried to focus back upon that part of the story.

"So where do I fit into this grand plot?" Jillian asked.

"As I said," Jeroch continued, "Talisia was cunning and careful in her construction of this plan. However, she made one glaring mistake, she underestimated the wrong person."

Again, the speed of Jillian's understanding impressed Jeroch.

"Raenera."

"Very good," Jeroch responded. "Sometimes being astute and careful is a better option than being arrogant and overconfident. Talisia did not think about all of the avenues that Raenera could influence her plan because of Raenera's history of detachment from her worlds. Raenera preferred to establish her complex and ordered system and let those empowered to manage those systems do so as they were intended. If she interfered, it would invalidate the very essence of her nature. However, when faced with the death of her world, and the corruption of those she had placed faith and investment in, she could not remain aloof. And so, while Talisia was syphoning away Dorovar's power and stealing the souls of the other members of the Adhradair, Raenera secreted away the one thing that Dorovar needed to make Talisia's plan work, the soul of her High Priestess. With it she took the one thing that only she could take, Dorovar's ability to connect to Raenera's divine power. Without those two things, Dorovar could never be whole, and could never successfully use the powers of the Dragon's Tear to unseat the Creator."

Jeroch took a moment, took a long deep breath, and then re-centered his gaze on Jillian. A moment later, he continued speaking.

"You have to understand, Jillian, the cost of this information is more than we could afford in this war, and the recent sacrifices the Brotherhood of Phasia have made in their fight against Dorovar may have been more than we can collectively bear. But Ranthall believed that saving the innocent, saving those who could not fight the horrors raining down upon them, was more important than his own life, or the lives of those whom others call heroes. It is this belief that brought you here. I don't know if it was some kind of preternatural foresight or maybe just dumb luck, but the end result is that you are here safely, and you are perhaps our greatest weapon in the days to come. Raenera hid the soul of the High Priestess, as well as the key to stopping the Dragon's Tear in the body of a very special child; the child of a hero of the light touched by the hand of two of the Children of the Creator, and a seer, touched by the hand of the Creator and possessed by Raenera herself during the conception. You, Jillian, were that child, the daughter of the Dark Seer Jehna Feris and Cedric Binosear, the Lord Lion of prophecy."

Both Jillian and Leonora had the same reaction, but for very different reasons. However, before either could put voice to their reactions, Jeroch cut them off.

"There is no time for this. There is no time for disbelief, or for recrimination, or for anything that would prevent us from doing what needs to be done. There will be time enough if any of us survive what is coming, and if we don't, then our protests will matter very little. Rhain has orders for us all, and the next days may very well prove to be our last. Remember who our enemy is. Remember what we have lost to make it this far."

Jeroch's voice trailed off, the words leaving him. Finally he simply nodded his head and turned to the door, opening it quickly and stepping into the hall. Leonora's confused gaze went to Jillian and the two women locked eyes. But Jeroch's voice again prevented any exchange.

"Leonora."

The blond woman frowned, turned to follow Jeroch and as soon as she made it to the door, pushed past him. Jeroch watched her walk away for a moment, shook his head and then looked back to Jillian.

"Take a few moments, and then Rhain wishes to see you."

Jeroch closed the door behind him, leaving Jillian with a mass of conflict and confusion, her very identity changed forever.

* * * * * * * * * * * *

The hour was late when Isabella Ranthall knocked on Rhain Seth's door. There had been many comings and goings since Isabella's arrival at the stronghold of the Shadow Guild, and very few had any explanation. Since their arrival, Isabella had been trying to attend to Marlae Tamerlane, but her encounter with Rhain had left the Divine Empress confused and distant. Denied her duty, Isabella turned her attention to learning all that she could about her surroundings as she was taught to do. Finally, the young woman named Taya had called for Isabella's appearance. There was a little trepidation as the door finally opened, but Isabella swallowed her concerns and entered the chamber. Rhain was sitting in a high-backed chair near a small fire that burned in the large stone fireplace. It was cold in the chamber, perhaps unnaturally so, and there was a palpable sorrow that filled the room. The woman who sat in the chair looked tired, older, as though she had aged a dozen years since Isabella had set eyes upon her earlier that day. A great weight pressed down upon her, one that radiated dread in all directions. Rhain looked up, pools of darkness under her eyes, and regarded Isabella for a long moment before indicating the chair across from her. Isabella moved deliberately to the chair, and sat, waiting for Rhain to speak. When finally she did, the voice was filled with the heaviness of responsibility.

"It has been a very long day, Isabella, and though I do not know you, I know enough of your parents and your family that I believe that I can trust you. Will you do as I ask for the sake of those parents and this part of your family that so desperately needs your help?"

Isabella didn't take even a breath to consider.

"My whole life has been leading to this moment, Rhain. I never knew my father until hours ago, and he was everything that I was told he would be. My mother and my grandmother have always spoken so highly of him and the family I had never known. If you have need of me, if you have use of me, I would do as you ask to honor him."

There was a lightness in Rhain's eyes for a moment; a hint of a smile tugging at the corners of her mouth.

"There are some who were granted power by my predecessor who need to be brought into the fold before the final act of this perverse little play begins. I have sent Saurn to meet with Orren Eldrath and Felicia Lorien, while Leonora goes to bring Alderin Terian back to his family. Though they have had issues in their past, Jeroch has gone to meet with your grandmother and attempt to broker a peace with the Church of the Creator and the forces of the Heart of Stone. Jillian and Taya go to meet with a group of rebels who are on their way to Aldere. All factions must be aligned if we are going to be victorious. For your part, Isabella, I need you to go to meet with your mother and to bring her here."

Isabella nodded, and sensing that was all Rhain was going to say, she stood and made her way to the door. Her hand on the handle, she turned back, her voice catching in her throat.

"Is my father dead?"

Rhain looked up for a moment, and then back down at the floor.

"I cannot feel him any longer, Isabella, but I do not know the answer to your question. Regardless, I still hold out hope."

Isabella nodded and left the room, leaving Rhain to her thoughts.

CHAPTER 104

"I have to believe there is enough hope left in this dying world...."

Under the Weight of Terror

*Year One of the Divine Empress and Child of the Creator
Marlae Tamerlane, Creator's Calendar Year 1871*

The sky above the private garden was beginning to darken when the talks between the four newly joined conspirators began in earnest. Above the group in the vine-covered arches a group of brilliant lanterns sparked to life as the light of the twin suns faded. These lanterns, coupled with those hanging from sconces around the perimeter of the garden were gifts from the Academy of Arcane Arts in Jelan. The lanterns, given in a time when relations between the Church and Academy were not at their best, were one a kind creations by a former Master of Fire, and burned with not only the primal elements of creation, but also a piece of the Master's own immortal soul. The gift, both priceless and eternal formed a pact between the two establishments that had remained unbroken for over a thousand years. The way the lanterns were arrayed, no shadows fell on the small sitting area that now served as a table for negotiation, and the light itself was warm and comforting. Baeata regarded the beings arrayed before her and in her mind constructed the starts of a joke that she might have heard once upon a time.

A dragon, a dark god, and a priestess are sitting in a garden….

"I think Lady Anabel," Baeata began shaking away her inappropriate thoughts about the situation, "that you should begin by explaining what exactly you and the Divine Empress expect of the people of Albitonin in this war between the Divine Empress and her disgraced father."

Anne hesitated for a moment and then adopted a more relaxed posture on the stone bench she sat upon. There was no easy way to go about the conversation that was about to occur, but the formality of titles and positions would make it even more difficult. The enemies of the Light and the future cared little for formality and even less for human-created strata of position and power. Dorovar, Emries, and the rest of the enemies arrayed against them killed regardless of what power pathetic humans felt they had.

"High Priestess," Anne began, "I need you to understand that this war is about more than control of Cadaria. It is about more than the soul of the people who dwell within her borders. This war is about the very survival of the entire race of humans, and all who set foot upon the face of any world within the Creator's realm. And because we fight upon that level, and because our very survival may depend upon what takes place in this garden tonight, I would ask that you call me Anne. I've learned that people will not fight and die for you if they do not trust you, and a friend will lay down their life willingly long before a servant or an ally of title or convenience."

Baeata considered for a moment and finally nodded.

"You understand, Anne, that appearances are important now more than ever for me. I was named High Priestess when Lady Ironheart was thought lost to us forever. Now that she has been confirmed as alive, my position is unclear. In much too short a time I will stand before the faithful of Albitonin and ask them to undertake the greatest series of sacrifices that has ever been asked of them, and I have no authority to do so. Perhaps it is vanity or perhaps it is pride. I have worked my entire life to attain a position of authority within this Church, and my elevation, while the culmination of a lifetime of work came at the expense of the life of a servant of the Creator whom I know I could never surpass if I lived another hundred years. The shadow is long that trails behind Hannah Ironheart, and I do not believe that I will ever be beyond it. That is why I have clung so fiercely to title, protocol and position. Perhaps I was trying to validate myself not through my own deeds, but through the trappings of title and perceived honor."

Anne felt her heart skip a beat for a moment and then the pain of her past hung around her like a fog. The past days had yet to fully hit her, and her involvement in the war was beginning to bring into focus the very things she had spent millennia avoiding. Whether it was seeing Logan once again, or trying to tutor a child wearing a great woman's name, her brother's lover, or the inevitable collision with the man who she had spent her life denying; the life she had built upon poise and focus was quickly sliding out of it.

"I understand your quandary, Baeata," Anne said finally, shedding the woman's title to speak to the person hiding behind it. "Unlike you, my title is not earned; it is simply a condition of my birth. Once upon a time, on another world, I was the daughter of a princess who had been chosen by a great king to be his bride. No one knew that my brother and I were actually the progeny of a scoundrel who shared her bed one night before she was to be sent to meet her future husband and become his wife and queen. We were raised as the heirs to a great responsibility. One that became even greater when the darkness crept across our world like a shadow. My brother, without any knowledge of what he was facing plunged headlong into conflict, his only aim to save those who could be saved. People were dying, and he had the power to try to stop it. That nobility infected so many people, and for a time, it looked as though our world was going to be better for it."

Here Anne fell silent. This was not the place to find solace for her own wounds, but it was important that Baeata truly understood what was at stake, and the little that she could actually contribute. She had a greater chance to obstruct what must be done than she did to make the situation better.

"But you see the truth of the war, the truth of any war is that you are ruled by what you know and are destroyed by what you do not. We were so sure, all of us, what it took to save our world. My father, my brother, our friends, the generations that came after. Thousands of people died for a lie. Thousands of people who trusted my brother, who trusted me, who trusted Logan and the others. All dead. Thousands who had no role in the war but to be victims of it, all dead. Thousands who knew only of the war through the stories of bards and others, all dead. A whole world, a history, lives and memories and hopes and dreams, gone. All gone. No matter how hard we fought, no matter how much we sacrificed. No matter how many battles we won, people we saved. Our world still burned. We still failed. All because we did not know the truth until the end."

Anne leaned forward, tears again trying to form in the corners of her eyes. However, the anger that was rising up in her burned them before they could take hold.

"And the greatest lie, Baeata, is the one we've been telling ourselves for these past millennia. The lie is that it would have made a difference if we knew the truth earlier."

Anne let the silence hold them all those next moments, hoping that the message would sink in. She didn't expect Serentis to add her voice.

"Dorovar.......story.......little........difference........perhaps........hero ....anothers........eyes........"

Anne was shocked by the statement from the creature, even more shocked when images flooded into her mind of a perfect pristine world of crystal and stone presided over by a group in white. There was prosperity unparalleled on that world, and at the center of it was the man who now wore the countenance of a demon, the man that once was a man of peace, Dorovar. The images in Anne's mind flashed to the betrayal of the dragons, the man holding his faith above all else, sacrificing his friends, his position, and in the end his world to hold on to the one true tenant of his core, his faith. In the end, he failed because he too was the victim of intricate deceptions perpetrated by the dragons, by Talisia and Emries, and by his own brethren. He held true, and his reward was floating in nothingness for thousands of years with only his pain to keep him company.

The relay of information took only a moment, but Anne felt drained by it. At first she thought that the dragon had shared the vision with only her, but when she heard Baeata's barely stifled sobs and saw the tears streaming from both her eyes and Rhya's, she knew that they all had experienced the same tragedy in their mind's eye. There was profound truth there, and Anne needed Baeata to understand it.

"I can't share the truths that I know as swiftly or as completely as our large friend can, but what I can do is help to put them in perspective for you. This war, if that's what you want to call it, dates back long before this world, long before my world, and long before Dorovar's world. We are simply trapped in the aftermath of something that transpired at the birth of Creation. A war of ideas but not of ideals. A war of concepts not consequences. A war that can never be won."

Anne's voice trailed off for a moment. There were so many thoughts swirling in her head, so many pieces of the puzzle that she had learned from Sabrina over the years. But she also knew that there was so much she didn't know. She hoped that the dragon would be able to fill in some of the gaps.

"There is one lesson that I can impart to you, Baeata, one that I have learned through considerable heartache and tears. There are truths and there is Truth. Truth is immutable; it is absolute, without bias and without intention. It is a fixed point that we all must acknowledge, no matter what we may think of it. There is no changing Truth. The same cannot be said for truths. They are at the mercy of how one looks at the Cosmos, how one looks at the world around them, and how they look at their own place within those constructs. For people like you Baeata, truths have little consequences past your own life. They influence how you deal with others, but you lack the power to influence real change. For me, and for other Dark Gods, our ability to influence the larger constructs is much greater. That comes with the power that we have been given through certain sources. These consequences are magnified further when you speak about the Children. Whole worlds rise and fall based upon their truths. Then there is the Creator."

Anne paused here. This was what she had been dreading.

"You see the Creator as this figure of peace and creation. A loving father who has given his people the path to become greater than he made them."

Baeata's nose wrinkled at the assessment, and she countered with a description of her own.

"The Creator has given us his laws so that we may follow them to glorify Him and His creations. Service and supplication are the duty of every being that owes its existence to the Creator. We are made in His image so that we can do good works in His name."

Anne began to respond, but it was the priestess Rhya's voice that took over the conversation. However, as soon as the woman began to speak, it was clear to Anne that the words came from elsewhere.

"It is unfortunate that the delusion of the Creator's image continues so long after the first humans were forged. While the lie had a different connotation when it was originally spoken, the lie has been perverted now into a major tenant of your religion."

Baeata looked as though she had been struck. Anne found her eyes moving to where the dragon hung coiled above them. The creature's eyes were closed, and it was clear that the ancient beast was speaking through the young priestess. Before Baeata's shock could manifest into words, Rhya's voice came out again. This time, however, it was clear that the words were the woman's alone.

"The dragon Serentis has chosen to use me to speak on her behalf. Serentis finds human languages tedious and incapable of properly conveying her words, therefore she does so sparingly. Because I have allowed my mind to be touched by Aerith Seth to deliver the words of Hannah Ironheart, Serentis is able to use that connection to convey her words. I have consented to be her voice for the duration of her time as liaison from the forces of Mariti Brightblade."

Baeata paused for a long moment, and then nodded her ascent. Certainly having Rhya as Serentis' translator would make things easier, and Anne hoped that the dragon would now carry most of the narrative. Anne was not disappointed when Rhya began speaking the next moment, her language stilted and formal, and slightly condescending.

"A central conceit of your worship of the Creator is that the Creator is responsible for the race of humans and thus were made in the image of the Creator. The Creator did not create humans. No one being created humans. There were versions of humans created by Emries. There were versions of humans created by Raenera. There were even versions of humans that were created by Talisia, but fortunately none of those vile things ever saw the light of a world beyond their birthplace. The phasia, who are children of Halicon are human after a fashion. The version of humans that walk upon this world are closest to those that Emries made."

Baeata's response was shaky, but predictable.

"Even if humans were made by the Children, they did so at the behest of the Creator. The Children themselves were made in the Creator's image, and thus humans are made in that image. It may be a matter of abstraction, but the conceit as you call it is still valid."

Rhya's barely restrained chuckle was both surprising and disturbing.

"Religion is such a miraculous invention. Humans have developed a way to make themselves important to justify their behavior without a single shred of reasonable proof or foundational knowledge. Moreover, any attempt to shake such beliefs only reinforces them. But I am not here to sway you from your misguided understandings. There are things you must know in order to serve your purpose however. Your understanding of these items is not required. Your belief however is."

When Rhya spoke again, there was a new power in her voice, and the young woman's body was physically shaking with the exertion of it.

"I was there at the beginning. In fact, I was the third of my race born. The Palace and the Golden Throne did not even exist at that time. There was only the formless void. There were nine of us in the beginning, the first and most complete expression of the Creator's curiosity. But the Creator was disappointed in our conjectures and lack of motivation to do combat over our ideological differences. It may have been an express flaw in the dragons that we for a great deal of time valued the lives of dragons above even our own beliefs. That was the most unforgivable sin, and was the only true law. No dragon would dare harm another. Of course, that changed in the war in the Heavens, and that changed here upon this world. And so if any creature were truly made in the Creator's image, it was the dragons."

All color drained from Baeata's face. However, Serentis was not trying to shock the woman into compliance. There was almost a matter of fact nature to the words. Even as learned as Anne was, she had not been privy to this information. It may have even been possible that Sabrina had not known this truth, or it may have been such an immaterial history that she did not think it important to impart. Anne had shed her naiveté long ago regarding the Creator, so knowing that the dragons were the first-born beings in the Cosmos mattered little. However, in order to shock Baeata out of her fervent devotion to the Church, she would need to face some hard facts.

"I tell you this not to elevate the dragons, but to express to you just how much you do not know about the cosmos that stretches around you. I am as old as Creation, and I do not know what lies in the darkness beyond the Creator's view. But there is more than just the halo of the Creator's love, and there is more than just the darkness that lies beyond. The Creator is not eternal, and the Creator understands this. What he does not understand is what comes next. That is why the Children were created. The Creator needed a way to shape that which he had Created and learn from the shaping of it. The Children gave him the one thing that the dragons would not. Not just differences of ideology, but clashes of ideology. Each of the Children believed that their view of Creation was correct, to the exclusion of all else. And while these clashes of ideal helped to shape Creation, as the conflict became more extreme, they also began to unravel it. We all believe that the Creator is close to ending this iteration of His Creation. This world is the final battleground, a place where one ideology must prevail over all others or all will cease to exist. All of Creation will be consigned to fire, with only the Heavens remaining to start again. And so, we fight alongside those who hate and fear us. We fight for one who should not exist, and we are willing to except extinction to prevent oblivion."

Rhya fell silent and Anne heard shifting above her. The dragon's eyes were open again, and it was moving toward a higher perch in the arches above. It seemed to Anne that the creature's patience had ended, and she watched in awe as the creature moved skyward. It didn't leap, it didn't fly, it simply seemed to slither from the solid structure of the arches to the openness of the sky. It was an awe-inspiring if not totally unfathomable sight. Baeata's eyes were fixed on the ground, but she did not seem undone by the dragon's words. Finally, she looked up and let her gaze meet Anne's.

"What do you need me to do?"

* * * * * * * * * * * *

Aelind was quick to accomplish her tasks as assigned to her by the High Priestess, but was then was left to simply wander the halls of the Heart of Stone while the negotiations continued between the High Priestess and Anabel Binosear. Aelind still did not trust the woman who was admittedly a Dark God, and she inwardly wondered if the entire trip to Hedorah had been folly. Perhaps this new Divine Empress was not what she appeared to be, and was in fact a test of faith. Perhaps the Creator anointed this pretender as a way to ensure that the High Priestess was worth of leading the faithful through the trials that lay ahead. Or, more terrifyingly, perhaps this Divine Empress and her advisors were exactly what they said they were. Perhaps they were the harbingers of some greater threat that was intent on destroying the world that they dwelled upon. Either way, they were matters for the High Priestess to tend to, and if she required Aelind's council on such matters, she would request it.

Aelind's wanderings finally brought her back to her modest little room that was mere feet from where the High Priestess's quarters were. The door to the High Priestess's chambers was at the end of the hall. There were doors on each of the adjoining walls of that hall, one leading to the quarters of the High Priestess's personal assistant, and one leading to a private study where the High Priestess could privately contemplate the Book of the Creator and its lessons. She slowly approached the High Priestess's door and knocked lightly. She didn't expect there to be an answer, but her duty would not pass the door without checking to see if the High Priestess required her service. It was a practiced ritual that while reflex had not been reduced to reflexive. Aelind took her duty to the High Priestess very seriously, and she was not one to partake in ritual for ritual's sake. She waited for several moments at the High Priestess's door, and when there was no sound from within the chambers, she turned back to her own door.

Like all quarters assigned to the priestesses and their aides, Aelind's quarters were small, with enough room for a small wardrobe, a simple small bed, a mirror on the wall and chair and table. Upon the table was her own copy of the Book of the Creator, the one that she had illuminated by hand as her final task as an initiate. It was said that only though the writing of every single word within the Book of the Creator did someone truly prove his or her dedication to spreading that word. If a single mistake was made in the illumination process, the work was abandoned and had to be restarted. Some initiates required years to complete the work, some still were making their attempts a decade into the process. It was a test of endurance as well as dedication as once the work ass started, it could not be stopped until completed. The initiate is only allowed small breaks for food and other physical needs, and sleep is confined to one hour for every eight hours of work. It was said that Hannah Ironheart had been perfect in her first trail, and had completed the task quicker than any initiate before. Aelind herself failed four times before finally succeeding. Baeata had taken two attempts, her first ending as she fell asleep in her chair while illuminating the final page.

Her hand on the Book of the Creator on her table, Aelind thought she saw motion out of the corner of her eye. When Aelind turned, she saw the motion again, this time however it was not her imagination or a trick of the light. The surface of her mirror rippled like it was the surface of a turbulent lake. Before she could approach, the shimmering surface turned black and Aelind's blood froze. A moment later an impossibly long, slender, delicate leg pierced the surface and stepped from the nothingness into the room. Aelind was petrified with fear as the alien form entered the chamber. The creature's limbs were thinner and longer than those of a human's, looking as though they would break by simply putting weight upon them. The face was stretched, pale and white with an elongated jaw and chin; eye sockets twisted upwards. The eyes themselves, roughly almond shaped were blacker than the blackest night, and seemed to drink in all light and hope. Long black tendrils of what could have been hair wreathed the creature's head, a shimmering black crown floating in the middle of the mass. Phantasmal black wings stretched behind it, and a cold malice radiant from the monstrosity like a fog. The cold dead eyes locked on Aelind, and she immediately fell to her knees in supplication. When the creature spoke, the somewhat feminine voice came out in several different pitches at once, a dissonant harmony of multiple octaves and voices. The voice sent shivers through Aelind, conveying terror and hopelessness with every syllable.

"Report, servant."

Aelind kept her head down, her face nearly against the floor. When she spoke, she was careful to keep all emotion out of her voice, not wanting to offend the powerful being that stood before her.

"My lady Talisia. We were brought back to Albitonin by means of a portal created by a man who called himself Logan Ranthall. He sent us here to keep us safe from the creature they called Conquest. The woman calling herself Anabel Binosear accompanied the High Priestess and is now in negotiations with her. Apparently, Lady Hannah Ironheart still lives, and she sent a message through a priestess from Aldere codifying an alliance between the Kingdom of Albitonin and a group of dragons led by the one called Serentis. The High Priestess does not know that I know about the alliance, and I have been kept from nearly all of the discussions. However, as the servant of the High Priestess, I was able to gather information while I was arranging for a gathering of the faithful."

There was silence for several long moments, and then Aelind heard something hit the floor in front of her.

"On the morning of the gathering, my forces will attack. We will overwhelm the pathetic flight of dragons stationed here, and we will reduce this place to a smoldering crater. But you, my little servant will most likely not live to see this fortress cracked open like an egg. No, I have a far more important task for you. Before my forces descend upon this place, you will plunge that dagger into Anabel Binosear's heart."

Aelind looked up slightly and saw the simple dagger that lay on the floor before her. It oozed hate and malice, and the thought of actually touching the weapon made Aelind's skin crawl. Talisia stepped forward and knelt down, long slender fingers reaching under Aelind's chin and seizing her face tightly. Cold radiated through the grasp. Aelind's face was wrenched upwards until she stared into the empty abyss of Talisia's eyes.

"Remember my little servant, if you do not do exactly as I say, I will obliterate everything you have ever cared about, and I shall do it slowly.

Remember it was my servant Korin that saved you from that fire long ago, and it is by my will alone that you have survived this long. I will reduce that orphanage to ash. I will find every person that you have ever known and I shall rip their hearts out. I will ensure that every living person upon this world knows that you are both a traitor and a coward. And if you survive the purge that is coming and live through your failure, I will ensure that your last moments stretch on into eternity. Do you understand?"

Aelind blinked hard as the hand that held her face would not allow any movement.

"I shall not fail you, Lady Talisia."

The hand released her face but seized Aelind by the throat. As the Child of the Creator rose from her kneeling position, she lifted Aelind off the ground, the squeezing of her neck cutting off every breath before it could be formed.

"You will kill Anabel Binosear, no matter what it takes, no matter what it costs, and even if it means the end of your own life. You will be the vessel of my retribution, and the daughter of Aerith Seth will know death."

Talisia's hard stare froze Aelind's heart. Her vision was beginning to go black, and the feeling had long since fled from her arms and legs. Just before Aelind blacked out, Talisia released her and let her drop to the floor. By the time Aelind's vision cleared, the Child of the Creator was gone, and Aelind sat on the floor rubbing her throat and looking at the viscous dagger laying on the floor before her.

Winding Clocks

Year Five of the Just Emperor Kaitain "Dragonsbane" Lorien, Creator's Calendar Year 1872

The Palace of the Creator in the Heavens stood quiet and empty. There was no angelic host guarding the entrance, no flights of warrior angels circling overhead. The crystal columns while still brilliant in the ambient white light seemed dull and pensive. It was as though the whole of the Heavens held its breath, waiting. There was something ominous on the air, as though the whole of the Cosmos was holding its breath waiting for the inevitable next action. Though the Creator oversaw thousands of worlds within the firmament of Creation, there was one that required nearly all of His considerable attention and resources. As Ayden Seth walked through the cold and immortal halls, he could feel the golden throne of the Creator ahead of him though he had not caught sight of it yet. Since becoming the Will, one of the Creator's trusted Servants, Ayden had not spent much time in the Heavens, and had instead received his instructions via the power of the Creator that flowed through him. Now though, the Creator had requested that he make his way to the Heavens, forsaking his role as the protector of the Divine Empress, and await instructions. Though part of Ayden wanted to return to Marlae's side, there was no disobeying possible.

Finally, the Golden Throne came into view, however its appearance did not coincide with the memories of the Will that flowed through Ayden. Normally, the Golden Throne vibrated with the power of the Creator; a great golden aura of divine energy wreathed around the largely symbolic structure. Now though, the throne appeared as any other mortal construct would. Yes, it was made of gold and crystal, but it did not pulse with the awesome power that was befitting of the very heart of the celestial domain. Ayden knelt at the foot of the throne and waited. Time operated differently in the Heavens, so it was unclear how long he was there before he felt another presence in the throne room. His curiosity may have been piqued, but he did not rise from his place of supplication.

"You may be there a while."

Ayden turned his head in the direction of the woman's voice, not recognizing it. At first, he did not see her, and then finally caught the glimpse of her out of the corner of his eye. The woman had been behind Ayden when she first spoke and she moved just into the cone of his vision. The woman was slight of build but not frail by any stretch of the imagination. She didn't wear any garb that would be considered normal for a Servant of the Creator, instead wearing simple black pants and a white tunic with long sleeves that came down over the backs of her hands, leaving only her fingers exposed. Her red hair was bright, perhaps more colorful than it had been in life, and her eyes were like glowing green stars filled with the power of the Creator. It took only a moment searching through the memories of the Will to identify the woman. In life, she had been Rachel Core, and now unless Ayden missed his guess, she was the new host to the power of the Spirit. Rachel leaned against one of the crystalline pillars and cross her arms.

"The Creator has withdrawn from the Heavens to consider the state of affairs, and has left me here to manage the war that rages on Espre."

Ayden slowly found his way back to his feet and then turned to face Rachel without moving in her direction. Though each member of the Servants acted at the direction of the Creator, they were still possessed with at least a part of the personality of the host the Creator chose. Though Ayden had memories enough to know who Rachel Core had been in life, he did not know her, and could not anticipate the manner in which she would exercise the leadership that the Creator had bequeathed to her. In fact, Ayden found himself unnerved that a newly resurrected and elevated Servant would supersede him. Why should he be relegated to the subordinate position? A sly smile came the Rachel's face.

"I suppose were I in your place, I might be annoyed as well. But the simplest explanation is usually the best one. The Spirit is the vessel of the Creator's power on the mortal plane, and therefore leads in the Creator's stead. No matter what happens, there will always be a Spirit. The same cannot be said for the rest of the Servants."

Ayden nodded, but Rachel continued.

"But I can give you another, one that you won't like. The long and short of it, Ayden, is that you aren't a leader. You're a boy who has known power all his life and is willful and arrogant. Given what has happened, the Creator does not want you going too fast and overreaching. Discretion and experience are needed now. Not exactly your strong suits."

Ayden bristled at the description.

"In life, I was a general. I know how these people we're fighting against think. I've fought alongside and against many of them. And if we're going to succeed in preventing the catastrophe that looms, then our tactics must change."

Ayden balled his fists and stood straight, his shoulders pulled back and his feet firmly planted. Rage was building deep inside him, but he was keeping it contained.

"Order me to move on my father. If I kill him, this will all be over."

Rachel shook her head.

"You don't understand anything, do you?"

Rachel could feel Ayden's scowl. The young man took a half-step forward, the prelude to adopting a fighting stance, and slightly shifted his shoulders to present a smaller target.

"Regardless of what you are, regardless of what experience you choose to lord over me, I would caution you that it is not wise to attempt to insult or belittle me. The Creator could ill-afford to lose either one of us, especially now."

Ayden's posture did not change, and the longer he stood, his body filling with divine power, the more menace he represented. Though Rachel did not actually believe that he would start a conflict at the foot of the Golden Throne, she knew that his volatility could not be underestimated.

"Ayden, you must understand what is happening around you. You must stop thinking like a mortal. Those days are done, and that time of your life is over. You are a Servant of the Creator, and you must see things beyond the moment and beyond your own hatreds. And your hatred of your father has always clouded your judgment."

There was a moment of stunned silence, and then Ayden straightened, shifting his shoulders so that he faced Rachel fully. Some of the rage drained from Ayden's face, replaced by indignation.

"I do not hate my father."

Rachel frowned.

"Lies do not become you, Ayden. It is clear from your actions and from the man you have crafted yourself into that you do hate your father. There is no other explanation. Look at yourself, Ayden, look at what you are. You were blessed from birth with unbelievable power, and what have you done with it? You refused to learn the lessons that were taught to you by your mother and father, refused to learn the lessons that were taught to them with bitterness and with blood. You have cloaked yourself with arrogance and irreverence without the experience to justify it. Responsibility has never been a word that you have ever gravitated toward, and because of that you fail to grow into the role that has been yours since the moment you first drew breath. A wealth of knowledge has been laid at your feet, both from your father and mother, and then again from the instructors of the Academy of Arcane Arts. And what have you done with that knowledge? What have you done with the opportunities?"

Rachel stood straight and added a deadly new edge to her voice.

"At every turn you have avoided and abdicated. You have amused yourself with pranks and jokes, turning your power into nothing more than a parlor trick. You jumped from bed to bed as though it had no consequence and you degraded and humiliated anyone who could possibly have claimed to love you through your cruelty and thoughtlessness. You saw yourself as above those who were your betters, and you risked the lives of those who would have supported you through your carelessness and pride. In the end, you have run from everything that should have meant something to you, and you have been the beacon for the hopelessness and fallacy of this world."

The defiance returned to Ayden's eyes, and when he spoke it was with a growl that Rachel could feel deep into the core of her being.

"I am the Will of the Creator!" Ayden thundered. "I was chosen to be a vessel of His power on the mortal plane, the personification of His will. I am the protector of His hand-picked ruler of His faithful."

Rachel waited for the wave of anger to pass and then slowly and deliberately crossed the distance to the dangerous and violent young man until she stood less than a pace from him. The Creator's divine power had not yet reached her eyes, but filled every other part of her body. She would be prepared if her next words triggered an aggressive reaction from the Will. When she spoke, her voice was calm and even, with just a hint of venom.

"A post you neither earned nor deserved. Ayden, you were a failure in life, and it was only at your end that you were granted this position. The Creator saw all the wasted potential in you, and pulled you back from the brink of death and imbued you with powers beyond description and a solitary responsibility. Thus far, you have been as successful in this life as you had been in your previous one. You see yourself as superior to your task. You see yourself as above the Creator's plan. Would you sacrifice the whole of Creation just to elevate your own ego? Or are you willing to finally do what must be done."

Ayden blinked twice and held his ground. If he stepped back and ceded the ground to the Spirit, he would be admitting not only to her but to himself that she was right. But if he held his ground or even pushed forward, he would be illustrating her point.

"Do you finally begin to see, Ayden?" Rachel said, Ayden's thoughts coming to her clearly. "The price for this gift you have been given is higher than you could ever imagine. Loyalty demands the highest price of any of the virtues that the Creator requires of his Servants. Power comes the easiest, but loyalty at times demands sacrifices beyond what mortals can understand."

Finally, Ayden relented and took a single step back from Rachel.

"And what price does the Creator demand to demonstrate my loyalty?"

Rachel nodded and turned away from Ayden. She took two long steps forward until she was within arm's reach of the crystal column that she had leaned against. She started speaking again, keeping her back to Ayden, letting the commanding tone of the Creator's power flow into her voice.

"Your mother has come into possession of information that she should not have, and she cannot be allowed to share that information with anyone, especially your father. However, this information may allow her to be useful in another task."

Ayden nodded absently.

"And I am to convince my mother to undertake this task?"

Rachel smiled. Perhaps he was not unsalvageably dim after all.

"Your charge, the Divine Empress is approaching a dangerous crossroads, and she must be persuaded to take the right road. There are too many influences around her that do not have her best interests at heart, and none of those loyal to the Creator can approach her to assist her in making the right decision. Your mother however, can approach Marlae in the refuge that she has taken and guide her."

Rachel paused, letting the positive portion of her message seep in before issuing the second command.

"She must also pay for her sin of pride against the Creator, Ayden. And the cost of that sin is to ensure the death of her daughter. You are instruct her to kill Rhain Seth."

Ayden's blood frozen in his heart. However, before he could react further, Rachel turned to face him, the color in her eyes gone, replaced by the blazing white divine power of the Creator.

"Will you carry out these instructions, Ayden?"

Ayden bowed his head.

"I shall obey."

Rachel nodded. When Ayden straightened, the visage of the young man had faded, his body wreathed in power, and his wings beginning to stretch outward.

"And if Bryn refuses to carry out her penance?"

Rachel shook her head. Ayden understood the unspoken order and allowed his wings to wrap around his body. A moment later, the divine light surged and Ayden was gone, leaving Rachel alone in the Palace of the Creator. Her eyes by this point had returned to their normal color, and she slowly made her way over to the foot of the Golden Throne, where she sank to one knee and bowed her head. Her knee had no more than touched the marble floor when the brilliant golden glow faded back into existence, cloaking the Golden Throne in radiance.

"I fear he will fail in his task," Rachel said, her head still low.

There was a long pause before there was any response to Rachel's statement. While she had expected the commanding thunderous voice of the Creator to ring forth from the golden cloud, it was instead a softer human voice, one she recognized as once belonging to Aryx Terian.

"Ayden's task is important for many reasons, and important to him for many more. One way or another he shall succeed, perhaps not in the way that would be most beneficial for the fate of this world. But he will succeed nonetheless. The information that Bryn has come into possession of will not find its way into the hands of Aerith Seth or any of his followers."

Rachel stayed where she was, head down.

"But Bryn would surely not turn on her own daughter."

The Creator did not answer. For several long minutes Rachel remained in her kneeling position, her mind working on all of the information she had available to her. Though she was a Servant of the Creator and had access to some of the boundless information that was the very essence of the Creator, she did not have unlimited access. The Creator only allowed her to know what she needed to know at the moment she needed to know it in order to carry out her instructions. Since she had only been counted among the Servants for a short amount of time, she had not yet gained full mastery over her abilities. Though Rachel had only recently returned to the mortal world, she still had the memories of her life before and all of the experiences that brought her. She had fought at the side of two of the greatest heroes in the history of the human race, and they had taught her much. That experience, together with her own intellect and guile, was allowing her to put together the pieces quickly. Perhaps it was not as quickly as the Creator would have liked, but if He had desired efficiency, He would have simply given her the answer.

"You want Bryn to refuse the offer."

The golden cloud pulsed in rapid succession for several moments, and Rachel interpreted it to something akin to laughter, but perhaps she was simply projecting her own feelings into the ether. There were so many complex strategies that were floating through her mind; so many different possibilities. However, it was almost impossible to determine what was actually happening and what were the potential outcomes that the Creator was exploring. The Creator saw every moment, every possible moment, and every outcome all at once, and sometimes the Spirit could see what the Creator was seeing, at least in part. It was all so confusing.

"A great many of the eventualities that must come to pass depend upon two clear factors. Of course, there are hundreds of smaller possibilities but this is the clearest path," the Aryx-voiced Creator responded. "The first of the factors has remained unchanged. Ayden Seth must be fervently committed to the path that he has chosen for himself, and must be steadfast on the path of service. The more he believes in the righteousness of his actions and the righteousness of our cause, the more powerful will his devotion to that cause become. This devotion must be absolute for the trials that are to come. The trials that will determine the fate not only of this world, but all others that spin in great orbits around distant stars, the ones that may continue to flourish and support untold life."

Rachel nodded.

"And the second?"

Only silence answered. Rachel stayed silent as well, wondering whether or not she should press the issue. But finally, she decided to speak.

"Forgive me, but in order to serve to the best of my ability, I believe I need to know as much as I possibly can about what is to come. You have entrusted this power to me because of who I was in life, and the woman that I was valued information and valued doing everything I could to succeed. Though I am not the mortal I once was, I still wish to succeed in the tasks that you appoint me."

The golden glow pulsed again, and then the voice came once more, but this time it was one that Rachel didn't recognize. It was a woman's voice, sweet and understanding but with a harder edge.

"There is more isn't there? Remember that there is not a thought that you have that you can hide from me."

Rachel swallowed hard.

"I think perhaps if your previous Servants had been privy to more information, or perhaps had been more curious, then perhaps you would not worry so much about the state of Ayden's devotion to your cause."

Laughter washed through the halls of the Palace of the Creator like sheets of soft rain.

"Yes, perhaps you are correct," the woman's voice returned. Rachel had been able to deduce that the voice was of Diana Terian. "Perhaps my Servants rely too much upon being told what they should know. But then perhaps if I had not allowed my Servants any measure of free will, none of these measures would be necessary at all. Your predecessor, Sabrina, asked a great many questions, tried to ferret out as many secrets as she could, and though I knew the end result of these inquiries, I allowed them to continue. However, were I to deny my Servants free will, why not deny it of my Children? Why not deny it of the creatures that roam all worlds under my eye? Would that not remove the need for Servants at all? Would it not also remove the need for any living beings? Diversity of thought and action is the lifeblood of this living Cosmos. We may seek to exert control, we may seek to shape and form it to our whims, but the one thing that we can never do is remove the possibility that the Cosmos will do as it wills. The more we try to control the Cosmos, the more we are shown that we cannot. And yet we continue to try, we continue to corral that which desires nothing more than to spread unchecked and unfettered."

Rachel's head hurt.

"I don't understand."

There were several rapid pulses of the golden light.

"Good. A lack of understanding is often the first step to true clarity. But often the lack of understanding is met with disdain and petulance, and therefore few achieve the clarity it offers. And so, because you have shown the initiative and you have admitted your misgivings regardless of the repercussions, I will tell you more than you will wish to know."

Rachel steeled herself.

"Bryn Aplee, through her guile, trickery, and stubbornness has come into possession of information that cannot fall into the hands of her husband or any of those who have worn his mantle."

Rachel lifted her head.

"You told Ayden this, and he was content with that explanation. I am not."

There was a low rumble like thunder, and Rachel could hear the crystal pillars shake with a sound like a thousand small bells.

"I do not value impudence, even if it is supposedly in the service of my will. Remember that you are but a Servant and can be replaced if you cannot discharge your duties in a manner that is acceptable to your post."

Rachel felt the rebuke as though she had been punched squarely in the chest.

"However," the Creator continued, "the observation is a valid one. Bryn managed to gain entry into a portion of the Heavens where dangerous information is kept. It is information that cannot be destroyed, for the very reasons that I have previously explained. A locked door must always have a key, or a manner in which to subvert the lock. The information that she procured, in the hands of certain individuals could forge a path by which an individual could conceivably force their way into the Heavens and challenge me for control of the Heavens. But the information is only a piece, and while the information itself cannot be destroyed, the bearer of that information can. When Ayden fails to convince Bryn to act on my behalf, he will end her life, thus preventing the information she carries from doing any more harm."

Rachel nodded absently.

"You still do not understand."

Rachel's eyes opened widely, and then reluctantly she nodded.

"Perhaps there is hope for you yet. This path is absolute, and can only be prevented in the same way that it is forged, through choice, and the consequences of that choice. And even if the path can be discovered, the very nature of its creation makes it nearly impossible to open and even more dangerous to walk. And even if there is one among the mortals who can successfully traverse the path; the cost of such an action defies all understanding possible to a mortal mind. And yet there will be those that will always seek this path. Ignorance and the thirst for power drive many. Idle resentment for that which they can never understand will drive others. In the end the mortals will all choose ruination."

Sensing that explanations were at an end, Rachel brought herself back to her feet and settled into an all-too-familiar parade rest.

"What are your orders?"

There was silence for several minutes, and Rachel stood patiently, trying not to fixate on the silence or the mass of information that she could not understand. In her heart and at her core she was a soldier, and that part of her more than anything simply wanted to be away from the Palace of the Creator and fulfilling her next mission. Finally the voice of the Creator rung out again.

"When Ayden's task is complete and Bryn has been eliminated, you will take my will to the Divine Empress and ensure her loyalty. Once that task is complete, all of the Children of the Heavens must be brought back to their rightful place and understand the loyalty they owe to the Heavens and to the Creator. They will not wish to come willingly, and so you must use all of the tools available to you to remove the impediments to their fidelity to our cause. They must return, there can be no other acceptable outcome."

Rachel bowed.

"I understand."

The golden glow brightened.

"There is more. This will bring you in conflict with those that you once considered to be your family, and you may be forced not only into conflict, but you may be forced to take lethal action against them. Are you prepared for this eventuality?"

Rachel inclined her head for just a moment, and then her eyes shone with the brilliant white light of the Creator's power.

"My first and only loyalty is to the Creator."

Chapter CV

Choices and Expectations

*Year Four of the Just Emperor Kaitain "Dragonsbane" Lorien,
Creator's Calendar Year 1871*

Sadrina Annis woke with a start. A thousand thoughts whirled through her mind at the same time with no context and no pattern. She tried to arrange them the best she could in the first moments of her wakefulness, holding to a stubborn practicality that had been with her through her entire life. Analyze the situation, determine the best course of action, act. This fastidious nature and logical mind had served her well in some aspects of her life, but not in all of them. And so, she began to work through the thoughts, dismissing many that were mirrors of one another. There were echoes of confusion, fear, and anger. There would be time enough for those things once the more important items were dealt with. First and foremost was the pain. Every inch of her body hurt. Her muscles all felt as though they had been tied into knots, and her joints felt as though they had been stretched to well beyond their limits. On top of that, Sadrina's skin ached as though it had been frozen and then boiled. She could feel the dry flaking skin cracking with every movement while at the same time feeling as though it were tearing like wet paper. It hurt to move, and it hurt to sit still.

Quieting her mind, Sadrina tried to put herself back in the temple where she lived as a child with her sister Hannah. From the moment they were born, Sadrina and her sister were both marked as special. Their mother was an acolyte in the Church of the Creator in Albitonin and was thought to be well on her way to becoming either a Reverend Mother or possibly even in consideration for ascension to the rank of High Priestess. Their father, though not truly a father, was a patrician from Zevarit. Before her sister later outlawed the practice, it was common for lifelong female members of the church who were on the path to greater things to be matched with members of the aristocracy of the Great Kingdoms in order to further perpetuate the blessed bloodlines as ordained by the Book of the Creator. The critics of the practice, of which Hannah was one, viewed the tradition as little more than prostituting vulnerable girls to rich lecherous men in order to secure a significant donation to the Church. Proponents of the practice pointed out that without the tradition, there would not be a guaranteed pool from which to replenish the ranks as the old guard succumbed to old age. Also, it was considered an alternative to absorbing those losses incurred when the young novitiates decided that they wanted to sew their wild oats before taking their vows. Some would become pregnant and choose not to return in favor of becoming a common wife and mother. Some would simply find themselves so scandalized and shamed by their wanton behavior that they felt they could never return to pious ways. Others unfortunately fell victim to those who could easily exploit their naivety in the ways of the world. Hannah and Sadrina never knew their father, never knew anything about him, and in truth never wanted to. Their mother and the Church was all the parentage they needed, even in the trials that lay ahead.

Twins were uncommon in both the Ironheart family and the family of the man who sired Sadrina and Hannah, which was the first sign that the girls were marked by the Creator. The second was that both were born during the Days of Star Fire. Well, almost both. Sadrina, the older of the two girls was born just prior to the moon entering its tortured path through the corona of the twin suns. Hannah was born as the first streaks of fire began to cross the sky. That fact set Hannah's path, a path that Sadrina also tried to walk in the early days, but eventually she would stray and fall under the sway of a mysterious and eccentric lord during her time away from the Church before she was to take her vows.

The twin girls were pushed to excel in every aspect of their lives, and they were constantly in competition with one another. When Hannah accomplished something first, it was proof of her fated excellence and charmed destiny. When Sadrina accomplished something first it was dismissed as a fluke or immediately invalidated with Hannah accomplished it within an acceptable period of time. If anything, Sadrina was almost equal to her younger sister, but Hannah was always considered superior by everyone who mattered in the girls' lives. Even their mother, before her mysterious death in a riding accident, seemed to dote on little Hannah and paid only token attention to Sadrina. Despite all of this, Sadrina never felt anything but love and devotion for her little sister, and when they were old enough to begin the more rigorous training demanded of their eventual role in the Church, they would lean on each other heavily just to make it through every day.

The Church rigidly adhered to three stages of development of those who were considered to be their next great leaders. The first was that of mental facility. Like all novitiates, the first responsibility was to memorize the text of the Book of the Creator and be able to recite any verse without fail upon command. This was accomplished through repeated reading, recitation, and testing by an assigned acolyte. For the twin girls however, this tenant was expressed through demanding physical trial along with the rigorous mental stimulation. Each of the girls were responsible for illuminating their own copy of the Book of the Creator. The Book had to be copied perfectly, no room for error, before they would be allowed to eat or sleep. These fasts, these purifications of the flesh, were supposedly necessary to leave the soul free to search for and absorb the knowledge being communicated by the Creator. More than once both Hannah and Sadrina succumbed to either hunger or exhaustion and were forced to undergo additional purification. They would be placed in tubs of hot salt water, so hot that it would nearly scald their skin, and then would be scrubbed with metal wire bushes in order to purge the unclean energies from their bodies. If they would cry out either because of the heat of the water or the pain of the scrubbing, the process would begin anew. The goal was to redirect useless physical discomfort and emotional outbursts into something far more constructive. Total and complete adherence to the teachings of the Book of the Creator required control over the promptings for emotion and to uphold the dignity of human nature. Those tasked with carrying the sacred teachings to the faithful of the world had to demonstrate wisdom through imperturbability in the face of the non-believers. Yet at the same time an unfeeling emissary of the Word would lack empathy and the ability to truly assist the faithful and those seeking their faith. Therefore, the goal of the denial of one's lower desires would serve to strengthen the acolyte's will and deepen spiritual power. It was viewed by the hierarchy of the Church of the Creator that the purity of mind and mental facility were necessary for properly communing with the Creator and relaying His love.

The second tenant became a reality as soon as the twins reached puberty. The changes of the body marked by the passage into womanhood necessitated a moral vitality that suppressed transitory bodily desires in favor of an investment in otherworldliness and a dedication to a commitment to divine servitude that eschewed defilement of the body and physically-oriented living. Sadrina and Hannah's diets were immediately changed to strict vegetarian, with the girls only able to eat that which they grew in the Heart of Stone's gardens with enforced fasts designed to liberate the body. Once per year the girls were sent on their pilgrimage to the coast of Albitonin, three days' walk away. They were to travel on foot, with no supplies, sit in contemplation and prayer for one full day on the beach and then return to Heart of Stone. Through the whole pilgrimage, they were not allowed to eat. If their journey took too long, or they slept too much, they would starve. This was the ultimate test of faith, the ability to move beyond physical limitation and the ability to find faith beyond suffering. It was the reaffirmation of the dedication to service to the Creator and all of His commandments. As they aged, the girls endured increasingly strenuous physical trials which were designed to harden the body against the material world and leaving it prepared for the world that existed beyond the veil. In the winter months they would often be made to meditate naked in the snow. In the hottest days of the summer, they would be locked in small metal boxes, barely large enough to fit into, and left in the hot sun all day. They were then expected to recite the words of the Book of the Creator as loud as they could while lesser novitiates circled around them, completing their own physical trials. These acts were devotions to the will necessary to carrying the burden for all of the faithful on Espre.

In addition to the tenants of mental facility and moral vitality was the virtue of spiritual surrender. In between the physical trials, education, and teaching of the Word to those less advanced in their training, the twins were expected to spend hours in meditation. These meditations were often guided, with the intention of examining personal flaws or character deficiencies that would hold them back from spiritual perfection. Oftentimes, these meditations would take the form of long introspective journeys into the natures of guilt, sun, death, life, punishment, and duty. Every aspect of the soul's journey in the light of the Creator had to be explored if one was to be able to answer all questions raised by the believers and those with doubts about the true path. The leadership of the Church of the Creator believed that the inner life was as important if not more important than the outward life. This life was best expressed through upheaval and torment of the soul; methodically cultivated fear and dread, sadness so profound that tears run out, and extreme anger and rage to the point that the blood felt like burning lava. In time, Hannah and Sadrina were separated for their own growth, and to break the bond between then that was perceived to be holding them back. The wedge driven between the two sisters was violent, painful, and would have unseen ramifications for years to come. But in the end, Hannah would prove to be everything that the Church of the Creator needed her to be, a champion, a faithful follower, and an inspiration for every member of the Church. Despite herself, Sadrina was always proud of what Hannah accomplished, first in her role as a member of the Knights of the Flashing Blade, and then as the High Priestess of the Church of the Creator.

As the thoughts of the rigors of the Church of the Creator filled her mind, the pain in her body began to wane. She had suffered more at the hands of those who were expressing the love of the Creator than she ever could at the hands of a little man like Kaitain Lorien. He was unclear and erratic in his questioning, and Sadrina as she passed in and out of consciousness soon began to think that the man was cruel for the sake of being cruel, as though he believed that it was expected of him. However, there was no mistaking the hate that fueled Kaitain. He hated the Dark Gods, he hated any who doubted his right to lead Cadaria, he hated the dragons, he hated the Church of the Creator; basically, he hated everyone who wasn't himself. But hatred was predictable, and had only one end.

Kaitain would die, consumed by his own hatred, but not before he took countless innocent lives down into the flames with him.

Sadrina forced herself to a sitting position and put her mind someplace where she did not feel the pain that rocketed through every part of her. Her first responsibility now was to figure out where she was and whether or not she had moved from one dangerous situation directly into another. The room was small with a little fire burning in a fireplace on the opposite wall from the bed. It was enough to keep the temperature in the room comfortable, but not enough to take all of the chill out of the air. Obviously, based on the time of year, the only places that would be this cold in Cadaria would be the farthest northern reaches of Rashaleb. Of course, Sadrina knew that the ability to use portals could have taken her anywhere on the face of Espre, from the southernmost tip of the Dark Continent of Mythryn, to the uninhabitable Northern Wastes. Fortunately, she did not have long to wait for an answer to her questioning mind.

A simple wooden door to Sadrina's left opened softly, and a woman with somewhat familiar features entered, her face passive but comforting. The woman carried herself with an air of confidence and control that Sadrina immediately recognized as someone who came from royal stock, but there was an ease to the movement, the same kind of ease that Sadrina had seen in Midarin Rice. Perhaps this woman was one of those that the Dark Gods referred to as the Forgotten, other divine beings that had been sent to the world of Onea but chose not to join the Dark Gods on Mythryn. The woman did not approach, she simply stood at the door and closed it gently behind her, letting Sadrina adjust to her presence. Sadrina could not shake the feeling that she had seen the woman before. There was something about her eyes, something that stirred unresolved emotions in the former Queen of Mythryn.

"How are you feeling?"

The woman's voice was soft and comforting, but not practiced. There was an edge to her tone that could have simply been passed off as nervousness, but Sadrina was sure there was something more.

"Like I've been tortured by a madman."

Sadrina's tone was gruff and direct. She did not have the time or the patience for the niceties of courtly manner, and though the woman before her presented as though she was royalty, there was no way to be sure, and no reason to be polite. The torture that Sadrina had suffered at Kaitain's hand would have lasting impact even if all of the physical infirmities completely healed. There was damage beneath the skin that she would wear the scars of for the rest of her life.

"That's probably because you were," the woman said with no humor in her voice, "at least two."

A flood of memories threatened to rush into her mind, and Sadrina did her best to hold them at bay. Like a river already swelled to its banks, her mind was not prepared for the stress of more information should the damn of trauma break and flood her brain with new thoughts and memories to process. It would all be too much, and it would likely be even more debilitating than her physical ailments. When Sadrina did not quip in response, the mysterious woman took a slow step forward, letting Sadrina see the movement coming before she made it. Sadrina was aware that the woman was doing everything in her power to keep her at ease.

"You've been Kaitain's prisoner for quite some time now, brought to him by Ivan Quicksilver, the culmination of a longer plan concocted by Kaitain Lorien before Ivan's false defection. The goal was for Ivan to learn all that he could about the inner workings of the Dark Gods, do as much damage as he could, and then bring him a prisoner whom he could extract information from and then publicly execute to prove his righteousness as leader of the Cadarian Empire. He would be the first to kill a member of the Dark Gods since Terrik Lorien."

Sadrina frowned.

"Except that I'm human, like he is. Everyone would know who I am, the sister of the High Priestess of the Church of the Creator, the most respected Knight of the Flashing Blade, and the moral compass of the entire Cadarian Empire. He wouldn't have accomplished anything."

The woman shook her head.

"You've been out of touch for too long, Sadrina. Your sister is missing and presumed dead. There is a new High Priestess of the Church of the Creator, and all of the members of the Knights of the Flashing Blade are either dead or marked as traitors. And even if she was still the High Priestess, Kaitain has outlawed worship of the Creator and has decreed that those who still stubbornly put their faith in the Church of the Creator will have their lands, belongings, and rights stripped from them and forced into servitude until they renounce their beliefs. That is, if they survive long enough to have that indignity forced upon them. This is a different Cadaria than the one you left when you joined Pike and the Dark Gods, Sadrina. One that is much darker and devoid of hope."

Sadrina felt the woman's words like a cold hand gripping her heart. Unlike her husband, Sadrina had no hatred for the Cadarians, and often sued for peace and reconciliation when she was allowed to speak to the Council. She had few allies in that chamber, least of all her husband and his pet Serrina, but some, like Midarin and Aryx seemed willing to listen. But there would be time to worry about recriminations later. Sadrina needed to know where she stood and what lay ahead of her.

"You seem very familiar to me, but I don't think I've ever seen your face before."

The woman took another step forward and stood merely one pace away from the side of the small bed. Though she had made every effort to not seem menacing, for the first time Sadrina felt threatened to her core. If this woman was indeed a member of the Forgotten, it was possible that she held a grudge against Pike and meant to exact some kind of revenge against him by killing Sadrina. Pike had always said that there were some who counted themselves among his allies that most days would rather let him die than come to his aid. While he was careful to say that he didn't think any of the other Dark Gods would act against him directly, he also didn't rule anything out.

"Until I plucked you out of Kaitain's clutches there in Zevarit, Sadrina, we had never laid eyes upon one another. But that doesn't mean that I don't know you. In fact I think I know you better than probably anyone on this world could."

The woman paused for a moment and then continued.

"But the reason I look so familiar to you is that I believe you knew my daughter, Sabrina."

Sadrina's eyes went wide for the briefest moment, and then once she took hold of her emotions nodded gently.

"Then that would make you Cairyn Binosear."

Cairyn smiled.

"In another life," Cairyn said, the smile reaching her voice. "I have not been that person for quite some time. I've worn the name Calindria on this world much longer than I wore the name Cairyn during my life. There was a time when I was embarrassed of my name and my linage, and wanted to run from it. I even considered changing it at one point. Thankfully I was talked out of it by one who was far wiser than myself, though I was the lady and he was the backwards farm boy. But there, regardless of my desires, my life divided, so too did the lives of all of us who survived the fall of Onea."

Sadrina recognized the partially vague words and interjected in an effort to let her savior know that she was learned on the subject.

"Pike has told me about the Dark Mirror, and I've gotten some information from the other members of the Dark Gods that lived through it."

Cairyn motioned toward the edge of the bed and Sadrina nodded her ascent. Cairyn eased herself onto the edge of the bed and began to speak again.

"The Dark Mirror showed us all who we truly were, whether we wanted to know it or not. And while those members of the Dark Gods who remain can root themselves in the reality they came from, they do have the memories deep inside themselves of what they were in that other place. Some of the memories are too painful to acknowledge and so the whole of that experience is buried beneath the denials, but those who wish to learn from the failures of either of the worlds understand the truth. My daughter

Sabrina opened my eyes to what I had been on the world known as the Light reality, though it was not my native home. My shame at my blindness and failures kept me from seeing the truth until I was forced to remove the scales from my eyes. I am better for it now, but at the time I cursed my own daughter for her deeds. One version of myself shares more with you than I would have wished upon anyone, as I was Pike's wife and was the victim of his rages and his wandering eye. That is the version of myself that I am most ashamed of, but is not the one that brings me the most pain. In the world I consider the one that gave me the life I have now, I was loved in a way I never thought possible, and yet it was a love that was not mine, but one that I was privileged to inherit for a time."

Cairyn's words trailed off, and then after a moment as if remembering her purpose fixed her eyes on Sadrina.

"We all make choices in this life Sadrina. Some we make on our own, some we are forced to make, and some we believe are made for us. In the end however, we have to make peace with those choices. I made peace with the woman that I was never meant to be and with the woman that I have become. Unfortunately, it has led me to a crossroads that I cannot walk alone. That, more than anything, is why I secreted you away from your captivity and brought you here instead of taking you back to your home on Mythryn."

Sadrina's frown was all the answer that Cairyn needed.

"I know you don't understand everything yet. If I'm honest, I don't either. But perhaps together we can figure this out. But there are two other people who would very much like to meet you, and have a great impact upon what we do next. Now, you are not a prisoner, Sadrina, and if you want none of this and wish only to return to Mythryn, that can be arranged. But know now that the Citadel of the Dark Gods has fallen and your husband, or at least the part of him that called himself that, has fallen to darkness and is now in the service of the beast Dorovar."

Sadrina wanted to be surprised, but she just couldn't bring herself to it. Pike tried his best to hide his darker natures from Sadrina's eye, and she was adept at letting him believe that he had been successful. Sadrina knew all about the affairs, the petty wars, the murders, and the secret graveyard which housed the bodies of his victims. While she had never seen Pike as evil, and perhaps she should have, she saw the hole inside of him aching to be filled. The one who could fill that hole, or make Pike think that it could be filled would the one who would command his loyalty. If Dorovar had succeeded in tempting Pike away from the cause of life, then Pike would become the most terrible weapon in his arsenal.

"I do not like being in the dark, Cairyn, and I feel that I have been kept there for too long. I will receive your compatriots and together perhaps we can make sense of this world gone mad."

Cairyn nodded her ascent and half-turned toward the door. With a simple motion of her hand, the door opened fully and after a moment, two women entered. The first was a girl who could have been no more than seventeen with long straight dark hair but eyes that belied a wisdom and burden far beyond her years. Her features were very reminiscent of Cairyn's and it was clear that the two women were related in some way. The appearance of the second woman filled Sadrina with a combination of joy and dread. The appearance of the Dark Seer Jehna Feris was never met with joy as her tidings were perceived to be of ill events that were unable to be avoided. However, Sadrina had always counted the woman as one of her closest friends and most trusted councilors. No matter what else Cairyn said in the time that followed, if Jehna considered Cairyn an ally, then so would Sadrina.

"Of course you know the Dark Seer," Cairyn said turning back to face Sadrina, "but let me introduce you to my youngest daughter, Isabella. She is recently returned from Hedorah by way of Bellnoc, and she has quite a few interesting stories to tell."

Jehna moved past Cairyn and took hold of Sadrina's hand.

"There will be time enough for tales, my Queen," Jehna said with a gravity that only her words seemed to be able to carry without seeming forced or melodramatic. "But now we must speak of the last vision I gave to you. Do you remember?"

Sadrina smiled.

"How could I forget? You said it would be the last time I would see you. That you were headed to meet your fate. You said that Fate is conspiring both for and against the Dark Gods. That it would not be the power of the Dark Gods, or even the Creator that will hold sway. Innocence and love would aid and hinder the world. Through tragedy would come hope, and through hope would come destruction. That one man would wipe away the tears of the dragon, and one man would mend the glass heart. That I would help fulfill the legacy of your clan, though doing so might mean the end of my life, but not my death."

Jehna patted the back of Sadrina's hand.

"Good. Good. I was resigned to my fate, and yet the Creator's angel of death passed me by and instead passed his grim judgment upon those I had deemed to be my successors, and those I had passed my secret to. The poor girls met their end, but they protected their secret from him. Unfortunately, others have learned the secret, some in pieces and some in whole. The legacy of my clan is in danger, my Queen, and in my hour of need, I pray that you will heed my words and help me to save the one who is most important to what is to come."

Sadrina, ignoring the pain that raged in her body sat up straight and looked the Dark Seer deep in her eyes.

"Tell me what I must do."

Jehna's words filled the room like smoke, the weight of the responsibility of their next actions coating them.

"The bearer of the legacy is in grave danger, as some who have discovered her identity go now to end her life. This cannot be allowed to come to pass or all is lost. All hope in this world will die, and blood will flow on the day the tear falls. We do not have much time, my Queen."

Sadrina could feel the weight and pain in Jehna's words.

"Who is this woman, and where can we find her?"

"The woman's name is Jillian Corven, my Queen," came Jehna's grave pronouncement. "And it is not she who we must save, but what she carries. It must not be allowed to fall into the hands of any who are loyal to the Creator or to the beast. And as far as where she can be found, that we leave to young Isabella, as she knows where Jillian's path leads."

Foundation Imperfecta

The royal palace of the Kingdom of Water, Thorigald stank. It stank with the smell of death, blood, and malice. Bodies littered the throne room as well as the receiving hall that lay beyond the shattered double doors that separated the two chambers. Blood, gore and viscera were thick on the walls and floor, and some blood had even sprayed high into the air to catch the newly hung tapestries that swayed high above the carnage. The palace had only been completed the year prior to the slaughter, and had been a true jewel in the crown of the royal family of Thorigald, and a fitting seat of power for the Kingdom of Water. The palace itself had been constructed on huge columns of stone built up from the land and from the water to form what could only be called a man-made island where two rivers met at the edge of a lake. The cliff-side and waterfall that overlooked and flowed into the lake was also incorporated into the construction of the palace. Part of the waterfall flowed past the palace, diverted by huge metal baffles inserted into the cliff face. The remainder of the waterfall's water was collected and piped through the palace so that waterfalls fell in the throne room as well as in the private chambers of the royalty. The water also found its way into small channels that ran from the throne room, through the receiving hall, down through the middle of a set of steps, and out to a pool in the center of the parade grounds. It was as architecturally brilliant as it was decadent. But now the singular stream that ran through the center of the throne room was more blood red than crisp blue, and in a matter of hours the pool in the parade ground would be a grizzly effigy to the bloody battle that had decimated the royal family of Thorigald and those loyal to their cause.

Grawn Aplee, the Lord Shark of the Brotherhood of Phasia stood beside the throne and rested his blood-covered hand on the top of the gilded edifice. Still the king's corpse sat upon the gold and silver monstrosity that he had called a throne, Grawn's sword of diamond thrust through his chest with such force that it had not only penetrated the pompous ruler, but had also cracked the thick throne back, erupting through so that the point of the blade could be seen protruding. From where he stood, Grawn surveyed the entirety of the carnage that he alone had been the architect of, and it felt good to be the monster that he had been bred to be once again. He reveled in the feeling of ripping a pathetic human apart with his bare hands, and loved the feel of their blood coating his skin. Even without command of the full powers of the Blaze, Grawn was still a formidable warrior, and a terrifying opponent on the battlefield. More than a match for the soft men and women that called themselves the elite guard of the Kingdom of Water. When he was certain that no more of the weaklings were going to attempt to stop him from his task, Grawn reached down and pulled the diamond blade roughly from the corpse and flung it across the room where it shattered and dissolved into sand. Grawn then took hold of the former king by the overly opulent robes and pulled hard enough that the body flopped from his perch and landed face first, draped over the top and the first step of the dais. Grawn stepped over the body and then sat down on the throne, ignoring the pool of blood on the seat and the thick red veneer everywhere else. Just as Grawn was putting his feet up on the corpse of his fallen opponent, three new figures entered the throne room. They did not walk cautiously, but they also made sure that they were loud enough to be heard by the man that they had offered their service to.

Grawn had felt the trio coming long before they entered his field of view. Even among the mass of pathetic humans, and even diminished as they were, being in close proximity to his kind could not escape notice.

And though Grawn did not trust these three, they were his blood, so much as that was worth.

"Report."

Rane Larion was the first to speak. Grawn knew her only barely from their days back on Onea, during the War of the Ram in the third generation of the prophecies, but what he did know said that she could not be trusted to act with anything other than her own self-interest. She was a monster to be sure, but a shallow one, whose vices and pettiness had led to her extermination in a very short amount of time. But Grawn could not really expect much from the youngest generation of the phasia. They were flawed, imperfect copies of imperfect copies. None of the generations of phasia that followed the original six could be counted on to be anything other than fodder. Their power was merely a shadow of what it could have been.

"The whole of the palace has been secured. A great many of the soldiers have surrendered and have pledged to follow the banner of the Shark in the battles that are coming."

Erdric Yarrow spoke next. Grawn hated the man. He was a coward, a sycophant, and an imbecile. However, his ability to assume the form and voice of any person he had ever come in contact with was one that merited letting the wretched annoyance continue breathing.

"The members of the so-called Church of the Creator have been convinced that the Kingdom of Water was always meant to be ruled by the Lord Shark, and to fight against such providence is futile. They will help the believers see the wisdom of following this calling."

Grawn's frown could be felt across the room.

"Is that all this world has to offer? Cowards and fanatics? Those that traded one banner for another cannot be trusted to not make it their profession to trade allegiances, and the faithful will look for signs in every action and can be more dangerous than any opponent if they feel that their faith has been violated. Kill them all."

The high-pitched and grating voice of Farax Soar hit the air next. There were two things about Farax that were clear to anyone who had dealings with the man. The first was that he was every bit the genius that he professed to be when it came to the creation of servants for the cause. The second was that it took every ounce of control not to choke the life out of him every time that he spoke.

"If I may, Lord Grawn, there may be a better use for these wretched humans."

Grawn's hands balled into fists at the sound of the man's voice, but he restrained his murderous intent and nodded slowly.

"Your points, my lord, are well founded, and of course the humans cannot be trusted. They are the creations of our mortal enemy, and as long as a single one draws breath, they are a threat to our existence. But, to simply waste good resources is not a sound strategy."

Grawn had spent much of his extremely long life with a woman who loved to hear herself talk, and would constantly show how superior her intelligence was through the recitation of obscure facts with even more obscure words. At least Ellis' voice had been pleasant to the ear. Grawn often thought that Farax chose to use more words than necessary because he knew the effect that his voice had on others. Perhaps it was nothing more than another manipulation that Farax could bring to bear in his dealings.

"And what is your solution, Farax," Grawn said through gritted teeth, "to eliminate the problem of the humans' frailty and potential threat."

Farax's smile could have curdled fresh milk.

"Though our dear brother Jeroch has yet to surface upon this world, his method of converting these pathetic humans into something more conducive to our goals has not been lost. I had a great amount of time to study the structure of his so-called Black Tower, and I believe that I can effectively replicate and transform our new slaves into all manner of much more lethal beasts. Of course I would like to request that the first batch are converted into Snags, since they were never truly given their chance to serve in the proper capacity, and are far superior to…"

Farax's words died in his throat as Grawn raised a single hand. There was no application of power as there would have been if they were back on Onea, power was too valuable now to spare on such frivolous expenditures; even if it would have made Grawn feel good to forcibly shut Farax's mouth. But despite the violence that Grawn felt towards his annoying brother, the revelation that Jeroch's conversion abilities had not been lost when Onea fell made a smile crack the features of the Lord Shark. However, there was a concern nagging at the back of Grawn's mind. Though he often did his best to tune out the conversations that raged between his siblings Bryn and Ellis, he had learned enough over the centuries that he could still easily be counted amongst the most knowledgeable of all of the phasia.

"How will you replicate Jeroch's tower without access to the full powers of the Blaze? If my memory serves, Jeroch had to draw so deeply to create that monstrosity that it nearly killed him, and he had the help of both Kamen and Aryx."

Farax shook his head.

"Fortunately, this new breed of humans seem to be much more capable of touching not only the arcane forces of this world, but also some of them seem to be possessed with a kind of divine ability. They are still not powerful enough to pose a challenge to us, even in our diminished state, but what they lack in power, they more than make up for in potential. I could slave several hundred of them to the construction project and use them as a conduit to draw power. What does it matter if we kill a thousand in the construction of the tower when we're going to convert the rest of them anyway? Besides, at the rate these pathetic excuses for intelligent beings reproduce, we should have a near endless supply to stoke the fires."

Grawn's expression was impassive, but inside he was mulling the possibilities. While he had never been the tactical equal of his more devious brothers and sisters, one thing Grawn knew better than all the other phasia was the application of force and terror. With a large enough force of Jeresei, Stone, Shadowwalkers and Kalbraks, the pitiful humans would have no choice but to accept Grawn as their supreme ruler until the end of time.

"Very well, Farax," Grawn said finally. "Take whatever you need to make this new Black Tower a reality. But mark me, if I see one of those balls of fur anywhere near this palace, I will make sure that I leave just enough of you left to feel excruciating pain for the rest of eternity."

The smile didn't diminish from Farax's face, but the threat was taken with all of the seriousness that it deserved. Farax bowed slightly, a concession to the strength and leadership of his brother that grated upon the both of them, and then turned and left. Rane watched the willowy figure pick his way through the carnage, careful not to get any of the blood and gore on his long gray robe. She opened her mouth to speak, but Erdric's voice instead hit the air, coincidentally expressing her thoughts.

"Why do you tolerate that fool?"

Grawn leaned back, an audible squish coming from the pool of blood he was sitting in.

"You've never understood the nature of this war, Erdric. For all your schemes and your plots and your manipulations, what did you gain? For all of Aldridge's infiltrations, how many of the heroes of the Light did he kill? How did Taron fare when he stood toe to toe with Pike Rhuiden? How did Jeroch fare one on one with Cedric Binosear, or Gwydeon Sandar? Do I need to remind you Rane of your failures against Wolf Ranthall and Lissa Terian? As much as we view ourselves superior, how much has that superiority advanced our cause? For all of Ellis' vaunted intelligence, how much success did she truly have? So while I may know that I am superior to Farax and that I could rip him apart with my bare hands, I also know that his annoyance pales in comparison to his skill in crafting an army that will fight beyond the point of death against any foe. And so, as long as Farax fulfills the function that he is most suited toward, he will continue to be useful to me, and to my cause. When that usefulness is at its end, I will be sure to give him a quick death."

Erdric grimaced, and Rane tried to keep her expression as impassive as possible. Grawn scared her in a way she never thought possible. When they had stormed the palace, she and Erdric had done their best to control the guards on the outside of the walls, and she watched as Grawn waded into the ranks of the enemy with little care for their abilities. Spears stabbed at his flesh, arrows pierced him all over, and yet the vicious warrior continued forward. Those he didn't slash into pieces with his diamond blade found their throats crushed or their necks snapped in his massive hands. He was a force of nature, crashing like a wave over the unsuspecting and helpless men. They cowered at his might, and still he killed. It seemed that the more he killed, the stronger he became. There was no stopping his onslaught.

"Erdric," Grawn said finally, "go to the foolish faithful in Albitonin and work your manipulations. Find us some worthwhile subjects for Farax's experiments. Rane, head to the south and patrol our borders. We're going to need to consolidate power here before we start moving toward unification. I have spies to the east that should be bringing me information about what the other warlords are doing. Before long, these isolated struggles for power will boil over into a continent-wide war. However, this time, there will be nothing to stand in the way of the phasia taking their rightful place as the rulers of humanity."

* * * * * * * * * * * *

Year Twenty-two of the Founding Wars, the Creator's Calendar Year 27

The war had been going well on many fronts, and Grawn found himself finally back in his palace in Thorigald, the banners in the receiving hall denoting each of the kingdoms that had bent their knee to him. Already Iltorp, Albitonin, and Hedorah had fallen in line, and he had been in contact with the warlords who controlled Menoris and Oradrim. They were ready to fall in behind him, if he scored one clear victory over the forces of the upstart Terrik Lorien. Lorien had managed to unite Zevarit and Celidar with Rashaleb. He was facing massive resistance to the south with Pellatori and Bellnoc, as well as Grawn's forces harassing him to the west. However, Grawn was not without problems of his own that were preventing him from truly focusing on the upstart and his utter destruction. The kingdom to the south, the Kingdom of Storms Saldarine, had been Grawn's staunch ally under the direct command of his fellow phase Rane Larion. However, something had happened within the borders of the kingdom that had put an end not only to the alliance, but also to Rane. A messenger had appeared in the palace of Thorigald not a month prior, and within a lined box was Rane's head and a note which read, 'Alliances like marriages are not made to last forever.' Planning was too far along in Grawn's next set of raids to abandon them to deal with the unknown quantity to the south, but now that Grawn had returned to Thorigald, he would be able to deal with the upstart rebellious kingdom. However, a new challenge had met Grawn upon his return. Farax had suddenly disappeared, and the Black Tower stood empty of both potential recruits and also the battery slaves that fed the furnaces. Grawn had dispatched Erdric to find out what he could about Farax's disappearance, but he could not help but think that the two incidents were related. Perhaps Farax had defected to Saldarine and had betrayed Rane. It was not out of the man's character to attack his allies. Grawn was in the middle of pondering his options when a page entered the throne room, his head bowed and his eyes cast down to the floor. As useful as the Jeresei and the other creatures under Grawn's command were on the battlefield, he still found it useful to have humans around for the menial tasks required to run a kingdom. There were floors to be scrubbed and chamber pots to be cleaned. Humans deserved to work in filth, and so the humans were kept alive and unaltered in order to tend to that work. Grawn waited several moments longer than he had to before he finally broke from his thoughts and let his voice ring out through the chamber.

"What is it?"

Grawn could see the page tremble in response to the bark, and while normally the response would have brought him pleasure, he was too annoyed to enjoy the fear that he created. The page kept his eyes down and then began to speak.

"A visitor requests entry into your divine presence, Lord Shark. He claims that he is an ally who brings information vital to the success of your campaign."

Grawn considered for a long moment. This was not the first time that a so called ally appeared at his door requesting an audience with promises of riches, or information, or power. Some were assassins, some were charlatans hoping to gain information that they could in turn sell to the other warlords for a greater profit. Some were just madmen who were looking for the quickest way to die. Part of Grawn just wanted to have the annoyance dealt with and summarily executed. However, something in his gut told him that the offer might actually be genuine this time.

"Very well," Grawn said finally, his voice barely above a low growl, "show this so-called ally in."

The page bowed very low and then turned quickly and practically ran out of the room. Finally, Grawn allowed himself a smile. The name and reputation of the Lord Shark had flooded through the whole of Thorigald, and had traveled across the whole of the continent of Cadaria. Like his father Shau-ling before him, Grawn had become the nightmare of men. The bedtime story that parents told their unruly children before bed. 'Do as your told, or the Lord Shark will come and devour you in the night.' And yet, in the end, it was the parents who found themselves trembling under their covers when they heard the horns and saw the banners approaching. There were several parchments on the low table beside the throne, and Grawn picked up one of the reports from his spies in Zevarit. Terrik had been dismayed by Grawn's attacks on his supply lines, and it had caused him to lose considerable ground in his war against Pellatori. It was then that Grawn heard the heavy footsteps enter the throne room.

Grawn wasn't sure what he was expecting when he looked up from the parchment, but the man who stood just inside the entryway was equally a threat and a boon. The shorter than average, barrel chested monster of a man looked more like he was chiseled out of stone than shaped with flesh and bone. The beard on his chin was much longer than the last time that Grawn set eyes upon his brother, but there was no mistaking that look of death in Warron Ysamaran's cold gray eyes. Grawn made no sudden moves, instead opting to remain in his position, the parchment still held in his hands. Warron stayed near the entrance to the throne room, until finally Grawn motioned the other member of the phasia forward. Warron stopped two full strides before the dais.

"The Lord Boar," Grawn said, his voice even, "I never expected to see you again."

Warron regarded his older brother for a moment and then crossed his arms over his broad chest. Warron had not had many dealings with the original members of the phasia, save for Jeroch, but the stories that he was able to learn after their return to the fold brought a grudging respect from the often violent and self-assured Lord Boar. Grawn and the others had killed thousands, perhaps millions. They had leveled whole cities, devastated whole armies with their bare hands, and stood toe to toe in combat with Emries and lived to tell about it. And now, even without all of his powers, Warron knew that Grawn was as dangerous now as he had been all those millennia ago. He was the perfect representation of his animal totem. He was a perfect killer, with only one path; forward and through anything that stood in his path.

"I had no such illusions, Grawn," Warron said finally. "It is hard to go anywhere in the countryside these days and not hear about the exploits of the merciless warlord Grawn and the banner of the Shark that means death to any who do not bow to its might."

Grawn repressed the urge to smile.

"What do you want Warron? I don't expect that you are here to join my crusade, and so your appearance here, at this particular moment is highly dubious. Perhaps you are here to attempt to unseat me and to take command of my armies yourself. I assure you, that I have contingencies in place to prevent one of our kind from attempting to assume command of my armies. Farax may be cleaver, but I have learned enough from our much more intelligent siblings over the years to ensure that my machinations are never against turned against me."

Warron frowned.

"I have no intention of becoming a warlord, Grawn, nor am I interested in toppling you. I am simply here to provide you with some information."

Finally, Grawn placed the parchment back on the table and pushed himself slowly off of his throne. For the first time Warron could see the dark patches that stained the surface of what must have been a brightly gilded work of artifice at one point. However, what could only have been blood had tarnished the surfaces of the throne. Grawn stepped down one step with his left foot on the dais, turning his body in to a more defensible posture, his eyes never leaving his visitor.

"And what boon would you request for this information, Warron?"

Warron frowned.

"I want nothing from you Grawn. The information simply came into my possession, and now I am delivering it to you."

Grawn looked down at the floor for a brief moment, and then returned his gaze to the shorter man, a wide malicious smile on his face.

"There is nothing in this world that does not come without the expectation of reward or reprisal, Warron, our father taught us that. Even if the only reward you can expect is to leave the confrontation while still breathing. So I ask you again, Warron, what is the price of this information that you have brought me."

Warron slid his left foot back, taking a more defensive stance, but did not uncross his arms or make any other provocative movement.

"Very well, Lord Shark," Warron said, letting his tone and his words carry both his disappointment and his irritation, "I would like to be given leave to travel through your lands to Menoris. I have been told that I might find something of value there. Something that will give me direction."

Grawn's eyes widened for the briefest of moments, and then he turned, returned to his throne and perched just on the edge, hunched slightly, but looking as though he could spring into deadly action at any moment.

"And who told you this?"

Warron kept his features impassive.

"The same person from whom I learned the information I have for you. However, I have been sworn not to reveal the source under any circumstances. If it means you will not accept the information, then I shall have to find another way into Menoris."

Grawn leaned back, his thick fingers drumming on the arm of the throne. His eyes looked away from Warron, into the shadows that lay in the corner of the throne room, pondering for several moments. When he spoke again, he did not look back at Warron.

"Very well, Warron, you may keep your secret. But while you were prepared to provide your information without thought of compensation, my magnanimity does not extend so far as to allow someone like you free movement through my kingdoms. So I will make you a counter proposal. I will allow you your errand in Menoris and to wherever else that takes you within my lands, on the provision that you, here and now, bend your knee to me and swear to become my general in this war. You may have no wish to become a warlord, but before this war is done, you will either serve me, or you shall be dead."

Part of Warron wanted to rush up the dais and choke the life out of Grawn. But that was the old Warron, the Warron that preferred to see his world burn than to work with anyone. But he was trying to find a new path. There were ways to do a little evil while still doing good, that much he was sure of. So, slowly, and never taking his eyes off of Grawn, Warron eased himself down to one knee and lowered his head.

"I give you my pledge, Grawn, that once my errand is complete, I shall return to serve you in whatever capacity you wish."

Grawn considered just how long he would leave his younger sibling in that position, and while there was value in prolonged displays of subservience, that value was only to be found when the displays were genuine. Warron's acquiescence was a matter of convenience, nothing more, and as such, there was no pleasure to be gained from it. Grawn flicked his hand idly, and then looked back in Warron's direction, his eyes still floating past the man to the shadows.

"And so what is this information that has cost you your loyalty?"

Warron eased himself back to his feet and tried his best to suppress the frown he felt tugging at the corners of his mouth. When he finally spoke again, Warron kept his voice even and calm, even as he felt the tension and anger growing on the throne.

"As you've already been made aware, your general, our sister Rane Larion was murdered by the new ruler of the Kingdom of Saldarine.

However, while you may have suspected our brother Farax, that is not the case. Farax is also dead."

This brought Grawn's attention firmly back to Warron. But Warron did not give Grawn the opportunity to ask questions that he was not prepared to answer.

"He never saw it coming. The assassin was simply in his room and his throat was slit before he knew he was dead. Once Farax was dead, your not-so-secret Black Tower was cleared out in a matter of minutes, all of the slaves either freed or killed. I wouldn't bother looking for those that escaped, they are all far beyond your borders."

Grawn's fist slammed down on the arm of the throne and his voice sounded like thunder at the edge of a destructive storm.

"Who! Who could have done this? Tell me now Warron, or I swear I will rip your heart out and feed it to you!"

Warron weathered the verbal assault that he knew was coming and let it pass over him. He had seen everything that was going to happen up to this point, and though he was assured that he would survive this confrontation with Grawn, there was doubt that was beginning to creep into the back of his mind.

"If I knew the name, my Lord Shark, I would gladly give it to you, but my information does not extend that far. What I can tell you however, is that the Kingdom of Saldarine has renamed itself. It is no longer the Kingdom of Storms, it is now the Kingdom of Fire."

The explosion that went off in Grawn's mind took several moments to bloom on his face. It started with a grimace of pain that tugged at the corners of his mouth, and then quickly moved to a snarl that showed teeth so tightly ground together that Warron thought they would snap. Grawn's cold gray eyes filled with rage and his brow furrowed so hard that deep lines appeared on his face. His fist came down on the arm of the throne and the thick gold and silver slab fractured, sending a wedge of precious metal crashing down to the dais.

"Bryn!"

Blood flooded from the cuts on Grawn's fist, but the tyrant paid it no notice. But just as soon as the outburst began, it was over, and placid malice returned to Grawn's features. His eyes shifted again to the shadows, and he relaxed back into the throne as though nothing had happened.

"You have held up your end of the bargain, Warron," Grawn said finally, "and so I shall be magnanimous and keep to my portion as well. Run your errand to Menoris, but I warn you, do not keep me waiting long. I have many pathetic humans for you to kill."

Warron took several moments, trying to process what had just happened. When his hesitations started to become obvious, Warron bowed a respectable amount and then turned and left the throne room. Once Warron was gone, and the doors to the throne room were once against closed, a lithe form emerged from the shadows. Grawn had seen the young woman with long brunette hair several times, and though he did not trust her or the force that she claimed to represent, thus far her information had proved to be incredibly useful in establishing his dominance.

"I told you that your business with your wife and her plaything would not yet be at an end," Sabrina Binosear said, her voice full of the power granted to her as the Spirit. "Now you know the depths of their betrayal and their hatred of you."

Grawn, though the fires of hatred raged inside of him, did not rise to the small woman's bait. He knew what she was or at least what she claimed to be. If he struck out at her, she either would easily destroy him, or would be exposed for the fraud that she was. Neither outcome benefited Grawn or his crusade. So, Grawn restrained himself, his murderous frenzy momentarily contained.

"They will be dealt with," Grawn growled through clenched teeth. "It's been too long since I choked the life out of Bryn and watched the light go out of her eyes. That was over much too quickly. This time I'll make her suffer."

Sabrina's features never shifted from passive contempt.

"The leaders of the Kingdom of Fire are being dealt with another way, Grawn," she intoned with perfect calm, "and the Creator has sent me to collect on the agreement we made which put you in control of this massive army."

Grawn bristled.

"I took your information, woman, and used it as I saw fit. There is no agreement for me to live up to."

A ghostly white aura flared into existence around Sabrina, and Grawn had to shield his eyes from the miniature star that had exploded to life mere feet from where he sat. Even with his eyes shielded, Grawn could feel the searing light that pulsed with Sabrina's next words.

"Nothing is free, Grawn, or do you not remember your warning to Warron? You took the information greedily when it suited you, now you shall dance to the tune the Creator plays. Do you understand?"

The light faded, and Grawn returned his gaze to the woman, no longer doubting the veracity of her claims.

"What is it you want from me?"

"Nothing more than what you do best, Grawn," Sabrina said, a hint of sadness tinging her voice. "The Creator bids that you murder Terrik Lorien's wife and infant child. However, for the time being Lorien is to remain unharmed. His fate has already been written."

Grawn frowned.

"Why should I kill some insignificant woman and her whelp? I'm going to kill Lorien anyway, I'll make sure they're dead when I take his head."

Sabrina's eyes flared with power.

"Your destiny in your existence Grawn has never been to understand. Your destiny is to be what you were created to be, an efficient killer. I won't insult you by calling you a blunt instrument, so don't insult me by trying to be intelligent."

Grawn's protest died in his throat when the woman fixed her stare on him, and he felt the tendril of power reach out and wrap around his throat.

"Do we understand one another?" Sabrina's voice was filled with the cold violence of a trained killer.

Grawn couldn't have spoken if he wanted to. He nodded twice in ascent, and after blinking back tears from the pain in this throat and chest, he saw that the woman was gone.

* * * * * * * * * * * *

A day's travel south from the Palace of Thorigald, Warron stopped just outside the start of what would most likely become a small mining town. Even with all of the fighting that raged across the countryside, the humans were persistent in their desire to create as well as destroy. Though it was just as likely that these settlers would all be murdered in a raid as they were to actually thrive in their little community, Warron had to marvel at their ability to ignore the looming specter of fate.

"Fate has never been what defines humans, Warron," a voice said from behind the ancient man, "it is their ability to defy it that makes humans so disruptive to the Creator's universe."

Warron turned, but was not shocked to see the man who stood several steps behind him. Though the long brown cloak hid the brilliant white wings, there was no mistaking the at times grim countenance of Gwydeon Sandar. When the two had first met upon Espre, Warron was sure that Gwydeon had meant to kill his old enemy, but instead the two had become collaborators in a scheme that Warron had no chance to see the full scope of.

"And yet they don't have the ability to see that they are the center of everything," Warron added.

Gwydeon walked past Warron and look at the budding bastion of civilization.

"That's what Emries always wanted; beings that were just intelligent enough to shake loose the shackles of the Creator's dogma, but not intelligent enough to see how they influenced the pattern. Fortunately for us, he didn't realize just how much he gave us the ability to see."

Warron ran his hand across his long beard.

"Don't you mean them?"

Gwydeon turned at the word.

"It's not exactly as though you are human anymore," Warron continued.

There was a flash of white light in Gwydeon's eyes for just a moment, but as quickly as it was there, it was gone. Warron wasn't sure what the reaction was; anger, regret, sorrow. Whatever the reaction, it faded almost as quickly as it appeared, and left only Gwydeon's impassive expression in its wake.

"Were you able to successfully deliver the information to Grawn?"

Warron frowned.

"As you expected, he wasn't interested in a trade, and so I had to agree to become one of his generals when I'm through in Menoris. But yes, all I had to do was tell him the new name of the Kingdom of Saldarine, and he made the exact assumptions I'm sure you wanted him to make."

Gwydeon nodded.

"Rumors of Bryn and Aerith should keep Grawn off-balance and distracted until we're ready to move on him. However, there are more pieces that must be removed from the board before we can safely proceed."

Warron's frown deepened.

"Is that why you want me to go to Menoris? Am I removing an obstacle, or am I being removed?"

Gwydeon put his hand on the shorter man's shoulder.

"You have nothing to fear from me, Warron, and my hope is that you have a very long life once all of this business with Grawn is behind us. I'm sending you to Menoris to meet with some old friends. And perhaps, if we're all very lucky, the three of you can figure out how to get us all out of this mess in one piece."

Loyalty Earned not Bought

Year Five of the Just Emperor Kaitain "Dragonsbane" Lorien, Creator's Calendar Year 1872

Gwydeon was finished tearing down the command tent by the time Midarin returned with the few belongings that had survived their multiple encounters with dragons and demons. Gwydeon had learned to travel light over his years as the wanderer Wynne, but Midarin had become adjusted to her life in the Citadel of the Dark Gods. Fortunately for both of them, with their abilities they wanted for little. Connor and Gabrielle Peregrim joined Gwydeon and Midarin at the site of the command tent. Both seemed uneasy in the early light of the morning, and Gwydeon wondered how much of it was the position of their new alliance with members of the Dark Gods.

"Arent and Strum have the troops mobilized. We should probably keep a steady pace today to keep the men's minds off what is going on around them. By the time we reach Aldere everything should have normalized, but for now they're being asked to shoulder a bit more than any of them bargained for when the rebellion was well and truly joined."

Gwydeon nodded. Connor's suggestion was sound. A steady pace would keep the men from thinking too much. They could have gone with a forced march, but that might breed resentment in the ranks.

"You know your men, Lord Peregrim, and so I trust your judgement. Midarin and I are not here to assume control of your army, so please be the voice that commands the men."

Connor remained silent for a moment before nodding and turning back toward where the soldiers were quickly forming ranks for their march toward Aldere. Gabrielle lingered, watching her husband go before turning back to the Dark Gods.

"Connor will never say it, but he's relieved that you are letting the men take his orders and are not assuming control. There was a lot of talk throughout the night of the secret meetings being held in the command tent. There is enough fear and uncertainty in our enterprise, and so whatever stabilizing presence can be leveraged to ensure the men behave as they know they should is welcomed."

Midarin did her best to force a smile.

"We're sorry that we did not include yourself or your husband in our deliberations."

Gabrielle raised her hand and shook her head.

"I am grateful for it," the lady responded in her most practiced political tone. "I do not pretend to know the affairs of the Dark Gods, nor am I arrogant enough to believe that I would have had anything substantive to add. We are here for Quyhn, and to deal with Kaitain. The rest, of which I am sure there is a great deal, is beyond us. Though part of me is grateful that you are here to deal with those things that we cannot understand, I am also fearful that your very presence will draw those horrible things to us. I am thinking of course only of the safety of those who have entrusted their lives to us and have been willing to cast away everything they have been taught to be loyal to in order to make a better world."

Midarin adopted her own regal tone in her response.

"And we are only interested in insuring that there is a world left for you and your men to make better."

Gwydeon thought immediately that Midarin's words had been too harsh. He remembered that night all those millennia ago when he sat at the table in the center of Logan's small farmhouse in Onea and listened as the great Aryx Terian terrified them with stories of monsters out of their nightmares that they were supposedly destined to fight. Fate was a cruel mistress. Gabrielle opened her mouth as if to speak, hesitated, and then promptly closed her mouth again. She forced a smile, nodded first to Midarin and then to Gwydeon, then turned to assist her husband in his task.

"I think your diplomatic instincts are little rusty," Gwydeon said rubbing the back of his head. "You scared her to death."

Midarin didn't look in Gwydeon's direction, but instead let her eyes follow Gabrielle back to the growing troop formation.

"Good. I know we're just supposed to help Quyhn get a foothold in Aldere to make her a more legitimate voice in the Empire, but you know as well as I do that our very presence here makes the chances of getting to Aldere without drawing the attention of our enemies quite small. And if we have to divide our attention between defeating our enemies and protecting these soldiers, we'll most likely fail at both. And I know you, Gwydeon, I know what you would choose to focus on."

Gwydeon frowned.

"I may not be bloodthirsty like some of our former friends and allies, but I understand the stakes. However, I can't get Aerith's warning out of my head. He warned me that we were out of our depth in this part of the war, and that even though we have the powers that we have, the Children and the servants of Dorovar are fighting on a completely different level. Aerith even threatened that he would turn against us if we got out of line and tried to take the fight to our enemies. The mandate is to protect the people and make sure there is something left for them if we make it through this."

Finally, Midarin turned to face her husband.

"You know as well as I do that the Creator isn't going to let that happen."

Gwydeon sighed and shook his head. Of course, Midarin was right. Everything was angling in the direction of complete and total annihilation. That had been Sabrina's fear all along, and the reason why she had spent the last of her energy insuring that there would at least be a shadow of a chance for survival. Gwydeon had to still hold out hope. They had lost too much, too many friends and too many innocents.

"If we lose hope," Gwydeon said finally, "then how can we bring hope to these people. We have to at least believe that there is a chance."

Gwydeon swallowed hard. He didn't want to say what he was about to say.

"The Dark Mirror taught me all about despair. There were days after a bloody raid that we didn't think we would survive to see the next sunrise. Too many times, you and I got separated on the battlefield and I didn't know if I would find you dead or alive when the arrows stopped flying. You never would leave your archers, and the Shadowwalkers loved to rain down fire on the walls as you were trying to slow the advance of the Jeresei and Kalbraks. I know there were many times when I was on the palace grounds surrounded by so many enemies that there was no way you could have caught sight of me. And there was more than once when dead bodies had to be pulled off of me just to see if I was still breathing. I don't know how many years we lived like that, going from one battle to the next, living from terror to terror, only marking the days by whether or not we had to bury more friends. We had to be the hope for so many that we didn't have the luxury of despair. But we had hope of victory, even in the darkest of days, and that made it easier to bolster the spirits of our charges. Everyone was willing to fight and die to protect that small patch of land that we were able to wrest away from the Shadow. That's what we need to instill in these people. They need to see hope in the advancing darkness, and they need to be willing to fight and die for Quyhn."

Midarin's expression did not change, but she could not suppress a deep sigh. Lives were on the line every moment and she knew the stakes all too well.

"We'll make sure they're ready. No matter what comes."

She turned away without another word and set about ensuring the horses that Connor provided for them fit her requirements. Gwydeon watched her go, his heart feeling fragile in his chest. A diminutive voice broke him away from his moment of weakness.

"Is that truly how you see our chances? Like we're clinging to the edge of a cliff with just our fingernails between us and the abyss?"

For a moment, Gwydeon cursed himself for not being more discerning about where and how he voiced his concerns. He turned to see Quyhn standing behind him, looking both regal and small in her pale lavender dress. Rhionna stood behind her, looking more imposing than she had the night before, proof that she took her position as the young Empress's bodyguard very seriously. Gwydeon drew himself up to his full height and did his best to project confidence and strength.

"It would be foolish of any of us to think that the forces arrayed against us will simply let us walk into Aldere and establish a foothold. Whether it is one of the Children, or Dorovar, or the dragons, or even Kaitain, someone is going to try to stop us. And don't mistake resistance for concern. I've fought too many wars simply because one side did not want the other to exist. No ideological conflict, no desire for land, just pure, unadulterated hatred. But don't mistake my caution for fatalism either. I have no doubt we'll have to fight to achieve our goals, but as long as we believe in the righteousness of our cause, I believe that we can prevail."

Quyhn regarded Gwydeon for a moment, nodding.

"My father always said that pretty lies are the most disconcerting."

Gwydeon started to respond, but Quyhn's smile disarmed him.

"I don't mean to call you a liar, Gwydeon, I'm simply pointing out that hope is itself the prettiest lie. I have no doubt that you believe we have a chance at success, and I'm sure without you and your wife, our enterprise would already be doomed to failure. I just want you to know, now, that you need not protect me from what is coming. A ruler unwilling to face the truth, is a ruler who will avoid it and create their own truth at all costs. My father always said power makes it possible to replace one reality with another, but that false reality always comes at the cost of blood."

Gwydeon could only nod in recognition of the old axiom.

"Your father was a wise man. I'm sorry I didn't get a chance to know him."

"I think he would have approved of what we are trying to do," Quyhn responded after a hard swallow and a slight shift of her stance at the discomfort of the subject. "He wouldn't have liked the circumstances that forced it, but hard times require hard actions."

Before Gwydeon could respond, Quyhn drew herself up again.

"I'm sure there is much to do before we depart, so I shall leave you to it. Hopefully we will be able to talk of happier subjects once we have reached Aldere."

Quyhn nodded to Gwydeon and turned quickly on a heel and made her way back in the direction of where her tent had been. Rhionna lingered for a moment.

"Your Quyhn is an impressive young woman."

Rhionna's look made it clear she did not appreciate Gwydeon's word choice, but the blank stare that answered her glare made Rhionna realize that he had not meant the words in the way she had taken them.

"Yes, she is," Rhionna replied curtly.

She turned to follow Quyhn, leaving Gwydeon standing alone and completely confused. Women were never his strong suit, and it had taken him lifetimes to just begin to understand the subtle hints that Midarin would give him with her tone and her body language. Pike and Logan had always been the ones who understood women better, or at least it always seemed that they did. Of course, Logan had been in love with one of the most headstrong and stubborn women on the whole of Onea, and Pike had been hilariously fated to be intertwined with a woman who could outwit him and out fight him. In the end, Gwydeon had been the one who ended up spending several lifetimes with the woman he loved, and despite their challenges had been able to craft something of a happy ending. When Midarin returned with the horses, any trace of annoyance with their previous conversation had faded, and the pair fell into a practiced confident silence. They knew what was ahead, and they knew that the only things they could control in the days ahead were their own reactions and their own fear.

* * * * * * * * * * * *

The first day of the march toward Aldere was uneventful, and that was the best thing that any of the leadership of the army of the Lordhill Rebellion could hope for. The soldiers quickly became accustomed to seeing the four Dark Gods riding on horses and not flying through the air like demons out of a nightmare. The pace was steady and after a few hours most of the men came to see Gwydeon, Midarin, Liara, and Mirana as nothing more than members of the command group that rode at the vanguard of the marching troops. Quyhn had forsaken riding in a litter and instead rode on horseback with Rhionna at her side and Mirana and Liara behind them. The four seemed to be endlessly chatting through the whole day, with Mirana and Quyhn carrying most of the conversation. Gwydeon caught sight of Duncan several times during the march, and he very easily blended in to become just another faceless soldier in the ranks. If Gwydeon didn't know to look for him, he doubted that Duncan would have stood out at all. Gwydeon spent most of the day speaking to Connor, Arent, and Strum, giving them a crash course on the tactics of their potential enemies. Most of their soldiers had never fought pitched battles against Jeresei and Shadowwalkers, let alone flights of angels. Gwydeon sought to humanize the inhuman enemies for his new allies, to give them hope that even mortals could survive engagement with the forces that could be brought to bear against them. Midarin found herself riding mostly with Gabrielle and her small retinue. The conversation was largely polite small talk until the two began a lengthy discussion about the royal practices of Midarin's original home of Brea. Gabrielle seemed fascinated with their system of government, one that Midarin took for granted. The afternoon saw the conversation turn to more theoretical discussion about the nature of power in politics and how to help Quyhn craft a better government in the face of the failures of Kaitain Lorien. As dusk approached, Quyhn joined the conversation, eager to learn from the two more experienced women. She soaked in as much information as she could, asking thoughtful questions when she felt it appropriate. As evening approached, Connor called for a halt and for the troops to make camp.

Unlike the night before, the soldiers erected a simple marching camp with small fires and bedrolls instead of tents. The only tents that were erected were for Quyhn and Rhionna, Mirana and Liara, Connor and Gabrielle, and one for Midarin and Gwydeon. Gwydeon however was restless and would not be able to sleep. Fortunately, his nature as a Dark God allowed him to forgo human requirements like food and sleep for extended periods of time without deleterious effects. Instead, Gwydeon chose to walk among the soldiers, sitting with the night watchmen and sharing stories of battles and homes that would likely never be seen again. The men were naturally tense when Gwydeon first approached, but in time they began to see him as just another soldier. He spoke their language, and they appreciated a leader who would spend time with the rank and file instead of always riding above them. As dawn approached, Connor was up early, also walking among his troops. It was a clear demonstration of why his men trusted him as much as they did. The two old soldiers sat together talking about nothing as they watched the sunrise with the last watch. Connor quietly gave the break camp order to the watch, and the soldiers moved quickly to follow the orders leaving Connor and Gwydeon sitting together in the advancing morning light. As soon as he was sure that none of his soldiers could hear his words, Connor turned to Gwydeon.

"When do you think the attack will come?"

Gwydeon half-turned to Connor and regarded him for a moment before shaking his head. Connor reached out and put his hand on Gwydeon's shoulder.

"I'm an old soldier Gwydeon, and I know this feeling. It's coming, I can feel it in my bones."

Gwydeon sighed and nodded.

"I feel it too. Whoever is coming is aware of us, but only just. When will depend on how quickly they can marshal their forces. Unlike this army, those that are coming will not have the impediment of distance. And they can be upon us before we know they are there. We still have three days of steady march before we will reach the site of the Palace of Aldere. Of course, we could increase the pace, but then the soldiers would be worthless in a fight. Our enemy will know this, and they will time their attack when we are at our weakest. I would guess either tonight or tomorrow night before dusk. When our troops' bellies are grumbling for food and their eyes are drooping and their minds are thinking of sleep; that is when they will strike. And unfortunately, there is nothing we can do to stop them. All we can do is be vigilant. The first engagement will be the bloodiest."

Connor tensed.

"My men are up to the challenge, Gwydeon."

Gwydeon turned to face Connor.

"I don't doubt your men's training, Connor. But whatever floods through those portals or falls from the skies will be unlike anything your men have fought before. Our enemy will have the element of surprise, and they will be able to pick the ground upon which they want to fight. My only goal in the first engagement will be to keep the men from breaking and running. If they hold their ground despite the death and the fear, we may have a chance."

Connor rose and turned back toward where the troops were beginning to muster. He put his hand on Gwydeon's shoulder again.

"If you and the other Dark Gods can show my men that they can kill whatever comes, then I promise you, they'll hold."

Connor returned to his troops and Gwydeon was left looking at the sunrise. He couldn't shake the feeling in the deepest parts of himself that this would be the last sunrise that many of the men in the army would ever see. He knew that feeling all too well, and what disquieted him the most was the fact that that feeling had thus far never been wrong. He had been alive too long and had seen too many battles. And like Connor, he knew all too well the feeling of impending doom on the wind. Yes, their adversary was coming, and Gwydeon feared that this time it might be too much to handle.

* * * * * * * * * * * *

The damnable rain started at midday. There was not a cloud in the sky and then suddenly the storm was on top of them. A single streak of lightning followed by a peel of thunder was all that announced the storm moments before the deluge was unleashed. The hard rain fell in sheets immediately soaking the ground and turning the steady march into a turgid slog that ground nearly to halt because of the deepening mud. When another flash of lightning crossed the sky, Gwydeon thought he saw a form standing on a ridge far to the east, but when he blinked it was gone. It could have been a trick of the light and the rain of course, but deep in his heart he knew that there had been something on that ridge. Once the damage from the hard rain had been done, the pace of the rain slowed, and found a steady rhythm that would simply keep the march of the soldiers unbearably slow. Connor and the rest of the command group considered setting camp, but eventually it was decided to attempt to press on and outlast the storm. Three hours later, it seemed like a poor choice.

It was difficult to tell the time of day because of the steady rain and the voluminous black clouds that had filled the sky overhead, but through the cracks in the firmament, Gwydeon could tell that the sun was still up. Gwydeon had heard several of the men grumble something to the effect of what good was it to ride with Dark Gods if they couldn't stop the rain. Gwydeon had had the same thought of course. However, two things stayed his hand. The first of course was that if the storm was natural, using abilities to force it to move along or even dissipate it completely would have drawn attention from everyone with power for miles in all directions. Secondly, and most importantly, if the storm was not natural, the chances on overcoming the power behind it might have been futile and ultimately self-defeating. This wasn't a storm conjured by thousands of Jeresei, this storm reeked of divine power, and in the pit of Gwydeon's stomach, he feared the worst. At the start of the fourth hour of steady rain and miserable march, those worst fears were realized.

There was no warning when the strike happened short of the hairs standing up on the back of Gwydeon's neck. The first bolt of lightning lanced down from the dark clouds and struck the ground in the center of one group of soldiers. The resulting explosion sent several men flying through the air and landing in puddles of mud with sickeningly deafened thuds. Fortunately, none of the men survived the initial strike of lightning and thus were spared the pain of their fall back to the ground. The second bolt followed hard upon the first, striking the ground at the feet of Strum's horse, sending he and his horse tipping backwards where Strum struck the ground first, his horse falling atop him. Later they would discover that Strum's head hit a rock, snapping his neck and killing him instantly. It was a much more merciful death than it would have been otherwise. The third and fourth bolts came a split second later and were so blinding in their ferocity that Gwydeon could not see until it was too late what had happened. But when his vision had cleared, the horrific burning corpse of Gabrielle and Connor Peregrim were daggers in his heart.

Finally, Gwydeon had scrambled out of his saddle and embraced his powers. He had never attempted anything like what he was about to try, but if he did nothing, whoever was controlling the lightning would have been able to decimate the entire Lordhill rebellion in a matter of seconds. In his mind he could see his powers extending like a bubble from his extended arms, reaching skyward. At first the bubble was small, extending only a few yards, and felt weak. A moment later, Gwydeon felt another rush of power and out of the corner of his eye he saw Midarin mimicking his gestures. There was more action behind Gwydeon, and he knew that both Mirana and Liara had added their powers to the mix to strengthen the shield. An armored figure moved up beside Gwydeon and he too had his hands raised to the heavens, and Gwydeon silently thanked Logan that Duncan Rhuiden had been added to their number. A new cadre of bolts raced from the heavens, striking the invisible shield and dancing across it in a spectacular light show of sparks and shimmers. Had the display not been so deadly and dangerous it might have been considered beautiful. Dozens more bolts struck the shield in vain before the onslaught ceased. The rain too faded the next minute, but Gwydeon and the other Dark Gods did not release the shield. Then, several yards before the vanguard of the army, the thick mist created by the rain and lightning parted to reveal a single figure who approached slowly. When Gwydeon saw the face of the woman who approached, bile rose in the back of his throat, and he nearly lost control of the shield.

Rachel Core stopped three dozen paces from where Gwydeon stood, a bow in her hand and the power of the Creator wrapped around her like a cloak. When she spoke, her words carried through the whole army as though she was standing beside each person at the same time.

"I expected more," she said, her voice cold and hard. "After all of the sieges we planned together, after all of the pitched battles and hopeless odds, I never thought you would allow yourselves to be ambushed so easily."

Gwydeon swallowed hard, but did not let the stress show on his face. Of course, she was right, but that was another argument for another time.

"I see the Creator has found himself a new puppet."

The jibe passed between them, but no reaction showed on Rachel's face.

"What do you want, Rachel?" Gwydeon said moments later.

Rachel pointed toward the army, the intensity in her voice raising.

"You will surrender Mirana and Liara Ranthall to me and I will let you continue on your pointless quest to install your little princess onto her broken throne."

Midarin's voice returned, a feral growl mixed with it.

"And if we refuse?"

Lightning crackled in the sky above Rachel.

"Then you will all die, and I will take the children of heaven over your burned corpses."

Behind Rachel dozens of portals opened and flights of warrior angels burst through, flaming swords in hand. Beside Rachel two monstrously large angels, each at least fifteen feet tall simply materialized out of nothing, with spears twice their height in hand, tipped with flaming points that themselves had to be six feet long.

"Do not test me, Brother of Angels," Rachel said finally, "or you shall all meet your end at my hands."

Chapter CVI

The Traitor of the Mind

Year Four of the Just Emperor Kaitain "Dragonsbane" Lorien, Creator's Calendar Year 1871

Derelor stared upward at the stars in the darkening sky and breathed a shallow ragged breath. Out of the corner of her eye, she could see the remnants of her right wing. The membrane of the wing had been ripped nearly to shreds, and the wing itself had been torn from where it sprouted from her shoulder. The bloody stump still spilled thick red viscous vitae to the ground, and Derelor could feel the pain from its missing familiar weight rocketing through her body. But that was only one of a myriad injuries plaguing the proud creature. There were countless bones broken and even more numerous cuts that freely oozed blood. Talons on all four clawed hands were broken, and more than a dozen teeth had been sheared off nearly at the jawline. Laying on her side, looking up at the sky, Derelor felt the blood and bile rising up in her throat. The one called Maedoc had injured her venom glands early in the fight and deprived her of her ability to spew the noxious poison mist at her opponents, but the act had also had another consequence. Her own poison was seeping into her bloodstream, slowly liquefying her internal organs, and robbing her of her life faster than either of the Adhradair understood. She would have the final vengeance. The information they sought could not be rendered from her dead flesh, and they would gain no victory from their momentary triumph. But she had underestimated the two warriors at her own peril. How had they disarmed her and immobilized her so quickly? What abilities had they received from their patron Dorovar, and just how powerful had he become? Regardless of the answers to those questions, Derelor's time was almost at an end, and she would spite Dorovar with every last breath if she could.

"And now, dragon," Maedoc said coldly, his foot coming down hard on Derelor's neck, "you will tell us what we want to know. Tell us what became of the High Priestess's soul."

Derelor's wheezing laugh rasped from her injured throat.

"You fools have no concept of what you are asking, have no concept of what is really occurring, and I will gladly take what I know to the grave to thwart your misguided quest."

Luighsech pulled his compatriot away from the convulsing creature and knelt down so that he was eye to eye with the beast.

"We have spent thousands of years in captivity, Derelor, paying the price for the treachery that you helped to perpetrate. It was you, along with Stormbane and Shadowweaver that have led us to this point, and before the end, you will all be brought to account. But I give you this promise, dragon. Thus far, Dorovar and those loyal to him have indiscriminately targeted all dragons, their progeny and those who ally with them. If you tell us what we want to know, with no falsehood and no omission, Dorovar shall restrict his fury only to those directly associated with the fall of Loinn. They cannot be spared for what they have done, but you could save the whole of your breed from extinction."

Again Derelor laughed.

"And what good is your word, servant? How can you speak for the abomination when you are nothing more than a slave to his will? His vengeance will know no limitations. He must kill us all as he has sworn to do or he shall be impotent to his own desires. He wishes to rule above all Creation with no ability to rule himself."

Maedoc rushed forward with his sword raised, but Luighsech held a hand up to restrain his hot-blooded companion.

"The Adhradair are of one mind and one temper, dragon, and the words one speaks are spoken for all. While once we spoke in unison with the voice of the High Priestess and the goddess Raenera, we now speak with the voice of Dorovar. And if I say here and now that the dragons will be spared and allowed to find a place in the new Cosmos that Dorovar will create, then it is the will of Dorovar that it shall be so."

Derelor fell silent and closed her eyes. She seemed to consider Luighsech's words and then finally opened her eyes once more and spoke. Her voice was soft, barely above a whisper, but still loud enough that both members of the Adhradair could clearly hear.

"For supposedly intelligent beings, the wisest of your race, you are remarkably dim. You have yet to grasp even a fraction of what is at stake. Do you think for a moment that the Creator would allow your precious Dorovar his rebellion? Do you think for a moment that He would not intervene to prevent such an occurrence? Even the Children are not so foolish to believe that their schemes can escape his notice. They simply have the audacity to believe they are powerful enough to move beyond his reach. Remember mortals, and mark me well. We were there at the beginning of all things. We were there when the Creator made the Children, and we were there when the first of these foolish proving ground worlds were established. We have seen the raw power of Creation first hand. Your Dorovar, no matter how much power he has amassed, is not the equal of a Child of the Creator, and they could be crushed in the blink of the Creator's eye. Do you not see that it is not Dorovar's long game that is being played, but the Creator's? This is all a game for Him to get exactly what he has been looking for since the beginning of Creation. The means to transcend this Cosmos, to learn about the nature of His being, and to redefine the terms of reality. This is all just temporary, disposable, a façade. In the end, this will all be nothing more than a second in the space of eternity, and you will be nothing more than forgotten motes of dust floating in the formless void."

Maedoc's voice cut through the tension holding them both.

"If we are helpless to stop what is happening, and we are so insignificant, then there is no point in not telling us what we want to know. Where is the soul of the High Priestess?"

Derelor's low growl was one of frustration and pain. She knew she had little time, but the tediousness of the questioning made her wish that the two former humans would simply let her die. In the end though they would be taught the utter futility of their lives and their actions.

"Very well. Foolish and short-sighted to the end," Derelor said finally. "The soul…"

A shockwave of force knocked both Maedoc and Luighsech off their feet and sent them flying a dozen feet backward. Maedoc had to catch himself on a rock outcropping to keep from going off the edge of the cliff. Luighsech came to rest in a sharp bed of broken stones that slashed deep gouges down the whole left side of his body and blinded his left eye. When they both were able to look up, they saw the creature who had caused the disturbance.

Standing over the fallen body of Derelor was the incredibly muscular form of a dragon with mottled brown skin the shone with an almost iridescent glow in the moonlight. Short cruel spikes ran up the lengths of each appendage, as well as up both sides of the creature's long neck. The long row of spikes that ran from the back of the dragon's head all the way down the length of its back to the tip of its tail looked more like two foot long razor-sharp needles joined at the base by webbing that gave them considerable structural support. The dragon's head was on the smaller side compared to other breeds, without an elongated snout. Its brilliant red eyes were situated close to the middle of its head, just above where the upper and lower jaw hinged together. Its teeth were shorter and spread farther apart than most of the larger dragons. It stood only perhaps double the height of an adult human, but was so laden with muscle that it could have rivaled the strength of even the largest of the ancient monsters. The dragon's tail was twice as long as its body, neck, and head combined. It sat hunched over Derelor's fallen form, one clawed foot wrapped around Derelor's head. Its wings were stretched back, shimmering with odd patterns, bat-like and enormous. The top of the wings ended in hooked bony protrusions whose undersides glowed like razor-sharp daggers.

"I think that's quite enough of that," the dragon growled. "Derelor my dear, you were always too involved in your petty little intrigues to understand the true nature of what we were accomplishing for

Shadowweaver. But your time is ended, and I happily will be the one to end you."

The sickening crunch of Derelor's skull under the pressure of the new arrival's claw sent a wave of revulsion passing through both members of the Adhradair. Blood, brains, teeth and viscera spurted in all directions, and the dragon's red eyes flashed with pride at the violence. Now standing in the vital fluids of his former ally, the dragon fixed his gaze on the two former mortals who were just getting back to their feet.

"Stormbane the Traitor," Maedoc said with no attempt to hide the anger from his voice. "I've been looking forward to this day for millennia."

Stormbane's broken growl came out like laughter.

"Ah, if it isn't the Irrelevants, or the Erroneous, or whatever you called yourselves."

Maedoc's blood burned.

"The Adhradair."

To Maedoc the dragon's features took on something akin to a sneer.

"You humans with your quaint need to segregate yourselves from one another. Is it not enough that you are humans? You divide yourselves in such ridiculous ways. You divide yourselves by the color of your skin, by what line on a map you hail from, when you were born, and even how you give praise to the Creator for your pathetic little lives. For those who see themselves as vessels of the divine, you have done nothing but invent new methods of cruelty, divisiveness, and malevolence. And yet you laud yourselves for your altruistic intentions, and craft religions and systems of belief that praise you for the goodness in your souls. What hypocrites you are. On one hand you celebrate yourselves for your tolerance and drive to uplift your species while the other is brandishing a weapon to strike down someone whose only difference is one that has been invented by your own sick need for superiority. It is not enough to simply be, you must be more. Your greed is only outpaced by your vanity. And all the time you think yourself intelligent. You reason and you dream, but only succeed in creating ways to destroy yourselves. Were you to be half of what you dream yourselves to be, you might be worthy of acknowledgement by those with real power. If you had half the reason that you claim to have, you would have left behind your divisions long ago. But you are petty, and obnoxious, and should not even be considered true lifeforms. And so to us, you are nothing more than food, and a sour meal at that."

Luighsech, who was much worse for wear than his companion took a step forward and addressed the dragon. However, when he spoke, his voice had an obvious lisp due to the damage to his face.

"For one who claims to have such a low opinion of humans, you and the other supposedly superior dragons spend an inordinate amount of time interjecting yourselves in our affairs rather than, as you say, treating us as the food you see us to be."

Stormbane looked down his short snout at Luighsech.

"You are obviously the more clever one. I think your ally's head must have cracked several stones when he landed."

Maedoc held his ground, but Luighsech could feel the warrior's patience waning. Already his patience had been tested by Derelor's goading, and he would not be able to withstand prodding and insults from Stormbane. However, there were significant differences between the two dragons. Derelor, for all of her scheming and manipulations, was a warrior of the mind. She was much larger in stature than Stormbane, but the smaller more thickly built dragon was born for war. They had had a measure of surprise against Derelor, as she was not ready for the type of power that the members of the Adhradair had access to. However, that advantage would not be as pronounced against a creature like Stormbane. What's more, if they were unable to rend the information from Stormbane, the only remaining source of the information was the Demon Dragon Shadowweaver, a monster whose power was nearly unmatched within the whole of the ranks of the dragon race.

"But what you say, while pedantic, is true," Stormbane continued. "We have had to involve ourselves in human affairs because we broke the covenants of the Creator. We interfered in the war between two of the Children, and our actions resulted in blood being spilt in the Heavens. And so, we have been cast from the Heavens, never to return. In that way, we are no different from the so-called Dark Gods. Except our loss is far more lasting. So long as we are chained to these primordial worlds, we are diminished. And because we are diminished, we are divided."

Stormbane stopped for a moment, and then his next words came out with a growl filled with such ferocity that it threatened to shake both of the former humans from their feet once more.

"Make no mistake. The bane of dragon existence is the human, the pawns that think they're kings. You, like the Children, have no regard for the damage they cause. Raenera, Dorovar, Emries, Aerith, no difference. You fight, you lose. You win, you die. No difference. Advantage, futility. No difference. In the end, the humans will be destroyed. Nothing that you do will prevent that. Not Dorovar, not Kaitain, not Aerith, not any of them. The Children will be destroyed, those that are still alive. And now, it seems that even the dragons will be lost. Even Shadowweaver and Mariti Brightblade. The Creator has damned us all to fire. In a matter of days the whole of Creation will be consigned to fire."

Maedoc shouldered past Luigsech, his black armor stained with Derelor's blood.

"What do you mean days?"

Stormbane closed his eyes for a matter of moments, his head shaking slightly.

"And you are supposed to be exemplars of your race? How can you not feel it upon the wind? How can you not taste the power coalescing on your tongue with every breath? Does your blood not quicken with every moment that passes? We who have felt the touch of the Divine can feel the Winds of Creation slowing. The Creator has begun to withdraw his attention from his worlds and has focused it all here. When his focus has fully shifted to this world, the weight of his gaze will crush this pathetic ball of dirt into dust. There will be nothing left of us, and the Creator will be able to start again in another corner of the Cosmos. Perhaps the dragons will be reborn in another form, or perhaps the Creator will find new creatures to be the beneficiaries of his love."

Luigsech put his hand on Maedoc's shoulder and the two comrades locked eyes for a brief moment before Maedoc relented and allowed Luigsech to take up the parlay.

"Which makes our acquisition of the information regarding the soul of the High Priestess even more critical. With the soul, and the remainder of our Adhradair brothers and sisters, Dorovar will be able to supplant the Creator and protect that which has been slated for destruction."

Stormbane growled.

"Protect? Protect? You have the audacity to stand here and profess that Dorovar wishes to protect anything in this Cosmos? His only wish is to project his pain across all that the Creator has made, to make everything suffer the way that he suffered. What is worse, a world of indifference or a world of despair? Dorovar is a plague, a pestilence, and if he is allowed to spread his filth and poison across the face of the Cosmos, in time there will be no Cosmos left to be saved from him."

Luigsech raised one hand, the back of it toward the dragon.

"This is what Dorovar once was. Hard, unyielding, hostile. Dorovar was a man forged by three events. The first was the moment of his birth, when the High Priestess of that time read from the Great Tome of Order and gave Dorovar his place in the hierarchy of the Adhradair. Like all beings who dwelled upon Loinn, our places in the Cosmic Order were preordained. From the moments of our births, our courses were set. That was the strength of our world, the world that you destroyed. Our story was written from its beginning to its end, with no worry about fate or deviation from our purpose. When you and the rest of the dragons came to Loinn, you forced us to deviate from our appointed pattern, broke our covenant with the Cosmic Order, and changed the path of every life upon our world."

Stormbane's snort interrupted Luigsech's explanation.

"Never forget, we were invited."

Luigsech felt Maedoc's barely restrained rage peak again. But the wizened and oldest member of the Adhradair pressed on.

"Which leads to the second moment that has tempered Dorovar into what you believe him to be. The betrayal not only by our goddess Raenera, but by her siblings Emries and Talisia, in the bargain made with you that brought the dragons to our world. Stormbane the Traitor. You may not have been the architect of the destruction wrought upon Loinn, but you were certainly its instrument. You think us ignorant and arrogant about our place in the Cosmos, and yet the dragons are the most arrogant creatures in the whole of Creation. You see your place as unassailable given that you were there at the beginning. And in your minds, nothing could ever surpass you. And yet here you are, pawns in a game you are powerless to affect; nothing more than pieces to be moved as the humans and the inhuman are. But on Loinn, despite the betrayal he suffered, it was Dorovar that tried to hold us together. It was Dorovar that cautioned us from abandoning our principles and giving in to our baser natures. But we were drinking from the cup of vengeance, and soaked in the blood of futility. The more we fought and killed, the more we failed. And for every one of our failures, Dorovar stood more resolute, preaching for us to return to the teachings of our goddess. Even though we had been betrayed, deceived, and sacrificed to a conflict we could not even begin to understand, Dorovar stood firm in his belief in the goddess and her vision of Order. As we fell, our faith lost to our madness, Dorovar did not relent and acted as an anchor trying to hold together a world desperately trying to pull itself apart."

Luigsech paused for a moment and then continued, his hand still raised with the back out toward the dragon.

"But the world did pull itself apart, and Dorovar stood watching. It was then, his body broken and his mind failing, that rage first began to touch his heart. And so, once the dragons left him marooned in the nothingness between worlds, Dorovar had only his hate to keep him company, and it made him harder and more unrelenting in his desire to see the whole of the Cosmos ordered as Raenera intended. Over time he began to see that Raenera's vision was too limited and that the goddess herself was not committed to the order that she preached. So, to Dorovar, as he floated in the nothing, the only way to save the Cosmos was to burn all of Creation to nothing and rebuild it into perfect unyielding Order."

Stormbane scoffed.

"And so he burned worlds one by one, killing angels, killing Servants, and visiting his pain upon innocent populations all in the name of creating Order. And he did not see the fallacy in that?"

Luigsech balled his hand into a fist and held it aloft.

"Dorovar saw the Cosmos as a cold hard and cruel thing that only understood cruelty in return. And so he killed. And he killed. And he burned. And he killed. But there in the formless void, Dorovar began to see the futility of his actions. He began to see that no matter how much he destroyed, no matter how many angels he slaughtered, nothing changed. Dorovar found himself in an unending quandary; he knew that the nature of Creation needed to change, but he did not have the power necessary to affect that change. But he began to hear whispers of a place called the Vault of Terrors, a place where the Creator stored those things too dangerous to remain within the bounds of Creation. So Dorovar allowed himself to be captured and imprisoned there, knowing that he would be able to find something in those forbidden items that would allow him to resolve the quandary."

Luigsech opened his hand again, this time turning the palm to face the dragon.

"For many millennia Dorovar studied, and his rage faded. His anger was gone, and his hate was gone. All that was left was the goal. The Cosmos needed to be freed from the oppressive yoke of the Creator, and a new Order needed to be installed. Dorovar seeks now only to free Creation from its servitude, to be the guiding hand that will lead it to a new prosperity. But for that, Stormbane, we require the information that you have been withholding from us. We must know the disposition of the High Priestess's soul."

Stormbane was silent for several long moments, thoughts swirling in his head. Despite his brutish appearance, Stormbane was not a mindless thug. He was a skilled mediator and while not the manipulator or master of mind-games that Derelor had been, Stormbane was more than a match for the limited intelligence of most lower beings, including humans. Until this point he had never understood the creature called Dorovar; never understood the seemingly random and pointless brutality. But now with the new light shed by Dorovar's subjects, more of the abomination's motivations were clear. Through that, Stormbane saw an opportunity.

"Even were I to give you this information," Stormbane said slowly, careful to not seem too eager with his words, "there may not be enough time for Dorovar to bring his machinations to fruition. But if, as you say, Dorovar's motivations are not for conquest but rather salvation, I make you a counter-proposal that would ensure that the Creator is brought to heel and the whole of Creation is saved from fire."

Stormbane paused and let his words soak in for several moments before continuing.

"Within the Vault of Terrors is a device that will allow Dorovar to transfer the power that he has already accumulated into another host. If he were to transfer his powers into Shadowweaver, there is no power in the Heavens that would able to stand against him, not even the Creator. Dragons could take Creation into a new prosperity, one that would be free of the arcane and archaic rules set down by the Creator and his Children."

It was Maedoc that reacted first.

"Shadowweaver? That demon is as untrustworthy as the Creator. Shadowweaver hates every being that is not dragon, and would relish the chance to use these new powers the hunt down and destroy everything that would not bow to his will. No, we will not trade one tyrant bent on destroying all life on every world for another who would do the same with no less ruthless efficiency."

Stormbane did not react in the way that either of the Adhradair expected.

"Then choose another. Give the power to Mariti Brightblade, or Serentis, or Aspertis the Just. It does not matter which of my brothers and sisters that you choose. Find one that shares your view of how the Cosmos should be. Time is growing too short to have these debates. Action must be taken now before the stars begin to go out and the darkness takes hold of the sky. Once the cataclysm is triggered, and I feel it is close as surely as I feel my own heart beating, no one's schemes will matter any longer. Not

Dorovar's, not Aerith's, not Shadowweaver's, and not the Children's. All that will be left is fire."

Luigsech found himself simply staring at the dragon, his mouth agape. Could things really be so hopeless that the dragons would consent to such an arrangement? But then again, this could be another lie fabricated by the traitor in order to earn the trust of those he had already betrayed once. However, the more Luigsech thought about the situation, the less likely it was that Stormbane was lying.

"We will consider this proposal on one condition," Luigsech responded. "You will give us the information about the soul of the High Priestess, and we will take your offer to Dorovar."

Stormbane smiled.

"I will make a counter-proposal as I do not have the information you seek, at least not all of it. I know that the soul of the High Priestess is here upon this world, but I do not know where. Only Shadowweaver has that information. I will take you both to where Shadowweaver plans for our offensive against our enemies. Hear the offer from him directly, and if you find it to be an honest one, then summon your master so that he and Shadowweaver can deal directly. Regardless of whether Dorovar accepts the proposal or not, it will put him in the same location as one of his greatest enemies. If he is really as reformed as you say, he will not be tempted by his need for vengeance and will parlay with Shadowweaver. If he is the murderous monster that his reputation portends, then the information he seeks will be destroyed by his own hands."

Luigsech would have felt chills through his body if he had still been alive. As it was however, for a fleeting moment doubt entered into his mind as to the veracity of the claims he had made of his master's newfound benevolence. Stormbane seized on the moment of hesitation.

"Do we have terms?"

Luigsech looked to Maedoc whose eyes went wide and his head shook slightly. Finally, Luigsech sighed, turned back to Stormbane and locked eyes with the massive beast.

"Yes. We have terms."

Purgatories of Regret

Year Four of the Just Emperor Kaitain "Dragonsbane" Lorien, Creator's Calendar Year 1871

Pain. Pain resounded through Bryn's body, pulling her down further into the darkness that held her mind. It was the pain that kept her on the edges of consciousness; barely hanging on to the threads that kept her just above the tides of blackness. The pain receded briefly; almost letting her return to the waking world, and then it surged again, plunging her back into the nothingness between asleep and awake. This seemed to go on for hours, the tug of war between fight and surrender, between consciousness and nothingness. Then suddenly, as though it had never existed, the pain was gone. In its place was a luxurious softness that encased her entire body. As consciousness returned more fully to her mind, she began to place the sensations that tickled her bare skin. Beneath her was one of the softest feather mattresses that she had ever had the pleasure to lie upon, and atop her was a comforter of similar lightness. Her head rested upon a pillow that was slightly firm, but still was decadent in its silken covering. As more of her senses reawakened, the soreness in her muscles began to return. It was not pain so much as it was the stiffness and ache from overexertion and lack of rest. Finally, Bryn's eyes opened, and she looked up into the well-lit room that surrounded the opulent bed. The white walls, ornate carvings and colorful tapestries marked the room as part of either a palace or a keep, and the slight hint of salt in the air that flooded through an open window meant that the place must have been close to the sea. After a few too many moments enjoying the confinements of the bedding, Bryn pulled herself to a seated position. Though her nudity struck her odd, considering she had just been in the middle of a battle, it did not make her uncomfortable. She constantly had found the human taboos on nudity and sexuality to be counterproductive and foolish, but had felt no shame in turning those prohibitions and inhibitions to her advantage whenever possible. Her forwardness put people off-balance, her tactics often made it difficult to combat her advances, and she reveled in both the attention and the decadence.

From her seated position, she could still enjoy the comfort of the bed and take in more of the room. A large wardrobe stood in one corner with a smaller one standing beside it. The door to the room was in the other corner on the same wall. The opposite wall was taken up completely by massive floor to ceiling windows that were open and led out to a balcony. The balcony was at least several floors up in the structure. The headboard of the bed stood against the wall between the door and the window, while the opposite wall contained two large full-length mirrors. Looking at the mirror, Bryn noticed something irregular about her reflection. She shifted on the bed, letting her feet touch the cold marble floor. Bryn ignored the chill that ran through her and stepped lightly toward the mirrors. It would have taken merely a reflex thought to embrace her abilities and fill her body with warmth. At the moment however her mind was elsewhere, and the use of such power was unnecessary. That was not a thought that would have entered her mind before the last few centuries with Aerith and the children. She chose not to be irresponsible any longer. Her time in the Heavens with Liette had solidified that view. Power was a trap, it was a burden, and in the end, it would be the end of her. That was the one piece of information that had attached itself to her mind. Her time was running out quickly, and it was only a matter of time before her part in the war would be at an end.

Bryn made her way gingerly across the cold floor and stood before the mirror looking at the new deformity in her reflection. Her fingers moved to the base of her throat and slid down to the top of her sternum where the skin had scarred. The memory came to her the next moment of seeing the tip of the warrior angel's flaming blade emerge from her chest. Her fingers fluttered down the length of the sealed wound that ran from the top of her sternum, down the valley between her breasts to the top of her abdomen. It looked as though her skin had melted and dripped down like candle wax retreating from a flame. As Bryn stood looking at herself in the mirror, her analytical mind began to work. The blade as it passed through her body would have caused considerable damage, and likely would have pierced multiple major organs. Her nature and the newly increased access to the powers of the Blaze might have saved her from shock-induced death, and because the wound was caused by a flaming blade it was unlikely that she would bleed to death. However, the sheer amount of damage done to her body would have been enough to end even the life of a member of the phasia. Considering how much her body had already been taxed by the dual altercations with the host of angelic warriors, it was unlikely that she would have survived without assistance. So, whoever or whatever brought her to this place also was responsible for keeping her alive. It remained to be seen whether the savior was a friend or a foe.

Satisfied that she was in fact still alive, Bryn moved to the larger of the two wardrobes and opened the doors wide. A frown quickly tugged at the corners of her lips. Whoever this room belonged to had no taste in clothing. Everything was so chaste and reserved. So many of the dresses were blue or white, and a great many of them stretched from chin to floor with no respect for the form of the woman underneath. Frankly, it was disgusting. There was at least one part of the wardrobe that was not disappointing however. This woman, whoever she was, may have repressed herself in her clothing choices, but she did allow herself some decadence in footwear. Many of the shoes and sandals in the lower portion of the wardrobe looked as though they could have come from Bryn's own collection. Selecting a pair of small heels with straps that twined from her ankles all the way to her knees, she closed the doors of the wardrobe and stepped into the shoes. A quick gesture with her finger caused the straps to fasten themselves quickly around her calves and the sly knowing grin came to her lips. Perhaps she was not as reformed as she liked to believe. Not encouraged by the selection of garments, and with very little hope for anything the slightest bit decadent, Bryn moved to the smaller wardrobe and opened the single door. As soon as her eyes found the items inside, she could not repress the smile. The woman who called this room home had a wicked side. Some of the dresses that were in the smaller wardrobe could barely be called dresses at all, and a great many were sheer bordering on transparent. There was one dress though that immediately drew Bryn's attention. The dress itself was nothing special, off the shoulder, deep plunging V neckline, and a slit on one side that came nearly to the waistline. It was the color that drew Bryn's attention. The design gave the appearance that the dress was blood red during its inception and then one corner was dipped in the blackest ink. The tendrils of black spread from the right corner diagonally across the garment like a creeping shadow overwhelming a brilliant sunset. It was perfect. A snap of her fingers later, and the dress was wrapped perfectly around her frame, alterations to its fit done unconsciously. Regarding herself in the mirror once more, Bryn approved. Her new scar shown prominently thanks to the cut of the dress, and she intended to wear it as a badge for what remained of the rest of her life. It was then that Bryn heard rustling at the door to the room. Perhaps the prospective visitor had been astute enough to feel her slight uses of power, or perhaps it was coincidence. Either way she turned just in time to see the handle of the door begin to move.

There were several moments of trepidation and mostly-repressed fear before the door finally opened to reveal a familiar if surprising face. The young man who walked through the door was a welcome sight for a few moments before the gravity of the situation set in. It had been too long since Bryn had seen her son, and longer still since she had felt comfortable in his presence. He was his father's son to be sure, but there was something about him as he aged, a need within him that seemed to never be able to be filled. There was a restlessness that had no end. Perhaps that was one of the reasons that Bryn relented and allowed Ayden to be sent to the Academy of Arcane Arts to become Aerith's spy. She thought that the rigors of studying at the Academy along with the added responsibility of reporting back on the movements of the important people in Jelan would provide whatever was missing, or at the very least would keep him occupied enough that he would not feel the need to search for something else. But obviously Bryn was wrong as evidenced by Ayden's new feathered appendages. The young man's face was without expression, but his eyes were filled with the tell-tale marks of power.

"Hello mother."

Bryn nodded her head and clasped her hands behind her back.

"Hello Ayden. I trust you have a reason for bringing me here, wherever here is."

A smile tugged at the corners of Ayden's mouth but never fully materialized. Ayden walked fully into the room and left the door open behind him. He moved slowly and deliberately across the distance between them, and then walked past his mother in the direction of the window. Bryn turned as he passed and followed in step behind him until they had passed through the windows and out onto the balcony. For the first time Bryn was able to take in the view, and it was not one that she was prepared for. Stretching out below them was a cityscape that had been nearly completely devastated. The vast majority of the buildings in the city had been leveled, bodies lay in the street, and a full quarter of the city had been swallowed by a foot of water from the sea. Without looking back at his mother, Ayden stretched his hand out in the direction of the destruction.

"This was once a thriving city, mother, with thousands of people content to live their lives, raise their families, and make each day better than the one before. But that was before. That was before my father's war came here."

Ayden turned back to look at Bryn for a moment before returning his gaze to the city.

"Hedorah was a beautiful city once. Then the graft and corruption came at the hands of a group of arrogant non-believing royalty. These men and women who were supposed to protect their populace, empower them, and shepherd them into the light of the Creator's love chose instead to pursue profit. They used their soldiers to make shopkeepers surrender money that should have gone to feed their families. They killed those who spoke openly against them. And so, darkness gripped the soul of this place, and even those of the Church of the Creator began to feel as though Hedorah was outside the Creator's love. And then something miraculous happened."

Ayden turned back with a new look in his eyes. It was one of wonder and admiration.

"What is it that happened, Ayden?" Bryn asked, half not caring about the answer.

"You happened, mother," Ayden replied without missing a beat. "You were the catalyst that helped put pieces into position for the Creator's greatest triumph. Your actions helped transform a kingdom of decadence and fear into a shining beacon of possibility. You helped to will into being a place where the dream of a perfect world could have been realized."

Bryn shrank back as though she were struck. Could her actions truly have been a boon to the plans of the Creator despite her desire to do everything to oppose His will? Had she truly been the unwilling pawn that Liette had described her as? For all of her intellect and her arrogance, she was really just a small and insignificant creature; an ant trying to trip a giant.

"You helped push father toward his actions against Evan Sinn, and led to the necessity of a new Servant. You helped create the situation in which Jaccob Aldora found himself escorting a young man who had recently been expelled from the Academy of Arcane Arts in Jelan. That led to my being in the right place at the right time to see and confront Emries, which led to my injuries and also to Jaccob Aldora's execution with his own Sacred Weapon. The shattering of that Sacred Weapon let loose the first of Dorovar's servants, who latched itself to Jaccob Aldora's soul and enabled him to perform one last act in the name of the Creator and in defiance of Emperor Kaitain Lorien. It was your influence that put a hot-tempered morally ambiguous woman in the bed of the heir to the Cadarian Empire. That put her on the road to Albitonin, where she met up with a certain irreverent braggart who would arrogantly walk into the Church of the Creator thinking there would be no repercussions for his actions. The death of another Herald, the destruction of the Heart of Stone, the near death of Marlae Lorien, and all of which put Marlae and I in the same place, at the same time to meet our destinies. Marlae to become the embodiment of the Creator's law and leadership on the mortal plane, and I would become her protector and newest of the Creator's Servants."

Ayden paused only a moment and turned back to the cityscape again.

"And this was to be the throne from which Marlae would build a new world."

A new dark energy seemed to fill the room the next moment, and Bryn could feel the gloom and malevolence in the air.

"But the very convergence of actions that conspired to create the conditions which would lead to the formation of this new bright kingdom also could undo it. Evan Sinn's death set off a chain reaction in the Citadel of the Dark Gods. Pike Rhuiden's rage would incite the violence being felt in this world at the hands of Kaitain Lorien, and his own impotence and feelings of inferiority would lead him to turn to the seductive powers of Dorovar. Emries' hate of my father led him to strike against Logan Ranthall through his brother Korrd, while at the same time Dorovar struck at him through his own servants. These actions put Pike and Logan on a collision course assuredly, but the cruelest fate was perhaps sealed by the Creator's own actions. He allowed Anabel Binosear to become the councilor to Marlae. Allowed Logan Ranthall's daughter to become her personal servant, gave Marlae Logan's lover's name, and then allowed two of Logan's sworn enemies to become advisors to the Empress. Once Sabrina interfered in the nature of things, it put Logan on an unavoidable path to his confrontation with Pike Rhuiden here in the streets of Hedorah. And you see the result."

Ayden panned his hand across the vista and once again Bryn took in the level of destruction. She opened her mouth as if to speak, but Ayden's voice cut her off.

"This city was supposed to be the most holy, under the watchful eye of the Divine Empress. Guarded by warrior angels, advised by gods, and still there was no chance for that land to live upon this corrupted world. Pike Rhuiden appeared in his new guise as Conquest and killed warrior angels indiscriminately, his goal to eviscerate Marlae and present her head to his new master. And who came to her defense? What power was it that turned away the Herald of Dorovar before he could commit his bloody murder? Was it the powerful Servants of the Creator? It was not the Voice, as Gregor Quicksilver lay broken and dismembered at the hands of Conquest. It was not the Wrath, as his power were stolen by my father and Wolf Ranthall in an effort to save Sabrina Binosear's life. It was not the Spirit, because her path ended at the hands of the Herald Jerah, the corrupted phase you once knew as Caris Vale. And where was the Divine

Empress's sworn protector? Where was the Will? The Creator pulled me away from my charge to prevent Dorovar and Emries from acquiring information that could lead them to the last piece of the puzzle that might win them this pointless war. And all the while, mother, you were playing detective in the Heavens, fighting with warrior angels that could have been sent here to protect Marlae. And father was starting his own war in Albitonin, a war between angels and dragons, more forces that were unable to be leveraged to protect the Divine Empress. So, who was left to save her from all of the treachery that surrounded her? Who could protect her from the gods and monsters who sought to spill her blood? It was the man who stood between, the man who should not exist. Logan Ranthall."

The hatred in Ayden's voice was palpable, and Bryn identified with it in a way that few could. Though she was not directly involved in the first part of the war against Logan Ranthall and his compatriots on the world of Onea, her blood still burned at his very existence. He was the sworn enemy of the phasia, of Shau-ling, and the puppet champion of the demon Emries. But then something changed, something miraculous. Logan was not what he was supposed to be, and so he became the very thing that Ayden and the Creator hated.

"The inheritor of my father's mantle, a refugee from a world that should have never existed, a member of the Brotherhood of Phasia, a reinvented heretic who denounced the worship of the Creator at every turn, an ally to dragons, a killer of gods and angels. He is seemingly the enemy of all sides, and yet he commands the loyalty of every free person that has ever crossed his path. But you know as well as I do, mother, the fate of heroes."

Ayden pointed in the direction of the flooded portion of the city.

"There is where the confrontation took place. A holding action of sorts. Logan simply wanted to buy time for the innocents to flee the city via the docks to the north. He knew he couldn't save everyone, and he knew that every moment he bought for the people increased the likelihood of his death. But so clear was his sense of duty to prevent any more death at the hands of his friend, so great was his sense of responsibility that every life lost was on his hands as much as they were on Pike Rhuiden's, that Logan stood his ground against an enemy he could not defeat. And though he succeeded in defeating his friend and greatest adversary, he died. Right there, face down in the water as his life spilled out around him, he met his end. There will be no monuments, there will be no funeral and no mourners. Most of the people of this world will never know his true name, and he will be a folk tale if he is remembered at all. That is the price for heroism in this war."

Ayden turned back to his mother, and she recognized the look in his eyes immediately. They were the eyes of a remorseless killer.

"Now is the time, mother, to choose your own fate. Whether in this moment you shall call yourself a hero as your sister Ellis and your sometime brother Logan did, or you shall renounce this pointless crusade in favor of a place at the side of the Creator."

Bryn's jaw went slack. She could not believe the words that had just come out of Ayden's mouth, and despite her intelligence and the information she had just come into possession of, she could not reconcile any of it. The malice faded from Ayden's eyes. For a moment, just for the barest moment Bryn thought she saw the remnant of her son behind the Will's eyes. But that moment passed quickly, and the bemused look of the unrepentant killer returned.

"The Creator's chosen champion has reached her crucible. Saved from her past of decadence and privilege, she has been shown the path to benevolence and wisdom. Her tutors have shown her power, compassion, cruelty, vanity, and self-destructive self-interest. Now, at the crossroads between the now and the future, she will become the architect of everything that will come to pass from this point forward. She will be given the choice of what will befall this world. Should she stay on the right path, this world will be saved, ruled by her love and compassion for all who dwell upon the face of Espre. She may choose the path of humanism, forsaking the Creator and all those with divine power. This world could be cut off from the Creator's love, a purgatory that will burn just as Onea did. However, there is a chance that her better angels could be corrupted by greed and her old thirsts for power and control will resurface and turn her into the beautiful tyrant that some wish her to be. She would rule in the stead of an even more terrible power, and the viciousness that would be visited upon this world would make the cleansing fires of oblivion seem like a blessing. And yet an even worse fate is possible, one that throws not just this world but the whole of Creation into darkness; a cosmos of death and decay, where madness replaces reason and the cries of the dying are the chorus of supplication demanded of all. Regardless of the path she chooses, she shall be the instrument through which the Creator shall craft eternity."

Ayden paused for a moment, and Bryn thought she could feel a sadness emanating from the being, one that would have had to be coming from the part of the Will that was still her son. Part of him obviously cared for Marlae, and he was struggling with what was happening to her. He was also obviously struggling with his powerlessness in the situation. But why was he powerless? Surely had the Creator wanted, Ayden could have intervened in any number of ways. Something scratched at the back of Bryn's mind; something she was missing. What was it? Ayden continued the next moment, turning back to the cityscape.

"This could be the fate of this world, or the entirety of the Cosmos, and all rests upon how the Divine Empress comes through the other side of her crucible. To that end, mother, the Creator offers you a path to salvation and a way to cleanse yourself of the transgression that has been committed against the rule of the Heavens. You need only accomplish two tasks, and then you may take your place in the Heavens. The first and most important of these tasks is that you are to travel to the headquarters of the Shadow Guild in Bellnoc, rejoin the remaining members of your confederates in the Brotherhood of Phasia, and offer your support to the Divine Empress who has found herself taking shelter there. Guide her toward the message of the Creator's love, and insure that no corrupting influence finds a ways to sway her from the path of righteousness."

Bryn was unsurprised by that condition. But why send Bryn? Why would her voice have any more sway? The scratch in the back of her mind was getting stronger. There was something she was missing. It was there, in the corner of her mind, and the more she tried to grasp on to it, the further away it was. She had felt this feeling before.

"And the second task?" Bryn asked.

Even before Ayden's voice caught the air, Bryn's blood ran cold. She knew in her bones what his next words would be, and she now knew why.

"Your daughter, my sister, has inherited something that should never have come to her. It was a gift that could not have been given were it not for an extraordinary set of circumstances that was exploited by the will of those who did not understand their transgression against the natural order of things. This must be rectified."

Ayden turned his body toward Bryn, but did not look in her direction. He extended his hand toward her, palm up. A dagger appeared in his hand; a small simple dagger that could easily be concealed.

"You, I am sure are familiar with the principle of these daggers. The foolish leaders of the Cadarian Empire believed that these daggers could kill the Dark Gods, not understanding the nature of things beyond their own myopic universal view. However, the true nature of this weapon is to steal power. Power is connected to life, and as the life drains, so too does power. But instead of letting it evaporate into the Cosmos, this dagger allows the power to be sent to someone else, somewhere else. The daggers that Talisia crafted are crude, as her understanding of the nature of power is limited to her own vision. But this one, this one came from the Creator, and so its power is absolute. Take it, and once you have secured the fate of the Divine Empress, plunge this dagger into the heart of your daughter and restore the balance to this war."

The manipulation was so clear, so obvious, and at the same time, incredibly effective. The Creator could not act openly against the true threat against him, and could not remove the specter of choice from the soul of his chosen disciple. The whole of the war was about choice, about truth, and about the potential for every being in Creation to make the choice to walk in the Creator's light or to choose another path. Whether it was for one of the Children, or for Dorovar, or even for Aerith Seth. Bryn knew what she had to do.

"No, Ayden," she said finally. "If your Creator's champion is going to come to His light, she'll have to do it on her own. You and I both know that if the Creator wants me to sway her, then there is no chance that she'll follow willingly. The Creator wants a puppet; a pawn. He cares only for supplication and servitude. But that time is coming to an end. I will not serve."

CHAPTER 106

Bryn didn't see what happened next until it was too late. The dagger disappeared from Ayden's hand, but his other hand swung around, a different weapon clutched in it. The blade struck true in the center of her chest, in the middle of her new scar. Her knees immediately buckled, and she felt the cold stone floor beneath her. There was something warm around her, and just before the blackness took her, she realized it was her own blood.

Patience of Misfortune

Year Four of the Just Emperor Kaitain "Dragonsbane" Lorien, Creator's Calendar Year 1871

Dominique wanted to cry out. She looked on in horror as Chelsea dismounted her horse, drew Patience from her hip and charged at the man dressed in white. There was a menace about the man that was undeniable, and Dominique was truly afraid for Chelsea's safety. But the Wolf of Saldarine would not be denied. And so, Dominique could only watch helplessly as the combat was about to ensue. To her right, Dominque saw that Alderin was sliding from his horse, but he made no move to draw a weapon. That was perhaps the first time that Dominique realized that Alderin was not visibly carrying a weapon. The convention and characteristics of the Dark Gods were completely alien to everything that Dominique had ever known, and yet it seemed that the stories about them had underestimated them at every turn. They were not monsters imprisoned on Espre from some bygone era. They were not instruments of death that had been expelled from the Heavens. They were simply people who in trying to do the right thing, the heroic thing, had been trapped on the wrong side of a history intent on vilifying them without evidence. Dominique made a move to dismount her horse, but a raised hand from Alderin restrained her movements.

"If things start to get ugly, I want you to ride ahead as fast as you can. Get to the nearest town and hide out. If we don't come for you within a day, don't expect us. Circle back to Aldere and let everyone know what happened. I promised Gwydeon I would keep you safe, but I can't let one of Dorovar's puppets advance his cause."

Alderin didn't wait for a reply and turned his full attention to the white-clad man and Chelsea. Again, Dominique wanted to protest, but she knew there was nothing that she could say that would change Alderin's mind. As the man had painstakingly pointed out, Alderin was a killer. He and Chelsea had more in common than Chelsea would ever admit. Of course, Chelsea would never have seen herself as an assassin, but there was no doubt that she was a killer. On the battlefield she was renowned for her tenacity and cunning. Once the battle was joined, she would not stop until she had won. Dominique knew that this battle would be no different. But all the same Dominique worried. Only days before she had nearly been killed in the conflict with the Dark God Serrina, and though Liara had done a miraculous job of healing her wounds, Dominique could not get the picture of the bloody and broken Chelsea barely breathing in her lap out of her mind. Regardless, Dominique knew that she had to trust that between the two of them, Chelsea and Alderin knew what they were doing, knew their limitations, and would find a way out of the conflict alive and victorious.

To the uninitiated, Chelsea's charge might have seemed reckless. However, as she closed the distance between herself and the white-clad man, she began working out the specifics of the conflict in her mind. The man claimed to represent something called the Adhradair, and whatever that was, it was certainly not of Espre. It was also clear from the words he used, like mortals when referring to Chelsea and Dominique, that the man was more akin to the Dark Gods than he was to people like Chelsea. In addition, there was a disdain in his voice when he said Dark Gods, which meant that he wasn't a rogue Dark God like Serrina, he was something apart from them too. That left only one force that Chelsea could think of. This man, whoever or whatever he was, had to be working for Dorovar. Dorovar's Heralds had leveled whole cities with a wave of their hand, and so Chelsea knew that her chances against someone like that was low. But there was one thing that fighting against a superior opponent had taught

Chelsea. Sometimes the greatest advantage one had against a superior opponent was their knowing that they were superior. The combatant that is supposed to win and knows they are supposed to win can often make mistakes and let a lesser opponent surprise them. The greater the difference in power and ability, the greater the chance for a mistake. Chelsea knew she would not likely get more than one shot, so she would have to pick her spots very carefully.

The green glow around the white-clad man's hands intensified as Chelsea approached, and she waited for the inevitable strike. However, as she closed the distance over that matter of heartbeats, the strike never came. Perhaps he was waiting for Chelsea to close the distance so that he could be assured to destroy her in one blow. Nevertheless, Chelsea could not shake the feeling that she was missing something. Two more strides and she would be on top of him, and her guts clenched and her muscles tensed. She was a moment away from the strike and still the man did not move. In a quick deft move, Chelsea brought Patience up from her hip to her shoulder level, planted her right foot at the end of her stride, pushed off and leapt toward the man in white. His eyes caught hers and as she sailed through the air, Chelsea's eyes went wide. She was mid strike when she dipped her right shoulder and sailed past the man in white. Chelsea hit the ground shoulder first, tucked and rolled, coming up to one knee with Patience in front of her to shield herself from any potential counterattack. The move was purely instinctual, as her mind was busy trying to figure out two very important contradictory thoughts. The first was that the man in white had clearly wanted her to strike him down, and the second thought was wondering why she hadn't. The man in white turned, his mouth stretched into a frown and his head shaking slightly from side to side.

"So this is the great Wolf of Saldarine," the man said, his voice filled with ice and disgust. "Truly I had expected so much more. A woman who has made her reputation on the wholesale slaughter of her enemies without mercy suddenly cannot bring herself to strike down a defenseless man? What would your precious Seraph say?"

Chelsea did not take the bait.

"You and I both know you are far from defenseless. Why did Dorovar send you, and why do you want the Sacred Weapon?"

Coriden's left eyebrow cocked slightly.

"I suppose you are trying to surprise me, knowing that I serve Dorovar. But for someone such as you that would be an easy deduction. It is not as though I have made any effort to hide my identity. As to my purpose, well that I shall gladly teach you."

A moment later Coriden disappeared from where he was standing and reappeared right behind Chelsea. Alderin and Chelsea viewed the action in different ways. To Chelsea's eyes, the man simply disappeared. To Alderin's eyes, he saw the man in white moving very quickly, almost imperceptibly quick even to the eyes of a member of the Dark Gods. Alderin had two thoughts at the same time. The first was to call out to warn Chelsea what was about to happen, but by the time the words would have escaped his lips, it would have been too late. The other thought was to act. In the split-second he had to decide, instinct took over. Reaching into himself, Alderin touched the still unfamiliar powers of the Blaze. Instead of targeting the man in white directly, he targeted the spot where he thought the man in white's path would end. There was less than a heartbeat of hesitation before Alderin channeled the powers of the Blaze. He was still so unfamiliar with his new powers, but he also knew that if he didn't do something immediately, Chelsea would likely end up dead. And so, Alderin acted. The next moment, a column of fire appeared directly behind Chelsea. Chelsea for her part reacted to the two distinct actions in the same way. Her honed danger senses flared the moment that the white-clad man disappeared from view. The fine hairs on the back of her neck stood up and she knew that she had no time to act. She threw herself forward even before she felt the intense heat under the spot where she knelt. The dive was not as graceful as she would have liked, but it served the purpose of getting her away from what happened next.

Coriden came to a stop behind where Chelsea would have been and he reached down to try to grasp Chelsea by the back of the neck before she became aware of his presence. But what he was not prepared for was the pillar of fire that sprung up from the ground. The pillar was wider than Alderin had intended, and had Chelsea not acted as quickly as she did, she likely would have been consumed by it as well. The column burned impossibly hot, and Alderin kept channeling power into the pillar for nearly a minute. Just as he was about to release the flows of power to see whether or not the white-clad man was still standing, a spectral green glow appeared at the heart of the column. The glow spread as the seconds passed until it completely consumed the fire. Alderin's control over the flows of fire shattered. The column then disappeared, leaving an unscathed Coriden standing at the heart of where the column had been.

"I'm quite impressed, Dark God," Coriden said calmly, the spectral green haze hanging like a fog around him. "Dorovar does not hold your kind in high regard, despite the trouble you and your kind may have caused him in the past."

Alderin took a half step toward the man in white.

"You'll find that the Dark Gods are not all created equal. Some never wanted this life; some have only known this life. I was born a Dark God, and I was raised and trained to be a killer. And so, you will have to try a lot harder if you want to take the Sacred Weapon."

The man in white spread his hands wide.

"And how does it feel, Dark God, to be a killer? How does it feel to know no other life? Do you somehow feel noble? Do you somehow feel as though you have a purpose that you were born to fulfill? Does it fill you with a sense of contentment and peace when you are at your task?"

Alderin felt something cold run through him.

"Think about the moment you are standing above your kill. Do you look in his eyes? Do you watch the light go out? Do you enjoy the feel of blood on your hands?"

Coriden's face was impassive.

"Once I knew that joy, that sense of purpose. I was not bred to be a killer. I was not bred to be a warrior. Those concepts were alien to me. When my name was read from the Tome of Order at the moment of my birth, I was given everything I would ever need. My name was Coriden, and I was destined to be a scribe. Imagine that. Look at what I am now, standing here prepared to kill in order to save my sister from her prison."

Alderin and Chelsea exchanged quick glances as Chelsea got back to a crouching position. Coriden seemed to pay it no mind as he looked down at his glowing green hands.

"Once, the only worry I had was whether or not there was ink on my fingers. My task was to ensure that all scrolls and texts were preserved. As some of the paper and parchment aged, I would dutifully transcribe each word, each mark, each blemish. Everything preserved exactly as it had been, exactly as it would always be. All knowledge was sacred, and it was my sacred duty to make sure that it was available for every generation that would follow. But if there was a smudge of ink transferred from my fingers to a scroll, an unwanted blemish caused by my carelessness, days of work would be ruined. That was the only concern in my life. I needed only to prevent my own carelessness."

Coriden then locked his eyes on Alderin and raised a hand.

"It doesn't matter how much blood gets on my hands now, does it? Every life that I take in the furtherance of Dorovar's cause is an act of contrition for my crimes. My crimes, so vast and so bloody. My crimes against my goddess, against my brothers and sisters in the Adhradair, my crimes against my world, and my crimes against everything I was raised to value and trust. Had I only stayed in my workshop. Had I only ignored the cries and screams of the people who were defenseless against the terrors of the dragon horde. Had I only ignored the pressure from my brothers and sisters to take arms against the monsters. Had I only listened to Dorovar's warnings."

Chelsea could not process everything that Coriden was saying, but she got enough.

"Could you really have done that, Coriden? Could you really have sat idly by and let people die? You obviously cared about your world, obviously cared about your people. How is it a crime to want to protect them?"

Coriden's eyes looked down to the ground, and when he spoke again, there was a wistful quality to his words, as though he was trying to reason out everything that he was saying, trying to make sense of it all.

"You understand so little. Here, on this world, you have no structure. Look at you, Wolf of Saldarine. A woman. On this world women are largely marginalized. They are for procreation, for homemaking, and for keeping their men satisfied. But you, you defied that misogynistic standard and became a soldier. You escaped the perception that women made substandard soldiers, that they were weaker and less tolerant of blood, and became a general. You ascended in a way that few before you could, crafting your own narrative for your life. But how many other peoples' narratives did you destroy on your ascent to your place? How many lives did you cut short needlessly because of your arrogant desire to succeed?"

Finally he looked up, his eyes boring in to Chelsea's soul.

"On Loinn, we all knew our place. We all knew our role, and no one was sacrificed for the greater glory of another. But that all changed when the dragons came. Everything was thrown into the chaos that you live every day. The Adhradair abandoned their posts, farmers became soldiers, masons became medics. Everything was upside down. We were tempted away from our goddess and given powers beyond our imagining. And what was the cost for all that unrestrained power; power that defied Order? Our world was destroyed. Not by the dragons, not by the goddess, not by the Creator, but by our own hands. By the hands of the Adhradair. Hundreds of thousands dead because of what we did. Hundreds of thousands that would never be able to live up to their potential. All because of what we did. All because of our crimes. How many have you killed, Wolf of Saldarine? How many have you killed Dark God? Do you have the blood of hundreds of thousands on your hands? Even in this lawless chaotic morass you call a world, do you have that much blood to spill?"

Dominique slid down from her saddle, and approached slowly. Her heart was breaking at the sound of Coriden's words. Perhaps there was a way out of the conflict without any loss of life.

"Is that why you are here, Coriden?" Dominique said slowly and calmly. "Are you trying to save this world from the fate that your world suffered?"

There was a flash of puzzlement that crossed Coriden's features for a moment. His look passed first from Chelsea, to Alderin, and then finally to Dominique."

"Your world cannot be saved, Dominique Lorien," Coriden's pity-filled voice responded. "How can you not feel the doom in the air? All of these people, all of your people are going to meet their end when this world is reduced to ash. It doesn't matter if it is done by the dragons, or the Children, or the Creator, or by Dorovar. This world will meet its end all the same. The doom is clear all the same. Dorovar's vision extends beyond this world. On Loinn, each generation had its names written in the Tome of Order, each and every generation that was to come. We all knew our place from the moment of our birth, and we all were destined to succeed so long as we did as the Order dictated. That is the comfort that Dorovar wants to bring to the whole of Creation. He wants to save every generation of every world from the uncertainty and the fear that the Creator and his lies bring. How many more worlds will burn so long as the Creator allows petty conflicts between the Children? How many more worlds will burn when the Creator decides to allow his Servants or wayward heroes to change the course of events to such a radical degree that the only result is bloodshed and destruction? It will only end when the Creator is ended, and the Creator can only be ended by someone whose vision will not allow those failures to be repeated. Dorovar wants to save you all from yourselves. Wants to save you all from the Creator, and wants to save you all from the inevitable divine fire. You should stop fighting against us and see the wisdom of Dorovar's perfect Order. You need not join the Chorus of Souls yet. You need only help us free the rest of the Adhradair and stop those who stand in our way."

Dominique's stomach turned. The sheer madness of Coriden's words spoken not in the voice of a fanatic, but in the voice of a true believer was like a splinter in Dominique's soul. She could see the reason of it, even through its absurdity. But so long as Coriden was willing to speak, Dominique would try to extract what information she could.

"Is that why you need the Sacred Weapons?"

One corner of Coriden's mouth twisted into a frown.

"The perversion of you calling those things Sacred is perhaps the greatest insult you Cadarians have paid us. And while others of the Adhradair can chalk up the insult to your ignorance, I cannot bring myself to be so forgiving. I was a scholar and a scribe in my life, and I valued knowledge. I valued it above my own life. I understood the ignorance was bred not from a lack of knowledge but from a lack of will. Ignorance only exists because people are unwilling to acquire knowledge. The knowledge about the true nature of your so-called Sacred Weapons has been here on this world all along. Talisia has been here, and her servants have been here. They had the knowledge of what these things really were. But so too did the Lorien family. The first Empress knew what the Sacred Weapons were. She knew and she passed the information down to chosen seers in her line for generations. Arturious Demascious knew, and he wrote it down in his journal that was stored in Imperial Archives for almost two thousand years. And so for all this time, you have been calling these prisons Sacred, and rather than trying to find out the truth, you lived with the mystique, you lived with the mystery because it made you feel special."

Coriden shifted toward Chelsea and pointed and accusatory finger in her direction.

"And you, Chelsea Zarova, you carried one of those prisons on your hip for years. Did you not sense the soul inside of your so-called Tenacity crying out to be freed? Did not my brother Zaraven's voice fill you with his desire to once again roam the world? Did you ever wonder where that power imparted by Tenacity came from? Zaraven was a hunter. Perhaps the greatest hunter to ever draw breath on any world. He hunted what no other being hunted. He made sure the balance between the apex predators and their prey remained balanced by killing the apex predators. And you, Wolf of Saldarine, usurped that power for your own gain. You fed off of his power, you were his jailer, and you thought not once for the evil you did in his name."

Coriden's frown shifted into a snarl.

"And now you hold another prison, usurping its power. Do you feel the calm rushing through you? Do you feel the quiet in your mind? Do you feel the unnatural clarity in your thoughts and your ability to process information faster and more accurately than ever before? That is my sister

Judoc's power you feel running through you. She was one of the greatest thinkers that the Adhradair ever produced. She had the capacity to see through the vagaries, into the unknown and make sense of it. She heard the music of the Cosmos that the goddess Raenera left open for us to see. And while we lived by the Order that was dictated to us, we were still allowed to try to understand. I was responsible for writing down the things that Judoc saw in the Cosmos, the wonders that she loved beyond Loinn. She helped the religion of the High Priestess meet the philosophy of the Cosmos within the framework of Raenera's Order. She could make all the pieces fit. And now you hold her soul in your hand like some trophy."

Chelsea felt revulsion ripple across her skin. She felt dirty. Coriden's anger spewed through his voice like venom.

"But your husband," Coriden moved his finger from Chelsea to Dominique, "and your lover; he knew that what he felt from the weapon was unnatural. He knew that he could not be responsible for the denigration of another once he learned the truth. And when Dorovar brought his message to Seraph Kore, he saw the truth of it, and quickly consented to become Dorovar's Herald War."

The information detonated in both Chelsea and Dominique's minds, but both had different reactions. Dominique staggered backwards several steps, her mind racing and her chest heaving. She couldn't control the racing of her heart, and she felt as though her skin was on fire. Instantly the feeling of panic struck and she felt in that moment that the whole of the world was just wrong. Chelsea the moment she heard Coriden's proclamation knew that it was true. Seraph's late night visit, leaving Patience behind, the wedding ring, all of it. It all made sense. But now, she knew more than Coriden, and she knew how to attack him. Chelsea stood, a new calm and confidence filling her. She didn't have time to wonder if it was from somewhere inside of her or if it was from Patience. In the end it didn't really matter. All that mattered was what was about to happen.

"Seraph made his choices," Chelsea said calmly, "but he is not the true believer you paint him to be. If he did truly believe in what Dorovar had planned, then why did he leave me Patience instead of turning it over to Dorovar? He may call himself War now, but his goal is singular. He wants to make Kaitain Lorien pay for the horrors that he has visited upon

Cadaria. Seraph is just using Dorovar and his power for his own purposes. Seraph doesn't believe in your Order, he never did. You don't understand Seraph. If you did, you would understand how he thinks, and you would understand how you have been deceived."

Coriden growled.

"Dorovar sees all. Once Seraph gave himself over and became War, there are no secrets from the mind and will of Dorovar."

Chelsea calmly sheathed Patience.

"Then why do I have Patience? Why is your precious Judoc not free?"

Coriden's next charge had all the speed of the first, but this time Chelsea was ready and so was Alderin. Chelsea leapt out of the way a fraction of a moment before Coriden would have collided with her, and Alderin sent a stream of blue-white lightning pulsing in the Adhradair's direction. But Coriden seemed prepared for the strike, and instead of dodging the attack, caught the flash of lightning in his glowing green hand and sent it right back at Alderin. The Dark God was fast, but not fast enough as the redirected blow hit him square in the chest. Alderin was thrown backwards nearly thirty feet, knocked unconscious by the sheer force of the impact, his shirt burnt and smoking. Chelsea did not wait to see what would happen next. She rushed across the distance to Dominique and pushed her toward one of the horses. Coriden closed the gap impossibly fast, shoving Dominque down with one hand while the other took Chelsea by the throat.

"Give me the Sacred Weapon," Coriden growled, "or mine will be the last face you see."

Chelsea gasped for breath, but the next moment Coriden cried out in pain and was sent flying. Chelsea tumbled gracelessly to the ground, and after righting herself her hand went instinctively to her throat while her eyes scanned for whatever had stuck Coriden. The answer came in the form of a lithe female form stepping from a swirling blue portal.

"Don't worry, Chelsea," Leonora Wastri's voice was uncharacteristically hard, but no less welcome. "I'll take care of this."

Cold Blood, Flaming Hatred

*Year Four of the Just Emperor Kaitain "Dragonsbane" Lorien,
Creator's Calendar Year 1871*

Tess sat by the small fire at their campsite looking out into the forest, waiting for Cedric to return. He was taking longer than usual to return from his hunt, and she was starting to worry. Of course, she could have used her abilities and reached out across the whole of the continent of Mythryn to find him, but she dared not use her abilities so frivolously. That had been one of Cedric's first rules, and one that Tess had the hardest time following. After looking into Cedric's mind early in their relationship, Tess had learned something about the severe and stubborn man, something that had shaped everything that came after. Cedric was a man defined by pain, loss, and expectation. From the time of his birth, there were expectations. This was a place where Tess and Cedric had much in common. Cedric was thought to be the first-born son of a powerful king, and from the moment of his birth, he was groomed to become the leader of a kingdom. Tess was the daughter of the leader of the Dark Gods, and while she was not the first-born, she was certainly the one being groomed to lead. Her half-sister Darrien was a fighter like their father, a woman more geared toward the demands of the moment without seeing the ramifications that rippled into the future. As Tess thought about Darrien, she began to see that she and her sister were not so dissimilar. Darrien acted, without thinking. She was trained, she had experience, and she had the drive imparted to her by her station and the training of her father. The way to solve any situation was with the application of force and guile. When Tess's new abilities began to manifest, she thought those abilities were the solution to every problem. That very impulse was what Cedric was trying to correct in her, largely because of his own experience with power and the havoc it can wreak.

Unlike Tess, Cedric had no sense of power before he discovered his role as the chosen champion of the Child of the Creator Emries. Power to him was how his father extended the protection of his position, wealth, and status to those who could not protect themselves. How that power could create better trade agreements, could solve disputes, and be a force for peace in a world that constantly found its way to turmoil. But in his heart, when the time came too early to become the leader of that kingdom, he was unsure if he was strong or wise enough to shoulder the burden and use that power responsibly. The want for power was never inside of him. Perhaps it was because he knew the power would eventually come to him, or perhaps he understood the responsibility required for the use of that power. Perhaps, Tess thought to herself, it was something much more basic. Cedric was taught to wield power by one who wielded it thoughtfully and with great care. He was taught by one who showed restraint and a steady hand, one who hesitated in the application of the power he could wield. This stood in direct contradiction to the model that Tess and her sister had. Pike Rhuiden was a man that knew little restraint in anything that he approached. He drank too much, he raged at every little slight, he used power when it was not required, and he reveled in his excesses. Pike kept Darrien close to him, teaching her all of his bad habits and imparting to her the skills necessary to smite his enemies with a flick of her wrist. Both fortunately and unfortunately, Pike had little time or patience for Tess's inquisitiveness or naivety. Therefore, Tess's role models seemed to have a more restrained view of power.

Aryx Terian, the man of many lives, was a man born with power, and had learned to be humbled by it. His wife and daughter were fighters, and while they understood the application of power, they each viewed it differently from Aryx. Diana was a woman who saw power as a means to an end, and nothing more. She was born in a time when war was a specter that haunted everyone's footsteps, and she was among the heroes that stood against a living nightmare and walked away with her life mostly intact. Lissa Terian, in much the same way, embraced power as a way to protect those she loved. Her devotion to her family made her power a necessary part of her. Then there was Midarin. Midarin, the most pragmatic and strong-willed woman that Tess had ever met was intimidating in a way that defied description. She oozed power and strength in every breath without actually using any of it. It was part of her no different than her hair or her skin. Like Cedric, she was born to the mortal kind of power, but unlike Cedric she saw that power as a prison and ran away from it, only later in life being able to accept it for what it was, after she had been sufficiently humbled by both life and love. When she became possessed of a new kind of power, the kind that she never dreamed she would have access to, it only accentuated the woman that was already there. It seemed to Tess that was the lesson of all the Dark Gods. The powers that they gained did not change them, did not make them better or worse, but only accentuated that which was already there. It was a fact she had not seen until her mind had finally been quieted by Cedric's teachings. If only she had met him years ago, before her rages had endangered so many lives, before she had taken…

Her thoughts trailed off. She didn't want to remember. She didn't want to know what she had done when she had been taken by the power that was inside of her. Was what she thought of the Dark Gods true for her? Deep down, was she a killer? Was she like her father, one who could be so controlled by her emotions that she would not stop until any slight against her was remedied in blood? She looked down at her hands and for a moment she could see nothing by Devlin Rannoch's blood dripping from her fingertips. She had held his heart in her hands, and she had crushed the life out of him in her rage. She had murdered. And why had she done such a terrible thing? He didn't have the ability to threaten her life. He could not have known how he had wronged her. And had she truly been wronged by him at all? How could he have taken from her something that was not hers at all? This was the part of herself that she had tried so hard to hide from Cedric. She knew that he had sensed her shame and her guilt, as he had tried to teach her about responsibility and the prison it can create if you cannot allow yourself to grow from the mistakes you had made. He had once said that power not only creates opportunities, but it makes every mistake a thousand times larger than it would be for anyone else. When one has the power to move a mountain, or kill thousands with a thought, every misstep could be catastrophic. But it had not taken the loss of a thousand lives, or even a hundred, it had only taken one before Tess felt as though she was irredeemable. She knew now that that was the part of her that Emries had thought he could manipulate. If she hadn't seen into his mind when he asked her to conjure Cedric back from the beyond, she might have followed through with his bloody designs. But she was not the same now. She would prove herself worthy of Cedric's teachings, worthy of her abilities, and worthy of forgiveness for the life she took. And one day, she would be worthy of standing in front of Camille once again to beg for her forgiveness.

Camille. The love of Tess's life, the angel, the true heir to the leadership of the Dark Gods. She had a beauty inside of her that radiated in a way that could not be described with words. She was the embodiment of grace, of control, and of everything that could be good in the world. At least, that was how Tess always saw her. But Camille was her mother's daughter. She was strong and strong-willed, but controlled in a way that created a distance. The weight of her name was something that Camille took very seriously, and it was a responsibility that she would never shirk or disrespect. Camille had captured Tess's heart almost immediately, her fearlessness, her steadfastness, and her unshakeable faith in the potential for light to win out over darkness. She was a divine being, but her divinity was in the humanity that she took from her mother and father, and the love of that which she could have stood apart from. Even more than the twins Mirana and Liara, Camille was an anomaly among the Dark Gods, and she represented the best of what they could be. Thinking of Camille made Tess's heart flutter, and she swore she could almost feel Camille there with her, so close that Tess could reach out and touch her if she thought hard enough. But perhaps that was the power talking, the power that could remake reality and literally make Camille be there. Again, Tess shook away her thoughts and returned to those of Cedric, and the wonder for where he might be.

Cedric was patient with her, but he was stern. Thus far, he had spent most of his time helping her unlearn a lot of bad habits that she had learned in her time in the Citadel of the Dark Gods. And while at first these lessons in mundanity were frustrating and confusing, she had begun to see the truth of them. Like the stories that he told, there were always hidden meanings, and hidden lessons. Cedric had wanted more than for her to think like a mundane, he wanted her to think. He had once said that the enemies that they fight, the enemies that wanted Tess made into a weapon had existed since the dawn of the Cosmos, and that they were the very essence of everything that existed. Their plots and machinations stretched over the length and breadth of time itself, and their power defied anything that had ever been seen or experienced. The only way to fight such a foe was through thought, understanding, and attempting to see things in a way that their opponents were either unable to or unwilling to see any longer. In the same way that Tess had struggled to think mundane, so too did the Children of the Creator and the dragons. It the final stages of the war that was coming, humanity was the only true defense left. And so, Tess attempted to see beyond the lesson, see beyond the moment of the test and how the use of power would interfere with the act. The first time she was forced to light a fire without her powers was the hardest thing she had ever done, both physically and mentally. Before Cedric, it would have taken nothing more than an impulse, not even a thought, to construct the flame. She would have simply reached out with her abilities, grasped the primal forces of fire and then simply made it appear upon the pile of firewood and kindling. When she failed several times to use the flint and steel to make a spark that would more than cause smoke, she reached for her abilities and attempted to light the first that way. For a moment, the flame appeared and then was immediately doused by a combination of primal water and air. When Tess had looked up at Cedric, his face held no expression where she had expected to see either anger or disappointment. The fact that he had expected her disobedience grated at her nerves, and it took several moments to quiet her mind. When finally he asked her why the test was important, she began to see the answers. Cedric was far more practiced with his abilities than she was. Even though she was more powerful than he would ever be, she did not know the subtle and practiced flows the way he did. He was an artist compared to her instinctual clumsiness. So too would be the case were she to engage a Child of the Creator, or one of Dorovar's servants. Tess had watched Camille use every tactic and every power to fight off the beast Death, and Tess knew that she would have failed where Camille succeeded. That object lesson behind her, Tess redoubled her efforts, dedicated to never making the same mistake twice.

Lost in her own thoughts, Tess almost did not feel the subtle flows of power in the trees behind her. At first, she thought that it might have been Cedric using a portal to return to the campsite, but she immediately disregarded that theory. It was completely out of character for Cedric. Unless of course it was another one of his tests. He had said he wasn't going to take it easy on Tess after her failed attempt to ambush him. However, she remained suspicious. Getting to her feet, she recovered the long rod that she and Cedric used to stoke the fire and held it like a sword in front of her. She had never cared much for martial matters, and had never truly learned to fight. Perhaps that was Cedric's intention, to show her the necessity of being able to defend herself without her powers. There was a growing part of her that expected him to simply appear behind her and snatch the rod out of her hand and give her a lecture about her lack of awareness. But then she heard the slightest rustling in the tree in front of her. Whoever was moving toward her was doing their best to be silent, but Cedric's lessons and her quiet mind could detect even the smallest movement.

"I know you're there," she said with pride in her voice. "I felt your portal before it formed, and I heard you moving through the underbrush. But I'm sure you left just enough power visible that I could see it if I was paying attention."

There was another rustle from the undergrowth, but this time the approaching figure made no effort to obscure its approach. After several moments, a woman in a nearly transparent white dress emerged from the darkness. She was short by most standards, but her lithe frame was knotted with muscle and her every moved screamed of danger. Long blond curly hair streamed from her head like a waterfall, and she wore a silver band around her forehead that was encrusted with crystal. The band itself formed a V that dipped down above her nose and brought more attention to her slanted eyes. Those brilliant blue eyes were filled with power. On each of her hands she wore a dark leather apparatus that circled her forearm and wrist, and at the back of her hands erupted three long silver talons. Tess could feel the malice rolling off of the woman like waves, so thick that it felt like it could choke her. Just beyond the edge of the forest clearing, the woman stopped, her posture hunched like an animal about to pounce on its prey. When she spoke, there was hatred and contempt in her voice, the tone barely above a whisper.

"So you're what all the fuss is about," Alise said coldly. "I'm not supposed to kill you, but I'll hurt you if I have to."

* * * * * * * * * * * *

Cedric stood, tension flooding his body, and yet his mind had moved to that calm moment before the storm. A fight was coming, a fight in which he was most assuredly completely overmatched. Unlike his father, Cedric had not spent generations fighting beings that were above his level of ability. Yes, he had stood against Shau-ling, but that was on a slanted battlefield where the rules had been set so that Cedric would win. Still, it had almost cost Cedric everything, and he had had the help of so many powerful people. In his days as the Lord Lion, Cedric had never felt comfortable with his powers. They were as alien to him as those that Tess possessed. That was why he marveled at the girl's restraint. If he would have had the power to reshape reality as he saw fit, how much damage would he have done? Of course, he would have acted out of a desire to do good, but with that much power, it would have been perverted eventually. Already Tess had brought two people back from the beyond, an ability that was reserved for the Creator and the Children alone. Emries and his siblings had proven that they could only use that ability for their own gains, and the Creator seemed to do everything in furtherance of this perverted game that pit his children against one another. Not one of them seemed to care about the damage they caused with this power, and yet Tess had not been completely corrupted, at least not yet. The specter of the things she had done while under the influence of her abilities haunted her. She thought she had hidden the thoughts of the life she had taken, but the man's face was seared into her mind in a way that could not be hidden from one who knew how to look. Those were the types of thoughts that Emries sought to exploit. Her regret for the death she caused, the love she dared not speak of, and her admiration for those who taught her how to live in a world where she would be feared, hated, and hunted simply for drawing breath. And yet, she still resisted. She still desired a better world, a world in which she would be the author of a change that would resound through the Cosmos and save untold generations of lives on every world that existed or ever would exist. To Emries, the girl was a tool to destroy the Creator, destroy his enemies, and remake the Cosmos in his image, an image of strife, chaos, and turmoil. The danger was that Tess still was unable to see that the very expression of that power given form could destroy everything that she was trying to save and plunge the entirety of the Cosmos into a darkened desolate eternity.

That thought brought Cedric back to the present. His opponent was an emissary from the Creator, and while she gave a great speech about how Cedric should not have been back, and his existence was an affront to the Creator, something about the explanation rang only half-true. Cedric was sure there were parts of the picture that he didn't see, and he was doubly sure it had something to do with his father. Cedric had seen glimpses of what Aerith had been up to in Tess's mind, but there was more, so much more. This visitation however struck of desperation, something that should have been out of character for a being as powerful as the Creator. If He wanted Cedric dead, why didn't he just reach out and erase Cedric from existence? Or, why didn't He simply prevent Tess from bringing him back at all? Too many questions, and no time for answers. However, something kept gnawing at the back of Cedric's mind. The woman in front of him was familiar, and he could swear that he had seen her face before. She had something to do with Tess, and while Cedric could have reached across the distance and touched Tess's mind to find the answer, that would have alerted the girl to the situation Cedric found himself in, and she was liable to do something reckless. They were not far enough in their lessons for her to be trusted in a stressful situation, let alone a full-fledged battle. So, Cedric reached back through his own memories in an attempt to piece together those things he had gleaned from Tess's mind. However, his time was short. He saw the woman's hands begin to tense, and the wings begin to drawn in slightly. She was ready to charge forward, which in and of itself was telling.

In Cedric's experience, there were three kinds of people with power when it came to combat. The first kind were those like Cedric. They thought mortal first, relying on martial prowess or using their powers to accentuate their physical abilities. The direct use of power would happen from time to time, but it was rare and it was usually unpracticed and raw. The second type were those mortals born to power. They had the most well-rounded usage of power, and also tended to be more creative in the application of that power. Creatures like the phasia were the best example. Then there were the divine beings. They were power personified, and yet they seemed the most disinterested in innovative uses of power. They had so much at their disposal that direct overwhelming force seemed to be the only viable tactic. However, Emries and Halicon had learned from their mistakes dealing with humans and had started to become much more devious in their application of power. But the visceral instincts of the woman in front of Cedric belied a woman who relied on their training first. That meant she wasn't a warrior angel. She was something else, and that more than anything gave Cedric her identity.

"Do you know why you're really here, Camille?"

Cedric saw one of the woman's hands twitch and the blade in her right hand disappeared. However, she did not relax from her battle posture.

"So you know my name. While in some circles, names have power, in this situation, it matters very little if you know the identity of the person who shall be your end. And in answer to your question, I have already told you why I'm here. The Creator has decreed that you must cease to exist, and therefore I have been dispatched to insure that your end is quick."

Cedric kept his posture and tone even.

"But why you? Aren't you the daughter of two mortals? Mortals that once upon a time I would have counted among my friends and allies? Why wouldn't one of the Servants been dispatched? Or a flight of warrior angels? Why you? Unless there is another purpose for you being here. Do you know who it is that I'm training? Do you know who Emries put in my care? Or didn't the great and mighty Creator bother to tell you."

The light in Camille's eyes flared.

"Again, your arrogance and your ignorance prove the pointlessness of your continued existence. You spend so much time trying to figure out the nature of your existence, and you question the will of those who made you. Why do you believe that you are entitled to know the thoughts of the Creator? What makes you believe you have the intelligence to understand the grand pattern being laid out before you? I do not question the will of the Creator. I was given an order, and I am here to carry it out."

Cedric shook his head.

"And that, Camille, would be enough for me to pity you. You are not here to kill me. You aren't even here to remove me from whatever plan Emries has hatched. You are here for Tess."

The brilliant white light in the woman's eyes faltered for a moment and the eyes unclouded by divine power returned.

"Tess? She's here?"

Cedric nodded slowly and extended his hands out to his sides as a demonstration of his willingness to continue talking. However, he continued to let trickles of power fill him in case the parlay failed and the woman decided that action was the only course left.

"Emries brought her here to turn her into a weapon against the Creator. He means to use her abilities to kill the rest of his siblings and take the Golden Throne for himself. Tess pulling me back from the beyond is his idea of some kind of poetic irony. That he would use me to train the instrument of his final victory. I'm sure he intends to make me watch him tear everything apart before finally making me pay for my lack of faith and betrayal. But Tess is innocent in this. I'm trying to give her the opportunity to make her own choices and not to fall into the trap that Emries has made for her."

Cedric considered his next words very carefully. They could drag the winged woman more fully back to her mortal self, or it could push her completely back into the Creator's servitude.

"That's really why you're here. Emries controlling Tess is bad enough, but if she is left to make her own decisions, she could be a threat to the Creator because she could fall into my father's hands. That's what the Creator is worried about. I don't know what Aerith is up to, but I know he's the one that the Creator is the most worried about. I don't know how I know it, but I feel it just as assuredly as I feel how much you care of Tess. Do you want to be the one to kill me and then be forced to kill her? Could you do that? Could you see her look you in the eye as you choke the life out of her? Could you live with yourself with her blood on your hands?"

Camille blinked hard twice, and for a moment the other weapon disappeared from her hand. Her wings relaxed and her shoulders started to sink. However, before she had a chance to take any action, a blinding wreath of white energy sprang up around her, and a guttural, visceral scream of pain ripped from the woman's tortured body. The aura of white receded slightly and the woman's features came back into view. The brilliant white energy had returned to her eyes, and they burned cold with hate. Her hair had been lifted by the incredible power that radiated from every pore of her body, and twin blades of fire appeared in her hands. Whatever humanity had been reignited in the woman had been snuffed out by the Creator's intervention.

"Your words mean nothing. The Creator has decreed your death. Nothing will stand in the way of your execution."

Two things happened simultaneously, and Cedric was not able to process the sequence of events until after he hit the ground. A flash of power lanced out from Camille aimed straight for Cedric's chest. There was another flash of power from Cedric's right, and the shockwave from it sent the former Lord Lion flying through the air, landing hard on the ground at the base of a tree. Pain rocketed through his shoulder and his chest, and for a moment he wasn't sure if he was on the edge of death or simply suffering from several broken bones in his arm, shoulder, and ribs. When he looked up, another form stood where he had been merely moments before, a faint spectral green energy circling her stark white body. One hand was extended forward where it had intercepted Camille's strike. The tips of the figure's fingers looked as though they were covered with blood. The woman radiated cold in all directions, and she regarded Cedric for the briefest of moments before turning her full attention to Camille. When she spoke, her voice conveyed a power unlike Cedric had ever heard.

"Flee."

The power flared up around Camille once more, and then lanced out like a dagger in the direction of the interloper. A split-second before the strike would have hit, the stranger's hand batted the energy away. It struck a tree several feet away, breaking it free from the ground and sending it toppling and crashing to the ground. When the woman's voice came again, Cedric could feel the malice roll across him like a wave.

"Die."

CHAPTER 106

Chapter CVII

The Crucible of Conscience

Year Two of the Divine Empress and Child of the Creator
Marlae Tamerlane, Creator's Calendar Year 1872

Marlae Lorien awoke in her soft and luxuriant bed and felt the silk sheets lightly brushing against her pampered naked skin. She kept her eyes closed for several long moments, savoring the feel of the silk encasing her. The pillows that held her head were just soft enough, but not so soft that she felt as though her head had sunk into a cloud. Feeling the soft embrace of sleep beginning to flee from her muscles and joints, Marlae arched her back slowly, keeping her shoulders to the mattress and sinking her hips deeper into the featherbed. The covers pulled away from her body, sliding down from around her neck, across her chest, settling just below her breasts. The air in the room was cool, and she felt it tickle across her exposed flesh. Slowly she let her eyes begin to open and despite herself, she felt a smile come across her face. There was a soft light in the room, and it seemed to bounce off of the lightly colored walls, bringing the whole room the colors of early sunrise. Propping herself up onto her right elbow, she looked around her room and felt the smile deepen. A large wardrobe stood in the far corner of the room, the doors open, showing the collection of the finest gowns in all the Empire. Hanging from one of the doors was a black and burgundy dress that once belonged to her step-mother, Dominique, but it was torn and stained with blood. A fitting monument to the end of the woman's life. From the other door hung the crown that her father once wore when he reigned as the Emperor of Cadaria. It was cracked and tarnished now; his name nearly forgotten in the shadow of the greatness that Marlae had brought to the title.

Marlae pulled herself from the bed gently and let her feet softly touch the cool floor. She stretched her toes apart, first on her left foot, and then her right before stretching once more and standing up. Her soft and curly hair cascaded down her back, long enough now to reach the small of her back. A nearly transparent robe hung from the gilded footboard, and she recovered it and slipped it gently over her shoulders, but didn't close it. Wiping the last bit of sleep from her eyes, while stretching one last time, she ambled slowly away from her bed toward the door of the warm bedchamber.

Two delicately featured female servants snapped to attention as soon as the door to the bedchamber opened. Marlae paused only a moment, inspecting their scandalous attire out of the corner of her eye before continuing on down the corridor. She suppressed a small smile when she heard the soft footsteps fall in behind her less than two paces behind. While the young women may not have looked like much, they were the deadliest of assassins that could be found in Marlae's empire, and they were not to be trifled with. At the end of the corridor, two more assassins waited, and then led Marlae out of the corridor into the large common room that waited beyond.

The room was filled with people, representatives from each of the great kingdoms, and all manner of people who wished boons from the Empress. As soon as the corridor door opened all in attendance fell to one knee. Marlae hesitated at the door, enjoying the adoration for several moments before slowly walking through the throng and ascending the dais and standing before the golden throne. She stood waiting, looking over the assemblage before perching herself on the very edge of the throne, feeling the cold hard metal against her barely covered skin. As she looked out upon those gathered dignitaries and sycophants, a thought ran through the back of her mind. This all seemed familiar somehow, and it also seemed completely wrong. At that moment, Marlae became aware of another presence in the room, a powerful presence that defied description.

"Isn't this what you've always dreamed of?" a voice said from the doorway to Marlae's right.

Marlae wanted to crane her neck to take in the full features of the person who spoke, but she suddenly realized that she could not move. Only her eyes could dart in that direction, her impotent body rebelling against the directions of her confused and panicked mind. Marlae tried to respond to the question but she found that she could not even speak a response as her jaw and tongue had ceased functioning.

"How long have you fantasized about this moment?" the distinctly female voice said from the darkness at the edge of a torch's flickering illumination. "Your father defeated, disgraced, and summarily discarded like so much refuse. Your step-mother, the angelic whore brought low, her body broken in a ditch somewhere like the common filth she was in life. Everyone in Cadaria lusting after you. Every man and woman wanting to share your bed, offering their bodies, their wealth, their eternal love to the one and only true Empress of Cadaria. A true credit to the Lorien name. A return to the greatness that has led Cadaria for nearly two millennia."

Finally, the speaker came into view. She was not beautiful, and yet at the same time she was captivating. Her features were cruel and cold and the darkness around her eyes seemed to be pools of evil that directed you to stare into those heartless depths. The woman exuded hate, disgust, and rage. Her black and gold garments clung to her gaunt frame, and her pale almost dead-white skin seemed to absorb the ambient light of the chamber. Gloom and fear trailed off her like a cloak, and her steps were light but still echoed through the chamber like the tolling of the undertaker's bell. Her brilliant green eyes flashed, radiating lust and jealousy and avarice; a hunger that could never be sated. Full black colored lips drew into a prideful smile and long flowing black hair framed her statuesque face.

"What you wouldn't have given to be here. The world at your feet, at your beck and call. Have you given up on this dream, Marlae? Have you forgotten the woman that you wanted to be? Do you no longer wish to be loved by all who see you? Do you no longer wish to see the hunger in their eyes as they fawn over you? Do you no longer wish to have the power to destroy your enemies with the snap of your fingers? To see them brought low at your whim?"

The woman approached Marlae slowly, seemingly judging each of her steps; her hate-filled eyes never leaving Marlae's, sending nearly imperceptible shivers through the Divine Empress's uncooperative body. Cold had begun to fill Marlae, the cold of the grave, a cold that penetrated flesh and bone and could never be sated until it gnawed through every last visage of warmth, hope, and love.

"I am here to offer you that power, Marlae. I am here to give you the power to be not a Divine Empress in name, but in reality. I can give you the means to become a goddess. A goddess of such beauty that all who look upon you will instantly fall in love and will gladly spill the blood of your enemies or their own at your command. Not the love of a sycophantic pretender, but true unadulterated love that will burn inside of them until it wrenches their hearts and they go to the grave with your name on their lips. This world can be your temple, with millions of supplicants screaming your name. Isn't that what you always wanted?"

Marlae wanted to shake her head; wanted to cry out and shout down the words of the woman who jabbed at her soul. The hateful woman began to lean in, her fingers extending towards Marlae's face when suddenly she stopped and turned her attention to the darkness to Marlae's left. She took several steps back from Marlae and turned in the direction of the darkness. Marlae felt a new presence in the room, and out of the corner of her eye she could see a green glow begin to radiate in all directions. There, just at the edges of her perception she could see a figure appear at the center of the green glow. A gaunt figure of a man in tattered white robes, but a man whose power could be clearly felt. His long, thin, bony fingers arched into a steeple before him, and the heavily pointed chin seemed to perch there like a hawk waiting to swoop down on its prey. If the woman before Marlae was hate personified, then this man was the personification of fear.

"Do not listen to the witch" a raspy voice came from the gaunt man, though his lips did not move, "you need not her assistance to become that which you have been ordained to become. You need only turn your eyes away from the lie that is the Creator. You can be a queen upon this world, upon every world. There is a new Cosmos that will be created. One of perfect order as it was always meant to be. There will be no suffering, no death, no famine, no greed, no war. There will only be peace and harmony.

The vision of the new utopia is beginning to take shape, and as more voices join my Chorus of Souls, I move toward the ultimate realization of that vision. In that utopia, one that will stretch to every world within Creation, there will be no need for my Heralds. There will be no need for subjugation or for slaughter. There will only be the harmony of Order, brought to every world by the voice of my High Priestess. She will speak only of love, and the purpose of life. Each and every being in my new Cosmos will be born and bred for their purpose. No questions, no worries about the future. They shall live as they were meant to, and shall prosper accordingly. My High Priestess shall shepherd my flock for eternity, unwavering, revered, and beautiful. Very soon the soul of my beloved High Priestess will be in my possession, and you need only accept it, and you shall live forever in the perfection that I shall create."

The hateful woman stepped further away from Marlae and rounded on the gaunt man whom Marlae had immediately identified as the demon Dorovar.

"You speak like my fallen sister, Dorovar," the woman fumed. "You speak of a perfect order, like your precious world Loinn. But what happened to your world? Did it not burn even with your perfect order?"

Dorovar's expression did not change, but Marlae could feel the rage building within him. When he spoke again, the green glow around him pulsed with each word, and the pulses were accompanied by waves of anger, hate, and rage.

"My world fell because of treachery, Talisia, your treachery. My people were betrayed by you, by Emries, by the dragons, and in the end by our own goddess Raenera. But it was you who were the architect of our downfall."

Talisia laughed loudly and viciously. It was clear that the characterization as the destroyer of Dorovar's world pleased her immensely.

"And how much did it take to tempt your world into destroying itself, Dorovar? It took only appealing to your vanity. Your goddess appears to you in dreams, pushing you down a path you knew to be wrong and dangerous, and yet you leapt at the possibility to be special. To rise above the station that Raenera decreed for you. It was you, Dorovar who broke your perfect order. If you or your Adhradair had been satisfied with your stations, with your world, with your order, we could not have tempted you from your path. You failed Raenera, she did not fail you. You failed your world; it was not betrayed. This Cosmos you seek to build will fall just as Loinn did, because there is no perfect order, and there will always be a desire for more. You will forge a flawed perfection, because you are flawed and believe you are not. You blame, you rage, and yet you will never see that it was you and your Adhradair that failed all that you believed in. They are slaves to your failure, just as you are a slave to your own arrogance and desire for power."

The green glow began to pulse faster around Dorovar, waves of anger burst forth in all directions shaking the world around Marlae. But in the light, she caught a glint out of the corner of her eye. There, on a low table to her left, was a small hand mirror, obviously a nod to the vanity that Talisia was trying to prey upon, a holdover from her former life as Marlae Lorien. There was motion in the mirror the next moment, and a familiar and comforting face appeared. It was not her own, but it instead belonged to her new namesake, Elwyne Tamerlane. That moment, Marlae realized that her left hand and arm were able to move. She began to reach for the mirror, but before her delicate fingers could touch the silvery surface and blinding white light filled the room. Marlae could vaguely hear both Dorovar and Talisia cry out, but their voices seemed very far away. The light completely overwhelmed her senses, and she felt herself losing her hold on consciousness. She drifted there for several moments, on the edge of dreams, her mind trying to piece together everything that had happened and desperately trying to wake up. Brilliant white still held her vision, but she no longer felt nothingness around her. Where moments before she had felt the cold hard throne beneath her, in its place was a luxurious softness that encased her entire body. As consciousness returned more fully to her mind, she began to place the sensations that tickled her bare skin. Beneath her was one of the softest feather mattresses that she had ever had the pleasure to lie upon, and atop her was a comforter of similar lightness. Her head rested upon a pillow that was slightly firm, but still was decadent in its silken covering. As more of her senses reawakened, and again she was struck with the familiarity of the sensations. Finally, the brilliant light receded and Marlae's eyes opened. As she looked up into the well-lit room that surrounded the opulent bed, a pang of regret and one of joy filled her. The white walls, ornate carvings and colorful tapestries made the room unmistakable, and the slight hint of salt in the air that flooded through an open window meant that she could be only one place, her quarters in the Royal Palace of Hedorah, the place where she had become Marlae Tamerlane, the Divine Empress of Cadaria.

Marlae wasted no time in bounding from the bed, ignoring the cold of the floor as it hit her bare feet. She moved quickly to the wardrobe on the other side of the room and quickly selected a blue dress that had rapidly become her favorite. The shoulders and bust of the dress had patterns of lighter greens and blues that made the dress look as though it had been patterned after the sea, while brilliant gold filigree and embroidery were woven into the sleeves, below the bust-line, and down the hips to the floor. The dress hung low on her shoulders, but did not expose more than her clavicles. The Divine Empress no longer desired to display herself the way the old Marlae had. Instinctively she moved to the two full-length mirrors beside the wardrobe after pulling the dress on, but found that the mirrors were not there. Puzzled, she moved to her nightstand to recover her hand mirror, to find that it too was missing. She barely had time to process the strange absences when she heard a knock at the door. Marlae was just able to turn around before the door opened. She didn't realize that she was holding her breath until a woman entered the room, and the confusion forced her to breathe.

The woman who stood in the doorway was an enigma. She stood tall and proud like a noble, but the broader than lady-like shoulders and firmly set jaw made Marlae think that the woman had trained as a warrior. Her body was lithe but muscular, and she wore a man's pants and tunic with a green waistcoat that clung tightly to her shoulders. The woman's features were fair, with high cheekbones and full lips that were curled into a frown. Long red hair was pulled into a tail and hung over her right shoulder. Piercing white eyes locked on Marlae, and the young empress could not suppress a shiver.

"I thought perhaps you were tired of your uninvited guests, Empress," the woman said with a clipped accent that Marlae could not place. It was not from one of the Kingdoms of Cadaria, that much was certain. She sounded more like Elwyne. "The Creator wanted to be sure that you were not taken advantage of by agents who wish you nothing but harm."

The woman regarded Marlae for but another moment before moving to the open windows and onto the balcony overlooking the city. Marlae did not move from her spot, but turned to face the new arrival. The woman stood on the balcony for several moments before turning back to Marlae. Suddenly able to find her voice once more Marlae spoke, but when she did, her voice felt small.

"Who are you?"

The woman's frown deepened.

"The Creator wanted to be sure that you are still dedicated to the path that has been set for you, Divine Empress, and that you are not wavering when faced with all of these…."

The woman's voice trailed off and she turned back to the cityscape the stretched out beyond the bounds of the balcony.

"….distractions."

Finally, Marlae moved from where she stood and approached the windowed wall that led to the wide balcony. She kept some distance between herself and the mystery woman not leaving the security of the room for the uncertainty of the balcony.

"I assure you," Marlae said, feeling some strength return to her voice, "I will not waver."

The woman spun on her heels, her eyes flashing with power.

"Will you not now? Perhaps you're thinking that your former lover Rhain will come to your rescue, or maybe Logan Ranthall will set your blood on fire once more the way that he did when you first set eyes upon him. Are these mortal concerns more important than the Creator's command? Will you fail him after all that he has done to help you redeem yourself from that silly little girl who acted more like a whore than a ruler?"

The words from the severe woman made Marlae's blood run cold. But before she could respond, the woman thundered again.

"Because Logan Ranthall is not coming to save you. He will not save anyone ever again."

She pointed out from the balcony to the city.

"There he lies. His body broken, his heart still, his blood flowing into the water that is engulfing what was supposed to be the Creator's city. The Phoenix, the Dragon, the pretender, the hero, the legend, the villain, all he was to people on this world and the world of his birth is gone. Soon he will not even be a memory when the Creator wipes this world clean of the influences of his Children and elevates the faithful to their rightful positions. And you, Marlae Tamerlane, are to be the instrument of that rebirth."

Marlae's heart beat wildly in her chest.

"I don't understand."

One corner of the woman's lips twisted into the barest smirk.

"Understanding, my dear little empress is not required. Only obedience. You are a servant of the Creator, and you will do as you're instructed."

The woman took a step forward, and a sword made of pure holy fire appeared in her hand.

"Do you understand that?"

Marlae wanted to shrink back, wanted to run away, and for the first time she was truly afraid of a servant of the Creator. She had never been afraid of Ayden, or of the warrior angels, but this woman, whoever she was, was absolutely terrifying.

"The Creator will deliver unto you the means by which you will end this war. Already the weapon is being procured for your father. Once it is in his grasp, you will convince your paramour to commit all of the forces she has at her disposal to seize the weapon from Kaitain and to crush him and his forces. Then you shall be rid of him, rid of the scourge of the Lorien name, and free of the blasphemous attacks he has been launching upon the faithful that you are sworn to protect. Once the weapon is in your control, you shall use it to destroy your paramour, the children of Halicon, as well as Aerith Seth and his disciples. The angels and the marshalled forces of the Heavens shall gather at your back, and you shall sweep across the face of this world eliminating the dragons, the Dark Gods, the remaining Children, their followers, and any who are non-believers. Only the faithful shall be left on Espre. This is the command of the Creator."

As the woman finished speaking, Marlae caught motion out of the corner of her eye, and realized with a start why the mirrors were no longer in the room. Whoever this woman was had done everything in her power to prevent Elwyne from interceding on Marlae's behalf. That was why she interceded in the confrontation between Dorovar and Talisia. But Elwyne was not to be denied so easily. Marlae could see the woman's reflection in the window to her left, and she quickly angled her body so that she stood between the reflection and the mysterious woman. If she could stall the woman long enough to work her way toward the reflection, she might be able to rid herself of this endless nightmare.

"What is this weapon, and how am I to use it to do all of these things in the name of the Creator?"

"The weapon is known as the Dragon's Tear...."

The woman's voice trailed off. Her white eyes flashed and the frown on her face deepened.

"You cannot hide your thoughts from me, little Empress. I am the Spirit of the Creator, and I know all that moves within his Creation. You are an extension of his will, and as such your every thought, your every desire, and your every emotion is His to know. You will give me your thoughts, or I shall take them from you."

Marlae knew she had only seconds. Even as the brilliant white light began to flare in all directions centered on the Spirit, Marlae turned and dove toward the wall of windows and extended her hands toward the bare glint of the reflection of the long-dead woman who had given Marlae her name and her inspiration. Just before the light enveloped her, Marlae's outstretched fingers brushed against the glass.

The next moment, Marlae was no longer in the Palace of Hedorah, but was instead in what appeared to be a simple farmhouse. While in her life as Marlae Lorien she would have abhorred a place like this, now she found the simplicity peaceful and comforting. She was in the bedroom of the farmhouse, laying upon the thick quilt that covered the simple sheets. There was a slight chill in the air, and as she sat up, she heard a woman clear her throat from the doorway.

"I tried to warn you."

Elwyne moved to the edge of the bed and sat beside Marlae.

"No matter what you may think, Marlae, there are forces that are going to try to use you, going to try to make you do things you would never do all in the name of the glory of Marlae Lorien. They will flatter, they will cajole, and they will make you think that you are the most important person in the world. But all of this is not for you, you are merely a means to an end. You can only believe your heart, and you must use it to see through to the truth of these schemes."

Marlae's heart ached and her head throbbed. This was all too much.

"These people can enter my dreams. They can make me listen to them. They're too powerful."

Elwyne clicked her tongue.

"I wouldn't think you would give up so easily. I thought you were stronger than that."

Marlae instantly felt the color rush to her cheeks. She was afraid, but more than that she felt as though she had let Elwyne down. This woman who had been forced to sacrifice so much had given her the opportunity to be better than she thought she could be, and forced Marlae to recognize the truly ugly things about herself.

"I want to fight."

Marlae felt the words come out and knew that they were weak. While the conviction may have been inside of her, it did not shine through in her words. The next moment Marlae felt Elwyne's doubt. Marlae took a breath, focused her mind and spoke again.

"I want to fight."

Marlae looked at Elwyne and saw the woman nod.

"Better. Now. Remember that you are in control of your own mind. No matter how these other forces try to influence you and make you think that you are subject to their will, you are not. But as you have seen, you will have to work hard to find escapes from their machinations. What I can tell you, Marlae, is that the best way to resist is to root yourself in those things that you love."

Elwyne looked down at the floor and smoothed her dress.

"Once I was captured by the phasia and brought before Halicon to be tortured. He wanted to break me to use me against the people that I loved. And no matter how much it hurt, no matter what thoughts he tried to force into my head, I brought myself to this place. Logan's farmhouse. A place I knew I would always be safe, a place I would always find love and happiness. This sanctuary allowed me to escape the pain and the torment, and kept me strong. When they come for you again, and you know they will, you must find a place where you are safe and loved. The place where you want to be more than any other."

Slowly Elwyne rose from the bed and turned to face Marlae, a weak smile on her face.

"Now that the Spirit knows about me, she will cut off any route for me to speak with you. You'll have to find your own way now. Close your eyes and put yourself where you most want to be. Once there concentrate on waking up. And remember, you are in control and you must remain in control if you want to see your way through this. Your greatest strength has always been your independence and your will. Do not let them be bent to someone else's purpose. You have the chance to make this world better, and all it requires is that you believe."

Marlae closed her eyes and imagined the place where she wanted to be the most, the place where she felt safest; the place where she felt loved and protected. A warmth flooded through her. That next moment Marlae felt as though she were deep under water, held there by forces that she could not see. However, the grip on her had relented and she pushed toward the surface, out of the dreaming and back into consciousness.

The first sensation that came to Marlae was that she was very warm. Immediately she was able to place herself back in the large comfortable bed in the stronghold of the Shadow Guild, the thick comforter and sheet covering her. She was drenched in sweat and instinctively kicked the covers away to feel the cool air upon her skin. The next moment Marlae realized that she was not alone, and that there was a form sitting on the edge of the bed beside her. Wiping the sweat and sleep from her eyes, it took only a moment for Rhain's red hair to spark Marlae's recognition. Marlae flung herself in the woman's direction, wrapping her arms around Rhain and burying her suddenly tear strained face into her shoulder.

"It's alright Marlae," came Rhain's comforting voice as she stroked Marlae's hair. "I heard you cry out and I came to make sure you were safe."

For several minutes Rhain held Marlae as she cried, stroking her hair and holding her close. When finally Marlae calmed, she pulled back slightly and looked up to meet Rhain's eyes. Rhain smiled warmly and kissed Marlae lightly on the forehead.

"I see that your elevated status hasn't kept you from sleeping nude."

Marlae felt herself blush and then could not keep herself from laughing. Without a word she reached up and pulled Rhain's lips down to hers and kissed her more passionately than she had ever dared share with anyone. That next moment, as she felt Rhain's arms snake around her body and pull her close, Marlae knew exactly where she wanted to be, a place she would always be safe and feel loved.

Where Patience has Lease

Year Four of the Just Emperor Kaitain "Dragonsbane" Lorien, Creator's Calendar Year 1871

The stream of curses that flowed from Aerith's mouth brought an involuntary blush to Hannah's cheeks. He wasn't talking to anyone in particular, he was simply cursing at the sky, at a variety of those who had wronged him. Finally the torrent of profanity ceased and he dropped to the ground into a seated position, his left leg bent slightly, his right straight. His head hung, and for the first time Hannah could see the mass of scars and still-open wounds on the man. He had never looked so human as he did in that moment. The large black Snag bounced in his direction and sat regarding Aerith for a long moment before it bumped against his leg. Without looking, Aerith reached down and collected the Snag, letting it rest on his slumping shoulders. After several moments, Aerith's head raised again and he turned it slightly in Hannah's direction. With his right hand he patted the ground beside him and Hannah wasn't sure how to take the disarming gesture. Finally, the absurdity of it all was too much and Hannah found herself sinking down onto the ground beside her patron in one of the patches that was not completely covered in blood and gore. For a long time the two just sat there, looking at nothing in particular. Finally, Aerith lifted his head again and looked in Hannah's direction.

"So how has your day been?"

Hannah just stared at him, mouth agape. It was the most absurd question she had ever heard in her life. And then she could not help herself and began laughing. She laughed loud and long, and Aerith's chuckle joined hers in the advancing darkness. In the back of her mind Hannah even thought she felt the Snag laughing, a truly confusing and somewhat terrifying occurrence. When the laughter finally ended, Hannah became aware that the massive dragon Mariti Brightblade had ambled in their direction, looking at the two humans with a suspicious and disapproving glare.

"So this is the heretic? Somehow you are exactly what I was expecting."

Aerith looked first up at Mariti and then over to Hannah.

"I think she just insulted me."

Hannah's eyes were filled with caution and she shook her head slightly. She was not sure that Aerith's irreverence would have been accepted for what it was given everything they had all just gone through. Mariti was a proud creature, and she would not stand being condescended to, especially by a human. Aerith, as though processing and then wholly rejecting Hannah's warning, looked back up at Mariti.

"You know," Aerith said softly, "I met your Serentis. Strange creature, but seemed to like me pretty well, though she didn't appreciate my sense of humor either."

A low growl came from the dragon.

"I've lost brothers this day, heretic. I've watched many of my kind fall, and there will be more losses before this war is done, losses that the race of dragons may never be able to recover from. And here you sit, like some petulant child, like all humans, laughing at nothing and cursing at the gods for the blight that has been visited upon you. How have you survived this long?"

Aerith got to his feet and dusted himself off. He walked to where Mariti stood and looked up. The dragon lowered her head and stared down her long snout at the tiny human.

"I've lost too, dragon. More than perhaps you could ever perceive. I've lost people I love, and now my wife is gone, a girl I considered my daughter is gone, and perhaps my greatest champion is gone. And do you know what I've learned through all of this? Do you know why I'm sitting here cursing the sky and laughing at the absurdity of all of this? Because the Creator is afraid of me. Afraid of what we are doing. And I am committed now, more than ever to changing all of this, and setting it right. So if you dragons are true to your word, if you really do want to set right the mistakes that you've made, then you will fight by my side. If not, you just attend to your business and stay out of my way."

The massive dragon stared at the tiny creature for a long moment, and then raised her head, taking a long step back.

"We have an accord, heretic. And your protégé has proven herself to be worthy of the bargain that we have made to you and your followers. I go now to meet with Serentis at Albitonin to make plans for the next phase of the war with Shadowweaver and Dorovar. Even now, Shadowweaver is gathering his strength for a crushing assault. It will not matter if he is the only dragon left standing when the war is over. He cares only for his own survival and his own supremacy."

Without a response from either Aerith or Hannah, Mariti turned her back to the humans and with one hard beat of her massive wings, the huge creature burst into the air and flew to the south west in the direction of Albitonin. Aerith watched the creature go, and shook his head slightly.

"You know, I'm a little jealous." He turned back to face Hannah. "I've never had a chance to fight one of those things."

Again Hannah was left speechless by Aerith's disarming candor and his complete lack of an ability to take any situation seriously.

"You can gladly have the next opportunity."

Aerith smiled slightly and then turned back and watched as the massive dragon disappeared from sight over the horizon. When finally he turned back, the levity was gone from his eyes, and the weight of everything he had been through since the last time Hannah had laid eyes upon him was clear. She had felt ripples of anger and pain during their time apart, but now that he was so close, she could tell that he was barely able to keep himself moving forward. It was as if a part of him was missing, a part that he didn't know if he could ever replace.

"Well, things could certainly be better."

Hannah recognized the shift. Aerith had switched back to a mode of practicality. There was still the war to fight, and whatever he was feeling, he was going to push it down and compartmentalize it until there was a time and place for it. That time of course might never come to pass. He put his hand out to Hannah, which she accepted, and Aerith helped her to her feet. There was something in his eyes, a pain or perhaps a sorrow that had not been there a moment earlier. It was as though he was taking in Hannah's features in case he never saw them again.

"We don't have time for a full catch-up, Hannah, so I'll give you the short version. We're losing, and we're losing too quickly. Sabrina is gone, Logan may be gone too, and Dorovar has too many footholds. Talisia and Emries are dividing our forces, and the whole of Cadaria is turning itself into a wasteland. Hedorah is gone, Rashaleb is a graveyard, Zevarit is about to become a warzone, the Academy of Arcane Arts is gone, Menoris has been leveled, Aldere is a crater, and Galateria might as well be an enemy stronghold. It's like we're being herded."

Hannah did the quick math in her mind.

"That's why you sent the dragons to Albitonin. You want to make a last stand."

Aerith frowned.

"I don't like that word. I don't believe in last stands, but I like that my opponents do."

Hannah's eyes went wide.

"You're setting a trap? You want our enemies to commit all of their forces to attacking Albitonin."

Aerith grimaced.

"I needed a target. And I needed to use what little information I had against our enemies. Unfortunately, I did it without knowing what I needed to know. I made the trap too good, and I may have ended up trapping myself in the process."

Hannah frowned.

"I don't understand."

The admission brought a smile to Aerith's face.

"I'd be a little worried if you did. I don't understand it all myself, but I'm starting to see some of the pieces. They're all trying to use my family against me, against us all. The Creator, the Children. They've made it personal. I don't quite understand why. I think Bryn was starting to, and maybe that's why Ayden took her. The Creator didn't want her to tell me what she found out. But that didn't stop the Creator from slipping up and giving me more information than I already had. It wasn't arrogance so much as certainty. He's certain he's going to win, so it doesn't matter what he tells me. He doesn't think I'm smart enough to put the pieces together in time."

Being raised in the bosom of the Church of the Creator, Hannah reflexively blanched at the characterization of the Creator. It was blaspheme of the highest order, but Hannah was quickly realizing that blaspheme was the very definition of Aerith's existence.

"And you know what," Aerith continued, "he's probably right. I'm not smart enough. But I know people who are, and it's time to call in all my old markers."

There was a look in Aerith's eyes, one that didn't fill Hannah with a great amount of confidence. However, before she could give her concerns voice, he continued.

"I have to find out what's going on with my children. That's the piece the Creator let slip. All of my kids are in play, being used for some purpose or another. I thought Gideon and Cedric were dead, but apparently not. I have to figure out how this all fits together before we run out of time."

The next question was out of Hannah's mouth before she realized it.

"What about Bryn?"

Aerith smirked.

"As I have been reminded constantly today, Bryn can take care of herself, and as much as I want to go chasing after her to save her from whatever Ayden is going to do, I have to resist the urge. If Ayden had wanted her dead, he just could have let her die here. If the Creator really wanted her dead, we wouldn't have escaped the Heavens. She's still alive somewhere, I just know it, and so I have to keep us on track. Maybe the Creator wanted Ayden to take her to distract me, or to keep me off balance. I think it's just to keep that piece of the puzzle out of my reach. So, I have to go see Rhain. I have to figure this out before whatever is going on with Cedric and Gideon is too far gone for us to stop it."

Hannah looked past Aerith in the direction of the shelter in which the refugees of the Academy remained hidden. The structure looked completely undamaged from the twin conflicts, presumable because of some action taken by the Masters of the Academy. Aerith felt Hannah's gaze and turned to face the structure himself. He sighed deeply, shook his head, and then began walking in the direction of the structure. Hannah fell in step behind him and then immediately wished she hadn't.

"Maybe we all would have been better off if they had destroyed themselves," he mumbled to himself. "It might have solved a lot of problems in the long run."

Hannah tried to keep her emotions in check, tried to repress the wave of revulsion but she was unable to keep the bile from rising into her throat. Aerith stopped short, turned around and locked eyes with Hannah. There was the barest trace of sympathy there, but what came through the most in his gaze was cold and hard; the steely gaze of a man who had seen too much destruction, and been the cause of too much death.

WHERE PATIENCE HAS LEASE

"There are truths in this world, Hannah, truths that cannot be avoided. The masters of the Academy and their students are weapons that are just begging to be used by all sides of this war. And as much as I would love to have them fighting alongside us, I don't trust them. Perhaps there was a time earlier in this war when they could have been safely approached and engaged, but now they are afraid, they are desperate, and they wish for nothing more than to go back to the way things were before Alistair Ravenheart was murdered. When they could hide behind their vows of neutrality and using their abilities for defense only, they were predictable and sedate. Now, will they be moved to use their abilities to get revenge on Kaitain? Will they be able to control their abilities in the face of the stress of war and not reduce this world to a cinder? Despite their desires to do good, they are still humans, and thus are still going to fail. And don't forget, Emries and Talisia are still out there. Kaitain and others can only try to influence the Masters by intimidation, bribery, and cajoling. Emries and Talisia would not stop at mortal means, and they could easily reach into the minds of the Masters and turn them into puppets with terrifying power and no compunction about using that power. I guess you can say that we've been lucky so far that those with power who have approached the Academy have done so clumsily. That won't hold true much longer."

Hannah took in his words and tried to see the logic in them, but she could not. There were still things about her upbringing; the lessons of the inherent value of all life, that would never leave her. Regardless of the expediency that may have been served by the removal of the members of the Academy from the war, they still had just as much right to live as any of the other people that Aerith and the Dark Gods said they were fighting for. Sensing that she had dug her heels in, Aerith sighed and shook his head. Things would be so much easier if she just would see things his way. But unlike those they were fighting against, Aerith would just have to settle for letting Hannah come around to the truth in her own time.

"I'll be nice," he said finally, before turning back and placing his hand on the door.

A second later, he pulled his hand away, shaking it furiously. There was a spark of lightning that rippled across the door the next moment, and Aerith laughed in spite of himself before turning back to Hannah.

BRIAN C. KERSHNER - 341

"After you."

Hannah moved past Aerith and took a breath before putting her own hand on the handle of the door. There was no reaction as there had been to Aerith, and with a gentle push the door opened. She felt the next comment long before it came.

"I guess they like you better."

Hannah stifled her scowl and strode confidently into the structure, her eyes flowing quickly to where she knew the Masters of the Academy would still be waiting. Kiara was waiting there too, her ministrations to the students finished for the time being. Aerith stayed in step behind her, and before either could say anything, Aris Ebonsight spoke.

"I trust the danger has passed and we have you once again to thank for our safety."

Again there was a small wave of annoyance that came from Aerith, but this one was not one of irritation, but more one of humor at the lack of understanding that the Masters displayed. They may have been learned by mortal standards, but certainly not by Aerith's. The thought struck Hannah in a way she didn't expect. For a brief moment, when Aerith was thinking about mortals, she no longer counted herself among them. That in itself was enough to give her pause. What disturbed her more was the fact that she did not find the distinction disturbing. She now did see herself apart, as the other, the outsider with the ability to impact those who could not possibly understand the abilities she had at her disposal. Hannah shook herself away from those thoughts, refocused her intentions and spoke.

"The danger has passed for now, but that won't last for long. If anything the battleground has merely shifted."

Fiona nodded and looked past Hannah to Aerith.

"And this is?"

Hannah tried hard to suppress a scowl from coming to her features, but she knew from the slight widening in Aris' eyes, that she had failed. Aerith didn't move from his place over Hannah's shoulder, but she could feel his eyes moving across the Masters until finally they rested on Ashinica. When he spoke, his eyes never left her face, not looking at her exactly, more like through her.

"I'm Ayden's father."

There were stifled gasps, but Aerith paid them no mind. His eyes were still focused on Ashinica.

"You know, there are a lot of things that haven't made sense to me," Aerith started, moving slowly in Ashinica's direction. "And a lot of things that haven't made sense to those who have been working for me in this war. I've gotten pieces from Logan about what happened with the Academy, I've gotten pieces from Hannah, and I have a few from Ayden. Most of it came from my dear sweet Sabrina, though I doubt she knew all that she knew in the short time she had access to all of that information in the Blaze. Fortunately, I've had a lot of time to think and to reflect on what she found out, and the more I think about it, the more one thing becomes clear. The fall of the Academy doesn't make sense to me."

Aerith stopped, turned back to Hannah, and then cocked his head slightly.

"Does it make sense to you?"

Aerith didn't wait for an answer.

"Alistair Ravenheart dies mysteriously and then Kaitain expels the Academy from the Imperial Court isolating them, likely on the suggestion of Irene Drage. Or maybe it was someone else. But I'll get back to that. So now, the Academy becomes the must-have bauble for everyone with designs on winning this war. Either to have it or destroy it. We know that Pike and his people approached the Academy through Serrina Mistic, which didn't go well, and introduced Leonora Wastri to a new kind of pain and trouble. Which we know nearly got her killed were it not for the machinations of other members of the Dark Gods and a few members of the Knights of the Flashing Blade who couldn't follow orders."

CHAPTER 107

Aerith winked in Hannah's direction and then returned to his tale. Hannah wasn't sure what he was building up to, but he was enjoying his performance in a way that troubled Hannah's heart.

"So then of course, Kaitain in his thirst for power dispatches the unfortunate Bernhardt Yeoman to Jelan to secure the Academy for Kaitain, or to destroy it. Which is a fairly interesting and insightful ploy if I do say so myself. It's way above his level of course, but that is neither here or there. We know that Irene Drage was pulling the strings on behalf of Talisia."

Aerith felt rather than saw Hannah's horrified expression.

"Like I said," he said turning back toward her, "not enough time for a full catch up. But the fact that Kaitain is just a puppet on someone's strings isn't a surprise. Whether it's Talisia, or Emries, or Dorovar, the guy is just a disaster waiting to be unleashed in full. But that has been the point all along. Our enemies know the stakes in the game, and they need to keep everything off balance, in turmoil, in conflict. That's how Emries and Talisia like it; messy."

Aerith let his eyes pass over the Masters once more, and Hannah felt as though the temperature in the room had dropped several degrees.

"Where was I?" Aerith asked the air. "Oh yes. Kaitain declares a war against the dragons, supposedly in retaliation for the death of Alistair Ravenheart, but now we know that it was Kaitain himself that was the architect behind Alistair's murder. He may have made it look like an accident, but he asked the wrong person for help."

More barely stifled gasps filled the room. Aerith's look went from one of confidence to one of confusion.

"Didn't everyone know that already? Oh come on, it is so obvious. I'm not exactly a master at these palace intrigues, but it was the clear play for someone consolidating power. Eliminate Alistair, install Irene which would cast the Masters in the unenviable role of looking jealous and distracted. It gives him cover to fight against the dragons and the Dark Gods, lets him stock the Knights of the Flashing Blade with people who would be loyal to him, including Orren Eldrath, which would put even more distance between the Imperial Throne and Jelan. It makes you look like the renegades. Then when the wars start to turn bad, which they would inevitably do, he sends an envoy to 'ask' the Academy for help. Except this envoy who is above reproach, purely by accident, discovers that the Academy has been contacted by the Dark Gods. They are suddenly a corrupted entity. How long have they been corrupted? Are they a threat? Better send someone to deal with the Academy and bring them back under the control of the Emperor."

Here Aerith paused and turned back to Hannah again.

"And who did he send? Did he send Orren Eldrath, or one of the other members of the Knights who could have perhaps been reasonable in his negotiations? Did he send his Court Sorceress? No, he sent the worst possible person to send. He sent Bernhardt Yeoman. The one man who had an innate distrust of magic and the people who use it. It took only the slightest provocation and then you were at war."

Now Hannah could see the greater tapestry of machinations.

"But he couldn't have expected what happened next," Hannah said picking up the narrative. "Maybe he expected the resistance to send a force to try to recruit the Academy, and if this tapestry is as complex as you say, he would have expected it to be Leonora."

Aerith nodded.

"Of course it would be. She would come back to do her duty and defend her home, even if you and Marlae hadn't asked her to. So the traitor, corrupted by the Dark Gods, returns to the scene of the crime to finish what she started."

Hannah frowned at the characterization. She was about to take up the story again when Aris Ebonsight interjected.

"But what about the other Dark Gods; Rael and Trece? What about Talisia and Jerah? There are just too many moving parts to all of this for it to be a coordinated plan."

Aerith smiled and shook his head.

"Humans are so limited in their ability to see the way the world really works. But then I suppose with the information you have, it would seem like a series of terrible coincidences. But you have to look at the facts. Kaitain sends Bernhardt, of course Irene knows about it, so then Talisia knows about it. That explains how Talisia was there. Talisia employed a group of Jerah's followers, so that's how Jerah knew. Leonora was there because she was supposed to be there at that moment in time. And Rael and Trece were there because I asked them to go."

Aerith could feel Hannah's eyes boring into his back. He turned and met her eyes, and for just a moment she held on to the indignation, but when she saw the remorse deep in his gaze, her irritation softened.

"I couldn't have known that Talisia and Jerah would have been there. In my mind it was clear there was going to be a confrontation between Kaitain and Marlae by proxy. But what I didn't know at the time, what I couldn't have known, was the connection between Irene Drage and Talisia. If I would have known the war zone that the place was going to devolve into, I probably wouldn't have contacted Rael. But, knowing what I know now about what we gained from that war, I'm sure that Rael and Trece would accept their personal losses and do it all over again."

Aerith's gaze dropped to the ground and Hannah could feel the sorrow roll off him for a moment.

"Not that it matters now," Aerith said under his breath.

The moment of introspection lasted barely a second and then Aerith rounded on Ashinica again, all pretext of coyness gone, the voice of the killer returned.

"How long have you been working for Talisia?"

Ashinica's eyes went wide. There were audible gasps from some of the other Masters, and Jastra seemed the most offended by the accusation. After a moment, Ashinica narrowed her eyes and opened her mouth to reply, but Aerith cut her off hard.

"I don't have the time or the patience for denials. It's the only thing that makes sense."

Aerith turned back to the rest of the Masters, fixing his eyes on Fiona.

"Who was it that sponsored Irene Drage into the Academy of Arcane Arts?"

Not waiting for an answer, he shifted his focus to Jastra.

"Who insisted that Irene warranted the personal attention of Alistair Ravenheart?"

Now his eyes moved to Aris.

"Who insisted that she was the best choice to negotiate with the general of the army from Aldere?"

Finally, Aerith turned his attention back to Ashinica.

"And who was it that won my son's trust and beguiled him into revealing exactly who and what he was the night before he was to be sent on a secret mission to infiltrate Kaitain's rogue academy? Who was it that then informed Irene Drage that a Dark God was coming to Aldere in the guise of an expelled student?"

Aerith closed the distance to Ashinica until he was mere inches from her face.

"And because you told Irene, that meant Talisia knew, and because Talisia knew, Emries knew. Your reckless stupidity and treachery nearly KILLED MY SON!"

The last words boomed from Aerith and shook the foundations of the structure that sheltered them. He turned away from her and started to walk back in Hannah's direction. Hannah's eyes never left Ashinica. For a moment Ashinica's eyes were wide, and shock held her in her place. But that didn't last beyond Aerith's first two steps away from her. Her eyes narrowed, and a cruel sneer curled her lips. One hand came up, power beginning to coalesce like steam around her straining fingers. Part of Hannah wanted to cry out, while another part instinctively reached for her weapon and took hold of her powers. Hannah's eyes shifted toward Aerith's face, an unconscious attempt to warn him of what was about to happen. Aerith's face was calm, and Hannah realized immediately that Aerith knew what Ashinica was about to attempt and he had already planned his countermove accordingly.

Before the energy finished coalescing around Ashinica's curled fingers, Aerith spun around and a thin beam of white light erupted from an outstretched finger and pierced Ashinica's left shoulder. The beam of light then shattered into hundreds of pieces and wound themselves around her body like a net. Her arms were pinned to her sides, and she was pressed painfully against the back wall, her mouth held closed by the light net.

"I don't abide traitors," Aerith said coldly, his gaze turning back to Fiona. "And as much as I would relish ending Ashinica's life, I recognize that while she has betrayed my son, the worst of her transgressions came against the Academy itself. The Masters of the Academy should deal with this, not me."

Fiona smoothed her dress and took a step forward. Hannah could tell the woman was trying to hold on to some semblance of order and was about to give a kind of official pronouncement. However, Aerith was not in the mood for niceties, and it was clear to Hannah that he was barely restraining his more pathological urges.

"Let me make one thing clear," Aerith said, his tone filled with ice and malice, "the Academy of Arcane Arts is a threat to this world. Unlike my associate here, I think we would have been better off if you had destroyed yourselves. There are too many people in this world that see the power you wield and mistake that for real power, and they seek to use it to deepen and complicate this war, not to end it. And you, with your supposed intelligence actually see yourselves as above the fray. But your arrogance is only supplanted by your ignorance. If you had any true inkling of real power, you would run screaming from it and pray it never finds you and shows you your true insignificance."

Aerith reached into his pocket and withdrew a fist-sized black stone with flecks of red shot through it. He didn't even look at the stone before he held it out in Fiona's direction.

"So I'm going to give you an opportunity to salvage what little honor and dignity the Academy has left. This portal will take you under the Peaks of Patience to the conclave of the Order of the Flickering Flame. Their two most important members have left them to try to sway this war back in the direction of the people of this world. So now the Order seeks to fulfill their mission by providing comfort to those who have been displaced, persecuted, and vilified by the so-called leaders of this world who should be devoting their energy to protecting the weak and the helpless. You can go there and use your abilities to rebuild Menoris. You can create a haven where we can send those people who are trapped in the middle of a warzone in the same way you were. There are too many people at risk, and not enough places for them to be safe. Hannah and Kiara saved you and your students. Now you can repay that by saving countless others."

Aerith let his offer hang in the air for a moment, and then the voice of the killer returned.

"Or, you can try to fight. Try to be a factor in this war. Stand against gods and monsters and risk becoming monsters yourself. You can try to help not with mercy but with power. You can become killers, and for a while you can shake the world until someone more powerful squashes you like the bugs you are."

Aerith let his eyes flow across the Masters and then back to Fiona.

"And make no mistake, if you take that option, if you stand on the front lines of this war; then you won't have to look far for an enemy. I'll be there, and I will have no qualms about spilling your blood and the blood of every member of your Academy."

He took a step forward and lowered the volume of his voice to the most menacing sound Hannah had ever heard.

"And no matter what power you think you have, you will continue to breathe only as long as I allow it. I could kill you all with a thought, or I could make you suffer until the twin suns go out."

Aerith took a slow step backwards and then started toward the door. He stopped only briefly to hand the portal stone to Hannah before making his way back out to the blood-stained battlefield. Hannah watched her patron go, and though she wanted to turn to reassure the Masters that Aerith was truly a man dedicated to doing good works, she knew there was nothing she could really say. Aerith was right. As much as it galled her to admit, he was right. The Masters and the Academy were dangerous because they were the ultimate unknown quantity that could be turned to anyone's purpose. They had to be neutralized one way or another. She simply hoped that they were wise enough to see reason and relent.

Fiona's eyes followed Aerith as he left, and then her eyes scanned back toward the back room of the building where she knew that the students of the Academy were huddled. She knew they were confused, scared, and traumatized by the repeated near-death experiences of the past days. For several moments she stared at the door, and then finally turned toward the other Masters. There were no words exchanged, only a simple nod from Aris, and another from Jastra. Finally, Fiona turned her attention to Hannah.

"The Masters have decided that it is best that we turn our attentions to healing the wounds of this world rather than inflicting more. Please tell Ayden's father that we will ensure that Ashinica pays for her crimes, and we will do our best to prove ourselves worthy of the chance that he has given us. Aris, go and gather the students. Jastra, take custody of Ashinica."

Aris moved quickly to the other chamber while Jastra moved to where Ashinica remained caged. She placed her hand on the net of light gingerly, and when she found that it did not shock or harm her, she took hold and pulled it and the woman toward the center of the room. Hannah quickly pulled the portal stone open, and by the time it had begun to swirl to life, Aris returned with the students lined up behind her. Aris went through the portal first, followed by Jastra and Ashinica. Kiara and Fiona helped to usher the students one by one through the portal. After a few minutes, all of the students had been safely ushered through, and Fiona moved toward the portal. Hannah put her hand on the woman's arm just before she stepped through.

"Aerith really is a good man, despite his behavior."

Fiona forced a smile.

"I have no doubt he has good intentions, Hannah, but I do not think he can be confused with a good man. These are severe times, and as such severe men like your Aerith are a necessity. But the lesson he taught us today is that while men such as he are required for the moment, they cannot be what the rest of us aspire or allow ourselves to become. He has given us the means to be better. It is for that that he is to be lauded, and perhaps it is through these kindnesses that he believes that he shall be redeemed."

Fiona nodded in Kiara's direction and then stepped through the portal. Hannah turned her attention to the former acolyte and dragon hunter.

"Perhaps you should join them, Kiara. Your skills would be of great benefit to the refugees that will start finding their way to the Order."

Kiara didn't hesitate to answer.

"With all due respect, Lady Ironheart, I think perhaps the best use of my abilities will be at your side. If I understand what is about to happen, you will be heading into danger to rescue those who cannot escape the war. I can minister to those people and get them out of harm's way while you extend your protection and take the fight to those who would do them harm."

Hannah considered for a moment.

"I cannot guarantee your safety, Kiara."

Kiara smiled.

"It has become clear that there is very little safety left on this world, my lady, and I have to weigh the fact that my duty is far more important than my safety."

Hannah did not belabor the point, and let the portal stone close. It dropped to the ground and Hannah quickly recovered it. She started to put the stone in her pocket, but instead handed it to Kiara.

"I'll teach you to use that so you can get people to safety."

Kiara nodded.

"Yes, my lady."

Hannah started toward the door, and just before she pulled on the handle, she turned back to Kiara.

"If you're going to travel with me, you could at least call me Hannah."

Kiara smiled.

"Yes, my lady."

Revenge is Thicker than Blood

Year Five of the Just Emperor Kaitain "Dragonsbane" Lorien, Creator's Calendar Year 1872

The climate of the Royal Palace of Celidar had changed greatly since the deaths of Jerrard and Erika Mystic and a new force had taken to sitting upon the throne in the empty audience chamber. Where once the simple palace had been a beacon of light in the increasingly weary world around it, now the halls and passages were filled with a cold darkness that chilled the bones of all who were brave or foolish enough to set foot there. However, in the days following the announcement of the true nature of the Mystic family and the raising of the raven banner above the palace, the doors had remained tightly shut, and not even the palace workers had been allowed admittance. There had been some grumbling among the populace, but with all of the uncertainty and threats in the world, those who stood against the dark powers could not be begrudged what security they felt necessary. Inside the palace however, the climate was one of sorrow, fear, and regret for the one man who still walked the halls. As Feyd Lorien made his way from his quarters deep in the palace, he could not help but let his mind wander to all of the circumstances that had brought him to this point in time. The death of his wife, his banishment to the end of the world at the hands of his brother, the attempted assassination, his rescue by a member of the Dark Gods, the discovery of the true nature of two of his oldest friends, and then driving a dagger through the heart of one of those friends in the moment of her greatest sorrow. In that one moment he had turned his back on everything that he held dear and had sacrificed his soul to the only cause that seemed to still matter in a world gone mad; revenge.

As he stepped into the audience chamber, the man who was not a man, but instead was a Child of the Creator, Emries, sat silently on the throne that once had been the uncomfortable perch of Jerrard Mystic. Unlike Jerrard, Emries seemed completely comfortable in his place of power. Emries did not immediately acknowledge Feyd's presence, and did not turn his gaze to the man even as he approached the dais. For several moments Feyd stood at the foot of the dais looking up at Emries. Discomfort filled the man as the seconds passed and deep in his heart there was a resentment that blossomed as he understood the true dynamic. Feyd tried his best to keep the color out of his cheeks and the disgust out of his eyes as he slowly dropped to one knee. Feyd felt rather than saw Emries' glance shift, and there was a great weight that fell upon Feyd at that moment.

"Feyd, good. I think it is time that we turn our attention to your brother and get you the revenge that I promised you for your good deeds."

Feyd finally looked up and locked gazes with the brilliant blue eyes of the Child of the Creator. From the first moment that Feyd had been in the same room with Emries, he had been struck by how unimposing and unremarkable the being had been. However, power rolled off of Emries like waves, and it filled Feyd with the kind of fear that he had never known before. That fear had not diminished, and if anything knowing the malice the god was capable of had filled Feyd with an almost paralyzing terror.

"Now," Emries said, leaning forward on the throne, "let me tell you exactly what your brother has been up to."

＊ ＊ ＊ ＊ ＊ ＊ ＊ ＊ ＊ ＊ ＊ ＊

Though the twin suns were high in the sky, great clouds hung over the capitol city of Celidar obscuring most of the bright light that tried desperately to break through the haze. Since the hope had broken through the initial uncertainty of the announcement that Celidar had been ruled by members of the Dark Gods, there were many in Celidar who felt that perhaps there was an end to the years of wars that had embroiled the countryside. But as days passed and the palace remained silent, that hope dimmed. Word began to spread of Kaitain Lorien's crusade against the faithful to the Creator, and hope began to turn to fear. Petitions at the gates of the palace went without answer, and the city leadership began to debate drastic action. But, in answer to the growing anxiety, pages from the palace began to circulate telling of an announcement of the gravest importance on New Year's morning. It was just after dawn when people started arriving in the great open area outside of the palace of Celidar. As the hours passed, more and more of the townspeople arrived, and they were joined by citizens from the countryside who had made the trek to the capitol for this very event. Layers upon layers of conversation fluttered through the crowd, as fear and uncertainty tinged conspiracy theories collided among the masses. The crowd started to become one organism, surging and breathing fear, uncertainty, and anxiety. Just as the twin suns reached their apex in the dreary sky, trumpets blared from the palace and the doors opened. For several moments nothing happened and then finally a long figure strode slowly from deep within the palace into the light of the courtyard. The murmurs grew louder when people began to realize it was not their beloved leaders the Mystics that were coming to address the people but rather Prince Feyd Lorien. There had been much debate about Feyd Lorien since the announcement that Jerrard and Erika had thrown their support behind the younger Lorien brother. For most of the Empire of Cadaria, Feyd Lorien had fallen out of the view of the people once his wife died and he had gained his appointment to oversee Lordhill. However, most saw him as a Lorien in name only; a man who preferred to live a simple life, not a man who wished to live in sky-scraping palaces being pampered for the rest of his days. He was a practical man, who had raised a pragmatic daughter, and now looked to be a beacon in a growing storm of insanity that gripped Cadaria. Perhaps he was completely miscast for the role, or perhaps it was all of the reasons that he didn't fit the role of savior that made him perfect for the part. Either way, the next spoke of fate would turn on the words he was about to utter to the assemblage.

Feyd was dressed not in finery but rather common clothes that were the fashion for the foundry workers of the area. He looked as though he had aged several years in the few days since the last mass gathering which saw the raising of the flag of the raven above the palace. Feyd's eyes were trained on the ground as though he were afraid his steps would falter. After he came to a stop, Feyd looked up and spent several moments letting his eyes scan across the faces of the people before him. Voices in the crowd slowly quieted until there was nothing but the sound of the wind in the courtyard. Feyd then raised his head and let his voice project outward so that all could hear.

"Good people of Celidar, I speak to you today as a man who wishes he did not have to be standing here before you. I speak to you as a man who longs for the days of the past when we were one great united Empire, safe in our understanding that the Imperial family would do anything in their power to protect us. I speak to you as a man who wishes that his name was anything other than Lorien. But here we stand. All of us, victims of the same treachery and madness that reduced our beautiful countryside to a warzone. Rashaleb, our neighbor to the north, a kingdom who I am sure many of you knew people from, or had relatives in, is largely a wasteland. The creature known as Death walked among the people there and when he emerged, over half of the population of that beautiful kingdom would not see another sunrise. Pellatori, to our west, was the first to feel the terrible touch of the Herald Famine and her vicious Wasting Disease. The Grey Man Pestilence ravaged Bellnoc, our neighbor to the south, as well as the Imperial Province of Aldere. Further to our south has seen a disaster unlike any that this world has ever known. Power that should frighten every single one of us lifted the Peaks of Patience from where they have been rooted for centuries and brought them crashing down upon the citizenry, creating another massive graveyard where once a vibrant kingdom stood. Again this is at the hands of a creature calling itself the Herald of Dorovar, Conquest. This same Conquest, according to broken reports, has again visited his hate and violence on yet another kingdom, this time Hedorah, where now there is not a living thing to be found."

There were gasps of shock throughout the crowd, and the shock merged with hate, fear, and trepidation that had already grasped the people arrayed before Feyd. Something stabbed deep in his heart, something akin to guilt, but he had no choice now. He was committed to his course of action, and was committed to doing the will of the man who had promised that he would be able to end the life of his treacherous brother. It wasn't the promise of the throne of Cadaria, it wasn't the safety of his dear daughter, and it wasn't even the final vengeance for his fallen wife that drove Feyd. He could wear those emotions to rationalize his deeds to himself. Deep down though, there was only one motivation left. All of the other justifications had melted away, and all that was left was hate. Nothing in his life would ever have meaning again so long as his brother still drew breath. Perhaps killing his brother would fix nothing in Feyd's life, but that didn't matter any longer. Kaitain would die, or Feyd would give his life trying. Feeling the surge of emotion in the crowd, Feyd began speaking again.

"In the face of this daunting challenge, one that is unprecedented in the history of our Empire, what has our Just Emperor done? Has he brought to bear all of the resources of the Empire to discover who this demon Dorovar is and why he has brought this plague of death and destruction to our shores? Has he mobilized the army to fight against these Heralds? Did he empower his Knights of the Flashing Blade, the most elite fighting group ever assembled to hunt down and destroy this threat to the Empire? No. He has chosen to use abuse his power at every turn and assist this Dorovar in bringing Cadaria to its knees. From the moment he took power, Kaitain has been obsessed with embroiling us all in wars against enemies that only he could see. For hundreds of years we have lived in harmony and a fragile peace with the dragons of this world, a peace that Kaitain broke as soon as he took the throne. The first Emperor of Cadaria, my ancestor, risked his life and his fledgling Empire to create a truce with the Dark Gods, another truce that Kaitain was determined to shatter. And all that time, the real threat, the threat that has devastated half of this empire, continued to grow in strength and confidence. Four years my brother has been in power. In these four years our people have seen more bloodshed than in the entire history of the Cadarian Empire."

The surge of emotion heightened in the crowd, and a growing grumbling could be heard. Kaitain had created an incredible amount of rage, but that rage had largely been diffused through the populace, confused and broken with only pieces trickling down to the commoners. Even the royalty of the kingdoms were kept out of the loop as Kaitain's trusted circle continued to shrink. But there was more to it than that. More to it by far, and it was Feyd's intention to ensure that everyone within the sound of his voice would know the truth. At least a version of the truth that benefited Feyd's new benefactor.

"But Kaitain was not content to take his hostility and his venom and loose them upon the dragons and the Dark Gods. Kaitain knew that the first duty of the Knights of the Flashing Blade was to protect the Empire. Before my father's body was even cold and the crown was placed upon Kaitain's head, my brother was already plotting how to get the impediments to his rule out of the way. The first removed from the game was our friend, our hero, Alistair Ravenheart. He braved the wrath of the dragons to find a cure for the Crawling Plague. He was the only one willing to go where others would not, and only he could have discovered the connection between the Grey Man Pestilence and the real threat to our posterity. But Kaitain could not allow that. Alistair was a threat to all of Kaitain's schemes; he was too smart and too dedicated to the tenants of the Empire to allow it to be disrupted by Kaitain's unbridled ambitions. And so, leveraging the newly acquired assets within the Shadow Guild, Kaitain had Alistair murdered and ensured that the murder looked like an accident to the rest of the world."

The dam of emotion broke the next moment, and shouts of rage and anger exploded in a din of overwhelming dissent. Feyd let the crowd whip itself into a higher and higher frenzy and just as he felt it was about to tip into something completely out of control, he put both of his hands into the air. He didn't call out or try to shout over the cacophony, instead he simply kept his hands in the air. As more and more members of the crowd saw Feyd's raised hands, they urged those near them to calm down and return their focus to Feyd. Once the rage had once again been precariously contained, Feyd spoke once more.

"I was as shocked as you are when I learned the truth of Alistair's death, but I was unable to confirm it. There was not enough evidence to bring charges. Especially with what happened next. My brother has always had a history of taking terrible circumstances and twisting them to his own perverted ends. So, when Fiona Ebonsight wandered into Kaitain's trap, it gave him the leverage he needed to sever relations with the Academy of Arcane Arts. The distance would prevent them from interfering and give legitimacy to his hand-picked Court Sorceress and co-conspirator in the death of Alistair Ravenheart. For every traitorous action that Kaitain would take against the people of the Empire of Cadaria, Irene Drage would be at his side, benefiting as her patron did from the blood of the innocent."

A small chant of 'witch' began somewhere deep in the crowd and in a matter of moments had hundreds of voices. As the chant grew, it was infused with more words, until all were chanting 'burn the witch'. The fires and fever of revenge had gripped the entire community, and they all seethed as one. Once again Feyd raised his hands to quiet the mob.

"With the Shadow Guild firmly in his pocket, and the Academy of Arcane Arts at a distance, all that was left was the Knights of the Flashing Blade. But much though he would want to, Kaitain could not simply kill the Knights. The only course of action he could take was discredit them, and then through their failures either create circumstances where they would be killed, or following their failures remove them from their positions of power. Some of course were easier than others. Those who were old were forced into retirement, and those who were vulnerable were quietly eliminated. This allowed Kaitain to place those he could manipulate into their places; Jaccob Aldora, Tolon Morr, Orren Eldrath, and Devlin Rannoch. Of course, like most of Kaitain's judgement, his choices for new Knights fell short of his mark. They quickly grew out of his control. The damage however was done. In time he would discredit Hannah Ironheart, Gregor Quicksilver, Leonora Wastri, and Vallic Ultiv. Seraph Kore would be branded a traitor for attempting to do his duty and protecting the empire from the horror that Kaitain represented. Chelsea Zarova was reduced from one of the fiercest warriors in the whole of the Empire to acting as a wet nurse for her husband's mistress. Bernhardt Yeoman was sacrificed to fighting the needless war against the dragons, Xaran Firesoul mysteriously disappeared, and Natalia Pressen was hamstrung by her affiliation to the Shadow Guild. Now, a great many of our most powerful defenders are dead. Because their unity and purpose were shattered by Kaitain, they became targets for the true enemy; Dorovar and his Heralds. Tolon Morr and Gregor Quicksilver were murdered by Conquest, Seraph Kore by the Herald War, Xaran Firesoul was killed when the Imperial Palace was destroyed by the Heralds, Natalia Pressen and Bernhardt Yeoman by the enigmatic creature known as Jerah."

Feyd had known some of the facts were distortions from the moment that Emries had imparted them. Some events had been altered to fit the narrative of the danger that Dorovar posed and the ineffective leader that Kaitain had become. While many would assert that the truth was always the first casualty in war, and that the facts would win out in the end, Feyd had a different view. The truth is what made the facts matter, not the other way around. Yes the Knights that Feyd had named were dead, but the manner of their deaths were just as important. And as Feyd opened his mouth to continue his tirade against the injustices visited upon the populace, he could almost feel his heart breaking and a little piece of his soul being stolen from him.

"But it was by Kaitain's hand that Jaccob Aldora and Vallic Ultiv met their ends. At least Kaitain had the courage to look Jaccob in the eye before one of his agents severed Jaccob's head from his shoulders. When it came to Vallic however, Kaitain left the deed to one of his most accomplished assassins. These crimes against the people of Cadaria did not stop with those two Knights, no, they extended to the royalty of several of the Great Kingdoms."

Feyd stopped once more to take a breath. Here was the point of no return. The crowd was at the edge of a murderous frenzy, and if Feyd misplayed his next statements, the ultimate plan could possibly fail. He braced himself, knowing the lies about to spew forth.

"And no one seemed to be immune from this treachery. Not Thorigald, not Iltorp, not Saldarine, and not even Celidar."

It took several hushed moments for the true gravity of Feyd's words to register with the crowd, and while some were brilliant torches of hate that would burn brighter than a thousand suns, others were quiet caldrons of disbelief that boiled to the edge, waiting for that one push to explode.

"That is why I stand here before you alone. Kaitain has debased himself even further than what I thought was possible. Somehow, Kaitain's assassins infiltrated the royal palace of Celidar and launched an attack. Though Jerrard and Erika fought bravely, they were ultimately cut down by these assassins who displayed abilities very much like those that Dorovar's Heralds possess. Gabriel Shadowfall too met his end at the hands of these assassins. The brave Orren Eldrath and my own daughter Princess Felicia are tracking these assassins, but I fear that even if they are brought to justice, the cost will be far too high. Jerrard and Erika Mystic represented a heroism that is sorely lacking in this world, and their loss is immeasurable."

Feyd paused again, his words lingering in the air like a frozen breeze. Disbelief and sorrow flooded through the crowd. Feyd waited, seemingly out of respect, but more clearly out of the need to manipulate the temper of the mob. He had navigated the most dangerous news, and now it was time to whip them into a frenzy once more and put the final touches of Emries' plan into effect.

"This treachery and this deceit cannot be allowed to go on any further. In every way imaginable, Kaitain has not only declared war on forces that he could not hope to defeat, but he has declared war on the very foundation of the Cadarian Empire. The Knights of the Flashing Blade, the Royal Families of the Great Kingdoms, the Academy of Arcane Arts, and the Church of the Creator. He has decreed that everything you were raised to believe is a lie, and that your very belief and faith are traitorous acts. Only the weak and the zealots follow him now, and there are so few free Kingdoms still standing with the people or the will to oppose him. It has become clear now that Kaitain has been in league with this Dorovar all along. What else could explain the manner in which he has conducted his insane wars? What else could explain him ignoring the threat of the Heralds time and time again to focus his energies on the dragons and the dark gods, and ultimately the stability of the Empire itself? Why has he taken every action to destroy those who could protect us?"

The first shout from the crowd broke through the melancholy.

"Death to Kaitain!"

The call was seconded, and then a trio called out. More voices rose and there was a quiet rumbling in the crowd and Feyd seized on the shift in emotion.

"We can no longer stand by and watch as my brother destroys everything that we hold dear. It is not enough to simply declare that he is not our Emperor while he continues to shake the world. Where are the forces that are taking arms against him? Where are the brave souls to break his grip upon the throat of our Empire? He has stripped away all of our defenses, but he cannot take away the heroism that founded this Empire in the Founding Wars. So I say to you good people of Celidar, the time has come to do more than talk. The time has come to do more than denounce the actions of our rogue and traitorous so-called Emperor. It is time to act. It is time to stand for those who cannot stand for themselves, and fight for those who are either unwilling or unable to fight for themselves. The time has come to take back our empire by force, because it is the only language that Kaitain and his followers understand."

A great cheer went up from the crowd. Feyd put one fist in the air.

"Will you stand with me?"

The crowd did not hesitate to answer.

"YES!"

Feyd put his other fist into the air.

"Will you fight beside me?"

Again there was no hesitation.

"YES!"

Feyd left his right hand in the air punctuating each statement with a pump of his fist in the air.

"We will not be deterred. We will not be stopped. We shall march upon our enemy and take back every inch of ground that they have defiled. We are Cadarians! We determine our fate, and no one shall tear down what we have built!"

A great cheer came from the crowd, followed by a chant of Feyd's name mixing in with the chant to kill Kaitain. Feyd raised his voice once more, his own concerns and trepidations discarded. There was no more shame or fear. There was only the rage of the blood and the need for the death of his brother.

"Go now, my people. Let the word spread to every town and every village. Gather your weapons, gather your hearts and your rage. Tomorrow at noon all those willing shall march toward Zevarit, and we shall reclaim the land and the dignity taken from us. There shall be blood spilled and there shall be death, but there is no cost too high for our Empire. There is no price that we will not pay to take back what is ours. And through this crucible we shall reclaim what no one has the right to try to take from us; our dignity."

The crowd exploded once more in a cacophonous roar and in his heart Feyd knew that the man that he once was no longer existed. The blood on his hands was now his truth, and the expediency of the moment outweighed any trepidations that his own failings may have created. Everything was a means to a greater end, and no matter how many died, it would be worth it in the end.

Dangerously Irresistible

Year Four of the Just Emperor Kaitain "Dragonsbane" Lorien,
Creator's Calendar Year 1871

Darrien Annis stood looking up at the stars, her brilliant blue eyes flashing in the moonlight, marveling at not only her existence, but where it had brought her after so many years. As she stood admiring the vista above her, she felt the presence of the woman who had been stalking her for the past several days. Darrien had caught sight of the woman before, but did her best to pretend that she had not. And so, the slow chase had begun, moving from one untenable ambush position to another until finally Darrien had boxed herself in on the edge of a cliff that overlooked the sea. There was little about the Kingdom of Night Galateria that Darrien found beautiful, but the stars and moonlight sparkling on the rolling waves easily qualified. When Darrien turned to face her pursuer, she was half-shocked. The woman that she had expected to see was the so-called Fallen Angel Seraphina Masile, instead the piercing green eyes of the Child of the Creator Talisia stared back at her. The woman's cold white nearly corpse-like blue skin looked iridescent in the moonlight, and her soft black hair resembled the veil of a grieving widow. The black dress the goddess wore could have been a collection of spider webs, or simply the most delicate lace ever conceived. Black lips parted for the goddess to speak, but Darrien cut her off.

"It took you long enough."

Darrien felt her father's insolence in her tone. For so long she had strived to emulate the man she wished had had a larger role in the woman she had become. However, in her conversations with Wolf she realized that she had become her father's daughter, and she hated that fact. Now, with the road ahead, she would have only one chance to redeem herself for all of the terrible things done in his name. The expression on Talisia's face did not change, but she did pause to consider Darrien's words before speaking.

"I did little to mask my approach, or the interest that I took in you, little girl. Be grateful that I am giving you the honor of seeing my face before I rip my brother's soul from your undeserving husk."

Darrien did her best to keep the smile from coming to her lips.

"There is nothing about you that's honorable, nothing at all. If anything you've done everything in your power to be as despicable and horrible as your brother Emries."

The smile made Talisia's eyes sparkle with malice.

"Thank you."

A thin blade of brilliant white energy appeared in Talisia's hand that next moment.

"Tell me," she said with barely restrained hatred, "which one are you?"

"Darrien Annis."

If there was recognition of her name, it did not show in Talisia's face.

"One of Pike's bastards," Talisia said finally. "The girl with the stolen names."

The jibe hit Darrien square in the chest. While it was true technically that Darrien was a bastard, Darrien had tried hard not to give it as much thought as she probably should have. Again, things had changed for Darrien since she and Alderin had been dispatched from the Citadel of the

Dark Gods to fetch Tess from the Heart of Stone in Albitonin. She had had a great deal of time to soul-search in the Vault of Terrors. Finally, Darrien had been left with nothing but time on the long walk from the Great Crater to Galateria. And with that much time, she could do nothing but think, and inevitably those thoughts came back to her own place in the Cosmos, and the path ahead of her. While Wolf would not say so when she left the Vault, Darrien could not shake the fact that this was a one-way trip even if everything went to plan. So began the inevitable self-examination.

From the beginning of the life she could remember, Darrien idolized her father. But Pike was not a man who was tied to the moment, he was tied to the future and to the past. He was constantly trying to find a way to protect a future that might not ever come to pass, and running from things that he had done to get to where he was. There was a shadow hanging over Pike every day of the life that Darrien could remember with him. But regardless of how many times she tried to broach that subject, or many others with her father, he would shut her out or send her on some assignment that was supposed to advance the greater agenda. More often than not though, Darrien was simply cleaning up yet another in a long line of Pike's messes.

There were many things that Darrien didn't understand about her father, or about the other Dark Gods, and it took many years before she even began to glean the slightest fraction of what she would later understand, and what would fully crystallize sitting in the darkness with Wolf Ranthall. The Dark Gods were not immortal, they were not all powerful, and they were not bred to wield the type of power they did during their millennia of time in the Heavens and on Espre. Once Darrien had been speaking to Midarin and the older woman had let it slip that she did not look at her time on Espre as her real life. Her time as a member of the Dark Gods was something that was inflicted upon her. It was a Cosmic joke, and one that had ceased being funny long ago. This never-ending life had become a burden for some members of the Dark Gods, and a curse for others, including Darrien's father.

Darrien was a woman of privilege, moreover she saw herself as privileged. She was the first-born child of the leader of the Dark Gods, and as such she felt that she deserved the right to the attention and status.

She was, however, not the eldest of the new Dark Gods, far from it. Camille, Mirana, and Liara had all been born in the Heavens and had the distinction of being divine beings, and as such their level of power would always be greater than any of the other children of the Dark Gods that would follow on Espre. They also had the advantage that both of their parents were members of the Dark Gods, which changed how their powers manifested and the ease at which they could draw upon those powers. There was even more stratification because Camille always set herself apart even from Mirana and Liara. This division came purely because of parentage and style. Camille was bred to be every bit the warrior that her parents were. She was not a weapon only, because neither Gwydeon nor Midarin were blind to the danger she could pose if she had no concept of the consequences of her actions in the war. Camille was the perfect solider for this war. She had power, she had intellect, and she had the wisdom to understand when power needed to be applied, and when it was better to talk. She was as kind as Gwydeon was said to have been, and she was as ferocious as her mother could ever be. More importantly, she was loyal to her parents, loyal to her family, and loyal to the cause. Mirana and Liara on the other hand were not fashioned for a war of weapons and powers, they were bred to be soldiers on the battleground of ideas. They were both intuitive, questioners, and thinkers. They had been brought up with the singular tenant that all problems required the understanding of the prospective of all involved and all who could be involved. The Dark Gods had been betrayed only because they had not been able to see all of the sides of the conflict, because the information they were receiving was information they were fed. Lissa was determined that her daughters would not allow the Dark Gods to be led astray by those who wished to use the Dark Gods as pawns in their greater conflict. The three women were three sides of the same coin, always trying to find the right path through, even when no path existed.

The second group of children of the Dark Gods were the ones born on Espre after the fall. That group included Serrina Mistic, Alderin, Darrien, and Tess. Both Serrina and Alderin were older than Darrien, but unlike the divine children, their responsibilities seemed solely dictated by Pike and the Dark Council. Serrina was quickly fashioned into the Voice of the Dark Council. This was largely due to the fact that she was the child of two of the Forgotten, Jerrard and Erika Mistic, and she had learned the ability to mask her travels the same way her grandfather Basille had on Onea. She could appear to be many places at once, which helped to keep the location of the Forgotten and their allies a secret. It also enabled Pike to mask his own activities from the other members of the Dark Gods. Pike quickly ingratiated himself to the highly impressionable and naïve Serrina, and molded her into his doting acolyte and sometime mistress. Darrien had always found their relationship disgusting, but knew there was little she could do. It wasn't until she discovered the breadth of Pike's appetites that Darrien realized whatever relationship that he carried on with Serrina was only a show to ensure her loyalty and her capitulation to her role in his schemes.

Alderin's role in Pike's machinations was less clear, but no less self-serving and calculated. After her recent period of reflection however, more of Pike's motivations seemed to come into greater focus. Like Camille, Alderin was the child of two of the greatest warriors of Onea, though one generation further removed from Gwydeon and Midarin. Aryx Terian, by far the oldest of the Dark Gods, and one who had seen war on a scale that few could comprehend, had been a hero and a villain and everything in between. However, at the end of the day, regardless of which side he found himself on, Aryx Terian was a soldier. His wife however, was not bred to be a soldier. Diana Terian was the daughter of a farmer who happened to be the sister of a man who simply did not know how to quit or how to die. And so, when her brother entered the service of Cedric Binosear, Diana jumped at the chance to leave her farming life behind and become a hero. She, like the man she would come to marry, became renowned on Onea and inspired the next two generations of heroes. She and Aryx both instilled in Alderin the one trait that they revered above all others, and one that their son exemplified beyond measure. Loyalty. Unfortunately, that loyalty was soon subsumed by a man who demanded unquestioning loyalty in service not only of what was best, but also what was best for Pike. Thus, Alderin found himself, like Serrina first and then Darrien later, cleaning up Pike's messes and removing any obstacles to Pike's unknown self-centered agenda.

It wasn't until she was nearly a hundred years old that Darrien began to realize that she was not a part of Pike's plans either before or after her birth. Of course, that suspicion and horror had been confirmed by an argument that Pike and Darrien had when he was so drunk he could barely stand. He had never intended to ever have children, not after seeing what had become of the two children that his other self had sired in one of the fractured realities on Onea. He called them vain and selfish, lusting only for power; that they were not willing to do what was right when the time demanded it. He had vowed to set right everything that his other self had done wrong. But one drunken night of indiscretion had saddled him with a child. A child that he did not want, and a child that he did not intend to see become another burden upon the already troubled leader of the Dark Gods. Pike took great pains to avoid Darrien and to pawn off his parental responsibilities to anyone who would take the role. That more than anything began the revolving door of wives to the leader of the Dark Gods. Of course, none of the other members of the Dark Gods would have Pike as a husband, and Pike did not relish the thought of being with one person for the rest of eternity. Therefore, mortal women, preferably those who were naïve, were his caretakers of choice. They would barely live sixty to seventy years, and if they got too troublesome, he had his loyal agents who would remove those nuisances from his life.

When Darrien first saw the graveyard of Pike's conquests, concubines, and unwitting victims, she had fallen to her knees and thrown up. She had known that her father was a cruel man, but she had never imagined how cruel. It had been one of her first missions with Alderin, and while he had tried to convince her that she did not need to see the mission through to its end, she would not risk showing weakness or disappointing her father. At that point in time, she still believed that she could win his love by being the perfect soldier that he had always wanted her to be; the perfect soldier that he saw in Alderin and Serrina. Alderin did not relent easily, and even after the guardian of the young woman whose eye Pike had caught had been eliminated, he still opposed her continuing through the disposal of the woman's body. But in truth, Alderin could never deny Darrien for long, and after a mostly one-sided argument, Alderin relented and opened the portal to the secret graveyard tucked in a small valley in the northernmost reaches of Mythryn. The place was bitterly cold, cloaked in a mist that rolled down from the mountains that ringed the valley. There was some snow on the ground, and at first the environmental obstructions kept Darrien from seeing the full size of the site. However, as the two made their way wordlessly through the rows of tombstones, the enormity of the crimes committed by her father began to fill her mind and her heart. No more than five rows into the graveyard, Darrien fell to her knees and her stomach could stand the revulsion no longer. It was clear that Alderin didn't know what he was supposed to do, so he kept his distance, the body of the dead woman perched on his shoulder. Finally, when Darrien looked up, Alderin saw the tears streaming from her eyes. He started to say something to her, but her intent stare robbed him of his voice. There were no words in that moment, and in her mind at that time she wasn't sure there ever would be. But she couldn't bring herself to hate Alderin for following orders. What was he supposed to do? He was in an impossible situation. Pike was the recognized leader of the Dark Gods. Of course, Alderin could have gone to his parents and sought guidance, but Darrien knew that Pike would deny everything. Even if Alderin had wanted to bring his parents to the graveyard, there was no way that he could have prevented either Pike or Serrina from destroying the site before he could provide proof. It would look like an attempt at a coup, or perhaps something worse. The moment Alderin committed his first murder in Pike's name, he was committed to a course that seemingly had no end. Darrien dedicated herself that moment to ensure that Alderin would not have to walk that path alone, no matter what.

After the two had buried the latest victim of Pike's lust and greed, Darrien lingered looking back at the tombstones. When Darrien met Alderin's gaze, he understood her wordless question. He had told her later that he didn't want to take her to grave of her mother. He didn't want to answer questions about how she had died. Didn't want to confess that it had been his own hands that had ended her life. He didn't want to think of how Darrien's opinion of him would have changed. But for Darrien none of that mattered in the end. All that mattered was that they were in the mire of misdeeds together, and that she knew the truth. As Alderin led her through the morose path of land, Darrien's heart ached. She almost turned back every step, almost pulled on Alderin's sleeve and told him she didn't want to know. But she stayed the course, even as her chest hurt with every beat of her heart. It wasn't until Alderin stopped in front of a simple gravestone that she realized that she was holding her breath. Darrien wasn't sure what she was expecting when she looked at the stone. But there were no answers there, only more questions and a sense of dread that had held in her heart from the moment that she saw the single named carved there. Darrien.

The two did not speak of what they saw that day for a very long time, and when they finally did, Darrien made sure they were very far away from the Citadel of the Dark Gods. She couldn't risk either her father or Serrina hearing their conversation. Again, Darrien's quest for answers was cut short. Alderin knew little about the woman whom he had murdered. All he knew was that Serrina had requested his assistance in cleaning up a problem for Pike. When the two arrived in the simple bedchambers of the woman, she had been asleep in her bed, cradling what looked to be a newborn in the bed beside her. A nursemaid had been seated in the corner, but before she could even exhale, Serrina had snapped her neck and laid her gently on the floor as not to disturb either the mother or the baby. It took only a small use of power for the baby to be kept asleep, and as Alderin quickly and painlessly snapped the neck of the mother, Serrina recovered the baby. Alderin was to dispose of the two bodies while Serrina dealt with the child. Alderin had said at the time he was relieved because he believed that Serrina was going to kill the baby, and he wasn't sure he would have had the stomach for it. All he knew about the woman was a name, Darrien, and he wasn't sure it was her first or last. He didn't know anything about the nursemaid, so her grave ended up being unmarked. He related how Serrina had chided him for even bothering to make gravestones at all. That she believed it would have been more efficient to simply burn the bodies or obliterate them completely. But Alderin would not be deterred. He may have been a murderer, but he did not wish to be an unrepentant one. It wasn't until later, when Alderin returned to the Citadel that he discovered Pike's true intentions for the mission. He wanted the baby for his own, without the interference of the mother. And when Pike took to calling the baby girl Darrien, Alderin nearly stopped his bloody work. Instead, he decided that he would use the trust that he had garnered to save those that he could from Pike's wrath.

Alderin confessed to Darrien that unless he had been accompanied by Serrina, he had not killed anyone on Pike's orders since that day. He would wipe the memory of his targets and safely transport them to a place where they could start new lives with no memory of what transgression they had unwittingly committed against the leader of the Dark Gods. However, to keep up appearances, he would steal a body from another graveyard or crypt and then bury it in the secret cemetery. That way, Serrina would never catch on to Alderin's duplicity. Once Darrien learned the truth, she assured Alderin that there would need be no more killing, and that they would do everything in their power to keep the world safe from Pike.

All of this brought Darrien back to the moment she inhabited, standing face to face with one of the Children of the Creator, her life very much on the line. And while Talisia had hoped to disarm her with the jibe about her name, Darrien was proud of who she had become over the centuries. From a certain point of view she was a child with stolen names, but she had done her best to make those names her own. She had never known her mother, never known the woman that she had been or dreamed of being, and so she wore the name Darrien for the woman who couldn't and tried to use the centuries to bring dignity to that name. The name Annis had been one that was inflicted upon her father as an effort to strip him of his identity as a hero and cast him into the role of a villain that the Creator needed him to play. It was a curse and a burden to the proud man Pike Rhuiden. However, Darrien took that curse and made it into a blessing. Like Alderin, she was a child of a new world, and while she was intrinsically tied to a past she didn't and couldn't understand, what she was at her core was a hero in search of a battle. Though it had taken centuries, Darrien Annis, not Darrien Rhuiden, stood with her shoulders back, her head held high, staring down a creature that had been the death of countless worlds. Even if she failed in her task, no insult, no hidden past, nor any repressed shame would ever be able to take that away from her. These next moments would be her legacy that would live on until Creation fell.

"So, tell me," Talisia said, her expression passive but her eyes filled with malice unlike Darrien had never felt before, "what happened to that tragic little boy Wolf? I had hoped he would have been the one waiting for me. I would have liked to look him in the eye and tell him that his wife betrayed him and was the cause of his slumber. I think I would have liked to see the sorrow in his eyes when I told him how she died as I ripped his heart out."

Darrien felt a surge of power from deep inside of her and when she spoke again, the voice may have been hers, but the words most certainly were not.

"I never understood your penchant for cruelty, sister," Pyrrus' words flooded from the void. "With all of your ability to inspire and bend people to your will, you could have made this a place of wonder instead of one of horror."

Talisia's eyes flashed with recognition.

"You were always a fool Pyrrus, and that's why you were cut down."

Darrien shook her head.

"It's not foolish to believe that people can leave behind their destructive ways and find a better path. That was what you, Emries, and Raenera never understood. You tried to enforce your vision upon Creation and hoped to bend everything to that vision. Whether it was Raenera and her perfect Order, or it was Emries and his fixation on the survival of the strongest. Or even you sister, and your vision of a universe where everyone was out for themselves with no rules, only a need for survival. How could any of those things end? What did Raenera have to show for her vaunted plans? It took only a slight manipulation from you for everything to come unraveled. And I think what hurt Raenera more than your interference was the fact that she realized that even without you her world was doomed to failure. Emries wants to believe that his path is the best; the one where the strongest heroes and champions battle each other for supremacy and through the struggle, the course of fate would favor those who were deserving. But Emries doesn't have the patience or the control that Raenera does and so he cannot resist either tipping the scales how he feels they should go, or interjecting himself as a catalyst. In his mind, he is the greatest champion and should always be lauded as such. Thus, his conception of the universal could never come to pass without him at the head. A self-fulfilling and self-destructive prophecy at the same time. Then there's you, sister."

Darrien took a beat, letting her shimmering blue eyes bore a hole into the soul of her opponent.

"What kind of reality does not have the capacity for compassion and altruism? Why must all action come down to the basest desires of every being, even when those base desires will surely lead to the being's ruination?"

Talisia's voice was pure venom.

"Because our Father made this reality one of cruelty, pain, and suffering. The only truth of this reality is death. Those that do not hasten it through murder and malice are doomed to have those heinous acts inflicted upon them. Hate and villainy are the currency of this Creation, dear brother. We grow stronger by what we destroy, not by what we create. That is why I stand here, on the edge of my victory, and you are nothing more than a remnant of naivety trapped in the body of a forgotten girl who always pleaded for her father's affections. You were both disappointments when you could have been so much greater. Darrien always thirsted for love and approval, and instead of taking it by either ending that pathetic shadow she called a father, or showing her true power by crushing his enemies and taking his love, she whined about how unfair her life was and became a willing accomplice to the horrors he constructed in his addled mind. And you brother, always wishing for a fair and good universe, one that would see the value in all things, one that would reward those who helped and supported others. Those you trusted the most, those whom you hoped would become the stewards of your shining future were the first to turn on you in the rebellion that I led in the Heavens. The dragons that you had counted as your friends for so long could not stand your simpering and flawed vision because their place in it was not one befitting how they viewed themselves. You never understood that the dragons thought themselves even above us, and did not see the tools that Father designed them to be. I put them to their proper uses while you, you pathetic fool, trusted them to do the right thing for all of the creatures they viewed as nothing more than their food. They relished the opportunity to end you."

Darrien nodded.

"Perhaps you're right, sister. I never entertained the thought that I could be wrong, and I think that was the weakness all of us had. At least until Halicon returned from his defeat on Onea. Halicon saw a better way. Not because of some revelation of his own, but because he saw the struggles of those who had no chance to be victorious. That was why he took the actions he did on this world, and why he has inspired me to do the same."

Darrien stepped forward, her hands at her sides showing that she remained unarmed.

"None of us were right. And none of us alone can succeed in stopping Father for the horrible things he plans to do. He even now understands that we are too flawed to continue to exist. And soon now, he will wipe this place clean of all of his mistakes. The Children, the Servants, the dragons. All of it, gone in the blink of an eye. And he'll start the whole cycle over again, trying to learn the lessons that he cannot learn."

Finally, an expression came to Talisia's face. Her lips twisted into a mocking smile.

"That is why, dear brother, I am going to take your power and use it to defeat our Father. Together, along with what I intend to take from the rest of our siblings through Dorovar, we will reshape this pathetic excuse for a reality into something far more fitting."

Talisia raised the razor-thin blade and took a step forward.

"Yes, sister," Darrien's voice cooed, "we will be together."

Darrien darted forward, her hands clasping around Talisia's wrist and aiming the blade squarely at her chest before pulling the Child of the Creator forward. Darrien didn't feel the blade pierce her skin, pass through the bone, or enter her heart. But the explosion of power that followed, and the scream that tore from Talisia's lips reverberated in her head and for a moment Darrien thought her brain was going to rush out of her ears. Her body felt as though it was being shaken apart by the force of the scream, and then suddenly it was gone.

When Darrien opened her eyes, she realized that she was staring up at the sky. She didn't know how long she had been laying there, but from the moisture on her body, it must have been quite some time. As she sat up, the pain started. It first radiated from her chest, and then spread through her entire body like a fire. Wolf had warned her what would happen if she was successful. They had imprisoned the power of a Child of the Creator in a body that was not made to host it. What's more, the remnants of what Talisia was would seek to burn its way out of Darrien as quickly as possible. As Darrien fought her way back to her feet, she could feel the hate clawing at the back of her mind, barely contained by the sliver of Pyrrus' power that was being used as a temporary cage. If she didn't accomplish the second part of her mission quickly, there would be nothing left of the cage, and nothing to stop Talisia's malice from destroying Darrien from the inside out.

Her body threatening to rebel at any moment, Darrien turned her sights northward to the Kingdom of Stone, Albitonin, the Heart of Stone, and the person who would soon become the new vessel for Talisia's power.

Chapter CVIII

Foundations of Conscience in the Castle of Ideals

Year Five of the Just Emperor Kaitain "Dragonsbane" Lorien, Creator's Calendar Year 1872

The light rain continued to fall on the field that would soon see thick red blood mixing with the mud at the feet of the army of the Lordhill Rebellion. Despite the fact that three of the army's leaders had fallen to the otherworldly forces of the Heavens, the soldiers held their ranks and did not break and run. Arent Fox was doing his best to hold the troops together and to harness the rage that was overriding the fear that was filling them. Duncan had discarded his soldier's helmet and shield and was attempting to rally his regiment around Gwydeon as a sort of honor guard. Most had not noticed Duncan's elevation from simple soldier to a man with power, and they still saw and respected him as a fellow soldier. The ranks fanned out as quickly as they could with the difficult terrain and prepared themselves for the inevitable charge of the flights of warrior angels. Both Midarin and Gwydeon held their ground, eyes never leaving Rachel Core. It was Gwydeon whose voice cut through the din first.

"Get to Mirana and Liara. Make sure Quyhn is protected."

Midarin didn't budge.

"Midarin!"

The next moment, a bow made of diamond appeared in Midarin's hand. She brought it up and pulled the invisible bowstring back, a diamond arrow blinking into existence.

"Not this time Gwydeon," Midarin responded, her voice low, calm and even. Gwydeon barely was able to comprehend her words with the background noise. "Rachel is mine. You go and tend to Liara and Mirana. Do what you said you were going to do. Bring them hope. I'm going to do what I do. I'm going to kill our enemies."

Gwydeon wanted to argue, wanted to protect Midarin from her own urges, but he knew there was nothing for him to do. They were not what they once were. They were not two halves of the same whole. A distance had sprouted up between them in the days since Gwydeon's return from the dead, and while they had tried to find a way back to where they had been, it was clear that something was different, for both of them. Midarin had always had a streak within her, the streak of a killer. But she covered it with a charm and a disarming wit. But time holding the factions of the Dark Gods together, keeping Pike's rages at bay, and trying to raise a child without the man that she loved, had eroded that charm. What was left was not the princess who had lost her kingdom, or even the queen who fought desperately to keep her kingdom from falling to shadow. What was left was the warrior who faced down the forces of an evil god despite having nothing but a bow and her own tenacity. As Gwydeon fell back, soldiers rushed up around him. Some moved with him as he sprinted as best he could in the direction of Quyhn and her protection detail, while others flooded in to take his place at the vanguard. It didn't take long for Gwydeon to lose sight of Midarin, and from the moment she was out of his line of sight, he began to feel fear grip his heart.

* * * * * * * * * * * *

Midarin felt the mud under her feet begin to shift as she tried to set her stance. She dared not waste any power to try to stabilize the ground, she was going to need every bit if she was going to last more than a few moments against this new Servant of the Creator, as that was undoubtedly what Rachel had become. The woman Rachel Core was no more than a vessel, an empty husk into which the Creator had poured his power. The face that looked back at Midarin was not the woman that Midarin had come to see as a sister. Rachel was nothing more than a trick of the Creator's perverse mind, an attempt to keep them off balance. But Midarin was beyond the mind games. All that was left was the war. She brought her bow up so that she sighted down the length of the arrow, and her eye was locked on the heart of her opponent. Rachel did not disappoint, she brought up her own bow made of divine energy, an arrow of pure brilliant light perched on the bowstring. The flights of angels held their ground flanking Rachel, clearly waiting to be given the order to strike. Tension rippled through the ranks of soldiers surrounding Midarin, and out of the corner of her eye, she could see Duncan with his sword raised, ready to give the order to charge.

"Well, Princess Eagle-Eye," Rachel taunted, "are you ready to start a war?"

Midarin sneered.

"The person who gave me that name died thousands of years ago. It means nothing now, and it has no power to make me feel anything but contempt for the Creator and his games."

Midarin let loose of the bowstring and the arrow leapt into the air, crossing the distance between the two women with impossible speed. Rachel slid gently to one side, her feet gliding over the uneven and muddy terrain as though it were smooth as glass. The diamond arrow passed by Rachel's shoulder, the force of it rippling her blood-red shirt sleeve. There was a palpable wave of fear that rushed through the ranks of the rebels. Was that the sign that the battle was to be joined? Duncan's arm tensed above his head and the blade of the sword dipped slightly. But neither rank moved. The angels did not flinch even a millimeter. The soldiers of the rebellion stiffened and dug their back foot into the mud, ready for the inevitable charge. A moment later, Rachel released her arrow, and it sped to its target. Midarin did not make a move, and the arrow passed so close to her face that it left a faint blood trail across her right cheek. It had been clear to Midarin the moment that the arrow left the bow that it was not intended to kill. More mind games.

"Your nerve is still like iron, Midarin," Rachel said, her compliment sounding hollow.

Midarin drew her bow again, another diamond arrow appearing on the bowstring.

"What's wrong, Rachel? Are you not supposed to kill me? You missed on purpose, and it was clear coming off the string. I taught you better than that. If you shoot, you shoot to kill, otherwise when you try to kill you'll fail."

Rachel's eyes went cold.

"Alright Midarin. This time, I won't miss."

Midarin growled.

"Neither will I."

What happened next escaped the vision of most of the members of the Lordhill rebellion, but Duncan as well as the warrior angels were able to follow each stress-filled moment of the exchange. The arrow of light streaked from Rachel's bow, the trail of light impossible to follow to mortal eyes. However, Midarin was far from mortal. A split second later the diamond arrow launched from her bow and the two deadly projectiles lanced through the air between the two battle-hardened warriors. Near the mid-way point the arrow of light and the arrow of diamond struck each other in a violent explosion that sounded like a thousand windows shattering. There were dozens of miniature explosions of nearly blinding white light. Neither Midarin nor Rachel took notice of the impact as they had already launched their second and third volley by the time the first had detonated in dazzling light. Like the first volley, the second and third sets of arrow met in the space between the two women, colliding and exploding a brilliant cascade of light. Now both Rachel and Midarin moved faster than the human eye could perceive, arrows no sooner appearing on infinitesimally small bowstrings before being launched at the adversary. Three arrows became six, which became a dozen, which became two dozen. Each met the same destructive fate. It seemed that even the growing fireworks display in the center of the battlefield could not keep up with the speed at which new explosions were adding to the conflagration. Rachel and Midarin both began to sidestep and change the angles of their attacks, trying to find a way to break through the other's deadly accurate barrage. The collisions in the center of the battlefield began to slow as more and more of the projectiles found their way through. Each missed the other by barely an eyelash. Then finally Rachel was almost knocked off her feet as one of the diamond arrows found its mark, slamming into her shoulder. The plume of blood shocked everyone, none more so than Midarin. She had stopped truly aiming and was instead counting on her instinct and her skill to guide the shots. In retrospect she might not even consider that she was even using her abilities to influence her aim. For the moment both women arrested their assault, and Rachel straightened, the diamond arrow still protruding from the bleeding wound in her shoulder.

"First blood goes to you, Midarin," Rachel's voice cold and hard. "But I assure it, it will be the last."

The next moment, an aura of divine power rose up around Rachel like a fog. In life, Rachel had had long curly red hair and piercing green eyes. Now, in service to the Creator her hair was cropped short but still brilliant red, and as the aura intensified, the color drained away from her eyes leaving only brilliant glowing white. Color faded from the woman's skin also, the tone going from a sun-tanned bronze to a nearly porcelain white in a matter of seconds. The bow disappear from Rachel's hands, and she extended both arms downward, her palms outward toward Midarin. That next moment, four wings materialized behind Rachel. The two upper wings were brilliant white and shimmered with an almost blinding angelic light. The lower wings were charcoal in color and projected a wave of menace and malevolence in all directions. White feathers extended from Rachel's back and wrapped around her stomach and torso creating what looked like a layer of armor. When the feathers touched the wound in her shoulder, the blood as well as the diamond arrow simply disappeared.

"Now," the echoing angelic voice snarled, "you will bear witness to the power of The Spirit of the Creator."

With barely a beat of her wings, Rachel was propelled upward into the sky, the rain sizzling and fading into steam as it met the divine aura. Now perched high in the air, Rachel extended her arms to her side. In the space around Rachel appeared what could have been hundreds of the arrows of light. She pointed down to Midarin and her voice boomed.

"You have stood in defiance of the Creator and have been judged guilty of crimes against Creation. For that, you and all who follow you shall be cleansed from this world with divine fire."

She paused for a moment to let her pronouncement sink in before resuming.

"Angelic Host! Destroy the enemies of the Creator!"

At her words, the arrows of light rained down from above and the warrior angels brandished their flaming weapons and charged.

* * * * * * * * * * * *

Gwydeon skidded to a stop and nearly lost his balance due to the thick deep mud. Mirana and Liara had formed a screen in front of Quyhn and both appeared to be straining to maintain the integrity of the shield that was protecting the rebel army from the lightning that still was attempting to reduce the soldiers to ash. He was vaguely aware of the escalation of power coming from where Midarin and Rachel were facing off, and he felt that in only a matter of moments the conflict would be well and truly joined on all fronts. He could feel the nerves of the soldiers beginning to fray and they continued to be under assault without an opportunity to inflict damage upon their opponent, morale would suffer. Before Gwydeon could get a word out, Liara's strained and fearful voice found his ear.

"It's the Spirit," she said, her voice wavering, "she's here for us."

Gwydeon gritted his teeth and tried his best to sound reassuring.

"Don't worry Liara, I'm not going to let them take you. You or your sister. But we have to make sure that Quyhn is safe and the soldiers have a fighting chance. We've already lost too much."

Rhionna's question came in the form of a concerned look.

"We've already lost Connor, Gabrielle, Strum, and about two dozen soldiers," Gwydeon answered. "Arent is doing his best to keep the army from breaking or recklessly charging. Duncan is helping too. So far we're holding everything together, but it won't last much longer."

Rhionna set her jaw.

"Where do you need me?"

Gwydeon turned back in the direction of the vanguard.

"You have to keep Quyhn safe, no matter what. Whatever is coming is going to come right for Mirana and Liara to get them clear so that the Spirit can lay waste to everything without fear of causing them harm. There are two guardian angels here. I have no doubt they'll be the first to crash through the ranks. With their size and reach, they could inflict more damage than a dozen warrior angels, and in a fraction of the time. The Creator must really want the girls on his side."

It was then that Gwydeon saw the Spirit rise into the air and summon the mass of deadly projectiles. Her attack order rang out a moment later and the arrows rained down upon the shield. Mirana cried out and fell to one knee. But she did not release the shield. Despite the blood that began to flow from her nose at the exertion, Mirana fought her way back to her feet and pushed more power into the shield. Twin blades of fire appeared in Gwydeon's hands and he set his feet.

"Here they come."

* * * * * * * * * * * *

As the wave of warrior angles flooded forward, Duncan Rhuiden could only hear the beating of his heart in his ears, and the words of his patron in his new life on Espre running through his mind.

"When I was born, I was but a flickering flame, unsure of its direction but yearning to be more."

The first of the warrior angles flashed in, its flaming sword crashing against the shield that Duncan had recovered from where he had dropped it. He could no longer concentrate on reinforcing the shield above the soldiers. He needed to be what was needed at that moment, and that was a soldier. The flaming sword of the warrior angel dug a massive scar into the perfect polished finish of the shield. But Duncan saw immediately that the angel had overcommitted in its attack. It clearly thought that Duncan was just another mortal that the flaming sword would cut through as a scythe reaped wheat. However, the stubborn half-mortal was more than a match for the warrior angel's arrogance, and as Duncan shifted his weight and brought his blade up, he let the angel tumble past him, off balance, and brought the shimmering blade of his weapon crashing down on the back of the angel's neck. Head separated from body, and the two pieces of the angel crashed to the ground and disappeared in a flash of light. As Duncan turned to look for his next opponent, the litany resumed, this time loud enough that those around him could possibly hear.

"From my infancy I grew, I learned, and the flickering flame changed; it spread its wings and became the mighty Phoenix."

An explosion rocked the ground near Duncan, causing him to lose his footing for a moment. A dozen other soldiers were knocked off their feet, and Duncan moved quickly to give them aid and allow them to recover before they were cut down by one of the opportunistic celestial warriors. He directed the men toward the flank that a flight of angels was attempting to turn, and as the last one was just about out of earshot, Duncan continued, his sword ready as another angel charged.

"But from the day those wings spread to catch the air, I knew that there was a great fate waiting beyond; beyond what I knew, beyond my perception. I would make the most of my time as the Phoenix; learn all that I could learn, live a life that would make me worthy of what would come after."

The next angel was more cautious in its attack, but no less brutal. The first blow cleaved the shield in half, and the quick second attack would have cut Duncan from his shoulder to his hip had he not rolled out of the way. But the roll flowed into a strike as he was taught, and the scorched blade of his simple sword claimed the angel in the knee and severed half of the leg at the joint. The angel beat its wing wildly in an attempt to keep it balance, but Duncan would not give it the opportunity. He ducked under a wild slash bringing his sword up and cutting through the sword arm of the angel mid-bicep before bringing the blade crashing down again across the creature's chest. The angel fell back, exploding into light. Duncan bent to recover the flaming sword and as he stood, locking eyes on two angels that advanced upon him after cutting through half a dozen Lordhill soldiers, his hopeful voice projected out so that any in earshot could clearly hear.

"The Phoenix is not eternal. It returns to Flames when its life is ended, only to be reborn once more to continue its works."

A snarl curled Duncan's lips and he charged, the flaming sword in one hand and his mortal blade in the other.

"We do not live but one life."

A slash from the mortal blade followed by one from the flaming blade struck down the first angel, and Duncan ducked a blow that would have taken his head from his shoulders and then drove forward burying the tip of his steel into the heart of the second angel. As it exploded, a cheer went up from the soldiers around him. He thought he heard one of them order a charge, but he was beyond anything other than the voice in his head, the voice that echoed in his words.

"Like the Phoenix we live many. Some ending in fire, others in ashes, but all ending and beginning anew. My life before was the Phoenix. Now I am the flickering flame waiting to be reborn. Only through my deeds shall I become the majestic Phoenix once more."

An angel crashed down in the middle of a formation of soldiers, and Duncan sprinted in that direction, power flooding into his legs. He was not practiced in the use of his abilities beyond the simple applications that Logan and Kamen had taught him, but one thing he did know was how to make himself faster and stronger without thinking about it. That had been Kamen's lesson. Too many applications of the power in his blood would have required concentration. But in the heat of battle, it was the applications that came as a reflex that could be the most useful; strength, speed, healing, and endurance. Before the angel could bring its flaming blade down on the first of its intended victims, Duncan had crossed the distance, the steel blade flying from his hand like a spear. The tip was on target, crashing into the skull of the angel, sending it toppling to the ground before it faded in light. Duncan didn't wait for acknowledgement from the recovering soldiers. Instead, he took a spear from one of the stunned men and turned his attention to the fifteen-foot monster that was beginning to wade through the battlefield.

"I shall walk this world, the flickering flame. I shall lift up those who cannot rise by themselves."

The giant angel saw the threat approaching, spear in one hand, flaming sword in the other and jabbed in his direction with the flaming tip of his spear. The tip hit the ground just at Duncan's feet, cutting a furrow in the ground and sending soil and stone flying in all directions. Duncan was quick enough to sidestep the strike but still felt the heat of the flaming spear scorch the side of his face. Not giving up on its attack, the guardian swept the haft of its spear in Duncan's direction, intending to knock him to the ground long enough to allow the guardian to finish him off. When the haft of the massive spear came in Duncan's direction, he leapt into the air and used his enhanced reflexes to perch on the spear and begin running up its length in the direction of the guardian.

"I shall use this flickering flame to bring comfort to those who have none, to shelter those who know only the ravages of the world."

The spear flew from Duncan's hand the next moment, and before the guardian knew what was happening, the spear had pierced its throat, exploding through the back of its massive neck. The strike was not enough to fell the giant, but it did give Duncan all the time he needed for his follow-up strike. Just before he reached the guardian's hands, Duncan let the power explode from inside him and he rose into the air like a coiled spring released from a box. The guardian barely had enough time to look up before Duncan came crashing down, the flaming sword splitting the guardian's head wide open. The explosion of light and force propelled Duncan backwards, but he let the momentum carry him into a lazy backwards flip before he landed on his feet in the mud. When he spoke again, the tone was barely above a whisper but the force of his words radiated from him like a burst of sunlight.

"I am the flicking flame, and yet I am so much more."

Duncan took a moment to survey the battlefield. There were so many dead, more than he could count. Gwydeon and Rhionna were keeping a dozen angels at bay while Mirana and Liara continued to shield the remaining forces of Lordhill from the flashes of lightning and arrows of light that rained down from above. Had the shield not been in place, the battle would have been over before it started. At the edge of the shield, Midarin and the Spirit continued their dazzling light show of a conflict, sending impossible volleys of projectiles at one another and still somehow remained unscathed. But the small victories were not enough to stem the tide. The angels were breaking the ranks of the mortal soldiers. In a matter of minutes it would all be over, and Gwydeon and Rhionna would be overrun. Striking down a warrior angel who was unaware of how close its dodge from one of the soldiers had brought it to Duncan, the next words rolled from Duncan's tongue and froze his heart.

"Let this flickering flame be a beacon to all those lost in the darkness and let it lead them back into the light."

He knew what he needed to do. Looking over his shoulder, he caught Liara's eye, and sent a single thought across the distance. The girl's face twisted in horror, but Duncan was already committed to his course of action. She tried to reach out, tried to tell him to stop, but Duncan shut himself off from everything but the voice in his head. Logan's voice was driving him on, and also his father's voice. There was so much Duncan needed to make right, so much he had to atone for. And it was time for that debt to be paid in full. As he drew on all of the power inside of him, Duncan thought of the stories that Kamen and Logan told about the battle that made Logan into the man that he had become; the story of the birth of the Lord Phoenix. He remembered the story Kamen told of the day that he relinquished his position in the Brotherhood of Phasia and became the Living Flame. Had they known what would come to pass? Had they taught him what he needed for this moment?

"Through these deeds and through grace this flickering flame shall spread its wings once more to become the mighty Phoenix, whose might shall protect all those who take shelter in its magnificence."

Power flooded through Duncan, and the green flames of the Blaze crackled to life on his skin. The aura of flame intensified, and Duncan found himself being lifted into the air.

"Until again I shall return to the flames."

The Blaze exploded around Duncan, his body disappearing in the conflagration. The human-shaped shadow inside the roiling mass of fire disappeared, and the flame grew in intensity as it rose into the air. It drew upon every living thing on the battlefield. It drew upon its kindred powers found in Gwydeon Sandar. It fed upon the power in the blood of the former Dark Gods. It called out to the blood of all creatures across the face of Espre that would stand in opposition to the destruction represented by the Creator. And finally it reached through the blood of Rhionna Winter, the blood of the man who had been Duncan's salvation. It reached through the Ranthall blood and drew power unlike Duncan had thought was possible. The mass of flame exploded in a blinding flash, and when everyone's vision cleared, above the battlefield hovered a majestic bird, wreathed in flame, a piercing cry erupting from its golden beak. The cry froze all of the angels where they stood, and in the mind of every mortal on the field of battle, the cry sounded like Duncan's voice.

"I am the flickering flame, and yet I am so much more."

The Last Full Measure of Devotion

*Year Five of the Just Emperor Kaitain "Dragonsbane" Lorien,
Creator's Calendar Year 1872*

Nathan Sandar's body ached. It had been far too long since he had done anything that did not utilize his abilities. As he walked across the familiar landscape, he could feel the muscles in his legs contract and release, resisting every step that he took. He had lost track of how many miles he had walked since Gideon had dumped him in the middle of nowhere, but his destination was starting to come into his field of vision. Yes, he could have walked the other way. Yes, he could have just found some ignorant little town somewhere that was outside of the coming conflict and live out the remainder of his short life as just another mortal. Maybe that was what his father would have done if he found himself in the same position. Robbed of everything that made him special, Nathan could see the high and mighty Gwydeon Sandar going back to the simplicity and squalor in which he was raised. He would probably find some little farming community out in the middle of nowhere, ingratiate himself as a tradesman; a blacksmith, or a carpenter, or some other such nonsense. And there, among the insignificant trash of humanity, he would live out his days. He would reinvent himself, his identity, as he needed as he outlived those who knew him. In time, he would fade into insignificance himself, lost to his own failings.

Nathan would never allow himself to be brought so low. He had suffered a defeat, a series of defeats in fact, and now, left alone and outside the favor of his patron, Nathan existed with a death mark hanging over his head. While Emries might not waste the time necessary to track down Nathan and make good on his threat to erase the former *Coromor* from existence, it would not prevent those who served Emries from carrying out his execution should he encounter any of them. Nathan had learned in a short time that there were more creatures loyal to Emries than he had ever imagined. Between dragons, lords, emperors, would-be emperors, and others Emries had stretched out his hand across the entirety of the world of Espre, shaping events to his will, creating the opportunity for a final victory over his rivals, his siblings, those who had stood against him on Onea and in the Heavens, as well as his father, the Creator. The emergence of Dorovar's Heralds was the sign that conditions were right for Emries' master plan to begin its final phase. And so Emries loosed his most visible agents on their missions to destabilize and demoralize all that stood in his way.

The plan had been brilliant in its early stages and demonstrated how clearly and completely Emries had thought through his war against not only his siblings, but also those who had humiliated him on Onea and also in the Heavens. Of course, Nathan had only seen the plan from the outside at first, but as soon as it was executed the brilliance of it became clear. Emries allowed the *Erieal* from the first generation of the prophecies of the *Coromor* to be easily discovered and hunted down. He knew that Aryx Terian would have a connection to those members of his generation, and thus would know they needed to be removed from the Creator's game. Emries allowed Cedric Binosear to believe that he was acting independently and that he was an ally of the girl Sabrina and his father Aerith. The tactic was intended to make the enemy believe that only the first generation *Erieal* were brought to Espre for the final act in the Creator's grand ideological war. The whole of the second generation of *Erieal*, including the *Coromor* Korrd Ranthall were firmly in Emries' control, with the exception of Pike Rhuiden and Gideon Viruci. The Dark Mirror version of Pike Rhuiden had had his connection to Emries severed. However, Emries did not view Pike Rhuiden as a threat, and fully expected him to self-destruct when given the opportunity. Of course, Nathan was sure that Emries had not foreseen Pike falling to the wiles of the creature Dorovar. However, the more time that Emries' enemies spent fighting each other, the less time they had to focus on what Emries was actually doing. Gideon Viruci on the other hand was a problem, and an unforeseen one. Emries hated nothing more than an unforeseen issue. Emries had mentioned that Gideon's tie to him had been severed, but gave no details into how that might have occurred.

That brought Nathan's mind to his generation of the prophecies. Storm, Taya, and Gwillim were clearly dedicated to serving Emries, as was Nathan. The only outlier from the third generation was Lissa Terian, but Emries through Talisia had neutralized her before the Dark Gods were cast down to Espre. The manipulation that Emries and Talisia were able to enact regarding Lissa had also given Emries the opportunity to empower the Light Reality version of Taya. All told, that left Emries with dedicated soldiers powerful enough to stand toe to toe with the Dark Gods and their Forgotten allies. The only true wrinkle in the plan was Cedric Binosear. He had not been fated to meet his end as he did, at the hands of Jeroch Yetre. But perhaps Cedric understood the plans that Emries had for him, and perhaps he had not intended to live the rest of his life as a hapless pawn. Which meant perhaps that Cedric did have a measure of free will, and was able to resist the demands of his sometime patron. Perhaps it was because Cedric held so much malice for Emries, though Nathan could not bring himself to understand that. Why would Cedric hold so much enmity toward the one who had given him everything he could ever imagine?

Now of course, the story of Cedric's true parentage was not a mystery to those who had become educated on the war. He was the first-born child of the eternal other, the cosmic mistake Aerith Seth. Cedric and his sister Anne were born of a dalliance that should never have been allowed to come to pass. But now Nathan understood that it was done as a measure of control over the uncontrollable powers of Aerith Seth. Both Emries and Halicon had their designs on the man. Emries needed Aerith Seth as a conduit by which Emries' powers could be forged into a weapon. Of course, Emries could have acted directly against Halicon, but to do so could invoke the wrath of the Creator. However, if by using Aerith Seth's powers, Emries could coax one of his followers to destroy Halicon, then his hands would be mostly clean in the deed, and perhaps he would be able to escape expulsion from the Heavens and remove one of his greatest impediments to the Golden Throne. Halicon on the other hand saw Aerith

Seth for what he was, an archetypal thorn in the heel of anyone who thought to consolidate power. At the time, of course, Halicon was only thinking of his own creations, the phasia, as well as Emries and his armies. Eventually as the war moved from Onea to Espre, that definition expanded to include the Creator.

Emries had engineered the chance meeting between Aerith Seth and the soon to be queen of Marcwell, and ensured that their coupling produced an heir to Aerith's power and also to Emries'. Emries went to visit Cedric and Anabel when they were infants, but was disappointed to find that neither child had the spark of power inside of them. It was as though something inside of them prevented the powers from taking hold. Immediately Emries began to suspect that their hereditary tie to Aerith Seth was somehow blocking their ability to access the abilities that Emries desired to implant within them. And so Emries devised a plan, a plan that was both devious and dangerous. He had learned of the phasia's distrust of Shau-ling, and their desire to rise beyond their station as servants. And so Emries manipulated the most intelligent of the phasia, Bryn and Ellis, and allowed them to 'find' the way to defeat their father. However, this method would require the sacrifice of their sometime ally and Bryn's lover, the redoubtable Aerith Seth. And while Bryn could not bring herself to end Aerith's life herself, she was not above assisting in engineering his downfall. Basille, Jeroch, and Saurn were duped into doing the deed, not understanding exactly what they were unleashing.

Emries knew the moment that Aerith had been put to death. There was a ripple across the whole of Creation, like a star suddenly flaring to life in the night sky. When Emries returned to Cedric and Anabel, who by that time were toddlers, he immediately felt the power beginning to grow within them. It took little intervention to suppress the power within Anabel, and little more to delay the power's growth in Cedric. It needed to build within him without him becoming aware of it until the time was right. That would allow Emries to consolidate his hold over the young man and ensure that when the time came, Cedric would do exactly what he needed to do and never question his motives for doing it. All the while, Emries insured that Cedric would not be challenged or tested as he grew into adulthood. When it was time, Emries disposed of both of Cedric's parents, and made sure that the young king was placed in a position that would put him in direct opposition of the phasia. He would stumble upon his birthright and he would start the war that would lead to Emries' eventual victory. But something happened at the end of the battle between Cedric and Shau-ling, something that Emries had not expected. Of course, it had not been Emries that Nathan had heard this part of the tale from. He had heard the tale from his father long ago, part of the lessons that were supposed to prepare him for his role as the third *Coromor* of the prophecies.

Gwydeon took great pains in explaining to Nathan the nature of the war between Halicon and Emries, at least what they understood of it at the time, and the circumstances and hazards inherent in the conflict. In the first generation of the prophecies, the greatest enemy was not the phasia or the Jeresei or even the Shadowwalkers. The greatest enemy was ignorance. Emries wanted Cedric and those that he gathered around himself to be completely and totally dependent upon the little bits of information and disinformation that Emries allowed Cedric to become aware of. It was important that Cedric not be told about his role in the war between the two brothers, but rather that he stumble upon it on his own following the small breadcrumbs that had been left over the years. Emries made sure that the records of the Hand of the Light were appropriately modified to reflect not the truth of the conflict between the Moridon and the forces of Shau-ling, but the more idealist version of the conflict. The perception of abstraction was always much easier to control than the perception of fact, though at times truth was a greater ally in constructing a stilted narrative than a lie was. The key was understanding what people wanted to hear and then ensuring not that they were told what they wanted to hear, but that they would interpret what they wanted to hear from what they were told. Gwydeon always taught that the biggest mistake a person could make was assuming that a person would act in their own self-interest. Self-interest was simply a set of theoretical guidelines that often a person did not or could not understand totally. Based on a moment, self-interest could be manipulated to be the exact opposite of what it should have been. Emries was the master at manipulating a person to believe that they were doing what was best for them, when in truth following his advice would most likely cause nothing but harm.

The key advisors to Cedric were an eclectic bunch of misfits, cast-offs, and impossibilities. Pirates, priests, Moridon outcasts, farmers, hunters, and laborers from all walks of life. Cedric had the ability to collect outcasts and turn them into heroes. At the core of it all was Aryx Terian, Aerith Seth's father and Cedric's sometime foil. Aryx was a man with no past, no future, and no understanding of the contradiction that he represented. He knew only that he was drawn to the conflict, like a moth to a flame, and there was nothing he could do to break away from the fate that his two fathers had created for him.

His first father, Halicon, had instilled in each of the phasia characteristics that he believed represented the most destructive forces in humanity. The first, and perhaps the most unintentional, was Kamen and the characteristic of sloth. Kamen had power to spare, but was not moved to use it unless moved by others. Kamen was an experiment, and perhaps that was why he was excised from the Brotherhood of Phasia so quickly and replaced by more active and vicious progeny. Kamen was indifferent to his power, indifferent to the war, and indifferent to his own identity. His lack of feelings of self and purpose are what led to his linguistic affectation where he referred to the other members of the Brotherhood by their titles and not their given names. Next was Jeroch, a creature that despite his increased status and the favoritism shown to him by Halicon, always thirsted for the respect and elevation that others achieved. Jeroch felt pain at the sight of the success of others, and actively sought to inflict harm upon those he viewed to be attempting to subvert his station. This envy was eventually destructive to the generations of phasia that followed, as Jeroch's behavior became the template for the War of Ascension within the Brotherhood. Bryn, the object, the temptress, and the embodiment of lust demanded as much attention from her potential victims as she needed for her own self-worth. There was a longing inside of her that would never be fulfilled, a longing that Halicon had hoped would drive Bryn to destroy their enemies. The avaricious need for information, knowledge, and insight filled Ellis completely. The need was so profound that it created within Ellis a bottomless pit that could never be filled even if she spent a thousand lifetimes in the exhaustive pursuit of acquiring that knowledge. But Halicon knew that Ellis's need for information could be turned to the benefit of the Brotherhood, and the more information she acquired, the more they would be able to use that information against their enemies. Grawn lived in a constant state of barely contained rage. While at times the rage did not allow for Grawn to properly give weight to all of the factors of a situation, his adherence to violence in the application of his wrath made him the bane of the enemies of the Brotherhood of Phasia.

Then there was Aryx Terian, the personification of human pride. Halicon's application of pride within Aryx was meant to drive him to derive his sense of self-worth and place in the cosmic order only through the triumphs against the enemies of the Brotherhood, which would culminate in the defeat of Emries. But what Halicon had not expected was the duality that pride represented in the species of human. As much as it could have a negative connotation, so too did it have an antithetical positive meaning in which pride could lead to a humble and content state towards one's own actions or the actions of another. So powerful was this sense of pride within Aryx Terian that he saw the hopelessly inferior forces that served Emries and how they sacrificed themselves by the thousands in a futile attempt to destroy the phasia. No matter how many of their towns were destroyed, no matter how many were killed, they kept fighting. But Aryx understood the futility on both sides. There could be no end to the confrontation. The phasia would keep killing and the humans would keep coming. So complete was the human dedication to their service of Emries that there could be no other course. The pointlessness, the sheer hubris of both sides thinking that they could prevail simply by spilling the most blood forced Aryx to walk away from his first father and then straight into the arms of his second.

When Emries had leaned of Aryx's defection, he put all of his energy into using the creature for his own purposes. It took a great deal of manipulation and patience, but finally with the unwitting assistance of the phasia and the assistance of Emries' own *Erieal*, Aryx was put in a vulnerable state. His questioning nature and his desire to be at peace with the monster he had once been allowed Emries to cloud the edges of his mind. Eventually, even as his own son was raised in the depths of the mines of Quea, Aerith began to see himself as human. What he believe to be the loss of his first wife at the hands of those he had once seen as his family had softened his heart and allowed Emries to write forgeries in his mind. Forgeries that allowed him to simply forget that he was not a simple hunter who had lost his family and was desperately searching for meaning. Once Aerith Seth had fallen to the ignorant blade of the phasia, Emries was able to sever the last connections between Aryx and the Blaze and impart within him a strong connection to Emries' own power, making him the first of a new generation of *Erieal*. Next were the Geoffry siblings, Arathorn with his delusions of grandeur and Diana with her naivety about the way the world should have been. Last of course was Mailock who had fallen victim to the subtle manipulations that Emries had implemented into the Moridon teachings. Once the pieces of the puzzle were revealed, Mailock would be the one to ensure that Cedric was in the right place at the right time. Everything else would take care of itself.

And to a point, Emries was correct. The phasia, untried in their new incarnation, were overconfident and more focused on destroying each other than identifying and neutralizing the threat that Cedric and his confederates posed. The path to Shau-ling's throne room was largely free of obstacles, which left Cedric underprepared for his confrontation with his ultimate enemy. While Emries viewed the *Erieal* and the rest of Cedric's allies as expendable, Cedric did not. Perhaps it was because Cedric was Aryx Terian's grandson and a piece of that pride that was at the very core of Aryx's being had been passed on. Perhaps it was love for his sister, the other half of his soul. Or perhaps it was simply because Cedric Binosear was a good man. Whatever the reason, Cedric would not allow those who accompanied him into the depths of hell to meet their end for the sake of expediency. And that, more than anything, led to the eventuality that Emries himself could not predict. Cedric embraced the power that he was fated to destroy. He touched the Blaze, damning himself, in order to save those he loved. But what Emries could not have predicted, what Halicon could not have known, was that that act, that selfless altruistic act, started a chain reaction that would culminate in the war on Espre. The end of the ideological war that had raged since the beginning of time would see its end because of one man's act.

The Children of the Creator, for all of their power and all of their experience did not adapt well to new situations. That was in evidence by the way that both Emries and Halicon reacted to their direct conflict on Onea, and the way that their so-called servants threw off the yoke of oppression and charted their own courses; for better and for worse. What complicated the situation further was the fact that none of the Children understood what Aerith Seth was, where his powers came from, and how they reacted when mixed with the powers of the Children. Halicon and

Emries took completely different approaches to interacting with Aerith Seth.

Halicon preferred a hands-off approach. He had enough to worry about with his treasonous phasia, and the impending assault by Emries' forces. Aerith Seth and those that he sired were troublesome enough without trying to use them, manipulate them, or recruit them. Of course, the phasia kept their own council when dealing with Aerith and his progeny. Bryn, Ellis, and Grawn completely embroiled themselves in the drama created by a direct daily relationship with the infuriating troublemaker. Saurn tried to manipulate Aerith Seth and ultimately tried to use him as a weapon. Basille focused his energies on training Gideon Viruci, Aerith's son, into an asset that could be used in any way that would benefit the phasia generally and Basille specifically. Erdric tried first to manipulate Cedric Binosear posing as the jealous brother of Cedric's lady love, and then again tried to destabilize Anabel Binosear posing as a rebellious son. Then there was Caris, who replaced Cedric's lover and attempted to push him in directions that would benefit her and perhaps allow her to replace Shau-ling and Jeroch as leader of the Brotherhood. Emries on the other hand saw what Aerith Seth represented and would stop at nothing to control him, his father, and his children. Aryx and Gideon were made members of the *Erieal*. Cedric was the first *Coromor* of the prophecies. Anabel was given protection unlike anyone would ever experience, at least as long as she was considered useful to Emries' purpose.

In the end however, the two approaches that Halicon and Emries employed created an impossible environment. Emries had manipulated power in order to create his chosen successor, and Halicon had done nothing to prevent that chosen successor from touching the Blaze. The imbalance that was created within Cedric passed down through Emries' mantle and made his followers less likely to blindly follow his orders. At the same time, Aerith Seth's mantle was empowered in a way that could not be quantified. The powers employed by the followers of the Children of the Creator changed in one moment. From that, humans could be elevated to the Heavens, the war between the Children intensified, and the Creator began to feel the threat that those mortals represented.

While Nathan only could theorize at the motivations of the Children and the Creator, he had been given access to enough information to make some guesses. But what Nathan fixated on was the fact that even after all those millennia, even after all of the manipulations and abuses, Cedric Binosear still had the ability to choose his own course. He chose not to be a pawn. He chose to sacrifice himself. Aryx Terian pulled himself away from Emries not once but twice. He recovered his memories as an original member of the phasia, and stood against everything that Emries stood for. How had they rescued themselves? How had they found the gall to stand against Emries? Korrd, despite all of his losses and all of the threats to his existence, still followed Emries. Gwillim, manipulated by the gods, a man out of time, still followed Emries. Talon, a man who didn't believe in anything except for the strength of his family and his friends, still followed Emries. Arin Domae, a professional soldier who ate and slept duty, still followed Emries. Storm and Taya Mystic, from a family that despised Emries and fought tooth and nail to prevent being ground under his boot, followed Emries. But why? Why did Emries have such a powerful hold? And why now did Nathan think of any of this? Did the fact that Gideon had suppressed Nathan's powers finally allow him to see what Emries was doing clearly? His mind was in complete turmoil when the spire of the Royal Palace of Celidar came into view with the banner of the Raven still flying high. In a matter of minutes, he would be face to face with his fate, and he would most likely speak the last words he would ever speak.

* * * * * * * * * * * *

Emries sat on the throne in the main hall of the Palace of Celidar and let his thoughts pass through all of the events that were about to take place. He reached out through the void and touched the minds of each of his servants, reinforcing his hold. The time for his ascension to the Golden Throne was at hand. As soon as Tess was ready, Cedric would be eliminated and Emries would have the weapon that he needed to wipe out all of his enemies in a single stroke. Emries was only barely aware that the doors to the throne room had opened, and was even less aware of who it was that walked through the doors. The figure stopped several feet short of the dais and waited to be acknowledged. When Emries finally looked down and saw who was standing there, he wasn't sure whether to laugh or frown.

"I don't see a heart," Emries said finally. "And I see that Gideon did significant damage to you. I feel no power coming from you, and the light in your eyes seems to have gone out. You may as well be dead."

Nathan was about to respond, but Emries put his hand up.

"I don't know why you even bothered to come back here, Nathan. You are a disgrace. Were you too much of a coward to end your own life? So you had to come and waste my time by forcing me to make good on my threat to end you myself?"

Nathan felt something rise up inside of him, something that he had not felt in a very long time. His heart was beating wildly and his chest ached with the exertion. And then, suddenly and inexplicably, Nathan began laughing. Emries' eyes went wide, and he leaned forward trying to figure out what was happening.

"And just what is funny, Nathan?"

"I came back here, Emries, because I wanted to see the look on your face when I tell you what Gideon told me. He wanted me to tell you that you should look in on your secret weapon, that you may not like what you find."

Nathan's laughter rang out again, but it was choked off immediately as Emries crossed the distance to the young man and seized him by the throat.

"You dare to face me with that silly smile on your face and speak of something that you know nothing about? You deliver this message from Gideon, a man I sent you to kill, with such glee? I'm going to snap your little insignificant neck and send you back to the void that I rescued you from. Would you care to use these last breaths for an apology, Nathan?"

Nathan's vision was starting to go black, and Emries' voice was nearly drowned out by the pounding of his pulse in his ears. Despite the agony in his head and in his chest, Nathan tilted his head forward to look Emries dead in the eye.

"My name is Nathaniel Sandar," his voice rasped. "And the only apology I have is to my mother and father."

The sound of the bones snapping in his neck was the last sound Nathaniel Sander ever heard.

Sweat, Tears, and the Sea

*Year Five of the Just Emperor Kaitain "Dragonsbane" Lorien,
Creator's Calendar Year 1872*

The capital city of the Kingdom of Water, Thorigald had seen more conflict in the last few weeks than it had in nearly a three hundred years, despite the fact that Thorigald had been in a near constant state of conflict with their neighbor the Kingdom of Fire, Saldarine. Since the formation of the Cadarian Empire, the majority of the Great Kingdoms were able to find a way to live in peace and cooperation. After the Founding Wars, the first Emperor of Cadaria, Terrik Lorien, had many promises to keep and many more bruised egos to mend. The small group of kingdoms that backed the Lorien faction during the Founding Wars pushed for the dissolution of the kingdoms that fought for the warlord Grawn. While most of these calls died quickly with the help of Terrik's firm will, one would not relent. Some of the fiercest fighting took place between Saldarine, Thorigald, and Iltorp in the Plains of Steam. Thousands of soldiers from each of the three Great Kingdoms lost their lives during the Founding Wars, and in the time of unrest that followed. It took Terrik Lorien marching the newly formed Imperial Army to the border between Saldarine and Thorigald to create a blockade that would stop the fighting. The Imperial Army, including emissaries from all of the other Great Kingdoms held the blockade for nearly six months while Emperor Terrik Lorien tried to draft a peace agreement between the two kingdoms. However, Terrik's attempts consistently were met with obstacles that he was unable to overcome. Each time one side of the conflict would agree to conditions, the other side would return with additional demands. After the first three months of negotiations, both sides started to become disillusioned with Terrik Lorien and began threatening to withdraw from the infant empire. At the end of the sixth month of fruitless negotiations, tensions boiled over.

After a particularly heated session of negotiations where both sides walked out after traded insults, the night saw an unprecedented escalation in hostilities. Both the Army of Fire and Army of Water advanced on the Imperial Army who held the entire length of the border. Sensing that they were about to be overrun, the emissary from Iltorp quickly rode back to where the Army of Steam was garrisoned and summoned the army to the impending conflict. As the twin suns rose, the four armies were prepared for a day of bloody battle. Against the advice of his retainers, Terrik Lorien put on his armor and took up his sword and stood in the center of the would-be battlefield alone. With hostile forces on all sides, the young emperor stood silent, waiting. For two hours the emperor stood alone, neither of the opposing kingdoms willing to be the one to strike a blow against the empire they had fought so hard to create. Representatives from Thorigald and Saldarine requested a meeting with Emperor Lorien to attempt to end the feud. Each of the advances were rebuffed, and Terrik Lorien remained standing on the battlefield. As day began to turn to night Terrik Lorien continued to hold his position, and the representatives from Thorigald and Saldarine were forced to go to the emperor. The representatives and their entourage brought tents and tables and chairs to where the emperor waited, but he refused to yield his place. He would not take a chair, would not allow those who brought them back to the brink of war to be comfortable. They would stand, all together, and negotiate a peace or there would be nothing to stop all of the sides from attempting to slaughter each other, with the emperor and the kingdoms' representatives being the first amongst the dead. In the end, after many hours of exhausting conversation in the highly pressurized environment, a compromise was negotiated. In the truest sense of the word, it was an agreement that none of the sides was happy with. Free passage would be allowed between the kingdoms, and each would share access to the natural resources the other possessed. The one condition however was that the two kingdoms would consistently be considered in a state of war, and border skirmishes were allowed to occur without threat of escalation.

It would be several more years before the compromise would be tested because shortly after the agreement was reached, the First Shadow War began. The conclusion of the war saw the creation of the thirteenth Great Kingdom of Cadaria, the Kingdom of Night, Galateria, and the formation of the Knights of the Flashing Blade. However, before long the old hatreds would bubble back to the surface and the kingdoms would find themselves at war once more. For the generations that would follow, the war would be marked with uneasy periods of peace interrupted by flashes of conflict. The border skirmishes were always brutal and bloody. Even while the soldiers died on the battlefields, the nobles talked, insulted, and negotiated. In the end, the peace returned, but the layers of hatred only grew. What helped to keep the conflict recurring was the fact that the war never touched any of the major cities in either of the kingdoms. The sons and daughters of Thorigald and Saldarine marched into the wilds never to return, and the nobles and their retinues were able to keep their hands clean. Thus, the horrors of war were stories from another place, another time. They could be put out of mind, or hidden from the populace behind an ocean of misinformation or outright lies. The other side was always the aggressor. There was an ambush. Agents were caught planning some nefarious scheme that would have resulted in the deaths of hundreds of innocents. They hate us. They are the enemy. The words of the nobles filtered down into the ears of the populace and the generations-long hatred continued to be stoked. There would never be a shortage of young men and women who were willing to die defending their home against their eternal enemy.

That all changed when Seraph Kore launched his insurrection and seized control of Thorigald from the nobles. Now soldiers walked openly in the streets, on guard for the attack that would eventually come. Rumors swirled about who the invader would be. Would it be the Imperial Legion? Would it be a coalition from the Great Kingdoms? Or would it only be the hated enemy Saldarine come to finally crush its bitter rival? It didn't matter. All that mattered was that everyone expected blood to finally flow in the streets of the capital city.

What none expected however was that the army that first set foot into Thorigald was one of unholy might. The vanguard of the invaders were dressed in the uniforms of ancient Thorigald and Saldarine soldiers, their visages so horrible that to look on them would chill the blood and turn even the bravest man into a coward. Pocked gray flesh hung from aged yellow bones, and ichor oozed from eyes, ears, and noses. Many had missing limbs, or at the very least looked so frail that a stiff wind would blow them apart. Still the army of horrors advanced. Any citizen that attempted to bar their path or simply escape their wrath was cut down indiscriminately. Women and children wailed as they ran, while the brave men with pitchforks and simple swords and spears tried to delay the advance to buy time for their families. But delay was all they could hope for. Even though several of the unholy soldiers fell to the fearful attacks, the advance was not hampered in any significant way. The fear was doubled when the people saw the army that closed in behind the force of rotting corpses. Mud-stained banners of the Army of Fire became visible in the distance, and curses rolled from the citizens of Thorigald and the suspicion was immediately cemented that the villains of Saldarine were behind the invasion. The twisted corrupted souls that festered inside of Saldarine somehow sank so low into their perverse vision of justice and fouled the righteous dead soldiers of Thorigald to be used against their own people. But then, for some unknown reason, the Army of Fire turned their blades on the unholy army attempting to strike them down, while at the same time defending the lives of the innocent Thorigald citizens. It made no sense.

Despite some early clashes with overzealous and fearful citizenry, the Army of Fire dedicated themselves to engaging the Army of the Dead while at the same time ushering the citizens of Thorigald to safety. However, even with the forces of the Army of Fire combined with those able members of the Thorigald citizens who stayed to defend their homes, the Army of the Dead continued to press forward. They had nearly advanced to the center of the city when the rumbling tremors began to shake the paving stones of the city's streets. Moments later the hulking monstrous form of the Herald War entered the city. Its mottled bronze armor sucked in all light, and its brilliant red eyes fixed on the horizon rather than on the meager forces arrayed against it. After just a few long strides, War stood in the center of the city square, the streams that ran through the center of each street already beginning to turn red from the blood of the soldiers and innocents killed by the Herald's army. The combat circled itself around War, as though by its very will it drew the warriors to him. A single stomp from War shook all of the mortals from their feet, giving the dead soldiers an opportunity to strike their living counterparts. The cries of pain were immediately drowned out by War's booming voice.

"Hear me, Thorigald. I, the Herald War have brought to you the salvation of Dorovar. You have lived your entire lives in bondage, but one that you could not see. Every breath you have taken, you have been a slave. Every decision you have made, you have done so with a fear and a trepidation that you could not understand. You have bowed your head and bent your knee to an entity you have been told loves you, but that could not be further from the truth. The Creator sits upon his Golden Throne in the Heavens and he does not see you. The fact that you exist means nothing to Him, and yet you are expected to bow and be subservient to this being. You are expected to give of your time and your belonging to the Church that supposedly spreads the message of his love and forgiveness. You are paying your Master for the privilege of being in bondage. Every night you get on your knees and praise the name of the Creator, you are thanking him for your servitude. Every act and every word that glorifies His name only adds to your debasement. And all of this you have done and would have done for the rest of your lives because of the lies told to you. The lies of the Church of the Creator. The lies of your parents, the lies of the angels and the heroes and the so-called prophets."

A haze of green appeared around War, intensifying as he spoke. A gentle song seemed to emerge from the cloud, not one of words but one of emotion. There was rage there, but also peace. There was fear, but also elation. Dread, but joy. The song seemed to surge and fall with War's words and all who heard it could not help but be captivated by it.

"Dorovar does not come to conquer you. Dorovar comes to set you free. He has brought to you salvations in forms that you could understand but not comprehend. Dorovar has sought to show you the lies of the Creator. First he sent the Grey Man Pestilence. Pestilence was to show you the plague that you have already been fighting. A plague of your heart and your soul, a disease placed there by the poisoned words of the priests who speak their leprous falsehoods into your ears. The Crawling Plague was intended to show the indifference and powerlessness of those who claimed to know the mind of the Creator. If the Creator has truly loved the people of Cadaria, would he have allowed them to suffer such a horrendous fate? Would He have allowed Pestilence to do his righteous work in the fields and in the streets? Would not the priests of the Church of the Creator have been able to cure the ills of this world with but a wave of their hand? And yet the people suffered, and the lie of the Creator's love was exposed."

The green glow around War intensified and the Army of the Dead pulled away from the Army of Fire, but did not stop defending themselves. Already many of the soldiers from Saldarine had stopped fighting, transfixed by the words of the towering Herald. Some of the fearful people of Thorigald had come out of their hiding places also to listen, the words chilling them to the bone.

"It was then that Dorovar brought the touch of the beautiful Famine to Cadaria. The Wasting Disease that she spread far and wide was to expose the emptiness inside of you all. You have been fed platitudes and lies for so long that your souls have been screaming out for true nourishment. But you have been mislead for your entire lives and you have not been able to hear the wails of your soul. You have not been able to feel that hunger and need for true nourishment. Famine showed you the true hunger inside of yourselves, the hunger that can no longer be sated by falsehoods and self-serving doctrine. And so, just like those fortunate souls who were freed from their bondage by the Crawling Plague, those that were saved from their soul-wrenching hunger by the Wasting Disease saw the truth of existence, and the truth of the world around them. The only salvation was embracing the perfect Order, and embracing the salvation brought by Dorovar."

More people began to emerge from their hiding places, and all fighting in the capital city of Thorigald had ceased. People stood transfixed by the slow and calming words of the Herald. And though his voice boomed loud enough that it could be heard across the entire city, to the ears of those who heard it, it was as soft and comforting as a loved one whispering in their ear. The spectral green glow began to extend out from War, spreading like the early morning fog through the streets, carrying the calming glow of War's words along with it.

"What is it that you all fear the most? Of course, it is the senseless scourge that you call death. However, even that is a lie that has been told to you by the Creator and his black-hearted priests. You have been told that only through good acts and righteous devotion to your Creator that you will find a place in the Heavens. And if you do ill, and your heart is not a slave to the will of the Church, then you shall burn for eternity in a pit of blackness and pain. Of all the lies told by the Creator, this is the most heinous and reprehensible. That is why Dorovar next sent his Herald Death to Cadaria. The end of your lives should not be a thing that you fear, it should be a gentle passage onto your next incarnation. It should be a reward for a life filled with accomplishment and dedication to something that could not have existed without your touch. Dorovar's perfect Order gives everyone a place, everyone a role, and everyone a contribution. There is no fear of the end. That is simple the way of things. You fear Death because of what you have not done, what you could not do. The Creator's form of death is a thief that steals the potential of your lives. He steals your loved ones, steals your dreams, and threatens you with eternal torment for not serving him properly. How is this just? You live your lives in fear, and for what? What is your reward for a just life? The Heavens? Even that is a falsehood. Mortals do not find their way to the Heavens unless you are somehow useful to the Creator's perverse curiosity. You simply cease to be. That is what Death was sent to teach you. Your fear is unnecessary. There is nothing beyond your lives, and so your lives must be enriched through true service to the greater good of all humanity, through love of your family and your community, and through the perfect Order offered by Dorovar. There is no fear in the end of a life in the perfect Order, there is only contentment and peace."

Now the cloud of souls filled the entirety of the city of Thorigald, and there was not a person that was not enthralled by War's words. Everything that the Herald said made complete sense. The Creator was evil, and the love of Dorovar had come to save them all from their blind servitude.

"Thorigald and their neighbor Saldarine have been in conflict for nearly two thousand years, and despite the fact that they belong to the same empire, worship the same Creator, and share the same values, because one wears blue and the other wears red, you are intent on killing one another. The Church of the Creator claims that the message of the Creator is peace, love, and prosperity for all, and yet conflict is at the core of your lives. And it is not just here that conflict is felt. Your emperor sends you to kill dragons, sends you to fight against the servants of the Dark Gods. You quarrel with your neighbors over land, resources, who is trustworthy, who is lying. If the Creator truly believed in peace and love, then why is there conflict of this magnitude? The truth is that the Creator loves conflict. He forces it between his Children, and they express that conflict through the creatures that roam upon the worlds that they create. You are no different. You are aimless children fighting battles in a cage for the amusement of your abusive parents. And so Dorovar sent War to show the folly of an existence built on conflict. War has come to save you from your misguided notions of peace, by showing you the true atrocity that unrestrained conflict represents."

War raised its arms and the spectral haze pulsed like a heartbeat. Moments later, as the Army of the Dead retreated into a tight circle around War, a change came over the people of Thorigald. It started with one diminutive woman bending down and picking up a pitchfork that had been dropped by one of the men who had been covering her escape only moments before. Without a word and her face expressionless, she plunged the tines of the pitchfork into the neck of the man who stood beside her. Elsewhere in the city, without anything resembling a weapon available, two men who had been neighbors and best friends for their entire lives turned on each other. Their hands were at each other's throats, and in a matter of moments they both fell to the ground, choked to death by their best friend. In another part of the city, a child took up a large knife and began stabbing her father in the back until he fell face first to the ground, blood flowing everywhere. The ghostly fog pulsed again and the isolated pockets of violence quickly spread. In a matter of minutes, the whole of the city was a bloody, unrestrained mass of conflict. People threw themselves at each other, improvised weapons in hand, killing and dying by the dozens. Even the soldiers from the Army of Fire were not immune to the influence of the madness of War. They turned on each other and on the citizenry indiscriminately. In less than half of an hour ninety percent of the population lay dead in the streets while the remaining ten percent were well on their way. War swept one hand forward and the Army of the Dead was unleashed onto the remaining populace. It would take little time for them to track down and kill those that still drew breath in Thorigald.

"And so Thorigald is saved from da horrors of war."

War turned to his right and saw the diminutive man emerge from an alleyway. He was dressed simply, a loose-fitting shirt and pants and no visible weapons. He leaned against the side of a building and looked around the city's central square at the carnage.

"Dorovar visits his peace upon all of Cadaria. Aldere felt the touch of Pestilence, a salvation from the lies and oppression of the Creator's chosen leaders of this empire, the Lorien family and their puppets. Rashaleb was a kingdom of excess, a kingdom that did not understand the truth of its own existence. And so Famine saved it from the lies that had filled it for so long. Death tried to show Albitonin the error of the worship of the Creator, but was prevented by a child of the Heavens in a misguided attempt to save the supposed innocent. Conquest taught Menoris the folly of its arrogance in assuming it understood how Creation was organized in the spaces between consciousness and experience. Their kind of wisdom had no place in the perfect Order. And now, War will cleanse Thorigald, Saldarine, Iltorp, and Galateria of its misguided conflicts."

Still leaning against the building, the small thin man produced a dagger seemingly out of thin air and then began cleaning his nails with the incredibly sharp point.

"And den what? What happens when Dorovar has brought his love ta all Cadaria? Den is he gonna take his shot at da Creator? Bring his perfect Order ta da rest of Creation?"

War turned to fully face the man.

"That is the will of Dorovar."

Gideon hung his head for just a moment before standing straight and dropping the dagger. It disappeared before it hit the ground. He took two short steps toward the Herald and then crossed his arms over his chest before looking up at the colossus.

"Is it though? Is it Dorovar's will? Where did da perfect Order come from? Who is responsible fer it? Da will of Dorovar isn't even his. Raenera created da Order dat da Adhradair bowed to. Dey didn't know life wit'out it. And now, Dorovar pretends ta know how da people of dis world, people who have known only da word of da Creator dere entire lives, will react ta da perfect Order. So why would Dorovar not align wit Raenera instead o' huntin' her down and gettin' revenge he didn't deserve? It's 'cause Dorovar isn't interested in da perfect Order. He only wants ta kill da Creator and let da whole t'ing burn."

War's laugh resounded through the city.

"Your belief in Dorovar's motives is unnecessary. I am not a member of the Adhradair. I am not interested in a philosophical debate. Dorovar chose me because of my dedication to complete the tasks assigned to me by any means necessary. I have seen the horrors of war since the day of my birth, and I have had everything stolen from me because of war. Now, I will save the empire I have served, and I will help to bring peace to Creation."

The left corner of Gideon's mouth cocked in a half smile.

"It's refreshin' not ta have ta talk 'bout da finer points of which of us is right an' which of us is wrong. All dat's left is ta stop ya."

Again War's laughed resounded through the city, and the spectral glow pulsed with the laughter.

"And how do you intend to stop me? I have brought low those who claim to serve Emries. I have brought low those who claim to serve no master, and I have brought low dragons who have ruled Creation from the time of its birth. Now, I shall show you the folly of challenging War."

War raise its arms and the ghostly green fog pulsed once, twice, and then a third time before beginning to strobe faster and faster. Then the flashing stopped, and the haze was simply gone. Moments later, the dead citizenry and soldiers began to rise all over the city. Regardless of their wounds, they pulled themselves into a standing position and began marching toward the city center where War beckoned.

"All who have met their end on this world in conflict are mine to command. Whether ten minutes prior or two thousand years prior. They are all mine. Once you have been removed from this world, your corpse will fall into rank beside the rest and help to bring Dorovar's vision to the rest of Creation. How can you alone hope to stand against an army this vast?"

Gideon rubbed the back of his head and then looked back up at War, and he could no longer contain the smile that wanted to curl his lips. For the first time in over a thousand years, he finally felt as he did in the days on Onea. A confidence that he had once felt in his days a member of the People of the Dragon flowed through him. In those days, they walked into nearly every conflict knowing that they had a chance to not only survive, but to prevail. Now, Gideon knew, standing against War, that not only would he be successful, but that War was not prepared for what was coming.

"I never said I was alone," Gideon said in a power-filled non-accented voice. "Let me introduce you to my army."

Chapter CIX

Catching a Tear

Year Five of the Just Emperor Kaitain "Dragonsbane" Lorien, Creator's Calendar Year 1872

T ess stood straight as she could, trying not to let the fear that was filling her show in her posture or in her face. Despite the lessons that Cedric had been teaching her, there were a lot of gaps in her education, and more that were coming into focus in the past months. Tess had never considered herself sheltered, but her life had been spent in the Citadel of the Dark Gods surrounded by those that were hundreds even thousands of years older than she was. Even her own sister was centuries older than she was, and she was the youngest of the new generation of Dark Gods by far. Mirana and Liara had been born in the Heavens before the fall, as had Camille. Alderin had been born not long after the Fall, as had Serrina. Darrien was around a thousand years old, while Tess was only about five hundred. This left Tess more than a little isolated. Her formative years were spent at the feet of a revolving door of Pike's 'wives', who were little more than mistresses who could hold his attention for twenty or so years until he tired of them. It wasn't until long into Tess's life that she realized why Darrien had no time for these women. When they no longer amused Pike, it was her job, along with Alderin to dispose of them. Pike always told the rest of the Dark Gods that he returned them back to where they came from, their little villages or farm towns, with enough wealth to keep them comfortable well into their twilight years. It wasn't until one night when Tess heard Darrien and Alderin talking about their grizzly work that Tess knew the truth. She had tried not to see her father as a monster, but there was no escaping the conclusion from that point forward. Tess knew that once he had been a good man. Once he had been a hero. But the Pike Rhuiden who was the leader of the Dark Gods was a man whose ambition had been thwarted, not by his own hand, but by those he considered to be his family. Though Tess had never known Gwydeon Sandar, she understood what he had meant to the Dark Gods. However, more than once, Tess had heard one of Pike's drunken rages cursing his old friend. Pike bore so much resentment for the rebellion in the Heavens, so much resentment for the end of the war on Onea, and so much resentment toward what he viewed as his impotent life. The former blacksmith had refashioned himself into a warrior who knew nothing but meeting his enemies on the field of battle with an ax in hand and his head held high. In a way, the Fall turned him into the thing he hated the most; a being with the power to change everything, but without the ability to affect anything. He had become a domesticated wild animal, clawing at his cage every day, with no chance to ever escape. That was, of course, until the war came looking for him. Emries' war. But Tess knew that something had happened to her father. The part of her that could always feel him had gone cold some time ago, she wasn't sure when, but now even the coldness was gone. Perhaps her new training had simply dulled that instinctual ability, or perhaps Pike had finally found peace the only way he ever could, through death.

Which brought Tess back to the moment at hand. She could see death in the eyes of the woman that crouched at the edge of the small encampment. Her blue eyes were cold and full of barely restrained hate. The woman's muscles were tense like a coiled viper ready to strike, and the light gleamed from the impossibly sharp tips of the claws that protruded from the apparatus strapped to her hand that extended up her forearm. It was as if the woman personified viciousness. When she had spoken, her voice was disdainful and malicious, not attempting to hide her malevolence. Tess continued to keep her body rigid, as though the any movement would betray the uncertainty within her. She was trying to will herself to not tremble, but as her heart raced, she knew she was losing the battle. The assassin's mouth curled into a wicked smile.

"Scared little girl? You should be. I can smell your fear. I can smell the sweat starting to bead on your forehead, and I can hear your heartbeat speeding up. Do you taste that bitterness on the back of your tongue? That's your body trying to tell you to run. But you're smarter than that, aren't you? You know you can't outrun me. Besides, if you try to run, I'll have to hurt you, and neither of us want that."

Tess's golden eyes glowed brightly even in the advancing light. She was already starting to calculate if she could strike the woman without killing her. Would she be able to channel just a little of her power to make a point? As though the woman was in her head, she shook her head dismissively.

"Thinking about attacking me, are you? Well, I am impressed. I didn't think you had it in you. But think on this before you make a rash choice. I've killed Dark Gods. And if I wasn't instructed to take you alive, you never would have heard me coming and I would have ripped your throat out. But do not test my patience. I will hurt you if I have to, and I can make you feel pain in ways that will never go away."

Tess let the threat pass through her. Cedric had spent much of their time together teaching Tess that she could not afford to be ruled by her emotions. She had to take herself out of the moment, see everything around her. See the situation for what it was, and not let the situation dictate her actions. With her powers, with her abilities, she could turn any situation, so long as she saw and understood the consequences of her actions before she acted. Once she let her emotions take over, she would react rather than anticipate, and things could then go very badly. It was difficult to banish the fear from her mind, but she could feel the fog of it beginning to lift. The assassin seemed to like to talk, so Tess decided to let her.

"So what do you want?"

The assassin retained her posture, low to the ground like an animal ready to pounce.

"Trying to stall little princess? Hoping that your friend will come back soon? If he does, I'll simply dispatch him. So, let's make this quick. The

Emperor of Cadaria requests an audience, and I have been sent to convey you to his presence."

Several thoughts came into Tess's mind at the same time. When she was first dispatched to Cadaria, she was sent to sue for peace with the Cadarian Emperor. How much had changed since she first stepped off of that boat and was swept away to meet with her 'aunt' Hannah Ironheart? And now this assassin had been dispatched by that same Emperor. But now, Tess knew it would not be to talk of peace, it would be to talk of war, destruction, and how her powers could benefit him. Then her nightmares flashed into her mind.

The sky above a battlefield was a brilliant red as if the whole of the firmament above had been stained with blood. Clouds of smoke were rising from all around, stinking of sulfur and swelling to blot out the sun. The smell of death hung thick in the air, and all across the ground lay the broken bodies of soldiers. Many different banners and colors littered the battlefield, all of the major Kingdoms of Cadaria represented among dead. The Imperial Palace of Aldere lay in ruins, a smoking crater where the throne room had once been. There was a man with a terrible mask of rage and hate, his arm wrapped around Tess's throat, his other hand holding her wrists tightly behind her back. Tess frantically struggled against his grip, screaming incoherently, tears streaming down her face. Approaching, Tess could see Hannah Ironheart, and behind her a contingent of creatures from Mythryn and a group of the Dark Gods. The man in the mask calls out: 'You cannot stop me now! I have it, it is mine! You will never prevent my ascension to god-hood! I will unseat the Creator and this world will become mine! I will save us all from the Dark Gods!' At his words, fire emerges from thin air, and breathable air becomes poison. The next moment the world turns mad, ripped upside down and inside out. And then everything goes black.

Those dreams had plagued her since her powers first began to manifest, and as the days passed, they became more vivid. Since Cedric had helped her quiet her mind, more of the details came into focus, and more of the chances for those vision not to come to pass had revealed themselves. What had become clear was that moment, that terrible moment was not one that could be avoided. It was her destiny to be at the center of the next conflict, on that field of blood and death. What she did in that moment, before the world goes mad, before the blackness falls, would determine whether or not there would be a future. It was at that moment, all of the fear left Tess's mind. She knew what she needed to do. She had seen through the situation to the truth of it. The assassin however had misinterpreted Tess's sudden calmness. Her eyes went wide and she began to advance, as if to preempt Tess's assault. With a simple extended hand, Tess froze the woman in her tracks.

"There is no need for violence, Alise Modrall," Tess said finally taking the woman's name from her mind, her golden eyes flashing. "I will go with you to meet your master."

When Tess lowered her hand, Alise could move again. When the assassin moved toward her quarry, she moved slowly and deliberately with the grace of a hunter. Two full steps from Tess, Alise stood straight, and the two women were approximately the same height. Alise regarded Tess for a long moment before snapping her fingers which caused a portal to spring to life. Alise motioned in the direction of the portal and waited. Tess looked first at the portal and then back toward the forest. She hoped that Cedric was alright, but she knew that what she had to do next, she had to do alone. Confident in her course of action, Tess moved toward the portal and stepped through, into her future, and to her uncertain destiny. Alise followed behind the enigmatic girl, and just after she stepped through, the portal winked out of existence just as an explosion of power erupted deeper in the forest.

* * * * * * * * * * * *

Cedric Binosear was in pain, more pain than he should have been given the circumstances. All the woman in white had done was knock him to the ground and he felt as though Shau-ling had kicked him in the chest and then stomped on him. The amount of power at the mystery woman's disposal was incredible, and what was even more disconcerting was the fact that Cedric understood that she was trying to save him from Camille's strike. Had she wanted to, she could have struck him without warning and with such power that he would have been dead long before he knew he had been struck. What made matters worse, was while Cedric had powers and had had hundreds of years to practice with them, he did not have the comfort or the creativity with his powers that even some of his contemporaries had. To Cedric, his powers were a tool, and not an extension of himself. He wasn't sure that Tess had gleaned the truth of some of his lessons about taking the emotion out of the moment when using her powers. She was impulsive, angry, and possessive. She was ruled by passions she couldn't understand, but in her moments of lucidity she understood the gravity of her actions. Cedric was trying to make her see the moment first. But Cedric had his own demons, and perhaps by teaching Leah and teaching Tess, he could exorcise those demons. Cedric was afraid of his powers, afraid of what he could do with them, and afraid of what others could make him do with them. He had been a pawn of Emries, had been a puppet of Halicon, the unwilling casualty of the Creator and now again at the mercy of Emries. Nevertheless, Cedric had just gotten a glimpse of the future, the power necessary to fight on the level that the war would demand. Cedric looked deep inside himself as he pulled himself back to a sitting position against a tree. He had seen glimpses of a power there, a power that he didn't recognize. It did not come from Emries, and it did not come from the Blaze. It was something different. Something new. It would take time to unravel the mystery of this new power, time he probably did not have. However, if Camille prevailed over this new arrival, or if this benevolence shown by the new arrival suddenly evaporated, Cedric would be laughably outclassed in every way unless he was able to tap into this mysterious new power and wield it with any level of skill. He just had to hope that there was enough time.

From his position with his back against a tree, he got his first good look at the new arrival. There was no doubting that she was beautiful, but it was cold otherworldly beauty. Something like you would find in an artist's gallery. A beauty brush-perfect and totally unapproachable. Her skin was stark white, white like new pure snow. The dress she wore was also white, but to Cedric it seemed more like a death shroud or a burial gown. The woman's hair, white as well, had hints of grey at the root, but it could simply have been a trick of light and shadow with white hair layering upon white skin. Suddenly Cedric got the impression that her coloration, or lack of it, was more from a lack of color. It was as if all of the life and vibrancy and color had been drained from her leaving something akin to a sketch on the artist's palate. She stood in opposition to the Creator's living tapestry, a deviation of such proportion that it could not be ignored. The only exception to her monochromatic existence was the blood that oozed from each fingertip. It did not drip or flow, it just seemed to collect, as though she had clawed her way into this reality, and her every motion injured the fabric of the Cosmos around her. For just a moment she turned her head slightly in Cedric's direction as if ensuring that he was still there. Her brilliant green eyes flashed, brighter than any jewel, and colder than the emptiness of the abyss. Her face was passive, neither concerned nor tensed for the battle she had just stepped into. All at once, there was a familiarity to the woman that Cedric could not shake. He knew her. And for just a moment, just for a fleeting moment there was a softness in her eyes as though she acknowledged the connection that Cedric instinctually felt. The softness faded before Cedric could even process that it was there, and she turned her full attention back to Camille.

To the warrior angel's credit, Camille had not shied away from the challenge or threat that the otherworldly woman posed. Her wings were primed for a charge, and the twin flaming blades had returned to her hands.

"I know you, creature," Camille's voice infused with divine power called, "you are Jerah, the favored of Dorovar. Not one of his Heralds, but his slave nonetheless. Your master stands in opposition of the great design, and will be dealt with in due course, but his interference here is not warranted. In fact, the elimination of Cedric Binosear benefits Dorovar as much as it benefits the Creator. Let us simply erase this creature from his blasphemous existence and return to our more pressing business. I am sure that Dorovar's schemes require your attention elsewhere."

Jerah had no reaction to the words and stood completely placid against the world. The breeze did not lift her hair or ruffle her dress. The leaves that fell from the trees seemed to fall around her, creating a neat circle around her feet, which Cedric noticed for the first time did not contact the ground. Jerah hovered several inches about of the grass, the longer blades of which curved so as not to touch her bare bloody feet.

"Erroneous."

Jerah's single word response radiated out like a pulse of energy in all directions and hit Cedric like a punch in the gut. A moment later Jerah seemed to reconsider her first response and spoke again, this time with less power. Cedric read the reduced power wave like doubt.

"Irrelevant."

At that moment, Cedric felt the conflict that was growing within Jerah, and he began to guess the truth. Jerah was not there as an agent of Dorovar. She was there of her own accord. That added a new variable to the equation, and one that strengthened Cedric's feeling that he knew the woman that stood before him. Perhaps it was in another life, or perhaps it was just wishful thinking. Either way, Cedric knew that Jerah was there for him, to save him. Camille however was not content to let Jerah's will stand unchallenged.

The divine aura around Camille intensified, obscuring most of her appearance in the burning white haze. The blades of the twin flaming swords burned to a brighter intensity and then Camille shot forward, barreling straight toward Jerah. In response, a spectral green haze flared into existence around Jerah, and then the moment Camille would have collided with Jerah, the Herald of Dorovar disappeared from where she stood and reappeared behind the charging angel. A dozen phantasmal hands stretched from the boundary of the spectral field and seized Camille. Two hands took hold of her wrists, two more her ankles, and others seized her forearms, waist, and wrenched the swords from her hands. A guttural cry tore from Camille's open mouth and she beat her wings hard against her ghostly adversary. The brilliant white aura intensified again and it seemed as though Camille was starting to break away from the force holding her. However, Jerah had other ideas. She moved in as soon as Camille's full attention was on the spectral hands. Floating across the ground like a ghost herself, Jerah reached out and let her bloody fingers find the brilliant feathered wings. The guttural cry of frustration and anger from Camille became shrill the next moment, a cry of pain erupting in all directions. Again, Cedric felt himself assaulted by the force of the unfocused explosion of power, the shockwave pressed him against the trunk of the tree. What happened next, Cedric wasn't sure his eyes interpreted correctly. His disbelief held until the sheer brutality forced him into acceptance.

One moment, Camille was fighting against the pull of the nearly invisible force that was attempting to hold her in place, her wings batting wildly. The next moment Jerah's blood-soaked hands held the wings, arresting their movement and allowing Camille to be pulled into the swirling phantasmal green force. Camille struggled again, breaking one of her wrists free and attempting to torque her body so that she could strike at Jerah directly. Then, in a monstrous and vicious move, Jerah effortlessly ripped the wings from Camille's back. At that same moment, the phantom hands disappeared and Camille dropped to the ground, face first, the bloody stumps of her wings spilling bright red vitae in all directions as they still attempted to beat their amputated appendages. Jerah stood above the fallen angel, the wings still in her grasp. The woman's expression had not changed even after the brutal assault, and her eyes remain trained on Camille. Finally, she released the wings, only for them to ignite in mid-air and be reduced to ash. By this point, Camille had begun crawling. It was unclear where she thought she was going to escape to, but Cedric believed that instinct was simply telling her to get as far away from Jerah as quickly as possible. However, she was in so much pain and so disoriented that she could not summon enough power to heal her wounds, let alone open a portal.

Jerah watched the woman crawl for several painful moments before a long thin dagger appeared in her right hand. She stalked Camille for several steps as she crawled and then prepared to strike. At that moment, Cedric saw something in Jerah's eyes and in her movements. The careful grace of the hunter, the patience, the violence. She enjoyed stalking her prey, and she savored the moment of conquest. It was then that Jerah's identity clicked into place in Cedric's mind. Jerah raised the knife and was ready to strike the killing blow when Cedric's voice rang out above Camille's cries of pain and anguish.

"Caris, don't."

Jerah froze and turned her eyes in Cedric's direction. She watched as he pulled himself back to a standing position with the help of the tree and limped over in her direction. When he was mere paces from her, he could feel the aura of cold radiating from her like a fog. By this point, Camille had stopped screaming and had stopped crawling. Cedric stole a glance at the fallen girl to find that she was still breathing, but had passed out. The pain obviously was too great to fight against any longer. Jerah had floated back away from Cedric several paces, but the thin dagger had disappeared from her hand. Cedric at least had bought Camille a few moments. All Cedric wanted at that moment was to ensure that Camille survived. He knew that she was not acting of her own volition, and in Cedric's heart he knew he could not live with himself if he let her die as a puppet of the Creator's machinations. Moreover, Cedric felt that he needed to do for Camille what he had been unable to do for her parents on Onea. Gwydeon and Midarin were idealistic and naïve when they chose to take on Shau-ling. Cedric should have done more to protect them. Should have done more to help them. But he was afraid. He was still unclear what his role was, still unclear as to who was on which side of the conflict, and still uncertain as to whether or not Emries still had sway over his actions. He had thought then that the more distance he kept from Logan and his allies, the better chance they had of succeeding and surviving. But there was so much that Cedric hadn't known. He hadn't known about Aryx's true role in the conflict, hadn't known about the war between the Children of the Creator, and he hadn't known that it was Emries and not Halicon who was the true enemy. Maybe if he would have been more involved, things wouldn't have ended so horribly for Onea. But then, perhaps there was no way to prevent the fall. Regardless, Cedric had to take what responsibilities he could, when he could.

"This is Gwydeon and Midarin's daughter. It's not her fault."

Jerah looked down at the girl for a moment, then back up at Cedric. Finally, she knelt and extended a hand toward Camille. The bloody fingertips glowed green for a moment and then Jerah touched the middle of Camille's back. A green glow enveloped the angel's body, and the blood stopped flowing from the damaged stumps of her wings. A moment later Camille's wings began to regrow from where they had been ripped away, and in a matter of seconds it seemed that the young woman had been made whole. But Cedric immediately noticed a difference. The wings were no longer a pure white, bristling with divine energy. They seemed changed, diminished somehow, more a light gray then white. Finally, Jerah stood once more and returned her gaze to Cedric.

"Free."

Cedric immediately understood what Jerah had done. Somehow Jerah had used her new abilities granted to her by Dorovar to remove Camille's divinity, or at the very least seal off the influence that the Creator would have over her. No longer could Camille be turned against those who would stand in opposition to the Creator and his schemes. As Jerah said, she was free.

Cedric was about to speak when Jerah turned her head in the direction of the camp that Cedric and Tess shared in a clearing several hundred feet away. She put her hand up and for the barest moment Cedric thought that he could see the corner of her mouth pull downward into a frown. When her gaze returned to Cedric, he thought, again just for the barest moment, he saw sadness in her eyes. Jerah looked down at Camille and a portal appeared beneath her. She didn't drop through immediately as Jerah's will held her in place.

"Home."

It was only after Jerah spoke that Camille dropped through the portal and an instant later the portal winked out of existence. Finally, Jerah turned back to Cedric and another dagger had appeared in her hand. This one however was shorter with a wider blade and seemed to radiate malice and hatred. Cedric instinctively took a step back and was about to conjure a weapon himself when he felt a twinge in the back of his mind from the direction that Jerah had looked. It was the same feeling he had felt when Emries had come and gone. The Children didn't use portals, they simply willed themselves where they wanted to be, but it was still a use of power. Every use of power had a precursor and a lingering effect, if you knew what to look for you could recognize any use of power. Cedric had been forced to become much more observant when dealing with Tess, and so he was able to feel the subtle flows of Emries' impending arrival. Jerah obviously was far more attuned. She locked eyes with Cedric and then extended the dagger in his direction.

"Fate."

Cedric wanted to shake his head. He wanted to tell Jerah to take them both away from Mythryn. He was surprised how intense his desire to run was. He hated Emries, he wanted Emries dead. But for the first time in so long, he didn't want to die. He wanted to fight, and he wanted to make sure that Tess was safe from the monster who haunted her steps. Setting his jaw and squaring his shoulders, Cedric took the dagger from Jerah and turned toward the clearing and began his slow deliberate walk. It took only a few steps before he disappeared into the underbrush. Jerah floated above the bloody ground and watched him go.

"Goodbye."

She turned and started to will herself to her next destination, but she hesitated for just a moment, and turned back to look in the direction that Cedric had gone.

"Love."

The figure of Jerah had disappeared long before the echo of the word faded.

Aspiration of God,
Demon of Experience

Year Five of the Just Emperor Kaitain "Dragonsbane" Lorien, Creator's Calendar Year 1872

Dorovar stood on a ledge overlooking the ocean, but he was not seeing the rolling waves below him. He was not seeing the moonlight reflecting off of the turbulent waters, nor was he seeing the ships bobbing in the distance. His eyes were instead focused upward on the pinpoints of light in the sky above. The great and massive furnaces of gas, many of which he had floated past during his millennia long exile in the void. Time had little meaning as he was floating along on the solar winds, his chest squeezed by the pain of the vacuum attempting to burst his heart, lungs, and ribcage with every aborted breath. But he had felt the distant heat of the thousands of suns that populated the Creator's universe, and as he passed close enough to feel the ice in his eyes and his mouth slowly thaw, he began to have a new appreciation and love for the churning balls of gas and fire. But something was changing in the firmament. Some of the pinpoints of light had disappeared over the previous few nights. The mortals on this world certainly would not have noticed, and those that did most likely would have blamed high clouds, or a failure of their pathetic memories. But Dorovar knew the truth. The final days of Creation were upon them, and Dorovar could feel the creeping hand of the Creator's love beginning to close around his heart. As the stars began to go cold one by one, the advancing shadow that could be called neglect gained more power. Creation thrived because of the attention of the Creator and his Children. But the Children were falling one by one to the machinations of those who would call themselves heroes, not understanding the harm they were inflicting upon worlds they could not even imagine. As more and more of the Creator's attention focused on the world of Espre, and as more of his forces were marshalled there, more suns ceased to light the universe. Before long, the sky above Espre would contain only the twin suns, and perhaps in the moments before the death of the entirety of Creation, even they would cease to be. But that would only come to pass if Dorovar failed. And while Dorovar was not one to let doubt cloud his mind he could not ignore the possibility that there would not be enough time left for his plan to come to fruition.

Dorovar had not expected the opposition he had found upon Espre. Of course he had expected the Dragons to resist his crusade, and of course the Children, but he had planned adequately for them. The dragons were short-sighted and stupid for as old and as wise as they claimed to be. They would always protect their own, and could always be counted on to overreact to any attack made against their number. That was why they had been so easily goaded into a war with the Cadarians. The dragon hunters would be able to kill one or two of the weaker members of their number, and had the dragons not been so proud and vain, they could have simply ignored and absorbed the losses. Or, if they had not feared the repercussions, they could have launched a singular crippling assault and reduced the whole of Cadaria to a cinder. But the dragons hid their secret fear well. They lived and died at the whim of the Creator, and already they had been reduced to nomads, nothing more than cosmic trash begging for a place to call their own. All because of the actions of three of their number at the behest of the Children.

Dorovar had had many centuries to consider the plight of the dragons. Of course, during his time floating in the void, there was only hatred for the overgrown lizards. He wanted them all dead. But after a millennia of frozen hell, Dorovar had begun to think of the dragons as victims in the same way that he and his Adhradair were victims. Perhaps not the same, but similar enough that the minor distinctions mattered little. The Children had used the dragons against Loinn like a weapon, in the same way they had been used in the Heavens during Talisia's rebellion. And even if Shadowweaver had not been duped into following Talisia, those who were loyal to him had been. Pawns or puppets, in the end it was all the same. Just as the Adhradair, blindly loyal to their patron goddess who cared little for their plight as their world burned around them. A sociological experiment that had outlived its usefulness, cleansed from the Cosmos by the most efficient destructive force ever dreamed up in the mind of the Creator; War. For many long years, Dorovar thought that perhaps things might have been better for the Cosmos had Dorovar not made the second agreement with the dragons, the one that allowed them to flee Loinn. Then the dragons would have been destroyed along with the Adhradair, Talisia would be denied her weapon, and the Creator would be denied another piece of his puzzle. But would that have truly stopped the ideological war? Would that have prevented Talisia's attack on Pyrrus? Would it have stopped Emries and Halicon from nearly killing one another? Would it have done anything other than simply delay the inevitable conflict that culminated on Espre?

And now again, the dragons were at the mercy of the actions of Shadowweaver. For some reason again the ancient creature had tied its fate and the fate of all of its race to Talisia's machinations. Was there something perhaps in Shadowweaver's motivations that Dorovar was still unable to see? Had Shadowweaver had the foresight to predict this ending, and the lack of time that it presented? Dorovar was already aware of the offer that Stormbane had made to Luigsech and Maedoc, and so it was clear that at least Stormbane believed that Shadowweaver wanted to replace the Creator on the Golden Throne. But was that truly his motivation? After all of this time, had Dorovar and Shadowweaver truly been kindred spirits and not recognized the duality of their goals and their ultimate repeated failures?

Dorovar felt a presence approaching from behind him, but he did not turn to acknowledge the new arrival. Just as with the other members of the Adhradair, he knew the moment that Seisyll had been freed from her prison within the weapon Courage, and he knew the moment she had arrived on the island to pledge her loyalty to Dorovar. Like Maedoc, Seisyll was attached to the personal security for the high priestess. However, where

Maedoc was a reactionary who used his anger and his strength to his advantage, Seisyll was a far more cerebral warrior. When Seisyll was born her fate was the most unusual of all of the Adhradair, and it was one that Dorovar certainly had not envied once he was old enough to understand it. While Raenera's perfect Order necessitated that each and every person born upon Loinn was designated a role in society, the Creator still could influence the fates of those whose roles were supposedly well defined for decades to come. Deaths due to accidents and deaths in infancy were not uncommon, but those incidents could not be allowed to upset the perfect Order. Therefore, Raenera had built in a level of redundancy for key positions within the Order. While the Order would not be upset at the death of a farmer or a common laborer, the loss of the next High Priestess days after her birth would be catastrophic to the faithful. Therefore, when she was born, Seisyll was chosen to be the heir-apparent to the High Priestess should some unforeseen calamity befall the future High Priestess before she rose to her position and a successor was born and on path. Seisyll was taught alongside the future High Priestess given the same lessons, the same attention, and the same responsibilities. To those who were teaching her, Seisyll was considered to be the next High Priestess. Additionally, Seisyll was made to endure the training that was required of her to assume her position as a member of the Adhradair, and as one of the High Priestess's key protectors. Seisyll was perhaps the most talented, the most powerful, and the most intelligent of all of the Adhradair simply because of her depth of training and her commitment to the cause of the Goddess and the Perfect Order.

Dorovar could hear the carefully constructed black armor creak ever so slightly with every one of Seisyll's steps, and the rustle of her cloak as it moved across the shoulder plates and swept across the ground behind her. Seisyll stopped several paces short of where Dorovar stood and waited to be acknowledged. Dorovar hadn't expected Seisyll to kneel, and Dorovar knew that the powerful guardian still harbored a great deal of ill-will for Dorovar. But in the end, Seisyll was a pragmatist, and she understood, probably better than anyone, just exactly how difficult the last days on Loinn had been. Seisyll had also been one of the last of the Adhradair to consent to using the powers that Emries and Talisia had offered to take the fight to the dragons. Instead of following her fellows into ultimately futile assaults, Seisyll had remained at her post, defending the High Priestess.

Seisyll had also been there when the High Priestess was killed, as she had also lost her life in the process of defending her charge. Finally, the mystery of that last day would be solved, provided that the memory still lived in Seisyll after all of her millennia in imprisonment. When Dorovar turned to acknowledge her, he was immediately startled to see the crest of the goddess Raenera, the fiery white and red wings stretching across the breastplate of Seisyll's armor. Aside from the slight metal shimmer, there was no other color to Seisyll's abyssal black mail that stretched from her feet to her chin. The only skin exposed was that of Seisyll's face, and the sweep of her hair covered half of that. Her sullen dark eyes locked on Dorovar, and though he could only see one of them, he could feel them both piercing through him.

"Dorovar."

Dorovar could feel the contempt in her voice, and yet it was only his experience with the woman that allowed him to detect it. Seisyll had amazing control over her emotions and rarely would anyone be able to determine her emotional state unless she wanted it known.

"I'm happy to see that you are finally free from that unjust prison, Seisyll. We still have much to accomplish in the days ahead, and I fear that the Creator may not allow us to complete our goals."

Seisyll nodded for barely a moment.

"My freedom may have come at too great of a cost, Dorovar. Was the loss of Zaraven really worth my freedom? Did you so underestimate those that were in possession of my prison that you would let only Zaraven and Drust attempt to wrest me from their control?"

Dorovar felt his blood burn for a moment, but then let the wave of emotion pass through him. There was no time for recriminations or for unnecessary internal conflicts.

"Given our situation, Seisyll, I believe that the sacrifice was justified. We still have not identified the fate of the soul of the High Priestess, and should worse come to worse, I may need to call upon you for the sacrifice that you were born for. But in answer to your other question, what has become clear is that I have, at every turn, failed to predict the capabilities of the Dark Gods and their confederates."

Seisyll's impassive stare was broken only by a slightly raised eyebrow.

"I think perhaps that is an understatement, Dorovar. You forget that I was in the possession of Orren Eldrath, and you forget what he had come into possession of. He may be unpracticed with his abilities, but I am not. I have had thousands of years to attune myself with my prison, and extend my awareness to those who wielded the weapon as well as those in close proximity. Orren Eldrath, though a talented wielder of arcane ability, would never rise to anyone's notice outside of the limited understanding of the Cosmos held by those in control of Cadaria. Perhaps he is powerful in relation to others of his kind, but now he has stepped into a different realm of power and a different realm of understanding. Aryx Terian was perhaps one of the most powerful and practiced of the Dark Gods, and in passing his abilities to Orren Eldrath he has created an opportunity. But your short-sightedness has failed to recognize it, and now perhaps without Zaraven and Faelara, as well as Judoc, Vercin, and Ninian still imprisoned, and the High Priestess's soul still unaccounted for, we may not have the power to exploit this opportunity."

Dorovar was disheartened and confused by Seisyll's accusations, and yet what rose inside of him was an anger that he did not expect.

"And what is this opportunity?" Dorovar snapped, the anger thick in his voice. "What is this great opportunity that I have overlooked? Remember Seisyll that I have been awake and aware all of these millennia, and I have seen worlds, wonders, and horrors that you could never imagine. You have barely been free of your confinement for a matter of hours and now suddenly you have this great insight that has escaped me all these years."

Seisyll folded her hands behind her back, her calm expressionless features galling Dorovar even more.

"Do you hear yourself, Dorovar? Does this tone of yours ring as eerily similar in your ears as it does in mine? Remember the first days when your great dreams of prophecy came from Raenera and you strode proudly into the ivory spire as though you were the leader of the Adhradair. And there you stood, in front of all of us and proudly told us of the message from the goddess. You were oblivious to the damage that you caused to the Adhradair that day, to the confusion that you sewed into the perfect Order. The High Priestess stood on the dais, behind you, oblivious to the message that you were delivering. You were so proud; you were so satisfied with the potential that you had exceeded your chosen place. It was as though it justified the pairing between you and the High Priestess, as though somehow you were being elevated to be her equal. But you put her in an impossible position. Do you know what would have happened if she would have countered your pronouncement as the hubris we found out later that it was? Do you know the seismic catastrophe that it would have created within the ranks of the Adhradair?"

Dorovar immediately opened his mouth to respond but then found that his voice died in his throat. Seisyll's withering stare did not relent, and her pointed words pressed on.

"Your first proclamation put Maedoc and I in an impossible position. Would you believe that we actually had a conversation about how we would defend the High Priestess should the other members of the Adhradair decide that they had lost confidence in the ability of the High Priestess to commune with the Goddess? There was a thought that your pronouncements signaled a change in the desires of the Goddess and that for the first time in the history of our order that there would be a High Priest. Would we have been forced to defend the High Priestess against our own, or would we have been forced to turn our blades on the one that we were born to protect?"

The anger inside of Dorovar turned, and it pointed inward. In the days from the first dreams sent by Talisia in the guise of Raenera to the end of the world of Loinn, there was little time to think about motivations and consequences, at least for Dorovar. He had become so enamored with being the recipient of the Goddess's boon that he betrayed the very thing he thought he was exemplifying. He was every bit the traitor that the Adhradair believed Stormbane to be, but because Dorovar chose to martyr himself rather than accept the temptations offered by Emries he somehow saw himself as noble. The other members of the Adhradair followed

Dorovar on this new battleground because they were trying to expunge themselves of the shame they felt. They took an active role in the destruction not only of their world, but in a way of life that was designed to last forever. Seisyll had no such illusions, and had no such guilt. Unlike the rest of the Adhradair, Dorovar included, Seisyll never abandoned her post.

"Is that why you did not join the crusade? Is that why you accepted the power but did not leave your post?"

Finally, a frown cracked the impassive visage.

"I did not invite the dragons to our world. I did not start the war with the dragons. Nor did I wish to spend the last days of my life wading through the blood of our brethren in a pointless crusade that could not be won. I was born for a purpose. I was born to stand in front of the High Priestess and protect her from harm. That role would be mine until the day that I died. I allowed Maedoc to join the rest of the order in the crusade, but I stayed."

A tear rolled down Seisyll's face.

"What happened to the High Priestess, Seisyll? What happened in those last days?"

Seisyll's expression never changed, but her eyes went past Dorovar and her gaze went to the sky.

"The memory is seared into my brain. It was the last days of our world, and there was little that was still standing in the capitol city. Even the top of the ivory spire had been sheared off by a dragon attack. The High Priestess and I stood on the steps of the ivory spire looking out on the destruction. The smoke was so thick that we could barely see anything beyond the columns of fire that sprang up in the distance. There was so much ash in the air that it burned my eyes and made it hard to breathe. We knew how close the battle-lines had come to the ivory spire, and I fully expected that a flight of dragons could be over our head at any moment. In the distance, I thought I could see a form approaching us, and I didn't know if we would live to see another sunrise. However, whatever it was must have been a trick of the light and the shape was nothing more than a shadow. But the moment I relaxed, I felt the sting of sharp steel across my throat and the rush of molten blood flowing down beneath my armor. It was so impossibly hot it felt like it would burn my skin. The blade went so deep that it punctured my voice box and I couldn't even scream in pain. All I could do was moan in vague futile agony. My first inclination was to bring my sword to bear and spin around and strike down my attacker. But my sword was rebellious to my arm, and as I tried to close my fist around the hilt, my hand spasmed and the hilt slipped. But even if I would have wanted to turn and face my attacker, my body would not respond. My mind screamed for my legs move, for my waist to turn, for my eyes to focus, but the more my mind screamed, the more my body rebelled. My eyes began to glaze, my chest heaved in the little breath it could amidst the smoke and the blood, and my knees buckled. The next thing I knew, I was on my back, looking up at the sky. And when my vision cleared for a moment, I saw the face of the one who held the blade. And do you know who it was, Dorovar? Do you know who held the blade that ended my life?"

Seisyll's gaze returned to Dorovar's face, the rage clear in her eyes.

"It was our beloved High Priestess."

Dorovar could not keep the horror from coming to his face.

"She leaned down over me and smoothed my hair back from my face like the loving and caring woman she had always been and she could not keep the tears from streaming from her eyes. She said that Raenera had come to her and told her what was going to come to pass, and what she had to do. She said that it was the last true vision that she would ever receive from the Goddess and the price she demanded was the highest she could ask. The High Priestess told me that my soul was damned to a prison of my own making because I betrayed the teachings. Unlike the rest of the Adhradair, I had the teachings of the High Priestess and I never should have allowed what came to pass. That day you came before us with your false pronouncement, I should have struck you down as a heretic and let your role pass to the next generation. The dragons should never have been allowed to set foot upon our world, and they did so because I failed. That responsibility, that failure, was mine and mine alone. And so my punishment was two-fold. First, I would live on, imprisoned through the will of Talisia. But the second was the crueler infliction. Kneeling beside my fallen form, the High Priestess brought the dagger up, the same one used to slit my throat, and drew it across her own throat. She did not even flinch, and there was no fear in her eyes. Even as the blood flowed from the wound, and the light drained from her eyes, she smoothed my hair and remained proud. Even in defeat, she was dedicated to serving the Goddess, and she was victorious. But I was forced to watch every moment of her death. I was left to savor my failure."

Dorovar's shoulders slumped. He hung his head and looked down at the ground. Disbelief filled him and he could not wrap his mind around the revelations.

"Why?" Dorovar's voice was barely above a whisper. "Why would the Goddess order the High Priestess to take her own life? What did she know?"

Dorovar's voice faded away. He could not make sense of it all. He looked up again and locked eyes with Seisyll.

"I stood, face to face with Raenera, face to face with the Goddess and she said nothing. She said that I was visiting vengeance and hatred upon the whole of Creation, and that I crafted my Heralds not from a desire to save everyone from the Creator, but to punish them for what Emries and Talisia did to me and to the rest of the Adhradair. And now, standing in front of you I'm told that the woman that I revered, the woman that I was destined to marry, the woman who was the guiding star for our entire world, abandoned us."

Seisyll's thunderous reply shook the ground beneath their feet.

"You abandoned us, Dorovar. You put us on the path that led to our destruction. Your arrogance slaved our brothers and sisters to your perverted crusade because their guilt could not let them see a different way. But if they saw the High Priestess fall the way that I did, they would never follow you. And so, I will not follow you."

Dorovar gritted his teeth and measured his next words very carefully.

"You have no choice, Seisyll. You are here because we were betrayed. We were betrayed by the dragons. We were betrayed by Emries. We were betrayed by Talisia. We were betrayed by Raenera, and now you tell me that the Goddess corrupted the High Priestess and forced her to betray us as well. Perhaps that is why her soul has eluded us thus far. Perhaps Raenera again has stood against us and the soul of the High Priestess is not here to be found at all. And now the dragons have dangled a deal before us, trading control for information about the soul of the High Priestess. They lie to us yet again. They deceive us yet again. They use the situation engineered by the Creator to manipulate us into abandoning our senses. And now this manipulation has forced you to stand against me. You think you are making a reasoned decision, but you do not know what is at stake. You do not know what we risk. Are you willing to condemn hundreds of worlds to the fate that befell Loinn? Are you willing to let billions of creatures meet their end for your pride?"

Seisyll bared her teeth in defiance.

"You have the gall to stand there and speak to me about pride? It was your pride that doomed us Dorovar, and it is your pride that prevents you from seeing it. The final words from the High Priestess were that you were the doom that was coming for Creation. That your path had been irredeemably corrupted, and no matter what, you could not be allowed to be victorious. You could not be allowed to sit upon the Golden Throne or decide who will replace the Creator. You must fall."

Seisyll's shimmering black broadsword appeared in her hand. Dorovar took two steps backwards.

"Think before you act, Seisyll. Do not divide out family. Do not kill our order who stood in contra to three of the Children of the Creator, the whole of the race of dragons, and survived the death of our world. Together we can shake the Heavens. We can unseat the Creator, and we can extend the true perfect Order to the whole of Creation."

Seisyll pointed the tip of her sword in the direction of Dorovar's heart.

"The only thing that serves the perfect Order is your death. I will fulfill my last vow to the High Priestess, and I shall end you."

Epilogue

Failing Upward

Year Five of the Just Emperor Kaitain "Dragonsbane" Lorien, Creator's Calendar Year 1872

Emries stood in the center of the small camp and stretched out his awareness to the surrounding forest. Irritation began to bloom inside of him as he realized that Tess Annis was nowhere to be found. Cedric knew that he was not supposed to take the girl off the island, and he needed to spend every moment molding her into a stable enough state that Emries could use her to begin the final phase of the war against not only the so-called Dark Gods, but also his siblings and eventually the Creator Himself. The girl had enough raw power to spare, and in her uncontrollable state she would simply shake the world apart if pushed to the places that Emries needed her to go. Another time, on another world when the stakes were not so high, perhaps that would have been enough to force the Creator into the open. But now, with the supposed death of three of the Children, as well as the destruction of the Wrath, the Creator would be more cautious. Already with his appointment of the new Voice and Spirit, the Creator had taken on a war posture. Emries had to be sure of his footing before he set off the explosion that could change the nature of Creator forever.

Kneeling down to examine the small fire in the center of the camp, Emries felt the ache growing inside of him. He felt diminished. Each time one of his siblings had been cut down, he had felt it. At first, Emries had been unsure what it all meant, what exactly he was feeling. For the countless years that Emries and his siblings had been alive, and the countless years that they had been engaging each other in their philosophical conflicts, Emries had never felt anything quite like he did the day that Talisia ran her blade through Pyrrus' heart. At the time Emries almost felt as though it had been his chest that Talisia had trust her blade into, and perhaps, in a way, it had been. What Emries had not known, at least not until that moment, was how truly connected the five Children of the Creator were. Of course, they had battled each other over the millennia, and of course they had tried to do each other harm. But even in their defeats, they were still tied to the realms of Creation. But when Pyrrus was destroyed, something had changed. Something was different. His essence passed on to another host, but the being that was Pyrrus, the divine creation as old as Creation itself, would never draw breath again. Pyrrus had been reduced to something akin to life, but not actually alive. But in the back of his mind, Emries could still feel Pyrrus, could still hear the youthful exuberance and the love of all things that had life. But the connection was weaker, distant.

Standing up and turning his gaze toward the Heavens, Emries reflected upon the past in a way that he often did as the war ground its way to its inevitable conclusion. For so long the five Children of the Creator had existed apart from everything their Father created. And always their debates raged. Even separated by millions of miles, different planes of existence, they battled. It was not the same as when humans or even the dragons argued. They did not have to be in the same place to make their arguments to one another. And while they could always talk to one another, always feel one another, they were not able to read each other's thoughts and intentions. Nor were they able to precisely pinpoint one another's locations. However, when Pyrrus' essence passed from his mortal form into that of Wolf Ranthall, every other member of the Children was aware. At least, they were aware once Wolf regained consciousness after the Fall. Somehow in the tumult of the rebellion in the Heavens, he had been able to mask the transference. Halicon too had been able to mask his movement from a corporeal form into the half-dragon Knight of the Flashing Blade Devlin Rannoch. But when Raenera passed her abilities on to Gideon Viruci, the transition had been like a burning beacon. Emries wondered if Raenera wanted the attention, as though she were signally to the rest of her siblings that something terrible was about to happen.

That something horrible tugged at Emries' consciousness. There were only two of the Children left now, and while at one time Emries would have counted Talisia among his closest, if not his only ally, the situation had changed a great deal in their time on Espre. Talisia had become increasingly distant, wrapped up in her schemes to use the abomination Dorovar and the captive souls of his brethren to destabilize everything the Creator held dear. In some ways, it seemed to Emries that Talisia was no longer interested in winning the conflict, but simply wanted to inflict as much pain as possible. She had become obsessed with building her private army that she called the Hand of Chaos and using it to infiltrate all levels of leadership in the Cadarian Empire. Talisia loved to sew discord, loved to entice warfare and strife. However, now she had taken that to a higher level. Her followers had been mobilized to destabilize and disrupt Kaitain Lorien and make him vulnerable to the point that she would be able to recruit him. Talisia and Emries had shared the same vision of the future, the same dark vision that every path seemed to be leading them to. The vision had been plaguing Emries' mind since Kaitain Lorien took the throne of Cadaria, and its nature more than its content concerned the Child of the Creator. What could be so powerful besides the Creator that could place such a vision in Emries' mind unbidden? And what did it all mean?

All around there was nothing but blood and death. At the center of it was always a young girl, and while it took some time for Emries to uncover the girl's identity, he knew now that she was Tess Annis, the child of the intractable Pike Rhuiden and the enigmatic Raenera. Emries spent a great deal of time studying the details of the vision, and yet every time he thought he was making progress decoding the riddle, the details would change. While the girl was always a fixed point, the things around her were constantly in flux. Sometimes it was Kaitain Lorien standing in the center of the storm with his arm around her throat and laughter drowning out her words. Sometimes it was one of the Dark Gods, the faces changing seemingly at random. More often than not though, the eyes Emries saw belonged to either Gwydeon Sandar or Midarin Rice. Their presence was puzzling beyond words, and often made Emries doubt the veracity of the vision. Sometimes it would be a member of the Knights of the Flashing

Blade, standing on a mountain of the dead as the world tore itself apart. The last moments of the vision, the ones that struck fear into Emries' heart were always the same, and always contained the unstable Emperor of Cadaria. Yes, Emries had seen the other faces, but they never felt right. Closing his eyes, Emries could see the details as clear as crystal. The sky above the battlefield blood red, clouds of smoke blotting out the sun. The smell of death thick in the air, and all across the ground lay the broken bodies of soldiers. Many different banners and colors littering the battlefield, all of the major kingdoms represented among the dead. The Imperial Palace of Aldere in ruins, a smoking crater where the throne room had once been. More often than not, Kaitain Lorien clutching Tess Annis in his arms. She struggles against his grip and screams. All around on the bloody ground are the broken bodies of imperial citizens, the armies of the empire. Approaching is Hannah Ironheart, and behind her a contingent of creatures from Mythryn and a group of the Dark Gods. Lorien calls out: 'You cannot stop me now! I have it, it is mine! You will never prevent my ascension to god-hood! I will unseat the Creator and this world will become mine! I will save us all from the Dark Gods!' At his words, fire emerges from thin air, and breathable air becomes poison. The next moment the world turns mad, ripped upside down and inside out. And then everything goes black.

Emries had spent the entirety of Kaitain Lorien's reign dissecting the vision, and while it was a blink of an eye in the lifetime of a Child of the Creator, the time was perniciously slow. There were two things about the vision that disturbed Emries above all others, even above how it was placed in his mind to begin with. The first was that no matter how many permutations of the vision he had observed over the span of years, not one of the Children of the Creator appeared in the vision. While there were a great many people that did not appear in the visions, one thing was clear. If there was to be a cataclysmic even of such a scale that it could impact the whole of Creation, it would stand to reason that either Emries or Talisia would be there to either aid or prevent it. Emries did not like the implication of that thought. Could it mean that both Emries and Talisia were slated for slaughter as their siblings had been before the conclusion of the grand game? Or did it simply mean that the Creator was still hiding things from Emries' vision? The second issue, and perhaps the more disturbing one was that Dorovar and Aerith Seth did not make an appearance in any variation of the vision either. Emries assumption had always been that at the end it would come down to one of the two impossibly powerful forces, and whoever persevered through that conflict would be the one that Emries would have to challenge for superiority in Creation. Could Emries have been so wrong about the way this world would end?

Emries was not comfortable with the thought that he had miscalculated yet again. Onea had been an unmitigated failure. The plan had been so perfect. The humans would have been the perfect engine for Emries to build the case for his view of Creation. He could prove that the Creator was an unnecessary cog in a Cosmic wheel. If Emries would have been able to prove to his Father that He was no longer relevant, then perhaps the Creator would have willingly turned over the reins of Creation to Emries. Then Emries would have been able to deal with his siblings in a much quicker and more decisive way. What Emries had not counted on was how jealous and possessive the Creator was. At first, Emries wanted to believe that the Creator dispatched Halicon to Onea in order to test the veracity of Emries' work. If Emries were really able to expand his reach and influence across the whole of Creation, then he must be able to turn back a direct challenge from one of his siblings. And while Emries had been completely wrong about the Creator's motivations, he also significantly underestimated Halicon's abilities and just how far he was willing to go to carry out the Creator's orders.

Halicon had always been cagey, and his methods astounded even the perpetually good-natured Pyrrus. But unlike the other members of the Children, Halicon's views on the ideal shape of the Cosmos shifted. Pyrrus believed in the inherent good in all beings, and as such believed they could be trusted to determine their own futures even in the face of the horrific acts that they committed in the name of the Creator or in the name of survival. Talisia was committed to the absolute and complete darkness of the soul, believing that only through the expression of that darkness could the true nature of any being be understood. She believed that altruism and compassion were constructs inflicted upon those intelligent enough to understand such concepts and that they caused unnatural conflicts with the inherent desires for survival and reproduction. Talisia believed that unfettered by morality, the Cosmos could find its perfect self with alpha predators ruling over the rest of the chattel. Raenera's adherence to a perfectly ordered society where there was no possibility for creativity, independent thought, or variation outside of the rigid caste system was her eventual downfall. Raenera did not understand that any creature with a level of intelligence to perceive boundaries would be compelled to bend or break them. Creativity and a desire to know were the inherent characteristics of intelligence and such could not be constrained for long. One radical thought, one rebellious being who dreamed of more than its place in society, and the whole structure would be at risk of toppling down upon itself. Emries flaw had been characterized by not understanding how far that rebellions streak could go. While humans with a certain level of intelligence tended toward creating chaos with their thoughts, desires, and actions, they craved order in a way that often subjugated their own self-interests. And so while many would suffer under the yoke of oppression dreaming to be free, when the opportunity would present itself to rebel and claim that freedom they dreamt of, the oppressed would remain in bondage rather than risk their lives for a dream. Where Emries made his mistake is while he could prey on the masses making the choices that most often acted against their self-interest, he underestimated the singular voice that could stir even the hardest hearts to lay down their lives for an ideal. While those loyal to him would die by the thousands out of fear, a whole world was willing to burn for the likes of Aerith Seth, Sabrina Binosear, Gwydeon Sandar, Logan Ranthall, and Midarin Rice. In the end, it was the need for self-determination that was the end of Emries reign.

Halicon always believed there was another way. Often he would pick apart the beliefs of his brothers and sisters, posing the questions that they all should have been asking. But naturally, no one, save Pyrrus would ever truly indulge Halicon in his doubts when he would never put forth a view of his own. It wasn't until Halicon became Shau-ling that Emries truly understood what Halicon believed in. Halicon understood the wickedness of intellect, the thirst for self-determination, the soul of a hero, and the need for control. His first six children, the original phasia, were the prefect representations of what Shau-ling believed that humanity could become. Jeroch, the loyal yet conflicted soldier who constantly strove to prove himself but possessed a cunning even he did not fully realize. Grawn, the terrible mind who understood the application of cruelty and pain, but who longed only for quiet and an end to the terrible deeds that he committed.

Ellis, the cold intellect, who believed that reason was the only way to a solution while her polar opposite Bryn was a being of passion and fire who accepted that sometimes brute force was more useful than a sharp word. Kamen, the gentle giant who was as formal, wise, and calm as he was destructive and imposing and represented the limitless potential for growth and change. Then finally, Aryx Terian, the hero, the being of compassion and understanding who found killing as distasteful as it was effective. While apart they were flawed and vulnerable, together they were perhaps the most formidable force ever created. And yet, Halicon would not force them to be more than they wished to be, as he, like Pyrrus and to a degree Talisia, believed that self-determination was the only true path. Even fractured, Halicon and his phasia proved too much for Emries and his throng of sycophants and fanatics. And though Emries would gain some measure of success by using that self-determination and heroism against Shau-ling, in the end, even as Onea burned, it was Halicon who could have claimed the philosophical victory over Emries.

But Halicon did not lord his victory over his sibling, in fact it was quite the opposite. Halicon did not return to the Heavens after the fall of Onea, much as Raenera remained in hiding after the fall of Loinn. Emries did not understand at the time, but of course he too remained apart from the Heavens, half because of his wounds from the battles at the end of that world and half because of his role in Talisia's plan. Those forces that would rally to Pyrrus' side would have to be lulled into a sense of security and complacency if Talisia were to be successful. Of course, if things had turned on Talisia, Emries could have come to her rescue. What neither of them was willing to entertain though was if worse did come to worse would Emries have come to Talisia's rescue, or would he simply let her become the victim of her own shortsighted machinations. Even this far removed from the rebellion, Emries was not sure what he would have done had it come to it.

A sound came from the brush behind Emries and he was broken from his meditation on the past and prophecy. It didn't take much effort for him to reach out with his finely honed senses and feel Cedric coming his direction. There were two factors that made it clear that the approaching form was Cedric. The first was his tie to Emries' power which was unmistakable, and the second was the aura around Cedric that clearly marked that he was from another reality. Emries was unsure when he first challenged Tess to bring Cedric back how it would manifest. But instead of restoring Cedric from the grasp of death, she had instead pulled a version of Cedric through the void just before the moment of his death in another parallel reality. Emries was aware that other realities existed, and that the Creator held sway over them all, but the Children were never able to pierce the veil in the same way, and were forbidden to interfere in those other realities. The one exception of course had been the so-called Dark Mirror reality of Onea, which eventually culminated in the cataclysm that sentenced that world to burn. Perhaps that was why the Creator did not want the Children to interfere in other realities, or perhaps it was simply a level of control the Creator wanted to continue to exert upon his Children.

Cedric wasn't exactly sneaking toward Emries, but the Child of the Creator still felt it necessary to let Cedric know that his approach did not go unnoticed.

"I trust you have an explanation for Tess not being here."

Emries turned just as Cedric was breaking from the underbrush. It was clear immediately that Cedric had been in some sort of altercation, and for the briefest of moments, Emries wondered if Cedric had run afoul of the Annis girl's temper. But, if that were the case, it was more than likely that Cedric would no longer be drawing breath, let alone standing in front of his patron ready to answer his failure with his life. Cedric stood straight, looked beyond Emries at the small campsite for a moment and then answered.

"It seems your Father had other ideas about Tess's education."

For a moment, panic struck Emries' heart. If the Creator had learned about Emries' intentions regardless of all of the precautions he had taken, then the chances of actually succeeding in unseating the Creator from the Golden Throne had gone from slim to none.

"What happened?"

Cedric could feel the uncertainty and irritation in Emries' voice.

"The Creator coopted Gwydeon and Midarin's daughter and sent her here to kill me and collect Tess. I was able to fend her off, but I felt other portals form during the conflict, so someone else must have spirited Tess away. It could have been Wolf's daughters or it could have been one of the Servants. Either way I have to assume that Tess is now in the hands of someone loyal to the Creator."

In the moment Cedric wasn't sure why he lied and protected Jerah, but after hearing Emries' agitation at the mention of the Creator, Cedric felt it was better to feed into Emries' paranoia. Emries was gritting his teeth and his next words came out like a growl.

"And Camille?"

The next lie was easier for Cedric to tell as it had more than a kernel of truth to it.

"Gone. I'm not sure where she went, but I think she was only meant to distract me while Tess was secured. She talked about killing me, but I think that was only to keep my attention focused on her. I didn't realize how strong she had become."

Emries half-turned away from Cedric and looked up in the direction of the twin suns that were beginning their rise into the sky. He folded his hands behind his back and stood silent for a long time, fuming. Cedric kept his place, focusing on keeping his heartbeat as calm and even as possible all the while slowly feeding power into his muscles. He hoped that if he let the trickle of power go slow and steady enough that Emries would not view it as a threat. Finally after several minutes, Emries spoke, his voice calm, even, and stoic as it often was.

"I suppose I was naïve to think that my plans would escape the Creator's notice. But I don't think that it was a Servant that took her. I did not feel their power when I first came here, and I could only feel the remnants of a sloppy use of mortal ability to create a portal. It wasn't as refined as what the Dark Gods would use, and certainly far below the Servants or the Heralds of Dorovar. This was a mortal, likely Kaitain's pet assassin."

Cedric could not contain his reaction.

"The vision."

Emries whirled on Cedric and took a step forward before either of them realized the violence of the reaction.

"What did you say?"

Cedric kept his posture as calm as possible, and resisted the urge to immediately fill himself with as much power as he could muster. He did however keep up the slow buildup of power, more to keep Emries from noticing the change in Cedric that his reaction caused.

"Tess has had dreams that have disturbed her, dreams about being used by Emperor Lorien to destroy the world. They have haunted her since you brought her here. She said she has had them for a few years now, but they have gotten worse over the past days. I've seen them, and I know why they terrify her. A world of madness, blood, and horror. A world of death presided over by those so lost that death is a victory. But I've seen beyond her visions. She is trapped by her role in the vision. She isn't ready to know the truth."

Emries took two more steps forward and seized Cedric by the collar of his shirt. He pulled Cedric close and stared him dead in the eyes.

"What truth? Damn you Cedric you will tell me what you know or I shall rip it from your mind and leave you a drooling simpleton cursed to walk this world a living corpse until you are vaporized with the rest of the mewling pathetic humans."

Cedric's first instinct was to swallow hard and pull away, but he held his ground and continued to slowly draw power. He had almost filled himself to the point where Emries would certainly be able to notice the buildup. However, just as he had known a conflict with Camille would likely have resulted in his death, Cedric knew that a prolonged fight with Emries was futile. Logan and Aerith may have had the hubris and control necessary for a pitched battle with a Child of the Creator, but Cedric did not. He had planned for the eventuality of a strike against Emries, but without the Lion Sword, Cedric did not have the power necessary. Perhaps he could buy enough time to finish his preparations and use the weapon that Jerah had given him.

"Tess is too afraid to grasp the truth, even though it's right there in front of her. In her version of the vision she is pleading with Kaitain to stop, but her words are drowned out by his maniacal laughter. But cleared of her influence on the vision, anyone can see the truth. Kaitain screams that he will ascend to the Golden Throne, that he will unseat the Creator and that nothing can stop him. But at that moment he realizes what is happening and he starts screaming for Tess to stop. But it's his voice that is being drown out by her laughter. Her power completely unleashed with no control and only Kaitain's greed as fuel. She unmakes Creation, not for Kaitain, but because she has lost all control of her abilities and is a weapon unable to be used and unable to be stopped. This is the Creator's endgame, Emries. He doesn't need to unmake Creation, we're going to do it for him with our own stupidity, greed, and shortsightedness."

Emries' hold on Cedric's shirt tightened, threatening to rip the material. His eyes left Cedric's cast downward, his jaw working but no sound emerging. Cedric could feel Emries' thoughts, the disbelief and the confusion. Finally, Emries' gaze returned to Cedric's eyes, and Cedric saw something in those cold blue eyes he had never seen before; fear.

"I've seen the vision too, and so has Talisia. I'm sure Halicon, Raenera, and Pyrrus did too. It was Tess that put the vision into our minds. Was this a warning from Raenera of what could happen if her weapon was misused? Was the Creator interfering so we wouldn't discover the truth? I had her bring you back to teach her how to be in more control…"

Cedric frowned.

"All you succeeded in was teaching her how to harness her powers. Yes she no longer rages out of control, but if she is provoked and unleashes her abilities as I have taught her to do on your behalf, her power is limitless. You wanted her to be a weapon, Emries, and you got exactly what you asked for."

Emries pushed Cedric two steps backwards.

"She's my weapon. She's my path to eliminating the Creator."

Cedric knocked Emries' hand away and pushed the Child of the Creator back a step.

"She was never your weapon, Emries. You were played, again. The Creator let you think you were in charge on Onea, let you play your games when all along he intended to crush you. He let Talisia think that somehow she had gotten one over on him with Dorovar and his Heralds and the souls of the Adhradair, but He saw it all. Raenera thought she was so clever with the Dragon's Tear, and now it's going to be the death sentence for all of Creation. You and your family are making the same mistakes that Shau-ling's phasia did. They underestimated how much Shau-ling could see into their schemes, and they ultimately were defeated by their own arrogance. And now, the same fate befalls you as befell them."

Emries this time seized Cedric with both of his hands.

"No. No!"

The force of Emries words shook the ground upon which they stood. A tree's roots were dislodged nearby and fell to the ground with a loud crash.

"I will not be defeated again. You will help me return Tess to the fold. You will help me stop these visions from coming to pass. I will have that weapon. I will have the Golden Throne! I will be the new Creator and this Cosmos will bow to my whim."

Emries looked skyward and shouted at the top of his lungs.

"Do you hear me Father? I'm coming for you! I'm going to throw you down to one of your precious worlds the same way that you tried to discard Talisia! You will fall by my hand! You will know the wrath of your greatest creation! Do you hear me Father? Do you hear…."

Emries' cry to the Heavens was cut off abruptly as the pain radiated through his chest. He looked down to see the shocked face of Cedric Binosear staring at him, his jaw slack. Emries staggered back a step and looked to where the pain radiated from. Sticking out from his chest was the hilt of a silver dagger that pulsed with cold and hate. It took only a second for the origin and identity of the dagger to fill Emries' mind, and as he staggered back another step his hands went reflexively to the dagger. As the strength fled from his body, Emries tried in vain to dislodge the cruel instrument from his chest. His knees quivering, he was finally able to pull the dagger free, but in doing so expended most of the energy he had left and collapsed to the ground. Emries looked up at Cedric, blackness filling the edges of his vision.

"What have you done?"

Cedric knelt beside Emries, his face calm, his eyes smoldering with all the hate that had been repressed for centuries.

"You saw the vision yourself, Emries. Your time in this war is over. I'm just doing what's necessary. Long ago you chose me to be the first to wear your mantle in your war against Halicon. Now, I'm going to take your mantle and use it to defeat the Creator and save us all from the folly that you and your brethren created."

Emries eyes started to flutter closed, but just before he passed into the void, Cedric's last words rang perfectly in his ears.

"It was always going to end with us, Emries. You took everything from me, and now, I've taken everything from you."

Appendicies

Dramatis Personae

The Imperial Court

Terrik 'Godslayer' Lorien
Emperor Lorien I

Liette Lorien
Wife of Terrik Lorien
Empress of Cadaria
Seer

Kaldawyn Lorien
Emperor Lorien X
Father of Ender Lorien

Ender 'Justhand' Lorien
Emperor Lorien XI
Father of Feyd and Kaitain Lorien

Meara Lorien
Wife of Ender Lorien
Mother of Kaitain and Feyd Lorien

Kaitain Lorien
Emperor Lorien XII
Father of Marlae Lorien
Adoptive Father of Quyhn Lorien
Twin Brother of Feyd Lorien

Irene Drage
The Ethereal Sorceress
Court Sorceress
Protégé of Alistair Ravenheart

Galen White
Member of the Imperial Guard
Personal Guard of Felicia Lorien

Geoffry Aramour
Imperial Historian and Bard
Master of the Shadow Guild

Alise Modrall
Personal Assassin of Kaitain Lorien

The Lordhill Rebellion

Feyd Lorien
Prince of Cadaria
Brother of Kaitain Lorien
Overseer of Lordhill Province
Father of Felicia Lorien

Felicia Lorien
Princess of Cadaria
Daughter of Feyd Lorien
Host of Nightwing

Quyhn Ravenheart Lorien
Sorceress
Ward of the Empire
Voice of the Emperor
Daughter of Alistair and Estelle
Ravenheart

Dominique Arais Lorien
Wife of Kaitain Lorien
Former Mistress of Seraph Kore

Rhionna Winter
Personal Protector of Quyhn
Ravenheart
Archer from the Army of Fire

Connor Peregrim
Lord of Lordhill
Former General in the Imperial Guard

Gabrielle Peregrim
Lady of Lordhill
Cousin of Kaitain Lorien

Arent Fox
General in the Rebel Army of
Lordhill

Strum Anvilguard
General in the Rebel Army of
Lordhill

The Knights of the Flashing Blade
Bernhardt Yeoman
The Moonstone Knight
Kingdom of Iron, Pellatori
Wielder of the Hammer Gravity

Chelsea Zarova
The Garnet Knight
Kingdom of Fire, Saldarine
"The Wolf of Saldarine"
Wife of Seraph Kore
Wielder of the Katars Tenacity
Personal Protector of Dominique
Lorien

Devlin Rannoch
The Onyx Knight
Kingdom of Night, Galateria
Half-Dragon
Wielder of the Kopesh Discipline

Gregor Quicksilver
The Ruby Knight
Kingdom of Blood, Zevarit
Husband of Hannah Ironheart
Paladin of the Church of the Creator
Son of Ivan Quicksilver
Wielder of the Greatsword Valor

Hannah Ironheart
The Celestine Knight
Kingdom of Stone, Albitonin
High Priestess of the Church of the
Creator
Wife of Gregor Quicksilver
Wielder of the Mace Spirit
First *Chosen One* of Espre

Leonora Wastri
The Jade Knight
Kingdom of Soul, Oradrim
Wielder of the Naginata Wisdom
Trained by Cedric Binosear

Jaccob Aldora
The Topaz Knight
The Flying Kingdom, Hedorah
Former Member of the Academy of
Arcane Arts
Wielder of the Double Sword
Temperance

Natalia Pressen
The Sunstone Knight
Kingdom of Gold, Bellnoc
Master of the Shadow Guild
Wielder of the Rapier Perseverance

Orren Eldrath
The Sapphire Knight
Kingdom of Ice, Rashaleb
Former Member of the Academy of
Arcane Arts
Wielder of the Long Sword Courage

Seraph Kore
The Emerald Knight
Kingdom of Water, Thorigald
Husband of Chelsea Zarova
Wielder of Twin Sword Patience

Tolon Morr
The Amethyst Knight
Kingdom of Steel, Celidar
Former Gladiator
Wielder of Battle Axe Strength

Vallic Ultiv
The Serpentine Knight
Kingdom of Steam, Iltorp
Wielder of Scythe Harmony
Alias of Jeroch Yetre

Xaran Firesoul
The Tiger's Eye Knight
Kingdom of Knowledge, Menoris
Blind Since Birth
Wielder of Staff Faith

Gabriel Shadowfall
Member of the Imperial Guard
Personal Guard of Marlae Lorien
The Ruby Knight

Ivan Quicksilver
Former Ruby Knight
Father of Gregor Quicksilver
Advisor to the Dark Court

Tutio Illik
Former Onyx Knight

Heremon Tal
Former Amethyst Knight

The Academy of Arcane Arts
Alistair Ravenheart
Grandmaster of the Academy of
Arcane Arts
Master of Water
Imperial Sorcerer
Husband of Estelle Ravenheart
Father of Quyhn Ravenheart

Estelle Ravenheart
Sorceress
Wife of Alistair Ravenheart
Mother of Quyhn Ravenheart

Fiona Ebonsight
Master of Fire
Mother of Aris Ebonsight

Aris Ebonsight
Master of Air
Daughter of Fiona Ebonsight

Jastra Mythryn
Master of Energy

Ashinica Maupin
Master of Stone
Member of the Imperial Family

The Seers
Jehna Feris
The Dark Seer

Jania Maldovrin
Oldest of the Maldovrin Triplets

Jerrica Maldovrin
Youngest of the Maldovrin Triplets

Jordyne Maldovrin
Middle of the Maldovrin Triplets

The Dragon Hunters
Jillian Corven
Self-Titled Lady of Cadaria
Wielder of Scaleripper
Leader of the Dragon Hunters

Kiara Aren
Dragon Hunter
Former Priestess of the Creator

Angelina Lynn Sydor
Dragon Hunter

Jacqueline Escandi
Dragon Hunter
Former Member of the Iron Legion

The Chorus
Dorovar
The Destroyer of Worlds

Pestilence
The Grey Man
Carrier of the Crawling Plague

Famine
Formerly Isabel Relin
Carrier of the Wasting Disease

Death
Formerly Ardis Franel
The Collector of Souls

Jerah
Alias of Caris

Conquest
Alias of Pike Rhuiden

Haricos
Member of the Adhradair

Redissa
Member of the Adhradair

Coriden
Member of the Adhradair

Faelara
Member of the Adhradair

Zaraven
Member of the Adhradair

Drust
Member of the Adhradair

The Hand of Chaos
Dimitri Sulano
The Voice of the Lost

Syren Belloch
The Priestess of Blood

Torda Safrick
The Master of Secrets

Xavier Cormea
The Corruptor of Souls

Erik Relcan
Pursuer of Lost Love
Former Personal Assistant of Hannah
Ironheart

Seraphina Masile
Second in Command of the Hand of
Chaos

Korin Melcab
Captain of the Imperial Guard

The Children of the Creator
Emries
The First *Coromor*
Creator of the *Erieal*

Halicon
Formerly known as Shau-ling
Father of the Phasia
Powers imbued to Rhain Seth

Talisia Masile
The Dark Goddess

Pyrrus
God of Light
Powers imbued to Wolf Ranthall

Raenera
Goddess of Order
Powers imbued to Gideon Viruci

The Phasia
Rhain Seth
Mistress of the Blaze
Former Personal Guard of Marlae
Lorien
Daughter of Aerith Seth and Bryn
Aplee

Jeroch Yetre
The Lord Shadow
First Born of the Phasia
Father of Hawk Yetre

Bryn Aplee
The Lady Fox
Member of the Brotherhood of Phasia
Former Lover of Aerith Seth
Wife of Grawn Aplee
Mother of Gideon Viruci

Ellis Chandara
The Lady Leopard
Member of the Brotherhood of Phasia
Mother of Korrd Ranthall

Grawn Aplee
The Lord Shark
Member of the Brotherhood of Phasia
Husband of Bryn Aplee

Warron Ysamaran
AKA Blade
The Lord Boar
Member of the Brotherhood of Phasia

Basille Mystic
The Lord Raven
Member of the Brotherhood of Phasia
Father of Jerrard Mystic

Farax Soar
Creator of the Snags
The Lord Vulture
Member of the Brotherhood of Phasia

The Flame
Kamen
Personal Guardian of Shau-ling
Keeper of the Hall of Terrors
Originally known as Kamen, Member
of the Brotherhood of Phasia

Zarsi Aeron
The Lord Cobra
Member of the Brotherhood of Phasia

Aldridge Farran
The Lord Hawk
Member of the Brotherhood of Phasia

Saurn Macco
The Lord Viper
Member of the Brotherhood of Phasia

Caris Vale
The Lady Wolf
Member of the Brotherhood of Phasia

Erdric Yarrow
The Lord Scorpion
Member of the Brotherhood of Phasia

Taron Steen
The Lord Jackal
Member of the Brotherhood of Phasia

Draven Batoe
The Lord Crow
Member of the Brotherhood of Phasia

Rane Larion
The Lady Falcon
Member of the Brotherhood of Phasia

Stryfe Cadre
The Lord Python
Member of the Brotherhood of Phasia

Grimm Salde
The Lord Bear
Member of the Brotherhood of Phasia

Cash Griffon
The Lady Lynx
Member of the Brotherhood of Phasia

Nightwing
Member of the Dark Riders
Shau-ling's Assassin

Hawk Yetre
Son of Jeroch Yetre and Caris Vale

Natalie Yetre
Daughter of Jeroch Yetre and Ellis
Chandara

Jessica Chandara
Daughter of Ellis Chandara and
Grawn Aplee

The Court of the Dark Gods
Sadrina Annis
Queen of Mythryn
Wife of Pike Rhuiden

Darrien Annis
Half-Dark Goddess
Daughter of Pike Rhuiden

Tess Annis
Half-Dark Goddess
Daughter of Pike Rhuiden

Alderin Terian
Dark God
Son of Aryx and Diana Terian
Protector of Darrien Annis

Camille Sandar
Dark Goddess
Daughter of Gwydeon and Midarin
Sandar
Protector of Tess Annis

Serrina Mistic
Dark Goddess
Voice of the Dark Council
Daughter of Jerrard and Erika Mystic

Mirana Ranthall
Daughter of Wolf Ranthall and Lissa
Terian
Twin of Liara Ranthall

Liara Ranthall
Daughter of Wolf Ranthall and Lissa
Terian
Twin of Mirana Ranthall

The Celestial Court
Marlae Tamerlane
The Divine Empress
Chosen Representative of the Creator
Daughter of Kaitain Lorien

Ayden Seth
Son of Aerith Seth and Bryn Aplee
The Will

Anabel Binosear
Sister of Cedric Binosear
Mother of Cairyn Binosear
Daughter of Aerith Seth
High Council to the Divine Empress

Azure
God of the Heavens
Advisor to the Divine Empress

Krysis
God of the Heavens
Advisor to the Divine Empress

Terrance Aldora
Brother of Jaccob Aldora
Advisor to the Divine Empress

Isabella
Advisor to the Divine Empress

The Dark Gods
Aryx Terian
White Lightning
Fire *Erieal* of the First Generation of
the Prophecies
Husband of Diana Geoffry Terian
Father of Lissa Terian
Father of Alderin Parran
Former Host of Nightwing

Diana Terian Geoffry
Wind *Erieal* of the First Generation of
the Prophecies
Sister of Arathorn Geoffry
Wife of Aryx Terian
Mother of Lissa Terian
Mother of Alderin Parran

Pike Rhuiden
Water *Erieal* of the Second
Generation of the Prophecies
Refugee from the Dark Mirror
First Cousin of Logan Ranthall
Eldar Merin's Former Husband
Husband of Sadrina Annis
Father of Darrien and Tess Annis

Gwydeon Sandar
Brother of Angels
Husband of Midarin Rice Sandar
Father of Nathaniel Sandar
Father of Camille Renar
Also Known as Wynne

Midarin Rice
Wife of Gwydeon Sandar
Mother of Nathaniel Sandar
Mother of Camille Renar

Lissa Terian
Fire *Erieal* of the Third Generation of
the Prophecies
Daughter of Aryx and Diana Terian
Wife of Wolf Ranthall

Sabrina Binosear
Third *Chosen One* of the Prophecies
Refugee from the Dark Mirror
Daughter of Cairyn Binosear

Wolf Ranthall
Son of Logan Ranthall and Elwyne
Tamerlane Ranthall

The Forgotten
Aerith Seth
The First *Chosen One*
Husband of Bryn Aplee
Father of Ayden Seth, Cedric
Binosear, Anabel Binosear, Gideon
Viruci

Taya Viruci
Daughter of Gideon Viruci and Erika
Belnosian
Refugee from the Dark Mirror

Logan Ranthall
AKA Dane Rhuiden
Second *Chosen One* of the Prophecies
Brother of Korrd Ranthall
First Cousin of Pike Rhuiden
Father of Wolf Ranthall
Leader of the Order of the Flickering
Flame
Refugee from the Dark Mirror

Jerrard Mystic
Son of Basille Mystic
Husband of Erika Belnosian
Father of Serrina Mistic

Erika Belnosian Mystic
Wife of Jerrard Mystic
Mother of Serrina Mystic

Other Cast

Cole Breon
Freelance Assassin
The Living Shadow

Liandra Nightshade
Freelance Assassin
Death Blossom

Dane Rhuiden
Monk
Leader of the Order of the Flickering
Flame

Blade
Merchant
Purveyor of Oddities
Alias of Warron Ysamaran

Isa Shar
Companion of Vallic Ultiv
Alias of Ellis Chandara

Evan Sinn
Inheritor of Aerith Seth's power
The Voice of the Creator
Husband of Meredith Heron

Taya Mystic
Daughter of Jerrard and Erika Mystic

Meredith Heron
Emissary of the Creator
Wife of Evan Sinn
Murdered by Dorovar

Tera Dawnrunner
Guardian of the Council of the Winds
Guardian of the East
Last of the Tigrelle

Jander Eveningstar
Guardian of the Council of the Winds

Eldar Merin
The Spirit
Best Friend of Elwyne Tamerlane
Wife of Pike Rhuiden

Leane Torne
General in the Army of Rama
Former Member of the Army of Brea

Nathaniel Sandar
The Lord Ram
Third *Coromor* of the Prophecies
Son of Gwydeon Sandar and Midarin
Rice
Brother of Liette Forer

Gwillim Sandar
Earth *Erieal* of the Third Generation
of the Prophecies
Son of Korrd Ranthall and Gabrielle
Crill
Adopted Son of Midarin Rice

Storm Mystic
Son of Jerrard and Erika Mystic
Water *Erieal* of the Third Generation
of the Prophecies

Jared Vale
Son of Caris Vale and Cedric
Binosear

Cairyn Binosear
Daughter of Anabel Binosear
Niece of Cedric Binosear
Queen of the Kingdoms of Kandor,
Trelon, and Marcwell
Wife of Pike Rhuiden
Mother of Duncan Rhuiden and
Sabrina Binosear

Sabrina Binosear
Former Host of the Spirit
Third *Chosen One* of the Prophecies
Sister of Duncan Rhuiden
Daughter of Pike Rhuiden and Cairyn
Binosear

Duncan Rhuiden
Heir to the Kingdom of Marcwell
Brother of Sabrina Binosear
Son of Pike Rhuiden and Cairyn
Binosear

Talon Aielin
Wind *Erieal* of the Second
Generation of the Prophecies
Best Friend of Pike Rhuiden

Arin Domae
Fire *Erieal* of the Second Generation
of the Prophecies
Former Soldier of the Army of Brea

Gideon Viruci
Earth *Erieal* of the Second Generation
of the Prophecies
Killed in Battle with Shau-ling

Baeta Catrinel
High Priestess of the Church of the
Creator

Aelind Torral
Assistant to the High Priestess

Reverend Mother Amalia
Priestess of Hedorah

Heralds of the Creator
The Voice
Formerly embodied by Evan Sinn
Currently embodies Gregor
Quicksilver

The Will
Currently embodies Ayden Seth

The Wrath
Destroyed by Aerith Seth

The Spirit
Formerly embodied by Sabrina
Binosear
Currently embodies Eldar Merin

The Council of Winds
The Elder Dragon Tarot
Leader of the Council

Mariti Brightblade
Second in Command of the Council
Companion of Tarot

Khalas Skydancer
Friend of Xaran Firesoul

The Demon Dragon Shadowweaver
Chief Opposition to Tarot

Krangoth Granitewill

The Arcane Dragon Serentis
Ally of Mariti Brightblade

Brux Mightytide

Charnada Ivorytooth
Ally of Shadowweaver

Stormbane the Traitor
Ally of Shadowweaver

Sheyruushk Bottomdweller
Ally of Khalas Skydancer

Aspertis the Just
Ally of Mariti Brightblade

Derelor the Manipulator
Ally of Shadowweaver

About the Author

Brian Kershner is a life-long dreamer, writer, and problem-solver. He grew up absorbing anything and everything he could get his hands on, and as a child of the Star Wars era he constantly wanted to see the worlds beyond the little Indiana town he grew up in. There was no adventure too far, and no problem too big.

Emboldened by parents who always supported his curiosity and his thoughtfulness, Brian found himself bounding from Space Camp to Laser Summer Camp to Athletic Training Camp to Piano Lessons to Football Practice to Basketball Practice to Choir Practice and back again. Despite all of the roaming and traveling, his family remained close-knit and supportive.

Though he flirted with the idea of becoming a doctor, Brian's attentions always fell back to the computer world. He got his first computer when he was six, and not long after found his way into a word processing program and began crafting his own fantastic worlds and even more fantastic characters.

As he has grown and changed and experienced life, so too have his characters. He continues to write, craft, and create; whether it is websites for his customers, or characters and worlds for his audience.

www.ingramcontent.com/pod-product-compliance
Lightning Source LLC
Chambersburg PA
CBHW072333020726
47506CB00004B/874